THE WANTON PRINCESS

DENNIS WHEATLEY

DENNIS WHEATLEY

THE WANTON PRINCESS

Frontispiece Portrait by
MARK GERSON

Original Illustrations by
ROY SPENCER

Published by arrangement with
Hutchinson and Co. (Publishers) Ltd.

© *1966, Dennis Wheatley Ltd.*
© *1974, Illustrations, Edito-Service S.A., Geneva*

For the
Sales Representatives of the Hutchinson Group
in appreciation of their having sold
20,000,000
copies of my books,
and particularly for their Chief,
GEOFFREY HOWARD,
a treasured friend of many years' standing

CONTENTS

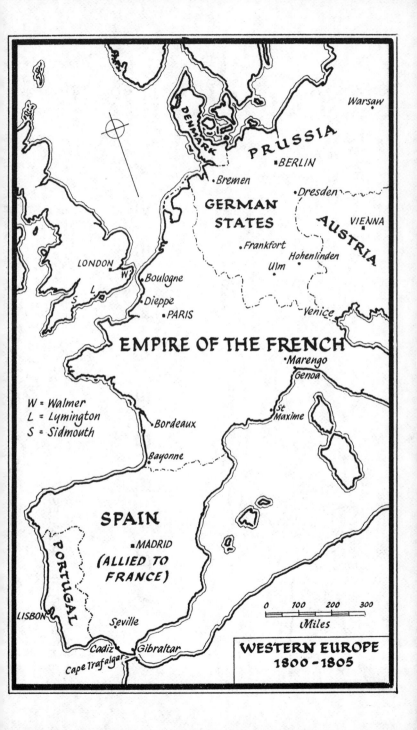

Warsaw

DENMARK

PRUSSIA

•BERLIN

•Bremen

GERMAN
STATES

•Dresden

VIENNA

AUSTRIA

•Frankfort

LONDON

Hohenlinden

Ulm

W

•Boulogne

L

•Dieppe

S

•PARIS

Venice

EMPIRE OF THE FRENCH

•Marengo

Genoa

W = Walmer
L = Lymington
S = Sidmouth

•Bordeaux

•St
Maxime

•Bayonne

SPAIN

PORTUGAL

•MADRID
(ALLIED TO
FRANCE)

0   100   200   300

LISBON

•Seville

Miles

•Cadiz   •Gibraltar

WESTERN EUROPE
1800-1805

Cape Trafalgar

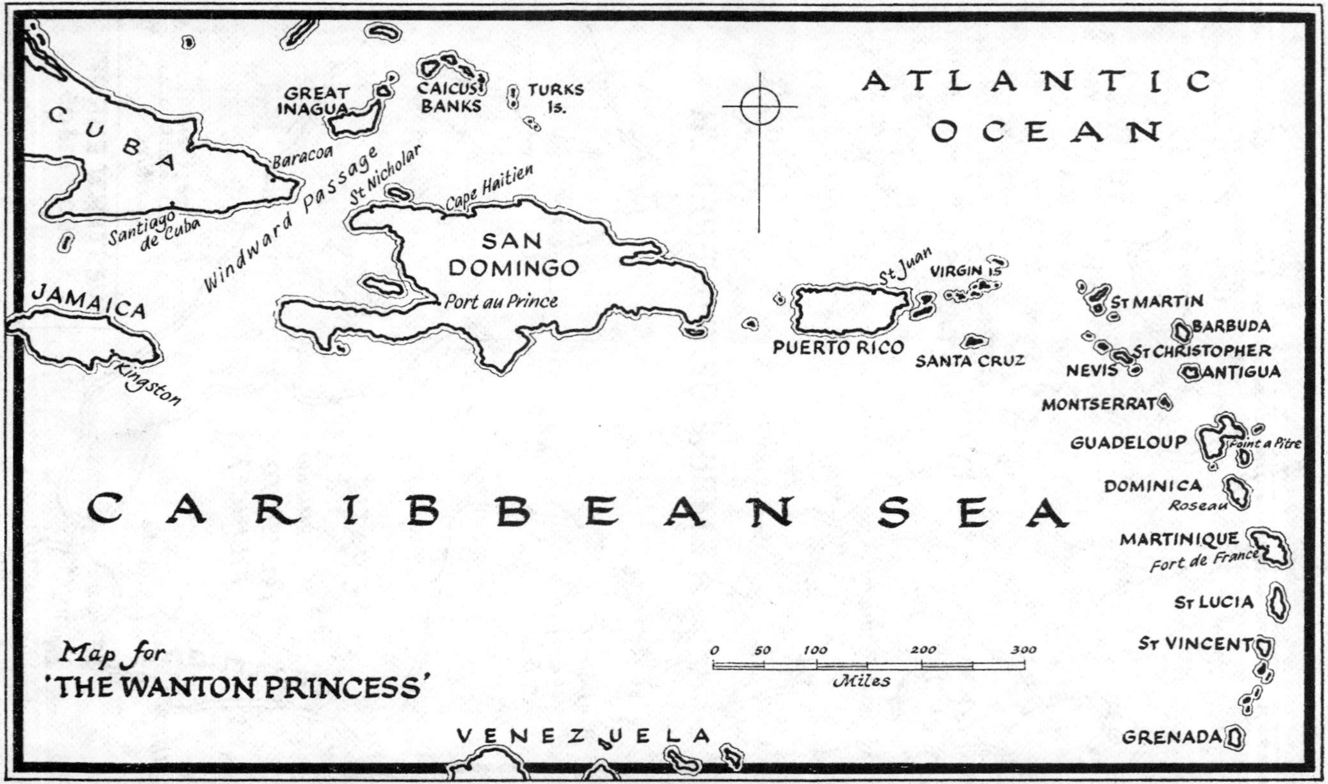
ATLANTIC
OCEAN
CUBA
GREAT
INAGUA
CAICUS
BANKS
TURKS
Is.
Baracoa
Santiago
de Cuba
Windward Passage
St Nicholar
Cape Haitien
SAN
DOMINGO
Port au Prince
JAMAICA
Kingston
PUERTO RICO
St Juan
VIRGIN Is
SANTA CRUZ
St MARTIN
BARBUDA
St CHRISTOPHER
NEVIS
ANTIGUA
MONTSERRAT
GUADELOUP
Point a Pitre
DOMINICA
Roseau
MARTINIQUE
Fort de France
St LUCIA
St VINCENT
GRENADA
CARIBBEAN SEA
0 50 100 200 300
Miles
VENEZUELA
Map for
'THE WANTON PRINCESS'

THE FAILURE OF A MISSION

I T W A S the first day of the new century. Seven hours earlier the bells of Ripley Church had rung out ushering in the year 1800. Not far from the village, at Stillwaters, the splendid mansion that was the home of Georgina, Countess of St. Ermins, the many servants were already bustling about, but Roger Brook had only just woken.

Normally, when staying at Stillwaters he would have awakened in Georgina's bed for, although circumstances had led to their being separated, at times for years at a stretch, they had been lovers since their teens and, although both of them had had many other loves, they still looked on one another as the dearest person in the world. But Georgina was ill. Only a few days ago her life had been despaired of; so Roger had slept in the room on the far side of her boudoir, to which in happier times he had retired for appearances' sake when her maid, Jenny, called them in the mornings.

As he woke his first thought was of her, and relief at the knowledge that she had turned the corner. His next was a bitter one for, on the previous day, he had learned of the failure of his latest mission. On December 28th he had arrived in England as the *Envoyé Extraordinaire* of General

Bonaparte who, on November 10th, as the result of the *coup d'état* of 18th *Brumaire*, had become First Consul of the French Republic. No more extraordinary envoy could have been selected for such a mission, as for a dozen years Roger had been Prime Minister 'Billy' Pitt's most resourceful and daring secret agent.

At the age of fifteen he had run away to France rather than be forced by his father, Admiral Sir Christopher Brook, to accept the hard life of a midshipman and make the sea his career. Four years in France had made him bilingual and had given him a second identity. Then chance had put him in possession of a diplomatic secret of the first importance. Realizing that knowledge of it might prevent France from going to war with England he had returned home post haste and seen the Prime Minister. Appreciating how well suited he was to such work, Mr. Pitt had sent him on a secret mission to the northern capitals. Other missions had followed. He had again lived in France during the greater part of the Revolution and the Terror. At the siege of Toulon he had first met Bonaparte, then an unknown Captain of Artillery, had been with him in Paris when he had become a figure of importance through suppressing the riots that preceded the formation of the Directory, met him again after his victorious campaign in Italy, saved him from being kidnapped, been made an A.D.C. and, with the rank of Colonel, accompanied him to Egypt. So the dynamic little Corsican artilleryman who had now become the most powerful man in France looked on Roger as an old and trusted friend while, owing to his audacious exploits, he had become known in the Army as *Le brave Breuc*.

Only two men in France knew him in fact to be an Englishman: Joseph Fouché the crafty ex-terrorist who was Bonaparte's Minister of Police and Charles Maurice de Talleyrand, the subtle and brilliant ex-Bishop who held the Portfolio for Foreign Affairs. The former had long been Roger's most deadly enemy but, recently, common interests had led to their burying the hatchet; the latter had, from their first meeting, been his good friend. As in those days it was

2

not at all unusual for a man born in one country to carve out a career for himself in another, as Roger had done in France, both of them now regarded him as a naturalized Frenchman and completely loyal to the country of his adoption.

Bonaparte and everyone, other than these two, who knew him in France, believed him to be a native of Strasbourg whose mother, an English woman, had died when he was quite young and that he had been sent to England to be brought up by her sister; then, when in his late teens, attracted by the epoch-making Revolution decided to return to the country of his birth. In consequence, on the rare, awkward occasions when he ran into anyone from one country who knew him in the other he was able to pass himself off as bearing a striking resemblance to either his French or English cousin of the same age, for whom they had mistaken him.

He even had a third identity which he used on occasion when in neutral countries and was liable to meet both Englishmen and Frenchmen who knew him either as Roger Brook or the *ci-devant* Chevalier de Breuc. For this he grew a short, curly brown beard, used his mother's maiden name, calling himself Robert McElfic, and posed as her nephew who had recently succeeded her brother as Earl of Kildonan. The McElfics had raised their clan in '45 to fight for Bonnie Prince Charlie, and after his defeat, like many other pro-Stuart nobles, followed their 'King' into exile in Rome; so very few people in either France or England had ever met this cousin of Roger's and he had never been challenged when using this name.

By the skilful use of these aliases over a long period he had secured himself from detection in the real part he played and now, apart from some entirely unforeseen catastrophe, had little to worry about on that score; but he was intensely worried at what he considered to be the criminal stupidity of the British Government and the report he would have to make on his return to France.

For seven long years, ever since 1793 when the French had guillotined their King, Britain and France had been at war.

3

To begin with, the Monarchist armies of the First Coalition had invaded France; but with fervid patriotism the ill-trained rabble of the Republic had driven them back, overrun Belgium and Holland and secured France's old frontier on the left bank of the Rhine. They had then invaded Savoy and piedmont. Young General Bonaparte's amazing campaign in '96 had made them masters of the whole of Italy, and Switzerland too had been dominated by them. But these victories had cost them many thousands of lives and, despite the vast treasure in indemnities and loot they had taken from the countries they had conquered, France was bankrupt. Exhausted both by the civil wars of the Revolution and these foreign wars to protect their newly won liberties the people longed for Peace, and Bonaparte had decided that the time had come to give it to them.

Internally, as a result of the Revolution, France was in a chaotic state. Civil war still simmered in La Vendée. Administration, other than in the Army, had entirely broken down. Taxes could no longer be collected, the paper money issued by the Government was almost worthless and the old laws protecting property were ignored. Roads and bridges had fallen into disrepair and the Post service had deteriorated to a point where it took three days to get from Dieppe to Paris instead of one. Industrialists were at the mercy of their workmen; a great part of the agricultural land confiscated from the nobility and the Church now lay fallow, with the result that food had reached famine prices; and bands of marauders, in some cases hundreds strong, roamed the countryside unchecked, robbing and murdering scores of people every week.

Eager, now that he had obtained the power, to concentrate on putting an end to this state of anarchy and restore law and order, Bonaparte had written both to King George III and to the Emperor of Austria proposing terms of peace. And, at Talleyrand's suggestion, Roger had been selected to carry the First Consul's letter to London.

Britain, too, was almost exhausted by her seven years of war and her people desperately anxious that an end should

4

be put to hostilities. So Roger had been overjoyed at being given the mission and set out with the conviction that he would be received in London as an angel announcing a new era of happiness and prosperity. But, to his amazement and disgust, the British Government had treated Bonaparte's overture with contempt.

As Roger woke he thought for a moment that his interview the day before with the Prime Minister could have been only an evil dream, but when he looked round the familiar room, he realized that it had indeed taken place. Getting out of bed he slipped on his chamber robe, pulled aside the curtains of one of the tall windows, glanced at the snow-covered landscape and the now frozen lake that gave the house its name, then crossed the boudoir and tiptoed into Georgina's big bedroom.

It was still in semi-darkness but he saw that Jenny, who since Georgina's teens had been her faithful maid and confidante, was sitting beside the great four-poster bed with its tapestry canopy, under which he had known so many nights of delight. There was no movement in the bed, and he whispered:

'How fares she, Jenny?'

'Doing well, sir, the dear Lord be praised,' Jenny whispered back. 'She slept the first part of the night, but roused when I came in to take the Colonel's place. So we gave her a draught of the wine that had the red-hot poker put in it as you ordered and she soon went off again.'

Roger smiled. 'Thank God for that. With plenty of sleep and the iron to renew her blood she will soon be herself again. I'll dress and go down to breakfast with Colonel Thursby, then come up here to relieve you.'

Half an hour later, shaved and immaculate in a blue cutaway coat, white stock, nankeen waistcoat and breeches, he made his way down the broad central staircase of the house. He was just over six foot tall, with powerful shoulders and slim hips. Although he was still in his early thirties the dangerous life he had led for so long made him look somewhat older and, as a result of having caught the plague

5

while in Syria the previous year, the brown hair that swept back in a high wave from his fine forehead now had a touch of grey in it. His mouth was a little hard, his straight nose aggressive, his strong chin determined; but his deep blue eyes, a glance from which had made many a pretty woman's heart beat faster, were gay and friendly. The little fingers of his beautifully moulded hands were long in comparison with the others, which would have told a palmist that he had the gift of eloquence and a special flair for languages; his calves, when displayed in silk stockings, gave his tall figure the last touch of elegance.

He found Colonel Thursby, Georgina's father, already in the breakfast room. The Colonel had attained his rank in the Engineers; then, already a man of means, used his good brain and practical knowledge to profit from the Industrial Revolution. His interests in the construction of canals, weaving machinery and the development of concrete had since brought him a considerable fortune. Georgina was his only child. Her mother had died when giving birth to her and her father had brought her up. To him she owed a far wider education than most women of that period obtained. Although he had two houses of his own, since she had become a widow he spent a good part of each year with her. They adored one another; and from his boyhood Roger had looked upon the kind, clever, quiet-mannered little Colonel as a second father.

After telling the Colonel that Georgina had passed a good night and was still asleep, Roger went over to the sideboard where, as was customary in big houses in those spacious Georgian days, there was more food than a dozen men could have demolished: a variety of egg dishes, bacon, kidneys, sausages, a mutton pie and the better part of a York ham. As Roger carried his first selection to the table the Colonel said:

'You appeared so worn out on your late return last night that I forbore to ask you what had passed in Downing Street Everything went well, I trust.'

'Far from it, sir,' Roger declared with disgust. 'Had not my Lord Grenville been there with Mr. Pitt and displayed the same obduracy of mind, I would have thought our Prime

6

Minister afflicted with a lesion of the brain. I can still scarce believe it but they have as good as instructed me to fling General Bonaparte's offer back in his face.'

'What say you?' The colonel put down his fork and looked up with swift concern. 'What possible reason could they have for wishing to continue draining away the lifeblood and treasure of the nation when given this chance to enter on negotiations? I can only suppose that General Bonaparte's terms were so hard as to preclude any possibility of accepting them.'

'On the contrary, sir. His one wish now is to be done with war so that he may turn his talents to rescuing France from the appalling state of disorder into which she has fallen. In consequence his terms were generous. The greater part of Italy was lost to France during his absence in Egypt. He asks only that France should retain her ancient frontiers, including the Belgian lands up to the left bank of the Rhine, and Piedmont. It was upon this last that Mr. Pitt and the Foreign Secretary hinged their refusal even to consider making peace.'

'In that they were no doubt influenced by our being bound by treaty to restore King Charles Emanuel to his domains.'

'We bound ourselves to our Austrian allies to make no separate peace which would not secure to them the return of the Belgian Netherlands. Had we ignored that pact we could have had peace with France in '96. And what was our reward for honouring our bond? A year later the Austrians went behind our backs and made the Peace of Campo Formio by which they gave up their title to Belgium in exchange for the Venetian lands, leaving us to fight on alone. King Charles Emanuel still has his great island of Sardinia. Is it so much that he should be asked to accept the loss of Piedmont permanently in order that this bloody war should cease and peace be restored to all Europe?'

'I judge you right in that. And, surely, had he proved difficult round a conference table it could have been arranged that he should receive some compensation for the loss of Piedmont?'

'Indeed it could. But the crux of the matter lies in the

blind prejudice that Mr. Pitt and his colleagues have against General Bonaparte. The Prime Minister stigmatized him to me as a proved liar, an atheist, a thief, a blackguard of the meanest order; while my Lord Grenville exclaimed of Talleyrand, "That revolting ex-priest. He would sell his own mother for a guinea. His corruption and immorality stink in the nostrils of the whole world".'

'One must admit that they are both most unscrupulous men,' the Colonel remarked mildly.

'That I grant you,' Roger returned swiftly. 'And who should know it better than I who have for so long been closely associated with them? But that is less than half the tale. General Bonaparte would go to any lengths to achieve his ends, but he is far more than a revolutionary who has become a bandit on the grand scale. There is no subject in which he is not interested, his knowledge is encyclopaedic, his grasp of new factors in a situation immediate, his breadth of vision enormous and his powers of decision swift. All this places him in a class apart and, as an administrator, head and shoulders above any of the scores of monarchs, potentates and statesmen with whom I have had dealings in the past ten years. Given the chance he will remake France anew. Of that I am convinced. But he needs peace to do it, and that is why his offer is no trick, as those fools in Downing Street believe, but an honest one.'

Standing up, Roger walked over to the sideboard to replenish his plate. While he was helping himself he went on, 'As for Talleyrand, of course he is a lecher of the first order and, following the custom of Foreign Ministers for centuries on the Continent—ah, and here too until Mr. Pitt came to power—he extracts huge bribes from Ambassadors to expedite their business. But he does not allow that to influence his foreign policy, and he is as well-intentioned toward Britain as you or I. To me, knowing I am an Englishman, he has never made any secret of his basic belief. It is that no lasting prosperity can come to either France or Britain unless they make an accommodation over their differences. I have heard him say that a score of times and for years past he has

8

been doing all he can towards that end. How I shall break to him this bitter blow of my failure with Mr. Pitt, I cannot think.'

'When do you plan to return to France?' the Colonel asked.

'Not for a week or so. I'll bide here until Georgina is well on the way to full recovery. But after I have reported my failure I hardly know what to do. This affair has sickened me of doing dangerous work for fools. I've a mind to retire gracefully from General Bonaparte's service, then return here and settle down to a life of leisure. Think you, after all these years, I could persuade Georgina to marry me?'

The Colonel was well aware of Roger's relationship with Georgina, and he replied at once, 'My dear boy, nothing could give me greater pleasure. I have oft wished it; and the bar to your regularizing your great love for one another has been that your work has prevented you from living in England except for a month or two at long intervals. I know she feels it her duty to marry again now that her little Earl has reached an age when he needs a man to bring him up, and as your Susan shares Charles' nursery, by marrying Georgina you could become a real father to them both. Go to it, and good luck to you.'

'Thank you, sir,' Roger smiled. ' 'Twould not be fair to approach her yet on such a serious matter; but I will as soon as she is well enough.'

After breakfast Roger went out into the garden, where the children were playing in the snow with their nurse. Charles St. Ermins was now a stalwart boy rising five, and Susan, Roger's daughter by his second wife, a pretty little thing just turned four. Her mother having died she was being brought up by Georgina and, owing to Roger's long absences abroad, the children knew him only as an occasional visitor of a rather special kind; but he was good with small people and was soon building a snowman for them.

Recently a new dance had found its way to Paris and London from Vienna. It was a great innovation as, in the formal dances of the past, the man had never touched his partner, except to link hands in certain movements, whereas in this audacious measure, called the waltz, the man put his arm round the woman's waist and whirled her away across the floor. Using the pyramid-shaped skirt of a woman as a solid base and sticks with snow packed tightly round them to support the legs of the man and the arms of both, Roger spent most of the day creating a waltzing couple out of snow. His efforts delighted the children and took his own mind off his frustration.

During the week that followed, between intervals of sitting with Georgina, he made the children a toboggan track that curved down a long gentle slope; then got out from the coach house Georgina's beautiful sleigh, which was fashioned like a swan. Having had the lake swept of snow, he tied the two children firmly into the sleigh, then put on skates and propelled them round the long oval of ice at a speed that made them squeal with excitement and delight.

These long days spent playing with the children gave him a pleasure that he had never previously experienced and dissipated the last doubts he had had about the wisdom of abandoning his adventurous life for good. Thankfully he realized that, the children still being so young, it was not too late to enjoy with them the best years of their lives. Soon his active mind began to make a hundred plans for their welfare and amusement and indulge in happy daydreams of a new carefree existence in which he would tuck them up in bed every night and wake with his beloved Georgina beside him every morning.

By January 8th Georgina's doctor declared her past all danger of a relapse. It was also Roger's birthday, so he and her father celebrated the double occasion by dining with her in her room. When in full health she was a ravishing creature with the full, voluptuous figure that was regarded in that Georgian age as the height of feminine beauty. Her face was heart-shaped, her eyes nearly black—enormous and sparkling with vitality. Her eyebrows were arched and her full, bright-red lips disclosed at a glance her passionate and tempestuous nature. Now, owing to her illness, she had lost several pounds

10

in weight, her cheeks were a little hollow and her lips still pale from the over-bleeding which had been inflicted on her before, on Roger's return, he had put a stop to it. But her eyes looked larger than ever, her white, even teeth still flashed when she smiled and, in Roger's eyes, her pallor made her more than ever desirable.

When they had finished dinner the Colonel left them. Roger then told her of his abortive mission and his decision to retire for good from Mr. Pitt's service.

At that she shook her dark curls and laid a hand on his arm:

'Dear Roger, disgust and disappointment may make you feel that way now, but I know you too well to believe that you would ever settle down for any length of time. 'Tis not in your nature, and you've been a rolling stone for too long. After a year or two the craving for excitement would drive you abroad again, if not for Mr. Pitt then on some other venture.'

'Nay,' he assured her. 'I'd like nothing better than to be done for good with courts and camps. I'm sick unto death of living a lie and risking my life to no good purpose. I mean that. I vow it, and 'tis high time you married again. Let us be wed, Georgina, and live happily ever after.'

She sighed, 'I would we could, but we've been over this time and again before; and you know full well that 'tis not alone my belief that you would not be long content to live an idle life that prevents my saying "yes". 'Tis only because we have never lived together for any length of time that we have never staled of one another, and when, at long intervals we are again united, both of us feel an immediate upsurge of desire for the other. The joy we derive from such a tenuous but enduring love far exceeds that to be hoped for from any marriage, and I count it too precious to jeopardize by becoming your wife.'

Roger knew only too well the soundness of her argument; yet during the past week he had so persuaded himself that only marriage to her could bring him lasting happiness that he endeavoured desperately to allay her fears, arguing that,

11

now they had both turned thirty and had had many love affairs, there was no longer the same risk that they would tire of one another physically and their marriage come to grief, through one of them developing a passion for someone else.

Finding Georgina adamant to his pleas, he played his last card and said, 'It is two years now since we talked of this, and you said then that you must marry again so that young Charles could be brought up properly by a man; yet you are a widow still. And why? Obviously because you have failed to meet a man whom you would care to have as a husband for yourself and as a father to the boy. Who better than myself could fill both roles; and even should your fears materialize that in time our desire for one another would wane, the children would form a lasting bond between us.'

She remained silent for a moment, then she said gravely, 'Roger, my love, it grieves me greatly to have to tell you this; but at least I find some consolation in that after your two years' absence you must have thought it probable you would find me no longer a widow. I have found such a man. He courted me all through the Fall, and although we are not yet married, we will be in the Spring.'

His hopes now utterly dashed, Roger stared at her in dismay. Then, recovering himself, he murmured, 'If that is so, dear heart, I wish you every happiness. All I pray is that he be a man worthy of you. Who is this monstrous lucky fellow?'

'A Mr. Beefy. He has . . .'

'Beefy!' Roger broke in aghast. 'Georgina, you cannot! For you to marry a man with the ridiculous name of Beefy is unthinkable.'

12

CHAPTER II

WAR OR PEACE ?

A M A Z E D and angry, Roger hurried on, 'You cannot mean it! For God's sake, Georgina, tell me you're joking, and I'll forgive the bad taste of your jest'

Giving him an indulgent smile, she replied, 'Nay, Roger, I am in earnest. If there be aught comic in this it is the expression on your face.'

'But dam'me, woman, do you become Mrs. Beefy you'll be the butt of every wit—the laughing stock of London.'

She shrugged her fine shoulders under the lace négligé. 'I care not a fig for that. 'Tis character that counts. He is a man of high integrity: kind, generous, of a most amiable disposition, only some ten years older than myself and handsome enough to please.'

'Be he plain roast or boiled I care not,' Roger stormed. 'I've never even heard of the fellow, so he cannot be a man of any consequence, nor of a family that has any standing. What in the world can have induced you so to belittle yourself? You've long been a reigning toast and accounted one of the most beautiful women in England. You have brains and talent. Here and in London you entertain the most distinguished men in the realm. Statesmen and ambassadors seek your influence to further their designs. You are very rich and will be still richer when your father dies. You have not only Stillwaters in your own right, but White Knights Park and the house in Berkeley Square as long as Charles remains a minor. By your first marriage you became Lady Etheridge, by your second the Countess of St. Ermins, and when you were a girl you vowed you would be a Duchess before your hair turned grey. Yet now. . . .'

Georgina threw back her dark curls and her gay laugh rang out. 'And maybe I will, should fate decree an early death for poor Mr. Beefy.' Then after a moment she added with a frown, 'Alas, on that score I have certain fears; for I have read his palm and saw in it that he will not live to make old bones.'

Roger had had ample evidence of the psychic gifts Georgina had inherited from her gipsy mother, and he said quickly, 'What point is there then in giving young Charles a step-father who is doomed to an early death?'

'That I did not imply,' she countered. 'Time, as you know, is difficult to assess by such hand readings. I know only that his death will be sudden but with luck it may not occur for ten years and, I pray, may be postponed much longer since I already feel a considerable affection for him.'

'It seems he does not reciprocate that sentiment,' Roger remarked tersely. 'Else how is it that during your desperate illness he has not even shown the concern for you to make his appearance here?'

'Since early December he has been in the West Indies. He has plantations there that are said to be worth a considerable fortune.'

'But Georgina, you have no need of money, and for a woman like yourself even a sugar nabob is a nobody. Among your acquaintance there must be a score of distinguished men who could meet your requirements just as well as he and who would marry you tomorrow. Why? Why, in Gods' name, enter upon this mésalliance that will place you outside the pale of high society?'

Her arched eyebrows lifted, giving her fair face an arrogant

14

expression. 'Nothing, dearest Roger, could put me so far outside the pale that I could not re-enter it whenever I wished. At least I have personality enough for that. But recently I have become plaguey wearied of the fashionable world. Gaming has never attracted me and routs and balls are well enough for a young woman seeking to acquire a beau. Of them I've had my share and more; so it irks me now to be cornered on all occasions by gentlemen pressing me to go to bed with them. My good John Beefy will be the perfect antidote to that. I'll become a country girl, and still have my painting for recreation. Should I tire of cows we can always make a voyage to his estates in the Indies.'

For a further half hour Roger argued with her; but it seemed that her mind was made up so, fearing that further talking would tire her too much, he kissed her good night. As he was about to leave her room she said:

'I fear my father will take no more kindly to my intentions than yourself, and I have not yet told him of them; so I'd prefer that you made no mention of the matter.'

With a cynical little smile Roger turned and made her a bow, 'About his attitude, Madame, you will undoubtedly prove right. And upon my discretion you may rely. I have never derived pleasure from noising abroad the follies of my friends.'

Despite the flippancy of his last remark, as he undressed he was sorely troubled. It was bad enough that Georgina should have brought tumbling to the ground the castles in Spain that he had been building for the past week, but still worse that she should be building one herself on so obvious a quicksand. She had for so long been a sought-after beauty in the gay world of London that he could not believe that she would find contentment in a humdrum life, however pleasant a fellow this John Beefy might be; yet, knowing of old how self-willed she could be, he feared it most unlikely that she could be persuaded to change her mind.

Still much disgruntled, early next morning he set out for London and by midday arrived at the Earl of Amesbury's mansion in Arlington Street. The Earl's tall, lanky son, Lord

Edward Fitz-Deverel—known to his intimates as 'Droopy Ned' from the short sight which gave him a permanent stoop—was Roger's closest friend. On enquiry Roger learned that his Lordship was at home but not yet down, so he went straight up to the suite that Droopy occupied overlooking the Green Park.

Clad in a voluminous silk robe, Turkish slippers and a turban, Droopy was about to sit down to breakfast. Hungry after his twenty-five mile ride Roger gladly accepted his friend's invitation to join him, and a footman was sent down for a second bottle of Claret.

It was close on two years since they had met, so they had a hundred things to talk of and Roger had no secrets from Droopy. Between mouthsful of Dover Sole, truffled Pheasant Pie and Pineapple grown in the Earl's hothouses at Normanrood, he first described the *coup d'état* of *Brumaire* then the expedition to Egypt.

Droopy showed special interest in the latter as, unlike the majority of the young nobles of the day, he took no interest in racing or gambling and abhorred blood sports. Instead, he collected antique jewellery, experimented on himself with strange drugs imported from the East and employed his good brain in studying ancient religions. This last had led to his forming an Egyptian collection, including a mummy, and he could not hear enough about the archaeological discoveries made by the scientists that Bonaparte had taken with him on the expedition.

At length Roger changed the subject to that of his current mission and, after he had been talking about it for some minutes, Droopy said 'Naturally, the knowledge of Bonaparte's offer and its rejection has not yet reached the *hoi-poloi*, but there will be a fine rumpus when it does. As for Charles Fox and his cronies, they can scarce contain their impatience to make capital out of it.'

Roger raised an eyebrow. 'You know already then of this business?'

'Indeed, yes. These past few days it has been the main topic in the clubs.'

16

'What is the general opinion in them?'

'Some, like Billy Pitt, think it an attempt to trick us; the majority that the nation needs peace so badly that we should take a gamble on the Corsican's intentions being honourable, provided the price he asks for peace be not unreasonable. From what you tell me that is the case; so it is a tragedy that his past acts have so prejudiced our Government against him that they'll not listen to him now.'

'In "prejudice" you've said the word,' declared Roger bitterly. 'They are so stuffed with their own righteousness that they'll not concede even the possibility of a man they have condemned being capable of using for the good of all the power he has won.'

Droopy nodded his narrow head, 'Stout Tory as I am, I fear the trouble is that our Prime Minister has been too long in office. 'Tis seventeen years now since he formed his first Government, and because he has always taken so much upon himself every one of them has been a year of strain. Brilliant as he was, he has become worn out with anxieties. From the beginning he has been self-opinionated and autocratic; now he no longer brings his once fine mind to judge events impartially but continues his old policies with dogged inflexibility.'

'I judge you right, Ned. Though I'd be loath to see him go, for I owe him much and have the greatest admiration for him. And who else have we? His cousin Grenville is little more than his mouthpiece on Foreign Affairs. Henry Dundas would act like a bull in a china shop. Addington is a poor weak fellow incapable of handling great issues. As for the Opposition, God forbid! From '89 Charles Fox became a partisan of "Liberty, Equality and Fraternity" with such enthusiasm that on all occasions since he has done his utmost to disrupt our war measures in favour of the French, and not long ago he publicly declared his sympathy with the extremists here who would like to see Britain a Republic. Even so, 'tis a bitter pill that Mr. Pitt's blindness to present reality should compel me to return to France with the report that I have failed in my mission.'

'How soon have you in mind to make the crossing?'

'Within a few days now. In Paris they will already be becoming impatient at my delay, but will put it down to the British Government shilly-shallying. As in time of war there is no French Embassy here I came over in a Revenue cutter which now lies below Tower Bridge and temporarily serves that purpose. Tomorrow I shall apply for clearance.'

Droopy Ned remained silent for a moment, then he said, 'I would not do that, Roger, but remain here yet awhile. Mr. Pitt is obliged to inform Parliament of General Bonaparte's offer and his refusal of it. In fact I learned at White's only yesterday that February 3rd has been settled on as the date for a debate on this matter. So strong is the feeling that a negotiated peace would be in the best interests of the country that, as a result of the debate, many Members may cross the floor of the House. That might well cause the fall of the Government. Should it do so you would, after all, be able to carry back to France a favourable reply to General Bonaparte's letter.'

Roger looked up quickly. Droopy Ned was an exceedingly shrewd man and had often advised him well in the past. 'Since you think that,' he said, 'I'll certainly stay on. After the great services Mr. Pitt has rendered our country, I'd hate to see his Government fall. But to bring about the pacification of Europe is of far greater importance. To accompany me I was given a small staff, including a professional diplomat named Broussalt as my Counsellor. I'll send him back with an interim report and myself remain in England until the result of the debate is known.'

'You will have nothing to lose by so doing,' Droopy said with a smile, 'I'll order your old room here to be prepared for you, and the longer you care to give me your company the happier I'll be. That is,' he added after a moment, 'unless you prefer to return to Stillwaters.'

'I must do so, to collect my belongings. But now that Georgina is out of danger I had meant to make my *adieux* there in any case; so I'd be glad to accept your hospitality for a few nights. Not for longer, though, as my present position in London is an anomalous one. Here I am naturally known

18

as Roger Brook, but there must be diplomats now accredited to the Court of St. James whom I have met abroad. Did I run into one of them he would assume me to be Colonel Breuc, and for my future security the fewer people to whom I have to explain that they have mistaken me for my French cousin, the better. As things are I'll take the opportunity to visit my old father at Lymington, then return here early in February.'

That afternoon Roger wrote his despatch, breaking the bad news to Talleyrand that the British Government were averse to entering into negotiations, then adding that a debate in Parliament on February 3rd might cause the fall of the Government, so he was remaining on with the somewhat slender hope that he would be able to return to France in mid-February with better tidings.

The following morning he waited on Lord Grenville at the Foreign Office and obtained clearance for his cutter, then went down river in a wherry to the ship. Having informed his Counsellor of the situation and handed over to him the papers he had brought, he returned to Amesbury House and dined *tête-à-tête* with Droopy Ned.

Next day he rode out to Richmond Park to visit Thatched House Lodge, a charming 'Grace and Favour' residence of which Mr. Pitt had given him the life tenancy as a reward for his services in the early days of the Revolution, when he had caused the National Assembly to annul the Bourbon 'Family Compact' by which treaty France was obliged to enter on war with England as the ally of Spain.

He had spent only a few nights there since he had lost his wife, Amanda, in December '95, but had left his faithful henchman, the ex-smuggler Dan Izzard there, with a house-keeper, to keep the place up during his absence.

As he expected, he found everything in perfect order. Old Dan was delighted to see him and still more so when Roger told him that, after a last trip to France in February, he intended to retire and in future would live there for a part of each year.

On the 12th he went down to Stillwaters and, that evening,

19

had another long talk with Georgina. Now that he had had time to recover from the shock of what he considered to be her extreme folly, he was better able to reason with her; but all his arguments were to no avail.

At length he said, 'You admit that you do not love this man, but only find him reasonably attractive; so, judging by your past performance, I take it you have no intention of being faithful to him!'

'In that you wrong me, Roger,' she replied, 'I have sown wild oats enough and hope to make him an honest wife. That is,' suddenly she smiled, 'with one exception, a certain Mr. Brook.'

With a laugh he seized her hand and kissed it. 'My sweet, you may be sure I'll hold you to that'

'How could I ever act otherwise, seeing what we are to one another.' With her free hand she drew his face down to hers, gave him a long kiss on the mouth, then murmured with a little giggle, 'Dost remember the night when we agreed that you should marry Amanda and I'd take my Earl, then we slept together?'

'Shall I ever forget it,' he grinned. 'Or that golden afternoon when I was but a boy and you seduced me.'

'You beast!' she cried with mock indignation. ' 'Twas the other way about. And for imputing me a slut I've a mind to punish you. I'm not yet strong but strong enough if you be gentle with me. Get your clothes off and I'll seduce you yet again.'

Next morning, with great reluctance, but knowing that a repetition of such nights would be bound to retard her recovery, Roger bade her a fond farewell, then had the footman who valeted him pack his valise and said good-bye to Colonel Thursby and the children. On the morning of the 15th, having travelled by night coach, he arrived at his old home, Grove Place, Lymington.

It was a pleasant square mansion looking out on the Solent and the western end of the Isle of Wight; not very large but with good, lofty rooms and some seventeen acres of garden, orchard and meadow lands. He had always loved it and on the way down had been happily contemplating now spending a lot of his time there with his widowed father, who had retired from the Navy the previous year.

Since he had run away from home in '83, Roger's only prolonged stay in England had been a period of two years in the early '90s; so, although he had many acquaintances in London, Droopy Ned was his only close friend; whereas in his youth he had had numerous playmates of his own age among the sons of landed gentry in South Hampshire and it would be easy to pick up with several of them again. Moreover, he knew that his father would be delighted for him to bring the children down to stay. At Thatched House Lodge there would be few amusements with which he could provide them, but at Lymington he could teach them to ride in the New Forest, to swim from Hordle Beach and to sail on the Lym river as well as spend happy days with them in the large garden of Grove Place.

He had informed his father by letter of his proposed visit, so the Admiral was expecting him and gave him the most hearty welcome. After Roger had unpacked, and had had a chat with the old houseman, Jim Button, who had known him from his birth, he spent a couple of hours exchanging news with his father. As they had not met for over five years they had much to talk of; but Roger refrained from announcing his intention of abandoning his adventurous life, keeping that as a pleasant surprise for his father after dinner. When the time came it was he who got the surprise, and it proved the second great blow to his hopes of happily settling down.

Pushing the Port over to him, the bulky, red-faced old sailor said gruffly, 'I'm glad you've timed your visit as you have, my boy; for had you made it later than March you'd no longer have found me here.'

Looking up with a start, Roger exclaimed, 'Why so, sir? While a state of war continues, travel on the Continent presents many difficulties. But perhaps you have in mind a voyage as a civilian to see again the scenes of your battles in the West Indies?'

'Nay, lad. I've had enough of a roving life, and for the

past few months after I'd swallowed the anchor I thought I'd be happy enough pottering about here until our Maker sent for me. But that's not proved the case. The cursed gout puts a ball and chain on me so that I can no longer shoot, ride or handle a boat, and I was never much of a fisherman. Our neighbours are kindly enough in asking me over now and then, but there are days together when I never leave the house. It's much too big for a man living on his own and with your dear mother gone it seems plaguey dismal and empty. So for three years from next Quarter Day I've let the place as it stands to one of the Drummonds. He's paying me a good rent, and as he is a banker I can be sure of getting my money.'

'But where will you live?' Roger asked.

'Over at Walhampton with my old crony, Sir William Burrard. He's in the same boat as myself, a widower with a house much too large for him; though he has a family that comes down to stay and that, at times, will make pleasant company for me. I'll have my own rooms, of course, and be free to come and go as I please. But when we are alone on winter evenings it will be pleasant for both of us to sit either side of a good fire and sip our grog together. Mrs. Hapgood is to remain on as housekeeper to the Drummonds, and they are taking the maids, but Jim will be coming with me.'

Roger forced a smile and said in a voice that he hoped sounded enthusiastic, 'I think it a most admirable arrangement.' But inwardly he was grievously disappointed at this unexpected wrecking of his plan to bring the children down for long visits. To speak of it now seemed pointless; so he took a swig of Port, turned the conversation to wine, told his father that before leaving London he had instructed Justerini's to send him down twelve dozen of the best current vintage and hoped that the gout would not punish him too severely for the drinking of it.

For the remainder of the month Roger stayed on at Grove, looking up old friends, going out on pheasant shoots with them and attending a few local dances. This pleasant round made him regret more than ever that, for the next few years at least, he would be unable to resume it by long visits to his old home. On February 2nd he returned to London.

On the evening of the 3rd he accompanied Droopy to the Strangers' Gallery in the House of Commons and they listened to one of the most memorable debates in all the long years that the younger Pitt had been Prime Minister. The Opposition attacked him with the utmost ferocity for rejecting Peace and, during a long oration in which he descanted on Bonaparte's rapacity and perfidy, and stigmatized him as 'This last adventurer in the lottery of Revolutions,' they frequently endeavoured to shout him down. Then Tierney, the Whig leader, defied him to state in one sentence, without 'ifs' and 'buts', the object of the war.

In reply Pitt flung back the retort, 'I know not if I can do it in one sentence, but in one word it is *security*; security against a danger, the greatest that ever threatened the world. How or where did the Honourable gentleman discover that the Jacobinism of Robespierre and of the Triumvirate of the Five Directors, which he acknowledges to be real, has vanished and disappeared because it has all been centred and condensed into one man, who was nursed and reared in its bosom, whose celebrity was gained under its auspices, who was at once the child and champion of all its atrocities and horrors? Is our security in negotiation to be this Bonaparte, who is now the sole organ of all that was formerly dangerous and pestiferous in the Revolution? ... If peace afford no prospect of security, then I say it is prudent in us not to negotiate at the present moment. This is my plea, and by no other do I wish to be tried by God or my country.'

It was a magnificent performance and made a profound impression on the House. At that time Bonaparte had barely started on his great regeneration of the French as a law-abiding people; so Members knew of him only as a grandiose bandit. In consequence it was not to be wondered at that the Opposition was shattered and Pitt left the House exhausted but triumphant with its sanction to continue the war.

Roger had feared that might prove the case, and there was

23

now no point in his remaining longer in England; so the following morning he went to Downing Street and requested an interview with the Prime Minister. After a wait of three quarters of an hour he was shown upstairs.

As he entered the room Mr. Pitt waved him to a chair and said, 'Your waiting on me comes as a surprise, Mr. Brook. I thought you had returned to France with the members of your Mission early in January. Or is it that you have again just crossed the Channel?'

'Nay, sir, I stayed on here,' Roger replied glumly. 'To be frank, distressed as I would be to see you personally defeated, I had hopes that Parliament might refuse to endorse your decision regarding General Bonaparte's offer.'

The Prime Minister shrugged, 'That they did not, demonstrates the soundness of my contentions, and I hope that by now you too are convinced of their rightness.'

'Far from it, sir. I am of the same opinion still, and in this matter believe you to be committing the greatest error in your career.'

'Indeed! In that case, Mr. Brook, I find it surprising that a man of your intelligence should fail to grasp the essentials of the situation. Our obligations to King Charles Emanuel apart, during Bonaparte's absence in Italy the French were driven from all but that country's northern part. The Austrians at this moment are mustering for an offensive aimed at regaining Genoa and Nice. Bonaparte has offered us terms only in the hope of detaching us from our allies; so that our Fleet should not support them in these operations and his own squadrons, now blockaded in Brest and Cherbourg, be freed to sail round into the Mediterranean. Do you not see how unthinkable it is for us to abandon our allies at such a juncture?'

'They abandoned us in '98,' Roger returned stubbornly. 'And both they and we could now agree a peace with France simultaneously, since General Bonaparte has sent the same offer to the Emperor as he has to His Majesty.'

'If his intentions are honest there is one way, and one way only, in which he could show it. That is by using the power

24

he has usurped to re-establish his rightful King on the throne of France.'

'Believe me, sir; even had he the wish to do so the French people would not permit it.'

'Then there is no point in our prolonging this interview. My Lord Grenville will provide you with passports enabling you to return freely to France.' For the first time the Prime Minister's face lit up with a smile as he added, 'Despite our difference of opinion on this present matter, on others in the past I have found your judgment excellent, and I have a great respect for your capabilities. In due course, therefore, when I receive from you further reports on affairs in France I shall continue to set a high value on them.'

'It was, sir, with the intention of disabusing any expectations that you might entertain on that head that I came here this morning,' Roger said gravely. 'You will receive no more reports from me, for I am not agreeable to serve you any longer.'

Mr. Pitt sat back and remained silent for a moment, then he said, 'I find that most regrettable; but from the outrageous manner in which you behaved towards my Lord Grenville and myself when last you were here, and I informed you of our rejection of Bonaparte's offer, I feared that it might portend a cessation of the good understanding between us that has endured for so long. Since you are determined to take no further part in secret diplomacy I assume you do not intend to return to France, but will at once retire into private life.'

'No, sir. I am under an obligation to report personally to Monsieur de Talleyrand on the failure of my mission.'

'In that I appreciate the delicacy of your feelings. So be it then. But that done I take it you will shortly be back here. Being not unmindful of the great services you have rendered myself and your country I should like to confer upon you some sinecure or provide you with an opening for some new career that you may think attractive. You possess both eloquence and a wide knowledge of foreign affairs, so would be a valuable man in Parliament. Without difficulty I could secure your nomination as Member for a Borough.'

For the past fortnight Roger had spent much time taking stock of his situation. Georgina's refusal to marry him and his father's having let Grove Place for three years had robbed him of his best prospects of living a happy life in which he could see a lot of the children. Apart from Georgina, he had no desire at all to marry again and the thought of living alone at Thatched House Lodge did not appeal to him. Lastly, he had come to realize that he had many more friends in France than he had in England, and that life there could hold much more for him. So he replied:

'I thank you, sir, for your good intentions; but here I am a nobody, whereas in France I have already made a career for myself that holds great promise. As an A.D.C. to General Bonaparte and the intimate friend of his Foreign Minister I am close to a seat of power that I am personally convinced will dominate France for a long time to come. To watch its growth and to grow with it offers me a far more interesting life than could being Member for a Rotten Borough. So I intend to return to the service of General Bonaparte and remain in it.'

The Prime Minister stared at him with slowly widening eyes. 'Mr. Brook!' he exclaimed. 'Surely I cannot have taken your meaning aright? I find it impossible to believe that you intend to become a traitor.'

Roger shrugged, 'Not that, sir. But many men born British subjects have made great careers for themselves in the service of other nations. For example, General Acton, who is Prime Minister in Naples, Admiral Sir Samuel Greig, who commanded Catherine of Russia's Navy, the Scotsman General Macdonald whom General Bonaparte counts one of his most able lieutenants. There are too the hundreds of exiles who still cling to the Stuart cause, such as my own cousin, the Earl of Kildonan, who live abroad. Many of them now earn their livings by the sword in the service of France, Holland, Prussia, Austria and other countries.'

'But your case is very different from their's,' retorted Mr. Pitt swiftly. 'They are no more than *beaux sabreurs* who

26

could have no influence on policy or events; whereas you, in the position you occupy in France and with your intimate knowledge of diplomatic relations, should you go over to our enemies could be of immense value to them.'

Again Roger shrugged, 'You need have no fears on that score. At worst I might be called on in a battle to kill an Austrian dragoon, or have him kill me. You may rest assured that I should never give General Bonaparte, or others, any information or counsel that could be damaging to England. And, to be frank, sir, I am not prepared to make any further contribution to your war against France, the sole object of which has now become the restoration of a set of decadent Princes.'

For a further ten minutes the Prime Minister remonstrated with Roger, but in vain. At length he said coldly, 'Very well then. Since you are determined to take this course I will send a message to my Lord Grenville informing him of it. At what hour do you intend to make your official adieux to him?'

'I had intended to wait on him at the Foreign Office and ask for my passports at about four o'clock this afternoon, sir,' Roger replied.

Mr. Pitt nodded coldly; Roger bowed and withdrew. Out in Whitehall he bought a news sheet in order to consult the column advertising the sailings of ships bound for neutral ports in the next few days; then he walked back to Amesbury House. There, over a bottle of sack, he told Droopy about his decision to remain in France and of his interview with the Prime Minister. When he had done, his friend said:

'I can well understand his fears that you might prove an asset to the French; but I know you to be clever enough to give them the impression that you are an ardent Anglophobe without disclosing anything that might advantage them in their war against England. When he thinks upon it he'll doubtless realize that to be a game at which long practice has made you proficient. As for your decision, I judge you right. Life as an aide to General Bonaparte can offer you far more than life could here.'

At a little before four o'clock Roger was approaching the

27

Foreign Office. Drawn up outside it he noticed a coach with its blinds down and standing near it two officers who, from their uniforms, obviously belonged to the Brigade of Guards. As he was about to enter the building the shorter of the two, a Captain, called to him, 'One moment, sir.'

Halting, he turned towards the officer who saluted him politely and said, 'Mr. Brook, the Prime Minister ordered me to wait for you here and request you to accompany us.' Then he opened the carriage door.

Considerably surprised at being summoned in this fashion, and wondering what new proposition Mr. Pitt intended to make to him, Roger got into the vehicle. Removing his tall bear-skin the Captain followed him, while his companion, an Ensign, marched round to the other side and got in there. As they shut the doors the coachman whipped his horse into a brisk trot and the Captain said with a bow:

'Mr. Brook, it is my unhappy duty to inform you that you are under arrest, and that I have been ordered to escort you to the Tower.'

CHAPTER III

THE PRISONER IN THE TOWER

'THE TOWER! Arrest! What the devil do you mean?'
Roger exclaimed angrily.

'Precisely what I said, sir,' replied the Captain calmly.

'Dam'me! There must be some mistake. You've confused
me with some other person of similar name.'

'No, sir. The Prime Minister gave me a very clear description of you.'

'God's blood! You can't do this! Show me your warrant.'

'I have no warrant.'

'Then you are illegally interfering with the liberty of a
subject. And the law is still maintained in England. Either
you'll let me out or I'll see to it that you answer for this act
to a Court Martial.'

'The Prime Minister's personal order, sir, is warrant
enough for me.'

'You may think so, but even Prime Ministers are not
entitled to order an arbitrary arrest. I demand that you take
me to him.'

To that the Captain made no reply so, after a moment,
Roger said:

'Inform me, at least, of the charge made against me.'

'I have no idea. Moreover my orders are to hold no discourse with you.'

While Roger seethed with silent rage the coach bowled along. For a few minutes he contemplated an attempt to open the door and throw himself out; but he was sitting on the back seat and the two officers were sitting facing him so it was certain that at his first movement they would lean forward and grab his arms. As the blinds of the coach were down he could not see the route it was taking but, by that time, he judged that it was probably in the Strand and approaching Temple Bar. Being aware of the ancient City privilege that no troops might enter it without the permission of the Lord Mayor he thought it just possible that, when they reached the Bar, there might occur a hold-up of which he could take advantage; but another ten minutes passed without the carriage being halted, so the chance of a Beadle opening the door and seeing the uniforms of his companions had by then gone.

When it did halt, the door was opened by a Guards sergeant at the entrance to the Tower. The Captain gave the password of the day then, as the coach clattered over the drawbridge, he put up the blinds. Roger caught a glimpse of the arches of the Middle and Byward Towers as he passed beneath them, and of Water Lane until, opposite Traitor's Gate, the carriage turned left up a steep slope and drew up in the square beyond it outside the King's House, in which the Mayor of the Tower had his residence.

After a short wait the Mayor, Colonel Matthew Smith, received them in his office and the Captain handed him a letter. Roger at once began a heated protest about his arbitrary arrest, but Colonel Smith sat down at his desk and, ignoring him, read through the despatch, then he said:

'Mr. Brook, this is an order from the Prime Minister to me to detain you here during His Majesty's pleasure. No reason for so doing is given and it is not for me to ask for one or to take notice of the protest you have just made. I am instructed to provide you with comfortable quarters and to feed you from my table; but you are not to be allowed to write to anyone and are to be held incommunicado; so your warders will receive orders not to enter into conversation with you.'

After a moment he went on, 'Enclosed is a letter which you are required to copy in your own hand. It concerns the collecting and bringing here of your personal belongings.' He then handed Roger the letter. It was addressed to Lord Edward Fitz-Deverel, and read:

'Dear Ned,

'Unforeseen circumstances have caused me to change my plans. Be good enough to have my belongings packed and handed to the bearer of this note. I will explain matters when next we meet. In the meantime my thanks for your hospitality.'

While the Colonel pulled up a chair for him and produced pen and paper Roger's mind was racing. His arrest had been so managed that no-one had witnessed it. And no-one, other than Droopy Ned, would be aware of his disappearance so set enquiries on foot about him. If he copied the letter, that would put Droopy's mind at rest, so it appeared evident that it had been designed for that purpose. Quickly he shook his head:

'No, sir. I'll not copy that letter and become a party to concealing Mr. Pitt's illegal and most extraordinary treatment of me. If I fail to appear at Amesbury House at latest by tomorrow Lord Edward will have the town scoured for me. There is a chance that he may learn the truth, and should he do so he'll raise all hell to get me out of here.'

The Colonel shrugged, 'I cannot force you to put pen to paper, Mr. Brook; but there is another passage in the Prime Minister's letter of which I have not yet informed you. Should you refuse his request his instructions are that I should put you in an unfurnished cell and your fare is to be bread and water.'

Roger's face went pale with rage, and he cried indignantly, 'By God, this is intolerable! He cannot keep me here indefinitely, and when I get free I'll see to it that he never hears the last of this. The stink made in Parliament when Captain

31

Jenkins produced his ear that the Spaniards had lopped off will be nothing to the stench I'll raise.'

'With what you may do in the future, Mr. Brook, I am not concerned. We are speaking of the present. And I must warn you, do you prove adamant you will find life here as His Majesty's guest most uncomfortable.'

Fighting down his fury, Roger let his judgment get the better of his urge to resist further. As he had been spirited away without trace, even if Droopy did raise a hue and cry for him the odds were all against his whereabouts being discovered. Realizing that he snapped 'Very well,' and plumping himself down at the desk scrawled a copy of the letter. Then, pushing it towards the Colonel, he said;

'And now, sir, I demand that you send for an attorney, in order that he may issue a writ of Habeas Corpus on my behalf.'

Colonel Smith shook his head, 'I have already informed you that you are to be held incommunicado. In any case, owing to the riots in the industrial centres brought about by agitators infected by the pestilence of the French Revolution, the right to issue writs of Habeas Corpus was among those suspended by the Government some considerable time ago.'

Picking up a hand bell on his desk he rang it loudly. A Sergeant of the Yeomen of the Guard entered. Clicking the butt of his pike sharply on the floor he stood stiffly at attention while the Mayor said to him, 'You are to take this prisoner to cell five in the Laathorn Tower, and he will be known by that number. If he mentions his name it is not to be repeated. He is to send or receive no letters or messages and no-one is to enter into conversation with him.'

Realizing that the Mayor and officers had only been doing their duty, Roger bowed to them and said, 'Gentlemen, I pray you pardon me for my rudeness towards you. It was caused by my having become somewhat overwrought from the shock of learning that my arrest had been ordered, for I know not what reason, by one whom I have always accounted a friend.'

All three returned his bow and Colonel Smith replied,

'You have my sympathy, sir, and my rest assured that I will do my best to make your stay here as little disagreeable as possible.' The two officers then saluted and took their leave; after which Roger followed the Sergeant out and, escorted by two other Yeomen who were waiting in the hall, was taken to the Laathorn Tower.

The chamber into which he was locked was lofty, spacious and reasonably well-equipped with oak furniture of a considerable age, most of the pieces having the names or initials of past prisoners carved on them. The early winter dusk had already fallen and three candles and a tinder box had been left for him. He lit two of them but the light they gave made only a pool in the centre of the gloomy room and, as he moved about, threw grotesque shadows of himself on the bare walls. On examining the bed he found it far from soft but he had slept on worse ones when in camps or passing a night at poor inns. Lying down on it, he stared up at the vaulting of the stone ceiling and considered his position.

When he had declared that he did not know the reason for his arrest he had been telling the truth; but, while sitting silent in the semi-darkness of the carriage on the way to the Tower, he had already made a fair guess at it for, preposterous as it seemed, he could think of no other. It was that Mr. Pitt looked on his decision to follow a career in France as one of Bonaparte's staff officers as so fraught with danger to the interests of England that he had resolved to detain him forcibly. In one sense it was a compliment, but in another a gross slander on his loyalty to the country of his birth; and he resented it intensely.

The more he thought about the circumstances of his arrest the more shocked he became at the Prime Minister's action. He had broken no law, yet here he was as good as in a dungeon. Since he had not been charged with any crime he was denied the right to a trial at which he might defend himself. Still worse he was being held incommunicado, so he could not write to friends asking their help to secure his release, or even to Mr. Pitt asking for an explanation. He had been picked up without warning, incarcerated in a fortress from which he knew it was impossible to escape and orders had been given to keep him there during His Majesty's—or what amounted to Mr. Pitt's—pleasure.

And this was England. The boasted Land of the Free. Not France in the days of the absolute monarchy when, at the whim of a King's mistress, her Royal lover signed a *lettre de cachet* consigning indefinitely to the Bastille some wretched scribbler who had lampooned her. But that was precisely what had happened to him.

It was said that at times such unfortunates had been forgotten and left for years in prison until they died there. But Roger endeavoured to console himself with the thought that such a fate was most unlikely to be his. It seemed reasonable to assume that Mr. Pitt had simply taken prompt action to prevent any possibility of his leaving London in a ship that was sailing on the night tide. Having insured against that the Prime Minister must think again, and produce either a bribe or a threat which might deter him from carrying out his intention of returning to France.

For a while Roger speculated on what form Mr. Pitt's approach would take, but his treatment of him and the aspersion on his loyalty made him more than ever determined to return to Bonaparte's service.

At seven o'clock a supper of cold meat and apple tart, with a bottle of passable wine, was brought to him and, not long after he had finished his meal, his valise arrived. Having unpacked it he was glad to find that it contained a book he had been reading; so he went to bed and read until close on ten, then he snuffed out the candles. For a while he mused on the extraordinary situation he was in, but he was no longer particularly troubled by it as he felt confident that Mr. Pitt would send for him next day; so he soon fell into a sound sleep.

But Mr. Pitt did not send for him next day, nor the next, nor the next, and gradually his anxiety about what the future held for him increased. His routine each day never varied. Every morning he was taken out for an hour's exercise and for the rest of the day he remained locked in his room. The

34

meals brought up to him were plentiful but plain, so he thought it probable that the Governor fared much better at his own table. Moreover the food lost much of its attraction from the fact that, having to be carried a long way from the kitchen, it was nearly always no more than luke-warm when it reached him; but the Governor sent him half a dozen books, for which he was duly grateful.

Several times he attempted to start a conversation with his gaolers, but they obeyed their orders in refusing to reply to him. In vain he racked his brains for a way in which he could communicate with the outside world. From the narrow, barred window of his room he could look down on the Pool of London. In it there lay scores of tall-masted ships, any one of which might have carried him to freedom, but he was as remote from them as though he were standing on the Moon; and, even if he had had writing materials, an appeal for help dropped out of the window would only have fluttered down inside the outer wall of the fortress.

Another three days dragged by. In vain now he endeavoured to concentrate on reading. For hours he restlessly paced his chamber cursing Pitt and vowing that he would get even with him. There were other long periods when he tossed restlessly on the bed endeavouring to gain freedom in sleep from his tormenting anxiety. Sometimes he dropped off for an hour or two, but that made it more difficult for him to get to sleep at night. And he found the long dark evenings almost insupportable. The shadows of the big gloomy chamber seemed to close round him making a prison within a prison and emphasizing his utter isolation. Mr. Pitt, he knew, had a thousand matters to engage his attention; so it now seemed to Roger quite on the cards that by this time the Prime Minister *had* forgotten him. If so it might even be many months before the thought would recur to him that on an impulse he had had his once most trusted secret agent arrested. Meanwhile Roger must continue to fret away the seemingly endless hours pacing up and down between the stone walls; for there was no way in which he could bring an end to his captivity.

He had been confined in the Tower for exactly a week

when, now to his surprise and sudden resurgence of hope, the Mayor sent for him. Fighting down his excitement he followed the Beefeater Sergeant, with his swinging lantern and bunch of big keys, down to the Mayor's office. In it were the Captain and his Ensign who had arrested Roger. Colonel Smith greeted him pleasantly and said with a smile:

'Mr. Brook, these two gentlemen have brought me an order for your release. I hope that it may prove a permanent one. But you must consider yourself as still under arrest while they escort you to the Prime Minister, who has asked that you should be brought to him.'

Roger smiled, 'I thank you, sir, for your good wishes, and for your fair treatment of me while I have been your prisoner. I hope that when next we meet it will be in happier circumstances.'

Five minutes later he was in the same coach that had brought him to the Tower, sitting facing the two officers. The blinds were again down so he saw nothing of the darkening streets through which they passed until the coach pulled up outside 10, Downing Street. They were admitted to the house and, after standing silent in the waiting room for some ten minutes, the Groom of the Chambers came to them. Bowing, he asked Roger to follow him, and requested his escort to remain there in attendance. With a firm step and a smile that had no trace of humour in it, Roger accompanied the servant upstairs. He was shown in to Mr. Pitt and the door closed behind him.

Giving him a nod of greeting that lacked any suggestion of cordiality, the Prime Minister indicated that he should take a chair. Instead Roger remained standing in front of the desk and said coldly, 'While I continue to be your prisoner, sir, it is more fitting that I should listen to what you have to say as would a convicted criminal in the dock before a judge.'

Mr. Pitt made an impatient gesture, 'So you are as stiff-necked as ever, and have failed to learn the lesson that I hoped a week in the Tower would teach you.'

'Oh, I've learnt it, and full well,' Roger flared, his dark blue eyes now nearly black with rage. 'It is that Charles Fox, whom I have long regarded as near a traitor, from his advocacy of revolutionary ideas, is in truth far from that and a true champion of Liberty. Whereas you, under the guise of patriotism, have taken on yourself the mantle of a tyrant. Your treatment of me has not differed in the least from that of King Louis XV when he had persons who were obnoxious to him flung into the Bastille without trial, justice or thought of mercy. How dare you behave towards a free-born Englishman in such a manner! Your conduct is an outrage and, Prime Minister though you be, I'll have the law upon you for it.'

The Prime Minister's grey tired face remained unmoved and he gave a slight shrug of his narrow shoulders, as he said, 'About any such intention, Mr. Brook, I must disabuse your hopes. Having been so long abroad you may not have heard how His Majesty's coach was stoned while on its way to Parliament, of the riots in Bristol, Norwich and other cities during which the mobs were incited to seize private property, or that twenty thousand Londoners congregated not long since at Islington to demand the abolition of the Monarchy and the establishment of a Republic here. To suppress such grievous disorders I was compelled to take strong measures. They included arrest without warrant, the suspension of Habeas Corpus and confinement in prison during His Majesty's pleasure. So I was entirely within my rights when ordering your detention.'

'But why?' Roger burst out. 'What possible cause have you for inflicting this ignominy and discomfort on me?'

'The answer to that is simple. When last we met you told me that you had been present at the debate in the House on February 3rd. You must then surely recall that the basis of my reply to Tierney's attack upon me was the necessity for protecting the security of the realm. You, Mr. Brook, threatened to become a menace to that; therefore I had no option but to have you locked up. I must add that my view about you remains unchanged. As an adherent of Bonaparte you could not be other than a danger to this country. In consequence I am determined not to permit you to rejoin him.'

37

'How do you propose to prevent that?' Roger inquired. 'By returning me to the Tower and holding me a prisoner there indefinitely?'

'I could, but I should be loath to do so. Under the emergency law, should more than four persons congregate in the street to discuss politics they could be transported to the plantations in the Indies. I could arrange such a voyage for you and it might serve to chasten you. At all events it would keep you out of mischief for many months to come. But again, in consideration of your past services, I am reluctant to be harsh with you. Therefore I give you a choice. It is either that, or you will proceed to New Holland—Australia as we now prefer to call it—and furnish me with a report on the facilities for our establishing a Colony there.'

'Should I accept, what guarantee would you have that I would ever go to this outlandish place?'

'Your word as a gentleman, which I am prepared to accept.'

'I thank you, sir, but I'll not give it. I will neither go to New Holland nor allow you to send me to the Indies.'

Suddenly Roger gave a harsh laugh, 'I warned you that you had made a grave error in rejecting General Bonaparte's overture. You have made a still greater one in sending for me today. In the field of politics I would never dream of challenging you; but you have had the temerity to challenge me on my own ground. We are face to face here in this room and, to my great regret, as enemies. You are set on thwarting my will. I am determined to regain the freedom of which you have arbitrarily deprived me and to pursue in future any mode of life that I please. In the past had some person sought to prevent me from bringing back to England secret information of great importance, do you think that I should have hesitated to kill him? Why then, since you are proving an obstacle to my plans, should I refrain now from killing you?'

Stepping forward, Roger swiftly snatched up the thick, two-foot-long ebony ruler from the desk that lay between them and waved it threateningly.

38

The Prime Minister sat back with a jerk, stared at him round-eyed and exclaimed, 'You would not dare!'

'Why should you think that?' Roger smiled. 'While in your service I've killed a score of people. And to kill you would establish me for life in General Bonaparte's good graces.'

'You are gone mad!' Mr. Pitt murmured. 'It must be so. 'Tis the only possible explanation of this threat to kill me.'

'I pray it may not come to that. But I must hit you on the head to render you unconscious for a while; and should your skull prove thin such a blow could make an end of you.'

Mr. Pitt did not lack courage. Coming to his feet, he held out his hand and said sharply, 'Mr. Brook, give me back that ruler.'

'Nay. I'll not do that unless you agree my terms unreservedly. And, for your skull's sake, heed this warning. Do you raise your voice above normal, or make the least motion towards your bell, I'll strike you down without further parley.'

'What are your terms?'

'That you should sit down again and write three brief documents. One, a paper for the officers downstairs stating that you have freed me from arrest. Two, an order to the Admiralty to have me transported back to France. Three, an acknowledgment that without just cause and for your own private ends you had me imprisoned in the Tower of London for a week.'

'Never! Your demands are outrageous.'

'It is through your own folly that I am compelled to make them. Had you allowed me to proceed to France without interference instead of acting against me as though I intended to become a traitor. . . .'

'You gave every indication that you might become one,' the Prime Minister broke in angrily. ' 'Twas clear to me that this ruffian Bonaparte had bewitched you. Once you had broken your ties with England, as you said you meant to do, the fascination he holds for you would have led you into becoming an enemy of your country, and a most dangerous one.'

'There you wrong me grievously. Having played a double game for so long, why should you consider me incapable of continuing to do so? I said only that I was no longer willing to act as a secret agent for you. It does not in the least follow that I would not aid the cause of England should an opportunity arise. And it well may. Britain and France are both nearly exhausted, and I am convinced that the time is not far distant when they must agree a peace. When that time comes, having the ear of Talleyrand and Bonaparte there is at least a possibility that I may influence them a little into giving us more generous terms than they at first had a mind to do.'

Mr. Pitt frowned, 'I will admit that view of the matter had not occurred to me. Very well, then. I withdraw my objection. You may return to France. But in no circumstances will I sign a paper admitting that I had you imprisoned without just cause. I did so in the belief that it was for the protection of the safety of the realm.'

'In that I believe you. Nevertheless, you must do as I require,' Roger replied firmly. 'You have made it clear that up till a few minutes ago you had lost faith in my integrity. How can I be sure that your trust in me is fully restored, that you will not after all prevent me from going back to France by having me again arrested before I can leave the country? Only your admission that you had me falsely imprisoned will protect me against that.'

'I'll not give it you!' snapped the Prime Minister. 'I'll see you damned first.'

'Then you leave me no alternative but to strike you down and, leaving you either dead or unconscious, make my escape by way of the garden.'

' 'Twould be the act of a madman. What hope could you then have of getting back to France? Within a few hours, on learning of such a brutal assault, every man in southern England would be on the look out to apprehend you.'

Roger gave a grim smile, 'You sadly under-estimate my resourcefulness. I'd not attempt to cross the Channel. I'd go only as far as Brooks' Club and seek sanctuary there. In that hotbed of your political enemies I'd tell my tale, then write it and give it to the newshawks for publication. Later I might hang for having attacked you. But, by God, the story of your having abused your powers to imprison a law-abiding subject would bring about your ruin. You would be hounded from the House.'

For a long moment the Prime Minister stared at this terrible antagonist whom he had made into an enemy. Then he sat down at his desk.

Two days later a British sloop under a flag of truce landed Roger in France.

CHAPTER IV

THE REBIRTH OF A NATION

L a t e i n the evening of February 17th Roger arrived at *La Belle Etoile*, a commodious hostelry no great distance from the Louvre. He had long made it his headquarters while in Paris, and its proprietors, the Blanchards, were old and trusted friends. They had first known him as a young assistant secretary to the Marquis de Rochambeau, seen him blossom into an elegant Chevalier who made one of Queen Marie Antoinette's circle at Versailles, given him shelter while he had lived in Paris disguised as a ragged, filthy *sans culotte* and, more recently, felt honoured that now, as a Colonel A.D.C. to the First Consul, he should continue to live at their inn rather than seek the more luxurious quarters that he could well afford.

Maître Blanchard greeted him with enthusiasm and took him at once into the private parlour, in which he had enjoyed many a good meal cooked by Madame. As the stalwart Norman landlord relieved him of his steeple-crowned hat and heavy, many-caped grey travelling coat, that portly lady said, 'You must be tired and hungry, *Monsieur le Colonel*. Sit you by the fire while I order your old room to be got ready and our biggest warming pan put in the bed. Then I'll make you

42

your favourite omelette with mushrooms and half a dozen eggs.'

Blanchard nodded his round head, on which the fair hair was now thinning. 'Go to it, wife, while I get up two bottles of good full-bodied Burgundy wine with which to celebrate the return of our distinguished guest.'

A quarter of an hour later Roger was attacking the huge omelette with zest, while Blanchard was giving him the news of the day. 'You cannot imagine,' he said, 'how greatly the state of things has been bettered here during the seven weeks you have been away. The First Consul has proved himself a miracle worker and is bringing order out of the chaos we have suffered for so long. Whereas for many winters half Paris has nearly starved, food is now plentiful and reasonable in price. There are no longer queues outside the bakers' shops, property is again respected and the streets have become safe, even at dead of night.'

'That is good news indeed,' Roger replied. 'And what of the new Constitution? Has it yet been passed?'

'Not yet, but it should be soon. There can be little doubt of that, for General Bonaparte's popularity is now immense.'

The *coup d'état* of *Brumaire* had taken place on November 9th. On the 11th Bonaparte, the Abbé Siéyès and his crony Roger Ducos had been appointed provisional Consuls and the sittings of the Legislative Assembly had been suspended pending the passing of a new Constitution. By December 13th its form had been agreed and the sanction of the people to its acceptance asked in a national plebiscite. On that day too Bonaparte had succeeded in getting rid of his troublesome colleagues and having them replaced by Cambacérès and Lebrun.

This new instrument of government, known as '*The Constitution of the Year VIII*,' was to consist of two Chambers: the Tribunate which could propose new laws but could not pass them, and a Legislative Assembly which had no power to initiate new legislation, but was to debate the measures put forward by the Tribunate and either pass or reject them. Superior to both, there was to be a Senate of conservative elder statesmen, whose function it was to appoint the members of both Chambers. Finally, on December 26th, the day Roger had left for England, the Consuls had announced the formation of yet another Body, that had not been mentioned in the Constitution. This was a Council of State, to consist of not more than forty members: Generals, Admirals, lawyers and others who had distinguished themselves either before or during the Revolution. Its powers had not been stated but Roger, knowing Bonaparte so well, at once foresaw that before long he would rule through it, and the Chambers be reduced to no more than debating societies in which the members could air their opinions.

Tired after his long and uncomfortable journey from the coast, as soon as he had finished his meal Roger thanked the honest couple, asked them to excuse him and went to bed.

Next morning he unpacked one of the trunks that were always kept for him at *La Belle Etoile* and donned his fine uniform with its gold epaulettes and the special sash of an A.D.C., then went out to call on Monsieur de Talleyrand. On his way to the Foreign Minister's he saw that, whereas when he had left Paris the streets had been filthy with litter, they were now clean and that the people in them, instead of having a sullen and often furtive look, were going about their business briskly with cheerful faces. These signs were the best possible evidence of the success of the measures that Bonaparte was taking.

On his return from exile in America, Talleyrand had at once resumed his old life as a *grand seigneur*, and now lived in a big mansion in the Rue du Bac. His major-domo received Roger as an old friend of his master's, said he would send in his name at once and showed him into a handsomely furnished room where a dozen people were waiting on the pleasure of the Minister. But Roger was there only for a few minutes, then the major-domo returned and conducted him across the hall to another room where Talleyrand was sitting, still at breakfast. With his usual charming manners he rose and invited Roger to join him. Roger had already break-

44

fasted but he cheerfully accepted a good portion of truffled *vol-au-vent* and a glass of Château Lafitte.

Charles Maurice de Talleyrand-Périgord was now forty-six. His grandfather had been a Prince de Chalais, so he was descended from one of the greatest families of ancient France. As the eldest son of a Marquis he should have inherited the title and estates but a careless servant had dropped him while still an infant, causing an injury to his right leg that, through lack of proper attention, had made him lame for life. This rendered a military career impossible; so his father had disinherited him in favour of a younger brother and forced him, much against his will, to go into the Church. Embittered by this, in '89 he had enthusiastically embraced the movement to curtail the authority of the Monarchy and nobility, and had become one of the most prominent leaders of the Liberal Revolution. When the National Assembly had repudiated the rule of Rome and sought to establish instead an independent Church in France, he had been the first Bishop to transfer his allegiance to it; but since his return from exile he had given up even the pretence of being a priest, and certainly no man could have been less fitted for such a role.

Handsome, elegant, witty, brilliantly intelligent, and dressed always as a layman in the richest silks and satins, he had from the age of sixteen devoted himself to a life of debauchery. Many of the most beautiful women at the Court of Versailles, and most of those in Paris who had graced the salons during the dissolute period of the Directory, had been his mistresses. He was a cynic of the first order and venal to the last degree, having, since he had become Foreign Minister, amassed a great fortune in bribes. But he was already proving himself to be the greatest statesman of his age.

Unfailingly courteous, preserving always an unruffled calm, graceful in movement despite his limp, he was an aristocrat to his finger tips. His slightly retroussé nose gave his face an autocratic look, but humour lurked in his grey-blue eyes under their heavy lids, and his deep voice was beautifully modulated.

As Roger took his seat at table, Talleyrand asked, 'Well,

45

Monsieur l'Ambassadeur, what news out of England? Do you bring Peace in your pocket?'

Roger now had reason to thank his stars both that he had sent Broussalt ahead of him with an interim report and later been imprisoned in the Tower for a week. The first had conveyed the information that the British Cabinet was averse to peace, the second had given time enough for particulars to have reached France that the attack by the Opposition on Pitt had failed to bring about the fall of his Government. With a smile he replied:

'Your spies, *Monsieur le Ministre*, must be a sadly inefficient lot if they have allowed you to suppose that I might have. It must be some days now since you learned how Mr. Pitt scattered the friends of peace like chaff before him in the debate on February 3rd.'

'Yes. He surpassed himself. One cannot but admire the man, ostrich-like though he has now become about realities.'

'True. I doubt though whether the First Consul will accept that as an excuse for my failure; and I am preparing myself with such fortitude as I can for him to order me to be bastinadoed.'

'Knowing how ill he takes any thwarting of his plans I think that in normal circumstances you might well fear to lose your epaulettes. But you are notoriously lucky, and your luck is certainly in that it should be today you must face him. The result of the plebiscite has at last come to hand. The voting was three million, eleven thousand and seven in favour of adopting the Constitution and only one thousand, five hundred and twenty six against.'

Roger looked up quickly. 'What staggering figures. No man can ever have had a more overwhelming testimony to the nation's confidence in him.'

'Yes, it is a veritable triumph; the more so as, against my advice, no attempt was made to rig the polls. Naturally, he is overjoyed; so I do not think you will suffer even a temporary eclipse from the radiance of our new *Soleil*.'

'You comfort me greatly. I had feared at least a period of some months before he would again wish to see me about

46

him. And your comparison of him with the sun is apt. He has already brought light and cheerfulness into the streets of Paris. It has become a different city since I left it.'

'That is no wonder; for he keeps us as busy as a whole hive of bees, working up to sixteen hours a day and every day issuing a dozen or more new ordinances. Moreover he loves his work, even singing at it in that awful voice of his. Nothing escapes him and he has a finger in every pie. One moment he is arranging for the formation of a National Bank of France to support trade; at another striking the anniversary of the death of Louis XVI and other holidays from the list of public festivals, so that more work will get done, the next planning a vast system of free education for all. Did you know that last year there were no more than twenty four Elementary Schools in Paris and they could take only one thousand pupils? There is no limit to the schemes that jostle one another in his fertile brain.'

'I can well believe you. But, well informed though he is on many subjects, I would have thought that he knew little about such matters as finance and education.'

While pouring Roger and himself another glass of wine, Talleyrand replied, 'That is so; but he is an amazingly quick learner. He attends nearly every meeting of the Council of State, listens avidly to everyone there whose experience of a subject entitles him to express an opinion, and only afterwards takes a decision. Neither is he too proud to accept advice from his Ministers. In that Fouché and I are specially favoured; for he decided that, unlike the others, who are required to carry their problems to all three Consuls, Police matters and Foreign Affairs should be discussed by us with him alone. Each time I see him he welcomes me warmly, and he has given me the opportunity to coach him for many hours on international relationships.'

'Then your position with him must be an exceptionally strong one,' Roger smiled, 'and I congratulate you on it.'

'Thanks, my dear fellow. It is certainly most satisfactory. Of course, his impetuous nature gets the better of him at times. But I have a remedy for that. My congenital idleness is known to you, and on occasion I make use of it. When he orders me to take some measure on which I think his judgment to be at fault I leave the matter unattended for a few days. By the time I broach it again he has almost always realized that to pursue it would be folly, and he saves his face by telling me to hold it over. Then no more is said of it.'

Roger laughed. 'I count him fortunate, *Monsieur le Ministre*, to have you in his service. With your guidance he should do great things for France.'

Talleyrand shrugged, 'If he lasts a year he will go far.'

'Surely you cannot doubt his lasting that long?' Roger said, much surprised. 'This overwhelming vote of confidence from the French people shows them to have taken him to their hearts.'

'The memory of the public is extraordinarily short. They will lionize a man one month and his opponent the next. In any case, should they still be loyal to him, their feelings will be of no account, because real power is never vested in the masses. Bonaparte has many enemies, and they may combine to pull him down.'

'I can well believe that several of his fellow Generals are mightily jealous of him.'

'That is so; Moreau, Bernadotte and Masséna particularly. But that is not his greatest danger. It lies in the fact that he has secretly abandoned the principles of the Revolution, yet at the same time is averse to a restoration of the Monarchy. Both factions will in due course seek to destroy him: the one because the Jacobins will find out that he has nothing but detestation and contempt for their doctrine of equality, the other because they will wish to replace him by a *coup d'état* with some other prominent man more likely to invite Louis XVIII to ascend the throne.'

'He is, then, walking a tightrope.'

'Exactly. And with commendable skill. He displayed it in his selection of his two fellow Consuls. Cambacérès was a member of the Convention which sent Louis XVI to the guillotine. Lebrun, on the other hand, played no part in the

Terror and is believed to be, in the secret, a Royalist. Again, observe his choice of his two most prominent Ministers. It was reported to me that he remarked to his brother Joseph "What revolutionary would not have confidence in an order of things where Fouché is a Minister? And what gentleman would not expect to find existence possible under a former Bishop such as Talleyrand?'

'Since he has made such a promising start, more's the pity that the war should continue, at least with England, and so divert his attention from the reforms he is undertaking.'

'With Austria too. Owing, no doubt, to the recent successes of his armies in Italy, the Emperor Francis has refused our offer to treat on the basis reached at Campo Formio. But matters might be worse. That timid, spineless creature, young Frederick William of Prussia, is more than ever enamoured of neutrality, so will continue to sit upon the fence; and the Czar Paul has recently withdrawn from the Coalition. It is our good fortune that he became disgruntled by the Emperor's treatment of the Army sent under Suvarov to aid the Austrians in Italy, and still more so at the mishandling by that stupid Duke of York of the Russian expeditionary force sent last autumn to Holland, which led to the surrender of the Allied forces there. We are now intent on wooing the Czar, and should we succeed in winning him over to us we'll cook the Austrian goose between two fires.'

'Is Moreau still commanding on the Rhine?'

'Yes. As a soldier he is rated second only to our little man; and since he must be regarded as a potential enemy it was a wise move to confirm him in his command. As long as he remains out of Paris 'tis unlikely that he will be persuaded to enter into any intrigue against the new Government. Masséna, too, might have proved a danger. Only four months ago, just before Bonaparte's return from Egypt, he had been acclaimed a national hero owing to his great victory in Switzerland which saved France from invasion by the Russians. But at present he has more than enough to keep him busy defending the Ligurian Republic.'

'From what I heard in London I gathered that things are going far from well with our army in Italy.'

Talleyrand nodded. 'That is so. Masséna is several times outnumbered by the Austrians, so is hard-pressed to hold his own. 'Tis my opinion that, should Bonaparte decide to take the field in person again, it is to Masséna's assistance that he will march in the Spring. But for the moment my instinct tells me that he is rather pleased than otherwise that his brother General should be taking some hard knocks.'

After wiping his lips with a lace-edged napkin, Talleyrand went on:

'And now, *cher ami,* you must excuse me. I'd willingly sit here gossiping with you all morning but, alas, to keep my position I must at times do a little work, and numerous people wait to see me. No doubt we'll meet again at the Tuileries this evening.'

'Is there a reception there then?'

'Yes, for the First Consul to receive congratulations on the result of the plebiscite. I would advise you, therefore, not to attempt to beard him in his den this morning, but to refrain from showing yourself until he is surrounded by smiling faces.'

Roger bowed. 'Your Excellency's advice has always proved invaluable to me, and I'll certainly take it now.'

The Minister smiled and laid a beautifully-kept hand on his arm. 'It will always be at your disposal. I'll never forget that you saved me from being sent to the guillotine during the Revolution.'

At seven o'clock that evening Roger joined the throng of men, most of whom were in brilliant uniforms, and silk-clad bejewelled women, that was making its way slowly up the grand staircase in the Palais des Tuileries. The last time he had done so was at Bonaparte's reception on Christmas Day, a date deliberately chosen by him to indicate that the Christian festival was to be revived and the persecution of the Church to cease. Since *Brumaire* he had occupied the Luxembourg, but now that the plebiscite had confirmed him in power it was being said that he intended to take up his

50

residence in the Tuileries permanently as from the following day.

At length Roger came opposite him and made his bow. Bonaparte was then aged thirty, a little under medium height and still slim. His large head was finely shaped, his forehead superb, his eyes big and luminous, his nose and mouth well modelled, his jaw exceptionally powerful and his face pale. His reactions to what people said to him were as swift as lightning and conveyed instantly pleasure, doubt, sorrow or anger. He had beautiful hands of which he was very proud and while conversing would often glance at them with complacency. When Roger had first met him at the siege of Toulon he had been an out-at-elbow Artillery officer with lank, ill-kept dark hair falling to his shoulders. He had since become fastidious in his dress, never wearing a shirt twice, and scrupulously clean in his person, frequently spending up to two hours a day in his bath while dictating to his secretary.

'Ha, Breuc!' he exclaimed in his rasping voice with its heavy Italian accent. 'So those pig-headed fools have kicked you out of England. Talleyrand told me this evening of your return. You must be glad to be back in Paris after surviving two months of London fog. What a country! But one day that fog shall prove the undoing of those stubborn people. Under cover of it I'll land there with a hundred thousand men.'

'My dearest hope is to be with you then, Consul,' Roger smiled.

'You shall,' came the instant reply. 'You've proved yourself little good as a diplomat, but you are still *le brave Breuc* and speak their uncouth language.'

'I thank you, General. Meantime I trust you will find me some suitable employment.'

'Since you wield a pen as ably as a sword, I can. Bourrienne is up to his eyes in work. Report to him tomorrow.'

Greatly relieved, Roger passed on and made his bow to Josephine. She was a few years older than her husband, an alluring brunette with a strikingly voluptuous figure. Her looks were marred only by her bad teeth and, from habit, she

51

kept her lips closed as she smiled at Roger. In more than one crisis in their lives they had rendered one another invaluable services; so she spoke to him most kindly.

Ranged in a semi-circle behind the First Consul and his wife stood the Bonaparte family. The mother, a tall, lean, handsome, commanding presence, whose expression showed a suggestion of disapproval at the adulation being showered on her amazing son. On her right her other sons: Joseph, a year older than Napoleon—an amiable man now becoming a little portly—with his wife Julie, already regarded as an angel of charity; Lucien, a short-sighted man with thin, gangling limbs—the firebrand of the family whose fervour for the Revolution had caused him in his teens to rename himself Brutus, but who had now, as the recently-appointed Minister of the Interior, become respectable—with his simple, sweet-natured, ex-barmaid wife Catherine; Louis, a handsome young man whom Bonaparte, while still a poor cadet at the Military Academy in Paris, had personally brought up; and Jerome, as yet only a youngster of sixteen.

On Madame Letizia Bonaparte's left were her daughters. Eliza most closely resembled Napoleon but, having heavy masculine features redeemed only by flashing black eyes, was the plainest of the girls. Beside her was her Corsican husband, a dolt named Pascal Bacciocchi. Caroline came next; a shrewd, ambitious, clever girl, good-looking and with a beautiful complexion but a bust and hips too large for her dumpy body. With her was Joachim Murat, Bonaparte's crack cavalry General, to marry whom she had only lately left Madame Campan's Academy for Young Ladies. Pauline stood alone, as her husband General Leclerc had been given command of a Division on the Rhine. She was such a ravishing young creature that she had been nicknamed 'La Belle des Belles'.

Roger knew them all, and that they were a grasping, scheming crew who thought of little but feathering their nests out of the pocket of their now rich and powerful brother. They were also bitterly jealous of one another and united only in one thing—their hatred of his wife. It was on Pauline that Roger's glance lingered, for he had long admired her; and, to his delight, she gave him a charming smile.

To the left of Bonaparte's sisters stood Josephine's two children by her earlier marriage to the Vicomte de Beauharnais: Eugene, a pleasant, round-faced young man whom, while still in his teens, Bonaparte had taken with him as an A.D.C. in both his Italian and Egyptian campaigns; and Hortense, a pretty girl with a mop of fair curls. Their stepfather was extremely fond of them and treated them as his own children.

The assembly was an extraordinarily mixed one. Men who had been responsible for massacres during the Terror, but who had been clever enough to save themselves from the reaction after the fall of Robespierre, rubbed shoulders with *ci-devant* nobles who had succeeded in getting permission to return from exile. There were financiers like Ouverard who had made vast fortunes out of supplying the Armies, eminent lawyers with Liberal principles who had lived in hiding throughout the worst years of the Revolution, learned men who were members of the Institute, the diplomatic representatives of a score of nations and many soldiers whose exploits had caused their names to become household words.

The looks of the women were much above the average for such a gathering because in recent years blue blood had become a liability rather than an asset and rich families had been deprived of their possessions; so, instead of seeking a wife who could bring them a coat-of-arms or a big dowry, most of the men who were carving careers for themselves had chosen brides solely for their beauty.

This was particularly the case with the soldiers. Several of the most distinguished were absent: Moreau and St. Cyr were on the Rhine, Masséna, Soult, Suchet and Oudinot were in Italy, Kleber, Desaix and Junot had been left by Bonaparte marooned in Egypt; but among those present were:

Berthier, Bonaparte's ugly, ill-formed little Chief of Staff in whose overbig head everything to do with the Army was filed like a vast card index; Marmont, the brilliant young Artilleryman who, at the siege of Toulon, had been

Bonaparte's first A.D.C.; Brune, who despite his very limited abilities, being opposed only to the hopelessly incompetent Duke of York, had, the previous autumn, destroyed the Allied armies in Holland; Davoust, clever, taciturn, the harshest disciplinarian of them all, whom Bonaparte had discovered in Egypt; Bessiéres, another discovery in the same campaign and, although still only a dashing young Colonel, now charged with making the Consular Guard into what was to become the finest élite Corps in the world; Ney, the red-headed son of a cooper, whose sole ambition was to win glory, with beside him the loveliest wife of them all; Augereau, the tall, terrible swashbuckler, who had saved the day for Bonaparte at Castiglione; Moncey, the hero of the Battle of the Pyramids; Lannes, the foul-mouthed little Gascon who, as a Brigadier in Italy in '96 and later at the siege of Acre, had won fame by his indomitable courage, and who also had an exquisitely beautiful wife; Bernadotte, another Gascon, still wearing his black hair long, who hated Bonaparte. He had, when Minister of War, proposed to arrest him for having deserted his Army in Egypt and, alone among the Generals, had refused to support him in the *coup d'état* of *Brumaire.*

Besides these there were the veterans of the Revolutionary wars; Carnot, once a member of the dread Committee of Public Safety, never a General but, from having created seven armies out of a rabble and kept them supplied, christened 'The Organiser of Victories'; Kellermann of Valmy fame; Jourdan, the victor of Fleuras; Sérurier, Perignon and old Lefebvre—still looking like a tough Sergeant-Major—whose wife had once taken in and washed on credit young Lieu-tenant Bonaparte's patched underclothes.

Chatting with them and their ladies were scores of Briga-diers, Colonels, Adjutants and A.D.C.s. All were wearing their smartest uniforms; the plumed hats they carried under their arms, their tunics and their sabretaches glittered with gold lace, and jewels sparkled in the sword hilts of the senior officers as they strutted, their spurs jingling, across the polished floors.

54

Roger was acquainted with at least half the civilians and soldiers there and, having served with most of the latter in Italy and Egypt, looked on many of them as well-tried friends. As he moved from group to group it was borne in on him that whereas he knew well comparatively few people in England, here he was hailed on all sides as a gallant comrade of the wars; so he felt more than ever that his decision to return permanently to France had been sound, and that few lives could be better than one lived among these gay, brave men and lovely women.

At one of the long buffet supper tables he ran into Joseph Fouché. The Minister of Police was the very antithesis of Talleyrand. He was tall and lean, his face looked like that of a corpse warmed up, his shifty eyes, with which he never gazed at anyone direct, reminded one of those of a dead fish. He was untidily dressed, his waistcoat was stained with snuff and, as usual, he was snivelling from the cold in the head that never left him.

He had been a Terrorist on the grand scale. As the convention's Commissioner in Nevers he had sacked all the churches and cowed the citizens by his murderous ferocity. In Lyons he had had hundreds of Liberals lined up—men, women and children—turned a battery of cannon on them and mowed them down with grape shot. When the reaction came he had been lucky to escape with only banishment from Paris, and nobody had ever expected to hear of him again. But, after for a while scraping a living breeding pigs, he had somehow managed to make money as an Army contractor then, by intrigue and blackmail, miraculously emerged as a high official of the corrupt Directory. Owing to his unscrupulousness, cold, calculating mind and immense capacity for work, he had now become, after Bonaparte, the most powerful man in France. With him was his dowdy, pathetically ugly wife to whom he had always been completely faithful.

While respecting Fouché for his great ability, Roger regarded him with distrust and dislike but, as the principal enforcer of law and order, he was now on the side of the angels; so for a while they talked amicably together.

55

He was rescued from this unprepossessing couple by Duroc and Hortense de Beauharnais, who had been dancing together. The former, a puritanical but charming man, had been Bonaparte's A.D.C.-in-Chief, and was one of Roger's closest friends. Now, after greeting him with delight, Duroc told him that he had just been given a new appointment as Controller of the Palace. From Hortense's starry-eyed expression as she gazed at the handsome Duroc, Roger guessed her to be madly in love with him; but he did not appear to be particularly interested in her and, pleading duty as an excuse, soon left her with Roger.

After dancing with her and returning her to her mother Roger caught sight of Talleyrand. Immaculate as ever, his hair powdered just as it would have been had his hostess been Queen Marie Antoinette instead of Josephine Bonaparte, he was limping gracefully away from the ballroom. Catching him up, Roger thanked him for having broken the news of his return to Bonaparte.

The *ci-devant* Bishop smiled, 'Think nothing of it, *cher ami*. You are too useful a man for him to have vented his displeasure on for long. I did no more than prevent him from cutting off his nose to spite his face by depriving himself of your services for a few months.'

An hour or so later Roger left the Palace having enjoyed a thoroughly happy evening, and entirely content with the future that he had chosen for himself.

Next morning he found Fauvelet de Bourrienne installed in his new office in the Tuileries—now rechristened 'The Palace of the Government'—and duly reported to him. De Bourrienne was the same age as Bonaparte and had been one of his few friends when they had been students together at the Military College at Brienne. Later he had entered the diplomatic service and during the early days of the revolution had been *en poste* in Germany. On the mounting of the Terror he had been recalled but, realizing that as an aristocrat a return to Paris meant for him the guillotine, he had wisely remained in voluntary exile. Then, after Bonaparte's victorious campaign in Italy, the General had written to him and invited him to become his *Chef-de-Cabinet*, De Bourrienne had accepted and neither had since had cause to regret this arrangement. Bonaparte found Bourrienne's swift grasp of affairs invaluable, Bourrienne delighted in enjoying the great man's complete confidence, and their intimacy was now such that he could go in and talk to the General even when he had just retired to bed with his wife.

It was towards the end of the Italian campaign that, owing to his having recently returned from Egypt and India, Roger had first attracted Bonaparte's special notice, for he was already dreaming of becoming another Alexander and making himself the Emperor of the East. These countries held such a fascination for him that, while an armistice with Austria was being negotiated, he had spent many evenings conversing with Roger about them. As a result, he had discovered that, unlike his other A.D.C.s, Roger was not only a *beau sabreur*, but also a well-educated young man with an extensive knowledge of international affairs. In consequence, as for the time being there was no fighting to be done, he had made him Bourrienne's assistant.

Roger resumed this work with interest and enthusiasm. It now consisted of drafting reports on the suitability of individuals for new civil appointments and making précis from a mass of information on the matters in which the First Consul was interesting himself, and they were innumerable.

There was the question of religion. In '97, when Bonaparte had overrun middle Italy, the Directory had ordered him to depose the Pope. Realizing that, regardless of the official enforcement of atheism since '93, the great majority of the French people were still believers in Christianity, he had been shrewd enough to avoid the act which would have permanently damaged his popularity, ignored the order and, instead, only extracted from His Holiness a huge indemnity. Now, appreciating that religion was a discipline of value in maintaining a stable government, he initiated measures to protect from further persecution such Roman Catholic priests as still remained in France, decreed that those willing to subscribe to the National Church should no longer be required to take an oath to the Constitution, but only give a promise of fidelity to it; and, having reclaimed a number of churches in Paris that were being used as dance halls and gaming hells, permitted again in them the public celebration of the Mass.

Another matter in which he showed concern was the situation of the émigrés. Since the fall of Robespierre some three hundred thousand *ci-devant* nobles and others had secretly returned to France, but under the laws of the Convention they were still liable to arrest. Now they were to be given security of tenure and, although he did not yet feel himself strong enough to defy the Jacobins and permit the return of the exiles still abroad, he passed a law that there should be no further proscriptions.

In order to reunite further the two factions that had torn France apart he was anxious to put an end to the insurrections in La Vendée. In '94 he had himself been nominated for this task; but again, foreseeing that the shedding of French blood would harm his future popularity, he had skilfully evaded being sent to Brittany. In January, favouring the methods of Generals Hoch and D'Hedouville, both of whom had in the past used conciliation to bring about temporary cessations of hostilities, he had sent General Brune to open negotiations with the rebels. The Count d'Artois had promised to support them by landing from England with a Royalist Army but, on his failing to do so, a village priest named Bernier had offered himself as a negotiator and, in spite of the violent protests of the fiery insurgent leaders, he had persuaded the others to agree a pacification.

But it was not only Brittany and Normandy that had long been in a state of anarchy. Every Province in France was infested with bands of marauders. Measures were being taken to put them down, others to make travel swifter by forcing Communes to have the roads put into sound repair, and others again to recreate a reliable service for posting along them by horse and diligence.

Closely associated with this policing of the Provinces was the restoration in them of regularly held Courts of Law, the dispensation of proper justice, and the collection of taxes. At the date of *Brumaire* there had been the huge sum of eleven hundred million francs owing and less than one hundred thousand in the Treasury. To deal with this fantastic situation Bonaparte had appointed Gaudin Minister of Finance. He had worked in the Finance Department for thirty seven years, was skilful, honest and industrious, and the sound measures he was taking had already led to a rise in the price of Government annuities from seven francs to forty-four, but a vast amount was still outstanding and, as a result of the Revolution, the collection of taxes had become nearly impossible.

In consequence Bonaparte resolved to revolutionize the entire administrative system of the country. His intention was to deprive the Communes of the right to elect their own officials, great numbers of whom were corrupt or inefficient, and replace the Mayors with men of his own choosing to be called Prefects. They would be accountable only to the Central Government, and in turn be given the power to appoint their own subordinates. This, in fact, would amount to a restoration of the old Monarchical system of Royal Intendants and would, at one stroke, abolish the freedom from rule by autocracy that the people had won in the Revolution.

The leading Jacobins saw at once that this concentration of all power in Bonaparte's hands foreshadowed his intention to become a Dictator. His brother Lucien led the Opposition, upbraiding him fiercely for seeking to pass a law contrary to the oath he had taken to adhere to the Constitution and preserve the liberties of the people; then, as Minister of the Interior, he had refused to lend himself to such a measure.

Bonaparte, determined to have his way, promptly dismissed Lucien. His other critics he could afford to ignore as, owing to his tremendous popularity, the vast majority of the people did not care how he ran the country as long as he continued to clean it up and give them the security they had lacked for so long.

There remained one danger—that his enemies might bring

the attention of the masses to his real intentions and cause them to rise against him. For long periods during the Revolution, the Press had been suppressed; but recently it had regained its freedom, and editors of the Left were already making full use of it to criticise the Government. In order to prevent discussion of his projects he instructed Fouché to bring the Press to heel. Henceforth only journals favourable to him were allowed to continue publication and even they were subjected to a severe censorship, with the result that without fully realising it the French people let him deprive them of their rights as citizens.

This replacement of democracy by a hierarchy entailing as it did the selection and instruction of a vast number of new officials meant an immense amount of work for Bonaparte and his personal staff; and on top of it there were the projects concerning education, the Church, finance, the posts, émigrés and many others; so throughout the Spring Roger was kept hard at it. But he felt that he was doing a tremendously worth-while job and tackled with enthusiasm the scores of problems that came his way.

The only relaxation he got was when on *Decedais*—the 'tenth-day,' substituted during the Revolution for Sunday—he accompanied Bourrienne to Malmaison, the charming property outside Paris that Josephine had purchased and furnished at great cost while Bonaparte was in Egypt. There she was under no necessity to receive her enemies—the members of his family. Such parties usually consisted of no more than a dozen people; her two children, a few close friends, Duroc and Bonaparte's personal assistants. With the latter he would spend hours walking under the trees of the avenue, his hands clasped behind his back, discussing new projects. But in the evenings he cast all cares aside. Gathered in the big drawing room they amused themselves with amateur theatricals and charades into which he threw himself with zest, crawling about the floor making comical grimaces and laughing with the abandon of a school boy. Sometimes he would make up and tell stories and, as he had a taste for the horrific, have all but one candle put out, delighting to make the women give little exclamations of fright in the gloom as he described ghosts and vampires. It was on such evenings that he displayed all his best qualities as an affectionate husband and father, with a love of gaiety for which he had so little time, a charming host and generous friend.

But as the Spring advanced his thoughts turned to war. In Germany, Moreau had crossed the Rhine, inflicted a series of defeats on the Austrian General, Kray, and was pushing him back upon the stronghold of Ulm; but things were far from well with the Army of Italy. Greatly outnumbered by the Austrians, the French Army had been cut in two. The left wing under Suchet had been driven through Nice and now, only with difficulty, was holding the line of the Var; while the main force had been compelled to retire on Genoa. Masséna and his other two divisional commanders, Soult and Oudinot, were putting up a stubborn resistance but they were now besieged in the city with only fifteen thousand troops, and a hundred and ten thousand civilians to feed. As a British Fleet under Admiral Lord Keith was blockading the port no reinforcements or supplies could be sent to them; so their situation must soon become desperate.

On April 20th an officer who had succeeded in passing through the enemy lines reached Paris and reported Masséna's plight to Bonaparte. He had replied that he would cross the Alps himself and relieve Genoa. In the meantime Masséna must somehow manage to hold out.

Had the public been informed of the situation they would have believed Bonaparte to have been caught napping as, to all appearances, he had no troops available to form another Army of any size. But that was far from being the case. On the rejection of his peace offers he had at once decided to take the field again in the early summer and had charged Berthier with creating an Army of Reserve. This had attracted no attention, as the units for its composition had been mustered and trained far from one another, scattered all over France. Now, they were already concentrating and on the way to Lausanne and Geneva, where large quantities of stores had been collected. To conceal his intentions for as

long as possible from the enemy's spies Bonaparte selected
Dijon as the Headquarters of the Army of Reserve, but in
March Berthier left that city for Zurich. As First Consul,
Bonaparte was debarred from taking command of an Army
so, nominally, Berthier remained its Commander-in-Chief.
But on May 6th Bonaparte set out for Geneva.

Roger accompanied him. As he mounted his horse he little
thought that he would come very close to death before he saw
Paris again.

CHAPTER V

MARENGO

WHILE CENTRED on Dijon the Army of Reserve constituted a threat to both the Austrian fronts, for it could have
moved with equal ease towards Swabia to reinforce Moreau
or down into Italy to rescue Masséna, and so swift was the
transition to Geneva that the Austrians had no idea that its
Headquarters had moved. Bonaparte's immediate staff was
aware that he intended to descend into Italy but he did not
make up his own mind until the last moment about what
route he would take. To cross the Alps by the Simplon Pass
was the obvious route, but the St. Bernard would bring him
immediately upon the rear of the Austrian Army, cut its
communications and force General Melas to fight him with
his back to Masséna's forces in Genoa. The difficulties of
conveying a large Army and all its gear over the Great St.
Bernard were immense, but after Bonaparte's engineers had
reported that only fifteen miles of the route were impassable
for carriages, he decided to take it.

Working tirelessly by day and through the greater part of
the night he dealt with the thousand and one matters necessary to ensure the success of the crossing. On May 15th,
satisfied that no more could be done, he ordered the crossing

to begin. Five days later he set out himself; not, as was afterwards depicted by the famous painter, David, on a prancing steed, but on a sure-footed mule led by a Swiss mountaineer of long experience.

Up in the mountains the cold was bitter, and in some places the many thousands of men had to progress along narrow ledges where a false step would have meant a fall into the abyss and death on the rocks far below. The horses could be led and the gun carriages carried in sections, so the great problem had been how to transport the weighty cannon. Marmont had solved it by having tree trunks hollowed out and the great iron barrels wedged inside them, then hiring hundreds of peasants to draw these home-made sledges. On the steepest slopes the peasants gave up exhausted; so the troops, filled with enthusiasm for this great adventure on which they were being led, volunteered to replace them. To the strains of martial music from the bands and singing patriotic songs, they managed to drag the cannons to the summit of the pass.

There stood the ancient monastery of St. Bernard. Bonaparte had sent on to it in advance a great store of provisions and the hospitable monks added to them from their own reserves. As the seemingly endless column of half-frozen soldiers passed the monastery, from behind long tables set out in front of it the monks supplemented their hard biscuits and cheese with bowls of hot soup and spiced wine. The troops then began to slither down the even more dangerous descent.

Lannes was in command of the vanguard and when Bonaparte reached the monastery, to his great annoyance, he learned from him that unexpectedly the descent into Italy was blocked. The Army had to pass through the narrow valley of Dora Baltea and at its entrance lay the village and fort of Bard, which was being held by an Austrian garrison.

Hurrying forward, Bonaparte personally surveyed the position. Marmont had got some of his cannon remounted but, owing to the position of the fort on a pinnacle of rock, it could not be bombarded; and the fusillades of musketry

directed at it by the French were having little effect on its stubborn defence by the Austrians.

Led by the intrepid Lannes, a body of infantry worked their way round the fort by a goat track and, on the 22nd, took the town of Ivrea; but it would have been impossible to follow with the guns, and without artillery Bonaparte could not hope to defeat the main Austrian Army down in the plains of Italy.

With his usual resourcefulness, Bonaparte devised a way to overcome the obstacle that threatened to ruin his plans. All the Austrian troops in the village had retired into the fort, so he ordered that when darkness fell straw should be spread thickly in the village street; then, taking advantage of a night of storm which further muffled the rumble of their wheels, the guns were sent forward. It was not until the greater part of the artillery train was through the village that the Austrians realized what was happening and when they opened fire their cannon did little damage.

Bonaparte passed the Alps with forty one thousand troops, only a handful of whom had become casualties, and his men acclaimed him as having achieved the impossible. But Roger, having read his classics, was secretly of the opinion that Hannibal's crossing had been a much greater achievement; for Bonaparte had met with only the slight opposition at Bard, whereas the Carthaginian General had been harassed the whole way by swarms of fierce Gauls and Helvetians.

Nevertheless, the Austrians, too, had thought it impossible, and their General, Melas, was taken entirely by surprise. Concentrating his Army as swiftly as he could in the neigh-bourhood of Turin, he planned to fall upon Bonaparte's flank as he advanced to the relief of Genoa.

Anticipating this, the First Consul decided on a new and bolder stroke. Further east Moncey was crossing the St. Gotthard with another eighteen thousand men and Tur-reau's division was coming over the Mont Cenis pass. By leaving Masséna temporarily to his fate and joining them instead, Bonaparte would have under him a force of seventy thousand. With it he could throw the Austrians out of Lom-

bardy, thus cutting Melas' lines of communications and iso-
lating him between two French Armies. Lannes had already
surprised and occupied Aosta. On June 2nd Bonaparte,
almost unopposed, arrived in Milan, the capital of Lombardy.

He was greeted with wild acclaim by the pro-French population, and at once re-established the Cisalpine Republic
which he had founded there in '96. For seven days he
remained in the city reinstating the officials who had been
proscribed when the Austrians had recaptured it during his
absence in Egypt. Meanwhile his troops had seized Cremona,
with its great store of enemy provisions and war material,
and he had despatched Murat and Lannes across the Po to
take Piacenza.

There they met strong opposition from an Austrian corps
under General Ott, but, with the aid of Victor's division and
Murat's cavalry, on June 9th at Montebello, Lannes inflicted
a crushing defeat on the enemy.

By the time Bonaparte reached Milan Masséna was in
desperate straits. In Genoa, horses, dogs, cats and rats were
being used as food and whenever a sortie was made from the
city thousands of the starving inhabitants followed the troops
out to gather grass and nettles to boil for soup. Driven to the
last extremity by Masséna's refusal even to consider surrender, they broke into open revolt. He put it down with the
utmost ruthlessness and gave orders that whenever more than
four citizens were seen gathered together they should be fired
upon.

But by June 4th his position became hopeless. Still refusing
to surrender, he informed the Austrians that he meant to
evacuate Genoa and if they refused to let him pass he would
cut his way through them with the bayonet. His courageous
defiance led to the enemy's allowing him and the eight
thousand troops that had survived the siege to march out
with colours flying and the honours of war.

Melas meanwhile was concentrating his forces round the
great stronghold of Alessandria and ordered his troops on the
Var to join him there. Suchet immediately recrossed the river,

recaptured Nice and furiously harassed their retreat. Now that the Austrians were almost encircled, Bonaparte was preparing to give battle. On June 9th he left Milan and advanced through Stradella. With Genoa open to him Melas' wisest course would have been to retire on the city and evacuate his Army in the British ships, but pride decided him to stand at Alessandria and fight with the hope of breaking right through the French. And, although he was unaware of it, his decision had much to recommend it; as Bonaparte's forces were now spread over a great area and when he arrived opposite Marengo, a village some three miles south-east of Alessandria, on June 14th, he had only eighteen thousand men under his hand to oppose the breakout of thirty-one thousand Austrians.

A few days earlier, Desaix had arrived unexpectedly upon the scene. This paladin was Bonaparte's favourite General; but as his decision to leave Egypt had been taken so abruptly and Desaix was then commanding a corps far up the Nile, he had had to be left behind. Having succeeded in getting back to Europe, Desaix had at once decided to rejoin his former Chief, and Bonaparte was overjoyed to see him. Detaching six thousand men from the twenty four thousand he by then had available, he sent Desaix off with them in the direction of Genoa to prevent the Austrians from retiring on the port and escaping through it. Now, as battle was joined, he realized too late that he had made a big mistake and was heavily out-numbered.

At dawn Melas opened the attack by pouring his troops across the Bormida river. They drove the French outposts back on Marengo but met with stout resistance from Victor, who was holding the village. This gave time for Lannes to bring up his division; but by ten o'clock the full force of the Austrian assault had developed. Marengo was captured and Lannes, although contesting every inch of the ground, was being driven back. An hour later Bonaparte came up from the rear to find his troops giving way in the centre and outflanked on both wings. He at once threw his only reserve, the Consular Guard, into the battle. For an hour its one thousand men, formed up in square, fought valiantly, and by their stand enabled Victor and Lannes to get their battered divisions back into better shape. But by two o'clock only St. Cyr, on the right flank, was holding his ground. All but five of Marmont's guns had been put out of action, and the flood of white-coated Austrians was again forcing back the centre and the left. Despite threats, pleas and exhortations from their officers and Bonaparte himself, many of the men were throwing down their weapons and several units were in full retreat. There could be no doubt about it, the French were being beaten.

Early that morning Desaix had heard the distant sound of gunfire and, turning his columns about, set off in that direction. Then, in mid-morning, one of Bonaparte's A.D.C.s came galloping up to him with an urgent order to hasten to his Chief's assistance; but to reach Marengo meant many hours of forced marching. Despite his doing his utmost it was not until five o'clock that he arrived on the field of battle. By then, although many French units were still fighting gallantly, the line was broken in several places and the Austrian cavalry through, cutting down fleeing men from shattered battalions.

As Desaix rode up Bonaparte said to him glumly, 'What do you think of it?'

Glancing at the terrible scene of carnage, Desaix replied, 'This battle is lost, but there is still time to win another.'

Bonaparte swiftly made fresh dispositions. Marmont had just brought up a reserve battery of thirteen guns from the rear. They were deployed to fire through the gaps torn in the French line. Desaix was despatched to take up a position behind Marengo village and a nearby hill. Kellermann, the son of the veteran General, was in command of the heavy cavalry. It had already done good service throughout the day and had suffered heavy casualties, but was still capable of making a charge, and was sent round behind Desaix to the extreme French left. When these troops had taken up their positions Bonaparte launched his counter-attack.

The sudden appearance of Desaix's six thousand tired, but still unused, troops advancing in parade ground formation over the hill put new life into the other divisions; their impact on the enemy stayed the retreat, but was not sufficient to force them back. For another hour the terrible struggle raged, swayed first one way then the other, and it remained uncertain which Army would emerge victorious.

Throughout most of the day, with his staff sitting their horses behind him, Bonaparte had been stationed on a rise in the ground watching the battle; now and then, after a glance through his spy glass, sending one of his A.D.C.s off with an order to the commander of a unit.

Now, with perfect timing, he turned, looked at Roger and snapped, 'Tell Kellermann to charge.'

Instantly Roger repeated the order, set spurs to his horse, and galloped off across the plain.

During the battle he had, like the other A.D.C.s, carried several orders, either verbally or scribbled by Bonaparte on a pad, to various senior officers, and two of his companions had failed to return. That did not necessarily mean that they had been killed or seriously wounded. When delivering their messages gallopers were, at times, caught up in the fighting and, although it was their duty to rejoin their General as soon as possible, two or three hours might elapse before they were able to do so. Nevertheless Roger greatly disliked such missions.

It was not that he was a coward. Far from it. He had fought several duels and would have met any man with sword or pistol. He had, too, never openly displayed fear in the numerous battles in which he had been forced to take part. But he had gained his sobriquet of '*Le Brave Breuc*' largely under false pretences.

Bonaparte had originally formed the impression that he was a courageous man because, within a week or so of their first meeting, Roger had, with the Corsican looking on, led on foot a charge against a battery of Spanish guns; but only because, in the particular circumstances, he had had no option. Admittedly he had personally and alone defended the General from an attack by a dozen conspirators while in Venice, and received a Sword of Honour as a reward for his gallantry; but that had been more in the nature of a duel against odds. The truth about his having brought a Turkish standard to Bonaparte at the siege of Acre was not that he had fought desperately to capture it, but that while unobserved he had simply picked it up from a dead soldier in a trench and walked off with it; while the exploit that had clinched his reputation throughout the Army for bravery was his having, presumably, been taken prisoner by the British at the Battle of the Nile and afterwards making his escape in full daylight with them shooting at him—but shooting to miss because he was escaping with their connivance.

So as he now rode at full tilt across the bullet-scarred ground, littered with dead and wounded, smashed gun carriages and abandoned weapons he felt none of the exhilaration that a Murat or a Lannes would have experienced. Instead he was praying that he would once again manage to carry out his orders without getting involved in the indiscriminate killing which he so heartily disliked.

As for twelve hours without cessation some sixty thousand men had been blazing off with cannon and muskets, a great pall of smoke hung over the battle-field creating a premature dusk on this summer evening. Smoke, too, obscured the greater part of the conflict that was still raging, so Roger could catch only glimpses here and there of groups of soldiers either firing volleys or going forward at an uneven run. The din was terrible, the boom of cannon and the continuous rattle of musketry being pierced every few moments by a shouted order or the scream of a badly wounded man.

When he crossed the ground over which Desaix's troops had made their first charge the fallen became thicker, and several times he had to jump his horse over twisted corpses or groaning men who were endeavouring to staunch the blood seeping from their wounds. Here and there groups of stretcher bearers were at work seeking in the murk to carry off casualties whose wounds they judged unlikely to be fatal, but their numbers were hopelessly inadequate to cope for many hours yet with the carnage that had taken place.

Behind the village the smoke grew denser. Many of the

buildings were already burnt out, but others were still blazing and the flames from them showed as patches of lurid glare in the semi-darkness.

The air stank of gunpowder, burning wood, sweat and excrement to a degree that made Roger want to vomit, and he was half choked by the smoke that he could not escape drawing down into his lungs with every breath he took. As he pressed on he caught the sound of cheering and the thunder of massed hoofbeats. A minute later there came surging towards him out of the murk a long line of cavalry approaching at a furious gallop. Instantly he realized what had happened. Young Kellermann had also judged it time for him to bring his heavy Brigade into action and, anticipating Bonaparte's order, had already launched his charge.

The onrushing line of horsemen was over a hundred yards long and three men deep. Roger was almost in the centre of it. There was no time for him to turn his horse and gallop clear of either end of the line. Kellermann flashed past him waving his sword on high. All Roger could do was to cause his horse to rear and swing it round on its hind legs. Even as he did so he found himself almost wedged between two dragoons yelling like maniacs. After being carried with them a hundred yards, he tried desperately to rein in his mount, so that the two rear lines of horsemen should pass him and leave him free to make his way back to Bonaparte. But by then, maddened by the shouting and thunder of several hundred hooves, his horse was out of control. After frantically sawing at its jaw for a minute he realized that, even if he could bring the beast up and pull out of the crush, it would afterwards be said that he had acted as a coward. There was nothing for it but, as had happened to other A.D.C.s in similar circumstances, to take part in the charge.

Within a few minutes they were crossing the ground from which Desaix had launched his first attack, trampling down dead, dying and wounded alike, it being impossible to avoid them. Through the smoke Roger caught a glimpse of the white-uniformed enemy. The charge, delivered on their flank, had taken them by surprise, but they were swiftly forming square in order to resist it. Irregular flashes of flame stabbed the semi-darkness as they fired a ragged volley. Roger felt a hammer blow well up on the left side of his chest. It knocked him right back on to the crupper of his saddle. His hands lost their grip on the reins, and his feet were jerked free of the stirrups. His mount jumped some unseen obstacle. He bumped in his saddle and was then flung off. In an attempt to protect his head from the flying hooves of the other horses he flung his arms round it. As he crashed to the ground the breath was driven out of his body. Gulping for air he felt the salt taste of blood in his mouth. The sound of the battle grew dim in his ears and then he lost consciousness.

Leading a charge only a little earlier the gallant Desaix had been shot through the body and killed instantly. But he, and Kellermann's charge, had saved the day for the French. At Bonaparte's Headquarters on the night of the battle the loss of Desaix was lamented as a great blow. Roger, too, was mourned as dead.

CHAPTER VI

IDYLL BY THE SEA

IT WAS several hours later when Roger came to. At first he could not think what had happened to him and knew only that his chest hurt excruciatingly. Then he became conscious that he was very cold. Slowly it dawned upon him that he had been shot during the charge, left for dead on the battlefield and was now naked.

The last fact did not surprise him, because he knew that swarms of camp followers always hovered in the rear of every army, and that among them were many human vultures who made a living by robbing the dead after every battle and stripping them of their clothes.

After some moments, making a great effort, he managed to half sit up; but the pain of his wound stabbed him violently, blood welling up into his mouth choked him and, his eyes starting out of his head, he fell back into a dead faint.

When he came round he lay still for a long time then, very cautiously, raised himself on one elbow. In that position he could make out by the moonlight his immediate sur-roundings. Here and there, some way off, he could see small groups of shadowy figures carrying lanterns. They might be stretcher bearers looking for wounded whose lives could be saved, or ghouls seeking fresh bodies to plunder; but he now had nothing to lose and he desperately craved water. Even body robbers might give him that, so he assayed to attract the attention of the nearest group by a shout. No sound issued from his cracked lips; a flush of blood strangled it in his throat.

Temporarily suffocated and half stupefied by pain he fell back once more, now convinced that he was doomed to die there. When he got back his breath he moaned at the thought. He had performed no gallant action, rendered no great service to his own country and had not even delivered the message from Bonaparte. That he should lose his life through having unwillingly got himself mixed up in a cavalry charge seemed to him monstrously unfair. Again he raised himself a little and endeavoured to attract the attention of the group by waving his arm.

It was then that he heard Georgina's voice. It came to him clearly out of the night. He recognized it immediately and it did not even occur to him that he might be the victim of an hallucination. Owing to her sensitivity as a psychic and the strong affinity that bound them, she had often felt unaccountably uneasy when he was in danger; and more than once when he was faced with a major threat to his life, during sleep she had come to him and saved him by her counsel. Now, she said urgently:

'Lie still, Roger! Lie still! Conserve your strength. 'Tis your only hope of remaining alive until someone finds you.'

In spite of the awful pains in his chest and back and his terrible thirst, he forced himself to do as she bade him, shut his eyes and lay there endeavouring to check his spasmodic movements.

Not long afterwards he was rewarded. Through his closed eyelids he became conscious of a rosy glow. Opening his eyes he saw a man with a lantern bending over him and a voice said, 'This is not he.'

Then came another with a heavy German accent, 'No. 'But! . . . But, *teufel nochmal*, 'tis *le brave Breuc!* . . .'

Roger knew that voice. It seemed to have some connection

74

with the Great Pyramid of Cheops. Then he remembered. It was that of German-born Colonel Rapp, and the other voice must be that of Colonel Savary. One sweltering day in Egypt he had climbed the Pyramid with them. They were Desaix's two A.D.C.s. From their next few sentences Roger dimly gathered that the General was dead and they were searching for his body.

While Rapp went to look for a stretcher party, Savary knelt down beside Roger and from his flask gave him enough water to rinse out his mouth. Ten minutes later, covered with a blanket, he was lying on a stretcher. After wishing him a good recovery, the two A.D.C.s resumed their search for their dead General, and he was carried away to a field hospital.

For some days he knew very little about what was happening to him as, to keep him quiet, whenever he roused from unconsciousness, he was given a draught of opium. Gradually, as the doses were reduced he learned from General Soult, who was in the bed next to his, where he was, and what had been taking place.

Soult had been wounded and captured some while before the battle, and the Austrians had put him in a special ward in their Military Hospital in Alessandria, Roger had been transferred to it two days after he had been wounded.

The General told him that on learning that Roger was still alive Bonaparte had sent his own doctor, Corvisart, to attend him and had given orders that he should be given the very best attention. A musket ball had passed through the upper part of his left lung and had gone out through his back. For some days his life had been feared for, but he was now expected to recover provided he made no violent movement that would bring about a hemorrhage. He must, however, resign himself to a long convalescence as it would be many months before he would be able again to exert himself without danger.

Kellermann's charge had proved the turning point of the battle. It had taken the Austrians completely by surprise and cut deep into their flank. The troops there who, a few minutes before, had still been fighting in good heart had suddenly ceased to resist and begun to run. The panic spread right through their army and it gave way along the whole front. The French everywhere attacked with new vigour and the withdrawal swiftly developed into a rout. A scene of wild confusion followed and, as night fell, thousands of Austrians were either being sabred by the pursuing French or plunging into the Bormida River. Bonaparte's victory was complete.

On the morning after the battle Melas, feeling his position to be hopeless, had asked for an armistice. Bonaparte had agreed to give it to him on condition that the Austrian army, and all its garrisons in Tuscany and Ancona, should retire behind the Mincio. It was a month to the day since Bonaparte had crossed the Alps and in that short time he had again made himself master of all north-western Italy.

Roger remained in the hospital at Alessandria for a month. Provided he refrained from putting any strain on his body, and from taking a deep breath, his wound was not especially painful and, owing to his good health, the flesh of his chest and back healed well.

When, in mid-July, he was told that he could be moved, he decided to go to a small château near St. Maxime in the South of France, that he had purchased some years before. That he should have been shot through the lung seemed a curious coincidence, as he had long established the belief that he suffered from a weak chest, and had used that as an excuse to obtain sick leave to spend periods in the sunshine of the South while, in fact, he had secretly returned to England to report to Mr. Pitt. But he had occupied the little château from time to time, keeping there an elderly couple named Defour as caretakers and to look after him on his rare visits.

Having always been subject to sea-sickness, and fearing that a bout of it might bring on a hemorrhage, he decided that instead of crossing by ship from Genoa to Toulon he would go by road; so he bought a comfortable carriage and took into his service a coachman and a valet. They made the journey round the Gulf in easy stages, so that the jolting of the carriage should not tire him unduly and, on August 1st, arrived at his property.

76

For the best part of a fortnight he did little but lie in the sunshine, acquiring a rich tan; then he felt that he might venture on a gentle swim each morning and, taking his Italian valet, Angelo, with him, in case he overdid it, he spent many pleasant hours on the nearby beach. By the end of August he could walk two or three miles without fatigue and was beginning really to feel his old self again.

By September the time of the vintage was approaching so one day he took a walk to see the condition of the grapes in his vineyard. It was on a slope and above it lay another that belonged to the owner of a pleasant little house on the top of the hill. On his previous stays at the château he had deliberately refrained from cultivating his neighbours on the grounds that the less they knew about him and his comings and goings, the better. But he was aware that the house belonged to a retired lawyer named Pasquier who had had a practice in Toulon.

While he was examining his vines, Roger noticed that a woman in a sunbonnet was doing the same thing in the adjoining vineyard. As they came closer he saw that she was rather short, about thirty, attractive-looking and well dressed; so, assuming her to be a member of Pasquier's family, he made her a polite bow and wished her good morning.

She returned his greeting with a pleasant smile, showing two rows of fine even white teeth between full lips set in a bright-complexioned face. Then she said, 'Monsieur must be the famous Colonel Breuc'.

He laughed, 'Colonel Breuc, at your service, Madame. But why you should think me famous, I cannot imagine.'

'Oh, but it is so,' she replied quickly, 'anyway hereabouts. Everyone knows that you are one of the First Consul's Aides-de-Camp. People still talk of your having brought him and many distinguished officers here for refreshments shortly after you had all landed at Fréjus on his return from Egypt.'

'That I did so is true enough,' Roger agreed. 'But I can claim no more than to bask in his reflected glory. I trust, Madame, that Monsieur Pasquier is well?'

She shook her head, 'Alas, Monsieur, my father died over

77

a year ago. He left me this property and as shortly afterwards I lost my husband, who was an officer in our Navy, I decided to sell our little house in Toulon and live here instead.'

Roger had been studying her large dark eyes with appreciation and, with a bow, he said, 'Madame, your misfortune is my good fortune. I expect to be here for some time, and it will be pleasant to have such a charming neighbour.'

Having heard in the village that he was convalescing from a wound, she inquired about it, and he gave her an account of the battle of Marengo. Then, after a few remarks about the prospects of the vintage, they parted.

For several weeks he had been too ill to wish for company; but recently he had begun to feel distinctly bored from lack of it, so it was hardly surprising that the following morning he again walked up to his vineyard, hoping that he might see Jeanne Meuralt, as he had learned his neighbour was named.

She was there, some distance away at the far end of her vineyard, but she did not appear to notice him until, after waiting for a few minutes, he called out and asked, on the excuse that he would like to compare her grapes with his, if he might join her.

For a short while they both made a pretence of sharing a great interest in grapes, then the conversation took another turn and, with frequent smiles at one another, they remained chatting for over an hour.

At the end of that time she said to him, '*Monsieur le Colonel*, you are a man with much knowledge of the world, whereas I am hopelessly ignorant where money matters are concerned. My affairs, alas, are in a shocking tangle. Would you think it trespassing too much on your time if I asked you to look into them?'

'Why, no!' he laughed. 'These days I have nothing whatever to do, and if I can be of assistance to you it would be a pleasure.'

Ten minutes later he was seated on the vine-covered terrace of her little house, sipping a glass of her previous year's vintage that she had just poured for him and about to look

78

through a portfolio of papers she had brought out. In spite of what she had said she gave him so lucid an account of her financial affairs that, having glanced through a few of the documents, Roger had no doubt about the reason for her anxiety. She was being swindled by a lawyer named Lacourbe, her late father's junior partner, and he had deliberately complicated the accounts he rendered her in order to cover up what he was doing.

Roger had a shrewd suspicion that Jeanne knew perfectly well what was happening and had asked his advice only to provide a reason for them to have further meetings. In consequence, instead of giving his opinion right away, he said that the matter needed going into carefully, and if he might take the papers away he would study them that night. He added that it was her turn to try a bottle of his previous year's vintage, then suggested that she should do so at the château next morning when he would be ready to discuss her affairs with her.

She willingly agreed to do so, and arrived at midday, dressed in a pretty gown of sprigged muslin and carrying a parasol: a small but well-made little person, pink-cheeked and smiling. Having given her his views about her papers Roger said they must later consult on what was to be done, then shelved the subject and took her on a leisurely tour of the château.

When she said that she ought to be getting back for her midday meal, he expressed surprise and told her that he had taken it for granted that she would have it with him. Seeing her hesitate, he went on with a smile, 'Surely you cannot be such a stickler for the old conventions as to count it culpable that two neighbours should enjoy a meal together just because they happen to be of opposite sexes?'

Despite the Revolution, Jeanne had been brought up with bourgeois traditions; but fearing that this splendid gallant from Paris might think her a country bumpkin, she gave way to her own inclination and replied a little hurriedly, 'Certainly not! Such ... such stupidities went out of fashion long ago.'

Their luncheon together was a great success, and she stayed on well into the afternoon. It was followed by others and two days later, when Roger asked her to brighten one of his lonely evenings by dining with him, she cheerfully waved good-bye to her reputation as of far less importance than pleasing this wonderful man who had come into her life. An hour or so after they had dined, Roger found little difficulty in seducing her.

That having been satisfactorily accomplished, there was no further point in continuing to pretend that they met mainly to discuss her inheritance, and Roger took her affairs in hand in earnest. Having sent for Maître Lacourbe to come over from Toulon for an explanation, he gave the lawyer one of the worst half hours he had ever experienced.

Displaying the cold, hard anger that he could simulate so well when it suited his purpose, he accused his visitor of having callously defrauded a woman whose interests, as his late partner's daughter, it was his sacred duty to protect, on the assumption that because she had no husband or brother to advise her he would not be found out.

For a few minutes Lacourbe protested violently and threatened to bring an action against Roger for slander. But Roger called his bluff.

'Go to it, then,' he snapped. 'And, by God, I'll see you rue it. As we are far from Paris and you have influence in these parts, no doubt you are counting upon some corrupt magistrate to give a verdict in your favour. But those days are gone. And you will find the arm of my master, the First Consul, long. Moreover he is swift to act. I have but to write him an account of this matter and before the month is out you will find yourself disbarred. Ah, and facing a charge of malefaction that, knowing the origin of the Prosecutor, no judge will dare set aside lightly.'

The outcome of this interview was that Lacourbe not only agreed to make restitution, but was blackmailed by Roger into paying such a heavy sum as compensation, for loss of interest, that he positively wailed with grief. Roger then arranged for all of Jeanne's money to be invested in the

Funds, feeling confident that, under the new government, they would continue to rise and so greatly increase her small fortune.

Little Jeanne gave expression to her gratitude in a highly practical manner and it was obvious to Roger that she derived great pleasure from doing so. As a 'sop to Cerberus' they continued to live in their respective houses but, as in so small a place it would have been impossible to conceal for long that they were having an *affaire*, they made no attempt to do so and spent the better part of each twenty four hours together. Naturally the servants talked, and this caused considerable tittle-tattle among the ladies of the district. A few of the plainer ones said some spiteful things about Jeanne; but the majority envied her her luck and maintained that to expect any young woman who had been a widow for over a year to resist such a dashing figure as the Colonel would have been asking too much. Some even thought that by acting as she was she stood a better chance of hooking him than if she had played the prude.

For a brief while Jeanne had herself toyed with the breath-taking thought that he might marry her. But in order that she should know where she stood Roger had disabused her of any such idea before persuading her to go to bed with him. With the beautiful Zanthé in mind, he had told Jeanne that while in Egypt he had engaged himself to a noble Turkish lady who might at any time arrive in Paris, refraining from adding that Zanthé had since married the young banker Achilles Sarodopulous and some three months before had given birth to a child of whom he was the father.

Quickly reconciling herself to the knowledge that her relationship with Roger could be only a temporary one, Jeanne had determined to make the most of it while it lasted and Roger found her a delightful companion. Her education left much to be desired, but she had abundant vitality, a happy nature and a ready laugh. For his part he found it a pleasant change to have a mistress who knew little about the great world and international affairs. It was a long time since he had enjoyed a spell of carefree idleness; so through the warm autumn months they were as happy together as two young people on a honeymoon.

Yet, after four months of this halcyon existence Roger's congenital restlessness again beset him. He had been given indefinite sick leave but it was getting on for six months since he had been wounded and, having taken good care of himself, his old capacity for physical exertion was almost restored. More and more frequently he found himself wondering how things had been going in Paris and what new schemes Bonaparte was hatching in his fertile brain.

At the end of the first week in December, not wishing to hurt little Jeanne by giving her to think that he had tired of her, he told her that he had received a despatch recalling him to duty. And after loving farewells, he set off next morning for Paris.

CHAPTER VII

AWAY TO PASTURES NEW

It was in Lyons that Roger heard about the Battle of Hohenlinden. It was common knowledge that after Marengo the First Consul had again offered peace to the Emperor of Austria on the basis reached at Campo Formio, but the Emperor had rejected it; so the war on the far side of the Rhine had continued throughout the autumn.

According to the bulletin in the *Moniteur,* the Archduke John, seeking to emulate the new methods of war introduced by Bonaparte, had formed the ambitious project of out-flanking the French and cutting off their retreat. But such operations depended for their success on swiftness of movement and to that the Austrians had never been trained. In consequence, after rashly leaving his strong position, the Archduke's deployment was too slow to take the French unawares. On December 2nd Moreau concentrated his troops round the village of Hohenlinden on an open plain in the middle of the forest that clothes the great plateau of Ebers-berg. To penetrate the woods the Austrians had to break up their formations and were unable to make use of their cavalry. Leaving General Grenier with a strong force to oppose the enemy as they approached the village, Moreau had executed a flank movement with the rest of his Army, led it through the forest and round to the Austrian rear. Caught between two fires, the Archduke's troops had surged back on themselves, broken and completely routed. They lost twenty thousand men in killed, wounded and prisoners, so it was a victory of the first magnitude.

Roger already knew that early in September Malta had surrendered to the English, and that on the same day that Desaix was killed, General Kléber, whom Bonaparte had left to command in Egypt, had been assassinated in Cairo. Then on reaching Paris he soon caught up with the other news.

The Blanchards told him of Bonaparte's triumphant return from Marengo and of how, as he was more popular than ever, great indignation had been caused in October by a plot to assassinate him. He was a great votary of the Opera, and said then to be having an *affaire* with a beautiful singer named Madame Grassini, whom he had brought back from Italy with him. On the 10th he had gone to a performance, and an attempt had been made to murder him as he left his box. The leaders of the conspiracy had been two Corsicans named Ceracchi and Aréna, and the painter Demerville. Most fortunately, they had been seized and overpowered before they could harm him.

From Talleyrand Roger heard the inside story. Demerville, being a braggart, had boasted of the plot to a penniless officer named Harel, who had been dismissed from the Army, and he had reported the matter to Bourrienne. On being informed of what was afoot, the First Consul had ordered that the attempt should be allowed to proceed while Fouché took precautions to protect him against it. In consequence, he had never been in any danger but made great capital out of the affair.

With lazy satisfaction Talleyrand then spoke of the success that had crowned his negotiations with Russia. Having detached Paul I from the Coalition the previous winter France had since been wooing him. The vain, feeble-minded Czar had taken a childish delight in having been elected Grand Prior of the Knights of Malta and had had a gorgeous uniform suitable to that dignitary made to strut about in. The British having captured Malta, he had expected them to hand it over to him and had taken great umbrage at their refusal. Bonaparte had then made him a present of the Knights' famous sword of Valetta, which had pleased him greatly. Declaring himself to be the friend of France, he had revived the League of Armed Neutrality, by which ships of the Northern Nations resisted attempts by the British Navy to search them for, and confiscate, any contraband-of-war they might be carrying; and this interference with their profitable commerce had resulted in Denmark and Sweden declaring war on Britain.

As a result of the armistice after Marengo, French and Austrian plenipotentiaries had met at Lunéville to discuss the possibilities of a permanent peace; but the Austrians had shilly-shalleyed for so long that Bonaparte had lost patience with them and, in November, declared his intention of resuming the war.

Brune had succeeded Masséna as Commander-in-Chief Italy. He had been joined by Macdonald, who had brought his army over the Splügen Pass—a feat much more remarkable than Bonaparte's crossing of the St. Bernard because the former had been accomplished so late in the year and in spite of vile weather. Brune had then crossed the Mincio in force, and the two Generals were now driving the Austrians before them up into the old Venetian lands. Meanwhile Moreau had shattered the other Austrian army by his great victory at Hohenlinden; so Talleyrand was in hopes that, soon now, the Austrians would at least see reason and throw in their hand. Murat, meanwhile, had been despatched south, had driven all before him, entered Naples and compelled King Ferdinand to accept a French garrison and sign a Convention closing his ports to British ships.

Roger's reception by Bonaparte proved not only disappointing but alarming. Later he put it down to the First Consul's being in an ill humour from having learned that for the past few days everyone in Paris had been saying that Moreau's victory at Hohenlinden was a much greater triumph than his at Marengo; as indeed it was, since Moreau had not first nearly lost the battle and he had inflicted more than double the number of casualties on the enemy.

It was in any case well known that Bonaparte, while a generous man in other ways, was always jealous of the success of other generals and mean in his praise of them. After Marengo he had claimed the credit for Desaix's splendid counter-attack and, instead of promoting young Kellermann for his well-judged action which had proved decisive, had merely remarked to him, 'You made a very good charge'.

Whatever the cause of his irritability on the morning that Roger reported to him, after briefly congratulating him on his recovery he said abruptly:

'Bourrienne no longer has a use for you. He has acquired a very able young man named Méneval as his assistant.'

'What then would you have me do, Consul?' asked Roger.

'I know not,' came the testy reply. 'If you can think of some way to serve me, come to me again.'

Roger bowed, turned and made for the door. He had nearly reached it when the harsh voice cried behind him, 'Stay! I am losing my wits. I'll forget my own name next. You travelled across India in the summer of '97, did you not?'

Actually, that after three and a half years he should have recalled such a fact about one of the hundreds of officers with whom he was in contact was a demonstration of his remarkable memory. Replying that he had, Roger turned about to find him perched on the edge of his desk swinging iis legs and now all smiles.

'Then, Breuc, you are the very man I'm looking for,' he said quickly. 'It is probable that you can inform me on many matters about which I am anxious to know.'

Slipping off his desk he crossed the room to a cabinet of maps, pulled one out, opened it, spread it on the floor, lay down at full length facing it and signed to Roger to join him. Having made Roger trace his journey right across the subcontinent from Calcutta to Bombay, during the next half hour he shot a hundred questions at him about the cities through which he had passed, the personalities of their rulers, the religions of the people, their like or dislike of the British, the climate, the navigability of the rivers and a score of other matters.

At length he got to his feet, playfully pulled Roger's ear and said:

'Breuc, your arrival is most opportune. I am preparing an expedition to wrest India from the English. You shall go with it as A.D.C.-in-Chief to the Commander. You will be invaluable to him. Report to Berthier, tell him I have nominated you for that post and that I wish you to work with him on the preparations for this project.'

The appointment meant promotion, so Roger hurriedly stammered his thanks, then left the room filled with dismay. With the possible exception of Egypt, India was the last place in the world that he wanted to go to again; but it would have been useless, even dangerous, to say so.

At Berthier's headquarters, he found the ill-made little Chief-of-Staff clad in one of the spectacular uniforms that he and Murat were so fond of designing for themselves; but where the tall cavalryman had the figure and panache to carry them off, they made this human filing cabinet only look ridiculous.

Having said that Roger's assistance would be welcome, Berthier informed him that General Menou had succeeded Kléber as C.-in-C. Egypt, and that before going on to India the new expedition would reinforce and secure his position there. He then spoke of Kléber's assassination. It had occurred on a spot that they had both known well—the terrace of a Palace that Bonaparte had occupied while in Cairo. Adjacent to the terrace there was an old, empty cistern which could be entered from the garden. The assassin, a young fanatic named Soleiman Haleby, had concealed himself in the cistern and, when Kléber had come out to stroll on the terrace, scrambled out of the cistern and stabbed him with a dagger. Bonaparte, when occupying the Palace, had often taken his exercise on the terrace in the evenings, and had been warned of the danger of leaving the cistern unguarded, but

had ignored it. They now agreed that it was fortunate for
France that it was not he who had fallen a victim to the
Mohammedan's dagger.

The following morning Roger started work with a group of
officers who were planning the expedition to India. In his free
time, he looked up a number of friends and paid his duty
calls.

The First Consul had offered his mother a suite of
apartments in the Tuileries, but she had refused it and was
living with her eldest son Joseph and his sweet wife Julie, at
their splendid mansion in the Rue du Rocher.

Although Madame Letizia was as yet only fifty years old,
the hardships through which she had passed, her great
strength of character and the uprightness of her disposition
combined to give her the prestige of a far more venerable
woman. Having questioned Roger closely about his wound,
knowing him to be intimate with her most brilliant son, she
spoke to him openly of her distress that Napoleon should
have quarrelled with Lucien.

She had not the least interest in politics and thought only
of the well-being of her children, maintaining always that she
loved best, at any time, the one who was suffering most. But
it could not be doubted that Lucien was her favourite son,
and she intensely resented Napoleon's having deprived him of
his office.

The only sympathy that Roger felt for Lucien was that he
had lost his simple, sweet-natured wife Catherine in the preceding Spring. Otherwise he regarded him as a dangerous
fanatic who might, if given the chance, endanger the First
Consul's regeneration of France. Further, Roger despised him
as the worst possible type of pseudo 'Friend of the People'
for he had used his position as Minister of the Interior to
amass a great fortune at their expense and to persuade or
blackmail into sleeping with him many pretty women.

Napoleon's oldest sister, Eliza, was also a great partisan of
Lucien's. After *Brumaire* her ineffective husband, Bacciocchi,
had been packed off to attend to certain administrative
matters in Corsica and Marseilles, upon which she had

88

happily settled down, Lucien's wife being ill, to take charge of his ménage in the Grande Rue Verte. They regarded themselves as spiritual affinities and both looked on the other as an astute literary critic. On the money that they owed to the First Consul's liberality they had a happy time gathering distinguished writers round them and encouraging them to write articles criticizing Napoleon.

When Roger called upon Eliza he found her dressed in an unbelievably ugly garb of her own design which she told him was to serve as the uniform of a new Literary Society she was forming and, knowing him to be an educated man, she invited him to become a member. Having pleaded that his military commitments were, at the moment, too onerous to permit him that pleasure, he bowed himself out of the presence of Napoleon's blue-stocking sister.

Young Caroline Murat he found equally discontented with the way things were going. She alone of Madame Letizia's children possessed the individuality and determination which, had she been a man, could have made her another Napoleon. As things were she could achieve her boundless ambitions only through her husband. As a girl of seventeen, when at Bonaparte's headquarters in Italy after his victorious campaign of '96, she had fallen in love with Murat, and he with her. To her fury she had then been sent to Madame Campan's Academy to acquire a finishing education. She had sullenly refused to take advantage of this opportunity; but those years of boredom had not deflected her from her purpose of acquiring Murat for a husband, and he had continued to regard her, as his General's sister, as a good catch. So much so that, on the night of 18th *Brumaire*, he had sent a couple of his Hussars to pound on the door of the Academy and shout the news to her that he and Bonaparte had saved the Revolution.

Immediately she had been freed from Madame Campan's tutelage she had badgered her brother to let her marry Murat. Bonaparte had demurred because by then he had good cause to dislike and distrust his brilliant cavalry leader.

Murat preferred to hobnob with junior officers because to

them he could boast of his exploits without fear of contradiction and not long since he had given a party for a number of them. At this party he had introduced a special Punch which, he said, could only be made with Rum from Martinique. He added that he had been shown how to mix it by a charming lady in whose company he had spent the whole day. Then he produced a new type of silver lemon squeezer which, he said, she had given him. On examining the squeezer one of his guests announced to the raucous laughter of the by then drunken company that on its base were engraved the initials J.B. This, and the connections with Martinique, plainly implied that it was the First Consul's wife with whom Murat had spent a whole day, and that he had enjoyed Josephine's favours.

Such was Caroline's doggedness of purpose that she had bullied Napoleon into letting her marry Murat; but when the story of the drinking party came to his ears, he had, after Marengo, sent Murat off to subdue southern Italy, and Caroline did not disguise from Roger her intense bitterness that Napoleon should have deprived her of her husband for so long.

Roger also called upon Pauline Leclerc. He knew that as a young girl, when Bonaparte was no more than a promising junior General who had never conducted a campaign, she had fallen desperately in love with the ex-Terrorist Fréron, and that Napoleon had firmly vetoed her marrying this unsavoury character, then old enough to be her father. His selection a little later of Leclerc for her as a husband had been due to the fact that Leclerc was outstanding among his officers as a gentleman, well educated and would prove an asset to the Bonaparte family. Pauline, who was extremely highly sexed, and by then eager to be allowed to get into bed with any good-looking man, had been attracted by Leclerc and readily agreed to accept him as her husband.

The marriage had been a great success, but not to the extent that Pauline was content to remain sighing for Leclerc when he had been sent off to the Army of the Rhine. Since then, rumour had it she had indulged in a triple *affaire* with

90

the Generals Moreau, Macdonald and Beurnonville simultaneously when they had been in Paris at the same time. She had early become conscious of her great beauty and her power to attract men. So now her greatest pleasure was to adorn herself in magnificent toilettes—the bills for which were nearly ruining the unfortunate Leclerc—and, reclining elegantly on a sofa, excite the admiration and desire of her male visitors.

The only other thing with which she concerned herself was her intense hatred of Josephine. The First Consul's wife had the advantage of her that, although she had never been presented at Court, she had been brought up as a demoiselle of the *ancien régime*. Her taste in clothes and décor was impeccable, she received her husband's guests with charm and dignity and she was now his greatest asset in helping him to bridge the gap between the societies of the old France and that which had arisen as a result of the Revolution. Pauline, on the other hand, was a vulgar little parvenue; but that did not detract from her beauty.

And there was another thing which attracted Roger to her. Greedy though she might be to get all she could out of Napoleon, she was the only one of his family who respected and loved him. He had always been her favourite brother and she placed his interests above all else.

With her Roger considerably outstayed the accepted formal call of twenty minutes. Reclining on a couch, clad in rich but revealing draperies, she was a sight to stir any man's desire, and she made no secret of the fact that she was enjoying Roger's undisguised admiration. When he at length rose to make his devoirs, she fluttered her long eyelashes at him provocatively and said, 'I find you most sympathetic, Colonel Breuc; I pray you come to see me soon again.'

But Roger was not destined to see her again for a long time to come. During the past few days he had been giving much thought to his future. On one matter he was fully determined—he was not going with the expedition to India. To avoid doing so he intended to pretend a relapse. It would be accepted without question that, with his normally weak chest and a lung wound scarcely healed, he had acted most rashly in leaving the South of France in mid-winter for the cold and windy streets of Paris.

What then, though? He had not the least desire to return to St. Maxime. His *affaire* with little Jeanne had been a pleasant interlude but her kisses had already begun to cloy before he left. If resumed it would soon become most wearisome to him; yet, if he went back there and broke it off, she would be terribly hurt. Besides, he had vegetated for more than long enough. Returning to Paris had brought home to him how greatly, if subconsciously, he had missed being *au courant* with events, privy to secret matters of importance, and the companionship of men and women of his world.

It then occurred to him that had he still been in the service of Mr. Pitt he would be about to feign a relapse, not to escape going with the expedition to India but in order to get away to England and inform him of it. Thinking matters over, he quickly came to the conclusion that no longer being a secret agent did not relieve him of his obligations to his own country. He might live and make his career in France, but that did not mean that he could stand by and watch a serious blow struck at England if he had the power to prevent it. And this threat to her rich possessions in India could develop into a very serious blow.

Having sent his excuses to Berthier, he retired to bed at *La Belle Etoile* and remained there for two days. He then wrote to the First Consul reporting that he had sadly overestimated the extent to which he had recovered from his wound and, greatly as he regretted it, there could be no question of his going to India. Instead, the state of his lung required that he leave the cold, damp capital and spend a further period in the sunshine of the south.

His good friend Duroc brought him in person Bonaparte's permission to go again on indefinite leave, condoled with him, sat beside his bed for a while and, much distressed, left him under the impression that his cough was so bad that it might lead to a consumption.

Duroc had not been gone long when it struck Roger that if

he took the diligence next day, he might, provided that he was not held up by bad weather in the Channel, be in England for Christmas. Accordingly he sent out to book a seat, with a message that he would be joining the diligence outside Paris. Then, after darkness had fallen that afternoon he drove in a hired carriage to the first posting stage on the road to Calais and put up at the inn there for the night.

He was sorry to leave Paris, as he had greatly enjoyed the week he had spent there before taking to his bed, and he thought the change the city had undergone in the past fourteen months more than ever marvellous. Cleanliness, cheerfulness and observance of the law were now the order of the day. Many streets were being widened and fine new buildings put up. Factories that had lain idle for years were now working again at full capacity. Trade was booming. The new styles in furniture created to make the sacked Tuileries again habitable, and Bonaparte's official receptions there, had created a great demand for luxury goods. The silk spinners at Lyons, the porcelain factory at Sèvres, cabinet makers, goldsmiths and jewellers, such as Jacobs, Biennais and Bohemer, who for long had been hard put to it to keep going were doing an enormous business; while the salons of the best modistes and dress-designers, above all that of Leroy, the veritable King of *haute-couture*, were making great fortunes for their owners. For France it had been a stupendous year and everyone knew it to be entirely due to the genius of the little Corsican.

When Roger reached Calais he went to a small inn on the outskirts of the town and there made contact with a smuggler who had put him over on two previous occasions. He was lucky, as a cargo was being run that night, and the following day, having been landed below St. Margarets-at-Cliff, he was in Dover. From there, instead of taking the coach to London, he hired a post chaise which took him and his baggage direct to Stillwaters, arriving there on the afternoon of Christmas Eve. In the past Georgina had always had big house parties there over Christmas and, knowing how fond she was of the place, Roger thought it probable that, whether she had

93

carried out her intention of becoming Mrs. Beefy or not, she would be in residence.

On enquiring at the porter's lodge he learned that the gamble he had taken had come off; also that Georgina had married in the Spring and now had nearly a score of guests staying in the house. Greatly curious to find out what sort of a man Beefy was, Roger proceeded on up the drive. He wondered, too, about Georgina's guests, as he could not imagine her cheerfully entertaining a number of merchants and their dull wives, yet doubted if her old friends would have accepted a sugar shipper into their circle.

On the latter question his curiosity was satisfied sooner than he expected. Half way up the drive he came upon a fine-looking man dressed in rich furs who was taking a brisk walk. Although it was a long time since they had met they recognized one another at first glance. The sable-clad gentleman was Count Simon Vorontzoff, the Russian Ambassador. At a time when Roger had been living with Georgina she had been temporarily attracted by the Russian and this had led to the two men each playing a scurvy trick on the other; but later they had buried the hatchet, so bore one another no ill will.

Having ordered his driver to pull up, Roger exchanged courteous greetings with Georgina's old admirer, then asked, 'How is our beautiful Mrs. Beefy?'

'As gay and delightful as ever, I am happy to say,' replied the Russian. 'But, my dear Mr. Brook, you will find no place in her good graces should you call her that. Married again though she is, she made it plain to all that she intended to continue to be known as the Countess of St. Ermins.'

Roger laughed, 'How like her. Has she then succeeded in maintaining her position in society and establishing her sugar merchant husband in it?'

'She has handled a difficult situation with great skill,' the Ambassador said with a smile. 'Had she been a man, her strong personality and tact, coupled with her great wealth, would have made her a most successful diplomat. She is, of course, no longer received at Court but she has retained the friendship of the *haut monde* by refraining from attempting to foist Mr. Beefy upon it. For brief periods she still occupies her house in Berkeley Square and entertains there lavishly, but she never takes her husband to London with her. While here, at Stillwaters, she has to stay only her older friends who, out of affection for her, had no objection to making his acquaintance.'

'And what sort of a man is he?' Roger enquired.

'A very pleasant fellow. Naturally he lacks the advantages bestowed by birth, but he has a simple goodness of heart that I find attractive and he carries out his duties as host very adequately. I feel sure you will like him.'

For Georgina's sake Roger had every intention of making himself pleasant to her husband; and, an hour later, after being received by her and her father with surprise and delight, when Mr. Beefy returned to the house from selecting the Yule Log, he gave Roger a hearty welcome.

John Beefy was in his early forties: a tall, broad, fresh complexioned man with pleasant brown eyes in an open countenance. He escorted Roger to a bedroom at the top of the house, apologized that he could not give him a better one as the more spacious were already occupied, said that he had heard a great deal about him from Georgina, and expressed the hope that his stay with them would be a long one.

Roger's only disappointment was with regard to the children. At their age a year was such a great stretch of time that they hardly recognized him and looked quite startled when he swept them up, one in each arm, and kissed them both heartily. As he set them down they both ran to John Beefy for protection, scrambled on to his knees and buried their small faces in his broad chest.

Glad as Roger was to see that Georgina's husband loved and was loved by them, he could not help feeling a slight twinge of jealousy; although he felt none when Georgina entered the room at that moment, joined the group and gave all three of them a fond kiss. The life-long bond between her and Roger had long since rendered him impervious to any affection she might display for other men.

Most of the other guests were people Roger had met and liked in the past. As he had no reason to conceal the fact that he had just come from France, he was able to entertain the company with accounts of the strange new society that now frequented the Tuileries, and the Christmas Eve dinner was a gay one.

Later that evening he managed to get Georgina to himself for a few minutes. Having congratulated her on the success of her marriage and her skilful handling of the social side of it, knowing she would not resent such a question from him, he asked:

'And how does the good John please you as a lover?'

She returned his smile, 'I have known several more accomplished, but I have no reason to complain about his virility and he is always most considerate.' Then in a whisper behind her fan she added, 'While here, with the house so full, we must be circumspect, but in January I'll come to London for some weeks. While there I'll let you nibble my ears again as oft as you may wish.'

On Christmas morning Roger produced for Georgina a *petit-point* reticule by Duvalroy and for the children a number of toys that he had had Maître Blanchard buy for him on his last day in Paris. The novelty of the playthings brought from France entranced the children and soon led to his regaining their affection. Later he enjoyed entering into all the old games and having again a real English Christmas dinner; turkey with all the trimmings, big dishes of mince pies and a huge plum pudding into which had been inserted a handful of guineas and a variety of lucky charms.

Boxing Day was traditionally the servants' feast. They all received their presents and, after a bumper dinner at which the guests served the food, assembled with them in the ball-room to dance. Georgina led off with her steward and John Beefy partnered the portly housekeeper. Roger danced with several of the prettier maids and took them out to be kissed under the mistletoe. Then, a little fatigued, he made his way to the small library to rest for a while.

There he found Count Vorontzoff studying a map of

96

Europe that he had spread out on a table. When Roger joined him he said, 'I fear this recent victory of General Moreau's may have a serious effect on the attitude of Austria. According to the latest reports I have received he is now no more than sixty miles from Vienna.'

Roger nodded. 'Things have certainly gone badly for our allies. It would not surprise me if, as they did before, they agreed to make a separate peace.'

'It is that I fear; and the more so as I have reason to believe my master, the Czar, intends to enter the war against them.'

Raising his eyebrows, Roger exclaimed, 'Should Your Excellency prove right that would be little short of calamitous. I was, of course, aware that there had been a rapprochement between His Imperial Majesty and the First Consul, but had no idea that it was likely to develop into an active alliance.'

'I can hardly doubt now that it will,' Vorontzoff said with a worried frown. 'As the Emperor Paul's representative at the Court of St. James, I should be the last to speak ill of him, but there are certain facts that cannot be ignored. He is of a most unstable mind and dangerously susceptible to flattery. The First Consul, ably abetted by Monsieur de Talleyrand, has played upon that weakness with great skill. The state of things in France has changed during this past year to such a marked degree that my master is now persuaded that he and his fellow Monarchs no longer have cause to fear the spread of the dangerous doctrines of the Revolution. He has become convinced that, under the First Consul, the French people have been restored to sanity, and that the war of Britain and Austria against them is no longer justified.'

'May I ask Your Excellency's own opinion?'

'It is that Bonaparte is not to be trusted, and that having upset the balance of power in Europe by making himself the master of Belgium, Holland, Switzerland, a considerable part of Germany and all Italy, he will remain a great danger to us all until that balance is restored.'

'If Austria collapses and Russia comes in against us, it certainly will not be for many a long year to come.'

'I agree; and with England left alone in arms against such a combination, how long can she survive?'

Greatly as Roger had been in favour of a general peace when Bonaparte had made his offer, since then the Corsican's resources had increased enormously and he had often said that nothing would give him greater joy than to crush the stiff-necked English. With Russia as his ally, secured from Austria attacking him in the rear, he might well be tempted to carry out his dream of invading Britain. Regarding the Ambassador gravely, Roger said:

'Your Excellency is right, that with nothing to fear on the Continent, Bonaparte might yet prove a terrible menace to this country. I have always been given to understand that you are a good friend to us; so may I assume you are doing all you can to restrain His Imperial Majesty?'

'Can you doubt it, Mr. Brook? Many of your country-men....' The Russian paused, then added with a slight smile, 'and women, are dear to me. Having been *en poste* here for so many years I look on England as something more than a second home. To have to ask for my passports would distress me greatly. So on this question my personal interests coincide with what I believe to be best for my country. But at a distance of eighteen hundred miles it is far from easy to reason with anyone—let alone a madman.'

'I had not realized that His Majesty's mind was in quite so parlous a state.'

'Unfortunately that is the case. My brother and others write to me that from unpredictable the Czar's behaviour has become intolerable. He will brook no opposition to his craziest whims, regards everyone about him with deep sus-picion and on an impulse will order the imprisonment of loyal subjects without cause.'

'Surely then, the time has come when he should be put under restraint,' Roger suggested. 'Here in England, as you know, when a few years back King George's mind became unbalanced, His Highness of Wales was by act of Parliament appointed Regent, and His Majesty kept more or less in confinement until he recovered.

'In Russia we have no parliament,' replied the Ambassador with a shrug. 'The only means of staying our tyrant in his course would be through a Palace revolution by which he was deposed and locked up in a fortress.'

'Think you, Your Excellency, that there is any chance of that?'

'It is difficult to say. Should he continue acting in his present fashion, his principal ministers may be driven to such a measure for their own protection. I only pray God it may be so, for naught else now seems likely to avert his entering into a pact with the First Consul to assist him in his war against Britain.'

This conversation gave Roger furiously to think. It foreshadowed a very different situation in Europe from that which had existed the previous year, and made him wish more than ever that Mr. Pitt had agreed to a pacification when conditions were so much more favourable to Britain. But there was nothing he could do about it; so he threw himself wholeheartedly into the many pleasures enjoyed by the company during the following two days and then, at Georgina's pressing, stayed on with a few of the other guests at Stillwaters to see in the New Year.

On the afternoon of January 1st, still with a slight head from an excess of Punch consumed the previous evening, he removed to London. Droopy Ned, he found, had returned there two days earlier after having spent Christmas at his father's seat, Normanrood, in Wiltshire. Over a supper of cold lobster, broiled marrow bones and champagne, they gave each other their news.

In Britain, during the past year, the foremost topic had been, not the war, but the Act of Union with Ireland. Pitt had long been in favour of such a union. To begin with, as far back as '85, and as a means of putting an end to the bickering between the two parliaments which prevented measures being passed that would have led to a great increase in trade between their countries, he had begun to work to that end. In '93 he had succeeded in putting through the Franchise Bill, which gave the majority of Irish people the vote; but as most Irishmen were Catholics the great majority of them were still excluded from sitting in their parliament.

Later there had arisen a much more cogent reason for uniting the two countries. From the outbreak of war with Revolutionary France, the French had sent hundreds of agitators to Ireland. They had succeeded in stirring up the natural resentment that the Irish Catholics felt at being debarred from any voice in the government of their country and the general discontent that had long smouldered among the Irish at being subservient to Britain. This had led not only to a strong movement aimed at achieving independence, but an open rebellion in '98 that had been difficult to put down. Added to this was the fact that the French consistently encouraged potential rebels with promises of military support, had actually on one occasion landed a small force and, on another, been prevented from succeeding in a full-scale invasion only because their Fleet and troop transports had been scattered by a great tempest. And for Ireland to be occupied by a French army with the willing consent of the majority of its inhabitants would, strategically, have been fatal to England.

The bases of Pitt's proposals were that the Irish Parliament, which was notoriously corrupt, should be abolished; that twenty Irish Peers elected for life and four Protestant Bishops should be given seats in the House of Lords, and that representatives of the Irish cities and boroughs should sit in the House of Commons.

It was also his intention that these newcomers to Westminster should not be required to take the Oaths of Supremacy and Abjuration but only the Oath of Allegiance, which would have been no bar to Catholics sitting.

In a speech to Parliament on the subject, Pitt had said, 'We must consider it as a measure of great national policy, the object of which is effectively to counteract the restless machinations of an inveterate enemy, who has uniformly and anxiously endeavoured to effect a separation between the two

100

countries.' And in September Pitt's Cabinet had, with one important exception, agreed to give him their backing.

This was Lord Loughborough who, as Lord Chancellor was technically, 'The King's conscience'. Loughborough apart, King George III was a deeply religious man, a bigoted Protestant, and held the belief that as Head of the Church of England, religious matters were entirely his concern and that Parliament had not even the right to debate them. So he refused absolutely even to consider allowing any Catholic to become a member of a United Parliament. Upon this liberal and wise innovation depended the real success of the measure, but the King's Veto had forced Pitt to shelve it indefinitely.

In the meantime Lord Cornwallis who, as a General, had been compelled to surrender to the revolutionary American colonists at York Town, but who had since directed a brilliant campaign in India, had been sent by Pitt to Ireland as Viceroy. By a policy of leniency he had won the goodwill of the greater part of the people, and had overcome the reluctance of the Irish Parliament. Finally, when Pitt put the temporal clauses of the Bill to the House, he had achieved a great triumph. The Act of Union had been passed by 236 votes to only 30 and had become law that New Year's Day of 1801.

As the First Consul's projected expedition to conquer India was still in its planning stage, Roger had felt no urgency about informing Mr. Pitt of it; so it was not until January 3rd that he rode out to Holwood House, just beyond Bromley, the home at which the Prime Minister always resided during Parliament's Christmas recess.

Having kept Roger waiting for over an hour, when Mr. Pitt did at length receive him it was standing and with a frigid mien. Roger had expected that and had in his pocket a remedy for it. Producing a piece of paper he said:

'Sir, this document has long outgrown its usefulness and I have, on occasions, thought of destroying it; but it seemed to me that you might prefer to do so yourself. I have shown it to no-one and by consigning it to the flames you will be assured that it will never fall into the hands of any malicious person.'

The paper was, of course, Mr. Pitt's admission that he had used his powers arbitrarily to imprison Roger in the Tower. A pale smile lit up his lined grey face and, accepting the paper, he said, 'I greatly appreciate your delicacy in this matter, Mr. Brook. Be pleased to sit down and inform me of the reason for this somewhat surprising return of yours to England, after your decision to remain for good in France. Is it that you have quarrelled with Bonaparte?'

Taking a seat and crossing his legs, Roger replied affably, 'By no means, sir. The First Consul and I continue to be on excellent terms, and I am still the happy recipient of Monsieur de Talleyrand's confidences. But they are now planning an operation which might have a most unfortunate effect upon Britain's interests in the East, so I felt it my duty to return and inform you of it.' He then told the Prime Minister of the expedition being planned to conquer India.

Mr. Pitt ran a hand over his sparse grey hair and said, 'Mr. Brook, I am grateful to you for your timely warning. I had no previous knowledge of this but it fits in with other intelligence I have received. The Czar, as you may know, is about to go over to our active enemies. His imagination has been caught by the old Russian project of conquering the Turkish Empire. In recent years it has become so effete that it is in no state to resist him. Given an alliance with Bonaparte he might well overrun it, move east through Persia and, by way of Afghanistan, aid the French in depriving us of our possessions in the East.'

After talking of the matter for a while, the Prime Minister said, 'I pray you, Mr. Book, remain on here to join us at dinner. With me I have Dundas, Castlereagh and Canning, now my staunchest supporters, and I should much like to discuss this matter further in their presence.'

Roger had long known Henry Dundas well. This bluff Scot, a heavy drinker who never hesitated to call a spade a spade, but was a glutton for work and ruled the Scottish members with a rod of iron in Pitt's interest, had for many years been a tower of strength to him. Viscount Castlereagh was the same age as Roger and George Canning a year his junior. These two had been Pitt's principal lieutenants in getting the Act of Union passed, and Castlereagh had recently been appointed Chief Secretary to Ireland.

When they talked over the meal of Bonaparte's designs against India Dundas, who as the head of the India Board was responsible for British interests there, exclaimed to the Prime Minister, 'Bloody my soul, Billy; but you see now how right I was to press you last October into sending an expedition to conquer Egypt. Does General Abercrombie succeed in that we'll spike the Corsican's guns in his plan to use the country as a staging base.'

'Loath as I was to agree, I'll now admit you were right in that, Hal,' Pitt replied. 'But the main thing we have to consider is can we by any means prevent this mad Czar from sending an army to take our Austrian allies in the rear and so putting them out of the war for good?'

Roger then related his conversation at Stillwaters with Count Vorontzoff and added, 'I gathered from him that we have many highly placed friends in St. Petersburg. Would it not be possible through our Ambassador there to incite them to take steps to restrain the Czar; I mean, if need be, arbitrarily?'

The Prime Minister looked across at him and replied:

'We are now without diplomatic representation in St. Petersburg. By last June the Czar's attitude to this country had already become so hostile that as a mark of our resentment I recalled my Lord Whitworth. When about to depart he asked leave to present Mr. Justinian Casamajor, our Secretary of Legation, as *Chargé d'Affaires*; but the Czar refused to receive him and sent him, too, a passport. There is though, just a chance that what you suggested might come about. On my Lord Whitworth's return he told me that Paul's principal advisers now go daily in fear that without reason he may suddenly turn upon them and send them to exile in Siberia. The Russians are a proud and violent people, and it would not be the first time that they had deposed a Sovereign.'

Canning took him up quickly, 'Could we persuade them to act, sir, our whole position would be saved. I am told that his Heir Apparent, the Grand Duke Alexander, is a most sensible young man: healthy, sane and, having been brought up by a Swiss tutor, liberal-minded, yet most opposed to Bonaparte and the revolutionary precepts with which he indoctrinates the people of other countries that he either conquers or becomes associated with.'

They all discussed the matter for some while, then the Prime Minister said to Roger:

'Mr. Brook, I appreciate that you have now become averse to acting against Bonaparte's interests in any other than matters that may menace the security of your own country. But by reporting his intentions against India to me, you have entirely regained my confidence. This matter of the Czar is a thing apart from any feelings you may have for your friends in France. Time and again you have shown yourself to be an extraordinarily able secret agent. Will you not now consider travelling to Russia on our behalf, make an attempt to rally the forces in opposition to the Czar, and endeavour to concert measures which will prevent him from joining Bonaparte against us?'

Roger considered for some minutes. In order to avoid being sent to India he must keep out of Paris for some months to come. He would soon start his liaison with Georgina again, but that would last only a few weeks and then there would be nothing to keep him in England. On the other hand, apart from the misfortune of incurring the displeasure of the Empress Catherine, he had much enjoyed his stay in St. Petersburg in '88. To spend a month or two in the Russian capital seemed an admirable way of filling in his time, and it would be intriguing to initiate a conspiracy with the object of rendering the mad Czar harmless. At length he said:

'Why not, sir? If I can succeed in serving my country and yourself in this way, I should be happy to do so.'

So the die was cast. Georgina arrived in London on January 4th and for a fortnight they took their old joy of one

104

another. During this time Roger paid a visit to Vorontzoff at
his fine mansion in St. John's Wood, which had for many
years been the Russian Embassy. To the Ambassador Roger
made no secret about the purpose of the mission upon which
he was being sent. In duty bound Vorontzoff refrained from
formally expressing his approval of it. Nevertheless, he furnished Roger with letters of introduction to a number of
people who he thought might prove useful to him, and gave
him much valuable information about the Court of St. Petersburg.

A few days later he spent an hour with Lord Grenville,
who briefed him on what had been occurring in the Northern
capitals. It had been towards the end of August that the
Czar's mounting antagonism towards Britain had culminated
in his inviting the monarchs of Prussia, Sweden and Denmark
to revive with him the League of Armed Neutrality, and in
November he had arbitrarily placed an embargo on all British
vessels in Russian ports. As the sea trade of both Sweden and
Denmark had suffered severely from the restrictions imposed
upon it by Britain, the young Gustavus IV of Sweden had
given Paul his enthusiastic support, while in Denmark the
peace-loving but ailing King Christian VII had been overruled by the pro-Russian Prince Royal and his Minister
Bernstorff. The cautious and vacillating Frederick William of
Prussia was still sitting on the fence but it was feared that he
would soon join the others.

Between them these Powers could muster a Fleet of forty
one ships of the Line, and the British Navy was already
severely stretched in the Channel, the Mediterranean and the
West Indies. Should it also have to engage the Northern Fleet
there would not be enough ships to continue the blockade of
France. That might well result in Bonaparte's invading
England; so the importance of Roger's mission could not be
overstressed.

They then discussed possible concessions that Britain might
offer to induce Russia to retire from the League should
another government replace that of Paul I. Finally, the
Foreign Secretary furnished Roger with a *Lettre de Marque*

105

to show as his credential should he find it possible to initiate negotiations.

On January 18th he took a loving farewell of Georgina and that night embarked in a ship that was about to sail from London to Bremen, as the first stage of his long journey to St. Petersburg.

CHAPTER VIII

THE MAD CZAR

CONSIDERING the time of year, Roger was lucky in the weather for his crossing of the North Sea, and four days later he landed at the Free Port of Bremen. As the city lay in the middle of Hanover and that country still was a part of the dominions of the British Crown, he received every facility for continuing his journey without delay. After covering the hundred miles to Lubeck in a coach he had to waste two days before he could get a ship that was sailing up the Baltic and, when he did, she had not been long at sea before he was regretting that he had not gone by coach via Berlin and Warsaw. But over icy roads in mid-winter the twelve hundred mile journey might have taken him anything up to six weeks.

The cold was bitter, even the furs he had bought in Bremen could not protect him for long from the icy, knife-like winds, his cabin was little more than a cupboard, and the food so revolting that, had he not brought aboard supplies of his own, he would almost have preferred to starve. But the weather might have been much worse; so he was sea-sick only on two days, and the brig landed him at Riga on her tenth day out.

Ice floes would have made it too dangerous for her to

proceed further north at that season, and St. Petersburg itself would remain ice-bound for at least several weeks to come. At Riga he hired a troika and, drawn by three powerful horses, proceeded on his way. The posting service proved reasonably adequate but the inns at which he had to spend the nights were atrocious.

The nobility always sent couriers ahead to make special arrangements for them and travelled with their own mattresses and other furniture. Lacking these amenities, Roger had usually to share a room with several people of both sexes, there was no linen and the sparse furnishings were always riddled with bed-bugs. After suffering stoically for a further eight days, he entered the Russian capital on the afternoon of February 12th.

During his earlier stay there he had found an excellent friend in the Reverend William Tooke, then the chaplain of the English 'Factory'—as was called a large enclosed area in which stood the warehouses of the British merchants trading regularly with Russia. Making his way to the docks, Roger enquired at the gate for the Reverend William, only to learn that nine years before he had come into a considerable fortune and had returned to England to enjoy it. However, his successor the Reverend James Peabody, received Roger kindly, said how agreeable it would be to have news from home and offered to put him up until he could find suitable accommodation.

Roger did not, of course, disclose to the Reverend James the purpose that lay behind his coming to St. Petersburg, but said that he found his greatest pleasure in travel, had enough money to indulge his taste and not having been in Russia for twelve years had decided to pay it a second visit.

The parson shook his head, 'I fear your visit is ill-timed, Mr. Brook. In the Empress Catherine's day, when you were last here, I'm told St. Petersburg was a wondrously gay city; but it is far from being so at present, and for an Englishman particularly so.'

'You mean, sir, that as we no longer enjoy diplomatic representation here I cannot apply to be presented at Court?'

108

'That, and the fact that you are an Englishman. Owing to the violent prejudice against our country with which the Emperor has been seized this past year, few of the nobility would be willing to give you a welcome in their houses from fear that the Czar should hear of it and vent his displeasure on them. Such is his rancour against us that last August, when he first announced his intention of reviving the League of Armed Neutrality to our detriment, he actually went to the length of seizing the goods in our Factory here and, on a trumped-up pretext, imprisoned a number of British seamen: both acts that any sane Monarch would have been ashamed to perform.'

'Indeed! But I take it that British travellers are still free to come and go without interference?'

'Provided they behave themselves, to interfere with their liberty, either in peace or war, would be an unheard-of barbarity. But I would advise that you keep a guard upon your tongue, and so give the Secret Police no cause to apprehend you for *lèse-majesté*.'

The chaplain was a bachelor so there were only the two of them at supper, and over the meal the Reverend James gave Roger an account of Paul I's earlier life and of the frustrations that it was generally accepted had caused his weak mind to brood for years upon revenge then, when he had at last ascended the throne, had made him a tyrannical despot.

It was not until he was forty-two that he had succeeded his lecherous, but great and liberal-minded mother. From boyhood she had kept him in a state of tutelage and denied him any say in the government of the country. For years the great nobles and ambassadors had fawned on Catherine's lovers while treating her Heir Apparent with ill-concealed contempt. She had even taken his children from him and permitted him no say in their upbringing.

The only liberty she allowed him was to play at soldiers. Like his father, Peter III, he was fascinated by the military achievements of Frederick the Great; so Catherine had permitted him to form his own regiment of Marines at Gatshina, his country place at which he passed a good part of the year.

There he had spent eight to ten hours a day drilling his miniature army on the Prussian model and enforcing the harshest discipline.

When he succeeded his mother in November '96, he had at once sent for his Marines, infiltrated them into the Brigade of Guards and promoted their officers to senior commands in these élite regiments. Before the nobles who officered the Brigade fully realized what was happening they found that they were under the thumbs of the newcomers. All leave was abolished and favoured courtier-officers, who had attended only one drill a year, were ordered to march up and down the barrack squares for hours at a stretch. Those who resigned were promptly sent into exile.

Once firmly in the saddle, Paul had changed the aspect of the Court overnight and, out of hatred for his mother, reversed all her policies. Her last favourite, Pluto Zuboff, had been deprived of most of his possessions and exiled to his country estate. Rastopchin had been one of the few ministers to retain his place; but only because formerly he had had the forethought to solicit the favour of wearing the uniform that Paul had designed for his Gatshina regiment.

Under the new régime, familiarity with Gatshina or past loyalty to Paul's father had become the only passports to promotion. The latter had never been crowned, so Paul had his body dug up, crowned in its coffin and laid in state beside that of the dead Empress who had instigated his murder; then the whole Court was required to kiss the hands of both corpses before they were buried side by side.

In the first months of his reign he gained some reputation for clemency by liberating the great Polish leader Kosciuszko and a number of other people whom his mother had imprisoned but, being strongly opposed to revolutionary ideas, he had initiated a ferocious and senseless persecution of the French exiles living in Russia; and had banned the use of French books, furniture, cooking and fashions, to the intense annoyance of his nobility whose culture was almost exclusively derived from France. Another of his pointless and infuriating orders had been that all carriage-owners had to buy a different type of harness and equip their coachmen in the German style. The Russian coachmen refused to part either with their kaftans or their beards; and the price of new harness soon became prohibitive, because the Czar had instructed his police that, after a fortnight, they were to cut the harness of any carriage on which the old style Russian harness was still being used. The upper classes had even greater cause for rage when he revived an old *ukase* decreeing that whenever a Czar or Czarina drove through the streets, everyone within sight must immediately abase themselves. This meant that even ladies in carriages must stop them, jump out and prostrate themselves in the snow or slush.

The lower classes, too, had cause for complaint. One of Paul's inexplicable idiosyncrasies was a hatred of round hats, and these were the general wear of the masses in Russia. After decreeing their abolition he gave orders to his police that any round hat they saw was to be snatched from the head of its wearer and destroyed; and many of the poorer people could not afford to buy others.

More recently, following his revival the previous summer of the League of Armed Neutrality, he had prohibited all trade with Britain. As Russia was almost entirely an agricultural country she had to import nine-tenths of her manufactured goods, and for close on two hundred years by far the greater part of these had come from England. Their present dearth was inflicting a considerable hardship on all classes of people and greatly increasing the rancour against the Czar.

Having listened to all this and more, Roger could only wonder that the Russians had put up with their crazy monarch for so long; but on reflection he realized that the masses, being bond slaves, would have been put down immediately by the military with the full backing of the nobility had they attempted to revolt, and that it was so ingrained in the upper classes to think of 'The Little Father' as almost an embodiment of God that they would never dare unite and openly defy him. Clearly the only hope of bringing his tyrannical reign to an end was by a *coup d'état* carried out inside the Palace by a few courageous men.

When Roger entered the city, the early winter darkness had already fallen, so it was not until the following morning that he again saw it by daylight. Unlike Paris, London and other ancient capitals, St. Petersburg having been built less than a hundred years before by Peter the Great, instead of having narrow, tortuous streets with the upper storeys of the houses nearly meeting overhead, had fine, broad boulevards lined with splendid mansions of stone.

As he was driven at a good pace along the Nevsky Prospect in a *droshky*, while enjoying the crisp clean air he recalled the names of several of the owners of the palaces but noticed that most of them were now shut, and that in the streets there was not a quarter of the handsome equipages that were to be seen in Catherine the Great's day.

He was carrying on him a letter from Count Simon Vorontzoff to his elder brother, Count Alexander, and when he reached the Vorontzoff palace he was considerably relieved to find it still occupied. Having left his letter at the door he spent an hour driving round the city, made a few purchases and returned to the Factory. That evening a running footman brought him a reply in which Count Alexander invited him to breakfast the following morning.

There were several people present at the meal and, as Russian gentry used Russian only when addressing their servants, habitually using French, English or German among themselves, Roger had no difficulty in entering into the conversation. For a pleasant hour they talked of general topics or of mutual acquaintances, either that Roger had met on his previous visit to St. Petersburg or that Count Alexander had made when for a short while during the reign of Peter III he had been Ambassador in London. Then, as Roger was about to take his leave he asked the Count in a low voice if he would give him a private interview, to which Vorontzoff replied softly, 'By all means. Leave with the others and return in half an hour.'

When Roger again entered the house he was taken to a small writing room, and there he told the Count the purpose of his mission.

112

As soon as he had finished, the Russian said, 'Mr. Brook, I must warn you that you are courting very grave danger. Should the faintest suspicion of your intentions get out you would find yourself locked up in a fortress for life.'

Roger smiled, 'I am aware of that, sir; and having had some experience of similar affairs you may be sure that I shall exercise the utmost caution. But, I pray you, tell me your view of the prospects of achieving such a *coup*.'

'Many people would welcome it. There can be no doubt about that. His Imperial Majesty is mad beyond question, and now dangerously so. For the sake of Russia he should be deposed. In fact if he is not, the country will be utterly ruined. I take it you are acquainted with the history of his short reign?'

'As far as a foreigner can be, sir. I know, of course, that he began by being ardently anti-French and sent his army under your great General, Suvoroff, to reconquer Italy; then, after Suvoroff's brilliantly successful campaign, the Emperor of Austria so misused his army that the Czar broke with the Austrians and recalled his forces. After the breach . . .'

'Do you know what has happened to General Suvoroff since,' the Count put in.

'No, sir, I have no idea.'

'When he was bringing his army back to Russia, His Imperial Majesty decreed that the General's entry into St. Petersburg should be a triumph equal to that any Caesar had enjoyed, made him a present of many thousands of serfs and loaded him with decorations and jewels. When Suvoroff reached Riga he received a despatch by courier. It told him that the Czar had deprived him of the command of the Army, of his rank as a Field Marshal, of all his decorations and of all his property. And this without any reason whatsoever. Suvoroff followed his army back a broken man. He refuses to see anyone or receive help from his friends, and now lies dying in a hovel.'

'Can this be true?' Roger exclaimed aghast. 'The great Suvoroff! The Empress Catherine's most successful General! The hero that all Russia has taken to its heart! I wonder that

113

the whole army did not mutiny at such treatment of its beloved veteran leader.'

Vorontzoff shrugged, ' 'Tis true enough, and it's not that alone that the army has to complain about. Formerly the troops wore a comfortable uniform suited to campaigning in all weathers: a pair of roomy pantaloons with the ends tucked into boots of soft leather, a loose jacket and hair cut short at the back of the neck below a round helmet. Under such a costume they could wear either thick underclothes or only a thin shirt as was best suited to the climate. But our crazy Czar has altered all that. He has put them into uniforms of the German pattern, such as he designed for his Marines at Gatshina. Now they must wear tight tail coats and skin-tight breeches, whether or not they shiver in the cold, long gaiters that cramp the legs, tall shakos that do not balance easily on the head and, a thing they hate above all, grow their back hair long then bedaub it with grease and flour to make it into a queue.'

'Then 'tis certain we'd meet with no opposition from the army.'

'From the army, no. But it is scattered far and wide. The capital is garrisoned by the Brigade of Guards. There are ten thousand of them and the majority of the officers and non-commissioned officers were formerly Gatshina Marines, so are loyal to the Emperor.'

'Then,' said Roger, 'if 'tis to be done at all, as I expected, it will have to be concerted within the Palace and the troops presented with a *fait accompli*. What is the situation there?'

Vorontzoff sadly shook his head. 'In recent years it has changed from a gay and happy meeting place, where the Empress Catherine gave a warmer welcome to artists, philosophers and literary men than they received at any other Court in Europe, into a vast, gloomy fortress hedged about with every form of defence against surprise attack. And through the empty corridors there now stalk bigotry, suspicion, cruelty and fear.'

'Your description implies that the Czar already fears that the people may revolt against him.'

'I imagine so; why otherwise these defences he has caused to be erected round his palace? One thing is certain. Fearing the same fate that befell his father may overtake him, he is now suspicious of everyone—even of his wife and sons.'

'Think you, sir, that they might be glad to see him put where he can do no further harm, and so be inclined to assist us?'

'I greatly doubt it. The Czarina Maria has suffered much. While at Gatshina he used to keep her sitting for hours upon a horse, often in pouring rain, upon a hill-top, simply as a marker of the place he wished his Marines to attack in some mock battle. She is one of the most lovely women at the Court of St. Petersburg, but he pays her scant attention. Nevertheless, she is of a faithful disposition and I think it unlikely that she would ever participate in a conspiracy against him. As for his sons, the Czarevitch is a charming young man. He could become an admirable ruler, but he is of such an upright nature that I feel sure he would not lend himself to deposing his father. His brother, the Grand Duke Constantine, I urge you to beware of. He is a fool and a loud-mouthed braggart, so all the odds are that by some indiscretion he would betray you.'

'What of Mademoiselle Niledoff?' Roger asked. 'I have heard it said that after having been the Czar's mistress for many years she has recently been displaced by a Mademoiselle Lopukhina. Out of jealousy, might she not perhaps give us her aid?'

'Have you ever met her?' the Count enquired with a smile.

'No, sir. I was little more than a youth when last in St. Petersburg, and that was near thirteen years ago.'

'You have lost nothing then. She is ugly and diminutive; squints, spits while she is talking and swears like a trooper. Apparently such conduct appeals to our military-minded master and after a day's manoeuvres they often get drunk together. But despite the Czar's new fancy for the Lopukhina, the Niledoff still has a hold on him; and without him she would be nothing, so it would be ill-advised to approach her.'

'Has he men favourites as well as women?'

'Indeed, yes. Apparently it gives him pleasure to raise up low-born servants and watch them being insolent to their betters. There is one in particular, his Turkish barber, a man named Ivan Pavlovitch. The fellow was a slave brought up in his house but now the Czar will do nothing that does not meet with this creature's approval, and has actually made him a Privy Councillor.'

'What of his Ministers, sir? Do you believe them to be loyal to him?'

'They would be as mad as he is did they not wish for a change of master. When in his presence the unpredictability of his mind keeps them in a state of constant fear. On being received in audience, should they fail to kiss his hand so fervidly that the smack of their lips on it is heard throughout the chamber he may impute to them a secret reluctance to pay him proper homage, fly into one of his violent rages and instantly deprive them of their fortunes. During this past year he has sent not a few but hundreds of officials into exile.'

'That being so there must be much suitable material to our hand.'

Vorontzoff shook his head, 'Perhaps to yours, Mr. Brook; but not to "ours". You must not count on my aid in this, because my circumstances are peculiar. Under the Emperor Peter I was a Minister and served him faithfully. I played no part in the *coup d'état* which led to his death, neither did I support his wife Catherine's usurpation. For that she never forgave me; so during her reign I lived in retirement. Upon the present Czar's coming to the throne, he recalled my loyalty to his father and on that account behaved most handsomely to my house, showering both myself and my brother with rich gifts.'

'My brother's situation is somewhat different from mine. Having lived for fifteen years in England he has become much enamoured of your country and has made the cause of Britain his own. As long as Russia continued to be at war with France he was entirely happy; but then, as we must in fairness admit, the Czar had some grounds for becoming

116

dissatisfied with his ally. As the elected Grand Prior of the Knights of Malta, to become sovereign of that island meant a great deal to him; but your country refused him that satisfaction. There was then the matter of the Russian force sent to Holland and its shocking mishandling by the Duke of York. Those, too, who succeeded in getting away with such English as escaped were sent to the Channel Islands and have since been treated as little better than prisoners. On that head I may mention that Bonaparte acted very differently. The Russians captured by the French in Holland were, in truth, prisoners of war; yet the First Consul not only sent them home without requiring an exchange, but had every man furnished with a new uniform before doing so.'

Roger smiled, 'Such a gesture was typical of both the generosity General Bonaparte displays at times and of his cunning. Agreeing, though, that the Emperor Paul had some grounds for dissatisfaction with Britain, and has now become so bewitched by the First Consul that he is determined to join him in his war against us, that has no bearing upon the facts, admitted by yourself, that the Czar is no longer competent to govern and has become a menace to his people.'

'There I agree. I was pointing out only that whereas my brother's love of England has overcome his gratitude for the benefits his master has bestowed upon him, so that he has at least tacitly encouraged you to undertake your present mission, I still consider myself bound by the benefits I have received from His Imperial Majesty to keep aloof from any attempt to bring about his ruin.'

'I appreciate your scruples, sir,' Roger replied quietly. Then, feeling that in the circumstances it would not be right to ask the Count for the names of any highly-placed men who might aid him, much disappointed, he shortly afterwards took his leave.

The next day being Sunday, he borrowed a pair of skates and went down to the Neva where a considerable number of people were skating on their own or propelling ladies in sledges swiftly over the ice. He had not been there long before he ran into a Captain Muriavieff, whom he had met the

117

previous day when breakfasting with Vorontzoff. When they had talked for a while as they glided over the ice side by side, the Captain invited him to a stag party that he was giving that evening, and Roger gladly accepted.

On his arrival at Muriavieff's apartment he found a dozen or more men assembled there, most of whom were officers of the Semenourki Guards. The Punch was mixed and they gaily set about an evening's drinking. By eleven o'clock they were on their fifth bowl of Punch, singing lustily and already slightly tipsy. It was then that a newcomer entered and, as he came into the room, a sudden embarrassed silence fell. Wondering at its cause, Roger looked at the tall, pale-faced young man, who was obviously very drunk indeed, and saw that although he was wearing the uniform of an officer it lacked both sash and epaulettes.

Advancing unsteadily on Muriavieff, the young man burst into a tirade of abuse against the Czar. From it Roger gathered that on the previous day the Semenourki regiment had been on guard duty at the Palace and when Paul had made his usual two hour-long inspection, examining minutely every man in the regiment, he had noticed that one of the men had a slight stain on his breeches. This had driven him into a furious rage and he had promptly reduced both the man's Company Commander and Platoon Commander to the ranks.

It was the outraged Company Commander who was now giving vent to his indignation, and he bawled at Muriavieff, 'How long are we to lie down under such vile treatment? The "Little Father" is no longer a father to us but a crazy imbecile. He treats us, scions of the noblest families in Mother Russia, as though we were no better than serfs. Why do you not speak to your Uncle and urge upon him that it is his duty to remonstrate with the madman? As First Minister Count Pahlen has his ear. Go to him, Muriavieff. You have always said you were my friend. Go to him and urge him to get me back my commission.'

At the name of Count Pahlen Roger pricked up his ears. Among the letters of introduction that Count Simon Vorontzoff had given him was one for the Minister. Knowing that at every morning levee his anteroom would be crowded with people submitting petitions to him, Roger had been wondering how, without making himself conspicuous, he could present his letter and secure a private audience. That Muriavieff should be the great man's nephew offered just the opening he had been seeking.

Clearly everyone sympathized with the degraded Captain, and joined in abusing the Czar. For half an hour the indignation meeting continued, everyone talking at once. Meanwhile, the Czar's victim was given several helpings of Punch and, being already drunk, at the end of that time fell flat on his face on the floor.

When he had been carried off to a bedroom and the clamour had subsided, Roger got Muriavieff aside, said that he had an introduction to his uncle and asked if he could arrange for him to meet him more or less in private.

Muriavieff, swaying slightly but not too drunk to register what was being said to him, replied, 'Nothing easier, my friend. Imperial Highness Alexander giving big reception two nights hence. We're his own regiment, you know. All invited. My uncle sure to be there. Take you with me.'

CHAPTER IX

THE CONSPIRACY

Two nights later, concealing his excitement at the promised meeting with Count Pahlen, which he felt might prove the key to his mission, Roger accompanied Muriavieff to the Palace of the Heir Apparent and was presented to him. He found, as he had been told, that the Prince was a delightful young man: handsome, well-made and of a most amiable disposition. For a man of twenty-four he seemed somewhat shy, but he had dignity and gave his wife a charming smile as Roger was about to make his bow to her. She had been Princess Louise of Baden and they had married when he was only sixteen, his grandmother having been anxious to see the succession secured before she died. In that Catherine had been disappointed; for Elizabeth Feodorovna, as Louise had been rechristened on taking the Russian Faith, had had no children. But she was a beautiful girl and the young couple had fallen in love at first sight.

An hour later Roger, who had been keeping a watchful eye on Muriavieff, saw him detach a tall, broad-shouldered man with a rugged, forceful face from a small group and lead him a few paces towards the embrasure of a window. The Captain then beckoned Roger who moved quickly over to them and the presentation was made.

Roger at once spoke of his letter from Count Simon and was about to produce it, but the Minister said quickly, 'I will take it as read Mr. Brook, and send you a card for some entertainment within a few days; but many affairs call for my attention and my nephew tells me that you wanted a word in private. Now is your time.'

'It was to give Your Excellency a sight of this,' Roger replied quickly, as he took from his waistcoat pocket a slip of paper. It had on it only three lines, which read:

'*Mr. Roger Brook is a confidential agent of the British Government. He is proceeding to Russia in the hope of bringing about better relations with the Government of His Imperial Majesty,*' And it was signed by Lord Grenville.

Having given the *Lettre de Marque* a swift glance, Count Pahlen handed it back with a dubious smile as he said, 'I fear you have set yourself a difficult task, Mr. Brook. My Imperial Master feels himself to have been most ill-treated by his late allies and is now firmly set upon entering the war against them.'

'Of that I am aware,' Roger replied in a low voice. 'But it cannot have escaped Your Excellency that his rule has made him many enemies among his own people. Should God in His wisdom decree a change of government here, I might be able to carry back to my Lord Grenville a very different answer.'

Having no official position Roger could not claim diplomatic immunity, so it was a most dangerous suggestion to have made. But, after the Czar, Count Pahlen was the most powerful man in Russia, and Roger had decided that this was his one big chance of getting to grips with his mission.

The Minister's smile left his face and, after a moment, he said, 'You are a bold man, Mr. Brook. In this country even to voice such a thought could be accounted a crime.'

Keeping his deep blue eyes fixed unwaveringly on those of the Count, Roger replied, 'I am confident that Your Excellency, too, would run great risks in the interests of your country and for the chance of restoring happiness to a vast number of people, I pray you at least to afford me an opportunity to put before you certain possibilities.'

121

'Do you speak German or French?' asked the Count.

'German well enough and French fluently.'

'Very well, then. German would be better. Be at my residence one hour after midnight and enquire for Alexis in that language. He will bring you to me and I will listen to what you have to say.'

Roger murmured his thanks, they exchanged bows and the Minister moved away.

For the remainder of the evening Roger continued to circulate among the guests, renewing an old acquaintance here and there and, through them, making a number of new ones. Moving slowly about the large, lofty rooms there were several hundred people and at the buffets the supplies of food and drink were ample; but the guests did not appear to be enjoying themselves. There was little laughter and an air of uneasy restraint seemed to afflict the whole company; so Roger found himself comparing the scene with those he had witnessed at the Winter Palace and the Hermitage in the days of the great Catherine.

The uniforms of her reign had been much more varied and brilliant, and the fêtes she and her favourites gave spectacles to marvel at. Lofty apartments were turned into Indian temples and indoor gardens, where tropical fish swam in great glass vases. Thousands of candles in huge crystal chandeliers had lit the scene. After the formal dances, led by the Empress herself, there were wonderful ballets each costing a fortune, parades of Kalmucks, Tartars, Circassians and all the other peoples of her Empire in their colourful tribal costumes. Then jugglers and acrobats performed their feats and Cossacks danced the Trepak to the wild music of gipsy bands. The long tables groaned under their weight of fantastic culinary creations on dishes of gold and silver, and the champagne flowed like water. At midnight the common people were let in by the hundred, given food and wine and presents of money, household articles and clothes. After the Empress retired the party became one vast drunken orgy, but it was not without reason that her people cried, 'Czarina, live for ever.'

Yet most of the time Roger's thoughts were on his coming interview with Count Pahlen, and he wondered with considerable anxiety whether he would emerge from it a free man.

At one o'clock in the morning he roused the sleepy night porter at the Count's palace, asked in German for Herr Alexis and, after a short wait, a lanky, grey-haired man showed him into the Minister's cabinet. Pahlen had discarded his stiff Court dress and put on a loose chamber robe. Waving Roger to a chair, he said at once:

'Now, Mr. Brook, let me hear what your Government has to offer that might induce Russia to change her policy.'

'A considerable modification of the measures that now seriously interfere with Russia's commerce on the high seas, Your Excellency,' Roger replied, 'and the return in good shape of the Russian troops now detained in the Channel Islands.'

'That is not much,' shrugged the Count, 'and would not weigh a straw with my present master.'

'Ah!' exclaimed Roger boldly. 'Your Excellency has brought us to the crux of the whole matter. You will surely not contest that the Czar Paul is rapidly leading Russia to ruin? Nine-tenths of your trade is already at a standstill. The fascination that General Bonaparte exercises on him may well prove disastrous. As allies, any troops he may send into western Europe must mingle with the French. Whatever change may have taken place in the First Consul's own views, his army is still imbued with the doctrines of the Revolution: "Liberty, Equality, Fraternity". You may depend upon it that your troops will be infected by their views and on return to their own country stage revolts which must end in the destruction of your system, under which by far the greater part of the Russian people lives in a state of serfdom.'

Count Pahlen nodded, 'In that being a danger, I agree with you.'

'Yet it is not that alone which must be a matter of great concern to you,' Roger hurried on. 'There is the parlous state to which the Russian nobility has been reduced. I learn that

123

within the past few years, not scores but hundreds of them have been sent to exile in Siberia.' He then related the scene he had witnessed two nights before in Captain Muriavieff's apartments and continued, 'Such arbitrary dismissals must immensely weaken your army when it is brought into battle, and by them the whole hierarchy under which Russia has grown great is systematically being destroyed. In this I tell Your Excellency nothing that you do not already know, and must surely feel calls for swift redress.'

With a grim little smile the Minister asked, 'What remedy for this, Mr. Brook, do you propose?'

'I'll make no bones about it,' Roger replied firmly. 'You should depose the Emperor and install the Grand Duke Alexander as Czar in his place.'

'Your proposal has no novelty,' the Count said with a heavy sigh, 'Your last Ambassador, Lord Whitworth, urged such a step upon me before his departure, and numerous other people have done so in secret. But a *coup d'état* of this kind is fraught with difficulties and dangers. The Grand Duke Alexander has no reason to love his father. In character the two bear no resemblance. On that account the Czar has always disliked and distrusted his son. The more so as he is aware that, but for the Empress Catherine's last illness having taken her off somewhat suddenly, Alexander would have succeeded in his place. Her Majesty had already had documents drafted to set aside her son and install her grandson on the throne. Alexander was aware of this but, being a youth of high integrity, refused to lend himself to supplanting his father. That is still his attitude. I have already sounded him on the subject several times, but he remains adamant in his resistance to proposals that we should depose his father and make him Czar. And, without his consent, such an act could lead to the death of all concerned in it.'

'I am much encouraged,' Roger said, 'by Your Excellency having confided in me that you are in favour of deposing his present Majesty, and I appreciate your difficulty. May I hope, though, that you will continue to urge upon the Grand

124

Duke the necessity of agreeing to this project for the salvation of his country?'

'You may, Mr. Brook; for our situation becomes more disturbing every day. But what of yourself? Whereabouts in the city have you a lodging?'

'In the English Factory, with the Reverend James Peabody, who has most kindly given me hospitality these past few days. But I am loath to burden him with my presence much longer and am seeking other accommodation.'

Count Pahlen thought for a few moments, then he said, 'As our only link with the Government of England I would like you to remain on in St. Petersburg, pending possible eventualities; but it is important that no suspicion be aroused regarding the reason for your presence here. In view of the present breach between Russia and England your pretence of being only a casual traveller is liable to become suspect before long; and it is most undesirable that the Czar's secret police should become interested in your movements. I think the safest plan would be for you to remove to my country house outside the city, as there you would be free from police surveillance. But I cannot place full reliance on my own staff, and it might arouse undesirable comment if it were known that I had an English guest there.'

Roger, now more than ever satisfied with the turn the interview had taken, smiled his thanks then suggested, 'As the Germans have always been looked on kindly by His Imperial Majesty, did I pose as one while your guest and my presence there come to his ears, he would think nothing of it. Particularly if you could provide me with some suitable employment.'

'That is an admirable idea,' the Minister replied. 'As a reason for your presence you could catalogue the German books in my library.'

So matters were arranged. Next day Roger thanked the Reverend James warmly for his hospitality and left the city to take up his residence in Count Pahlen's country mansion, under the name of Herr Professor Heinrich Below.

It was by then February 18th, and before the end of the

month Roger had several other conversations with the Minister, who kept him informed of what was going on. The Czar had despatched an emissary to Paris to end formally the state of war that existed between Russia and France. A glowing response had recently been received from the First Consul and with it a copy of a declaration he had issued. It gave unstinted praise to the Czar for his chivalrous decision to defend the shipping of all nations from the piracy of the English, then stated France's determination to render him all possible aid and not make peace with Britain until she agreed to recognize the 'Freedom of the Seas'.

Overjoyed by this, Paul had sent an enthusiastic reply of great length. In it he urged the First Consul to exert pressure through Spain on Portugal to force her to join the League, and to use his influence with the United States to the same end. He then proposed a vast, mad plan for conquering India. The French, under Masséna, were to cross the Danube, enter Russia then, by way of the Don and Volga, arrive at Astrakhan on the Black Sea. There they would be joined by a Russian army and by way of Herat and Candahar invade India.

Roger could well imagine how Bonaparte and Talleyrand would laugh over this crazy scheme; but it was certain they would flatter the Czar by pretending to accept it while making capital out of his hatred of England.

At several of Roger's talks with Count Pahlen, the Vice Chancellor, Count Nitika Panin, was present and, later, a number of other high officials, all of whom concurred that the Czar must, somehow, be deposed. But all were agreed that they dared not act until the consent of the Grand Duke Alexander had been obtained, and he continued obdurate.

Towards the end of February Roger learned that on the 9th, as a result of Moreau's further successes following Hohenlinden and his advance on Vienna, the Austrians had, at Lunéville, again signed a separate peace; so Britain was now left on her own to fight France, Sweden and Denmark.

But early in March the prospect of dethroning the Czar became more hopeful. Prussia had remained dilatory about joining the League, and had done no more than close the mouths of the rivers Ems and Weser to British shipping. Infuriated by Frederick William's lack of co-operation, Paul threatened to send an army of eighty thousand men against Berlin unless the Prussians at once invaded Hanover. For Russia to alienate her potential allies the Prussians, as well as the English, must prove disastrous; so Alexander reluctantly agreed that something must be done, but not for the moment.

Meanwhile Paul was becoming conscious that his tyranny was making him many enemies, and had begun to fear assassination. He had already turned the Mikhailovsky Palace, in which he lived, into a fortress and now he strengthened its defences still further. Suspecting everyone round him of treachery he became ever more gloomy and intractable. Even his devoted wife and his sons came under suspicion, and he told Pahlen that he felt convinced that they were plotting against him. Then, one day, he confided to his Minister that he meant to imprison all three of them and appoint the young Prince Eugene of Würtemberg as his successor. When Pahlen informed Alexander of his danger the Grand Duke finally consented to his father being deposed, but made the Count swear an oath that, when the Czar was arrested, in no circumstances should he be harmed.

Now, it seemed to Roger all that remained to be done was to evolve a carefully-thought-out plan for getting into the Palace without opposition and forcing Paul to sign a Deed of Abdication. But neither Pahlen nor Panin shared that view. Both were most averse to taking any active role themselves and agreed that, although innumerable Russians had come to hate Paul, they could think of no-one with sufficient standing who would have the temerity to face him and tell him he had been deposed. Roger thereupon volunteered to do the job himself, provided he was given adequate armed backing. But to that they objected that he was not fitted to take the lead in such an undertaking because he was known only to a few of the nobles who wished to force the Czar to abdicate; so the majority would refuse to put their trust in him and risk their necks by accompanying him into the Palace.

At length they decided to use General Bennigsen, a bold and ruthless Hanoverian in the Russian service. But he was commanding the garrison in a distant city, so Roger had to restrain his impatience as best he could while making a pretence for a further week of cataloguing Count Pahlen's library.

Bennigsen arrived in mid-March and, when informed what was afoot, declared himself willing to play the leading part, provided that others, equally resolute, were ready to give him their support. Pahlen assured him that he would have no difficulty in producing a body of such men shortly before the attempt. But now that it came to deciding on which night it should be made, there occurred yet another delay. Only Alexander's own Semenourki regiment could be relied on not to oppose the conspirators entering the Palace; so they must wait until its next turn for duty came round.

By this time, so many senior officers had been summoned to meetings by Count Pahlen and asked their views that it seemed to Roger that half St. Petersburg must know about the plot. Every day now he expected to hear that Paul had learned about it and had had his Minister arrested; and if that happened the whole movement would be nipped in the bud because the Count, as Governor of the City, controlled the police and should he be deprived of that post everyone else concerned would also be arrested.

With ever-increasing anxiety Roger strove to keep his thoughts on listing the titles of books and manuscripts until the morning of March 23rd. Still fearing that the Czar must know of the conspiracy and that they would all be seized at the last moment, he rode into the city to be present that night at a supper party Count Pahlen was giving for some sixty officers.

Among them were the three Zuboff brothers, the eldest of whom, Plato, had been Catherine's favourite at the time of her death. Roger had never previously met him, but had heard many accounts of his vanity, stupidity and insolent behaviour. Paul, on his accession, had deprived the brothers of the greater part of their wealth and they had since been

128

living uncomfortably in the country. Pahlen had chosen them to act as Bennigsen's immediate supporters and had sent for them in secret. Later it emerged that they, and many of the other officers present, were not yet aware of the reason for this gathering.

Soon after midnight, by which time large quantities of wine had been consumed, Pahlen addressed the company. He told them that that morning the Czar had carried out his threat against the dilatory Frederick William, and sent him an insulting message by the Russian Ambassador in Berlin declaring war on Prussia. When the exclamations of dismay had died down the Count added that this last insane act could mean the ruin of Russia so must be stopped, and he then immediately called upon them to join him that very night in forcing the Czar to abdicate.

Only four officers refused their aid; the rest enthusiastically hailed this chance to protect themselves from falling under the mad Czar's displeasure. In an excited mob they streamed out of the mansion and headed for the Palace. On the way there Pahlen succeeded in forming them into two groups: one that was to enter the Palace under Bennigsen, the other to remain outside with himself and overawe any officers of the guard who might attempt to make trouble. But there was no trouble. The senior officers of the Semenourki regiment were in the plot and had arranged that their sentries should allow the conspirators to pass.

Roger and the Zuboff brothers had joined Bennigsen's party. It was now close on two o'clock in the morning and all but a few of the inmates of the Palace were sleeping. Quickly the conspirators made their way across the great hall, up the broad staircase and along dimly-lit corridors to the Czar's apartments.

Outside them two *heyducks* were on guard and attempted to halt them. One was instantly struck down, the other managed to escape and, as he ran off shouting for help, several of the conspirators dashed away in pursuit of him.

Hearing his cries the Czar's valet, who had been dozing in the ante-room, appeared, his eyes round with terror. Knowing that he had the key to his master's bedroom, Bennigsen seized him by the throat, shook him as a terrier shakes a rat, and took the key from him. Two minutes later they were in the bedroom.

Roused from his sleep, Paul was sitting up in his huge canopied bed, but only vaguely discernible by the glimmer of a single night light. Bennigsen, waving his sword with one hand, with the other pulled from his pocket the Act of Abdication and shouted:

'You have ceased to reign! The Grand Duke Alexander is now Emperor. I summon you in his name to sign this document. Refuse and I'll not answer for your life!'

Protesting wildly, Paul slipped from his bed and made a dash for the door leading to the Empress's apartments. Then he pulled up short, suddenly remembering that he could not escape that way because, fearing that his wife might have him murdered, he had, only a few days before, ordered it to be blocked up. By his unworthy suspicions he had trapped himself.

At that moment there came the sound of tramping feet out in the corridor. Fearing that the *heyduck* who had got away had succeeded in reaching and rousing Paul's bodyguard and that they were now coming to his help, the conspirators panicked, faced about and ran back into the ante-room. There ensued a wild scramble as they pushed one another aside in their anxiety to get through the further door and away down the passage.

After a few moments Bennigsen regained his wits and bellowed, 'Stop, you fools! Defend the door! Give me five minutes and I'll force him to sign, then threaten him with death unless he orders his people to let us freely leave the Palace.'

Except for Plato Zuboff, his brother Nicholas and Roger the others ignored Bennigsen's plea and ran on. It seemed now that, if the coup was to be accomplished, every moment was precious. With no word said, all four of them turned about and dashed back into Paul's bedroom.

During their brief absence he had scrambled back into bed

130

and had endeavoured to conceal himself under the heavy rugs at its foot. Three parts drunk with wine and excitement, Bennigsen and the Zuboffs launched themselves at the bed and began to tear away the covers. One of them knocked over the night light and a moment later the room was plunged into total darkness.

Roger drew a sharp breath as it flashed into his mind that this contretemps spelled disaster. In the pitch darkness it would be impossible to make the Czar sign the abdication. At any moment now Paul's bodyguard might arrive on the scene. Even if Bennigsen carried out his threat to kill the Czar, there would be no escape for those who had brought about his death. All four of them would be overwhelmed and slaughtered.

Swiftly he assessed his own chances. Shouts and the noise of a desperate struggle came from the direction of the bed, but no sound came from the ante-room or the corridor beyond it. If he acted at once and abandoned his companions, there was still a chance that he might evade the guards, find some place in which to hide until the fracas between them and the conspirators had been settled one way or the other then, under cover of darkness, slip out of the Palace.

Heading for the door he fumbled his way out of the bedroom. The ante-chamber was almost as dark, being lit only by a faint glow that came from lights some way down the corridor. He halted abruptly, his mind still racing with thoughts of his perilous situation and all that hung on this attempt to force Paul to abdicate.

To achieve that end he had made the long, exhausting journey to St. Petersburg and for many weeks had tirelessly intrigued to bring it about. Barely five minutes earlier he had seemed to be within an ace of reaching his goal. Had he done so, it would have altered the whole balance of power in Europe to the inestimable advantage of Britain. If there was still even a slender chance that he could yet succeed in that, could he square it with his conscience to save himself rather than risk his life?

For another moment he was racked by awful indecision, then his sense of duty overcame his fears. The chance lay in quickly finding a light that he could bring to the bedroom, so that Paul could be coerced to sign the act of abdication before the arrival of his guards. Some way down the corridor there were lamps or candles burning. Resolved now, whatever the cost, to see matters through, he started forward and dashed out of the ante-room to fetch a light.

The corridor was deserted and still no sound came from further along it. Racing down it, he sped round the corner, then pulled up short as he came opposite a wall bracket holding six candles. Turning, he grasped one of them to take it from its socket. At that moment he heard distant footfalls. A glance over his shoulder showed him that a group of men was approaching from the far end of the passage, two of them holding flambeaux. Taking them for Paul's guards, he let go of the candle, instinctively drew his sword, and prepared to beat a hasty retreat.

As he did so, one of the advancing group hailed him by name. Next minute he recognized the man who had given the shout and, with a surge of relief, realized that it was not Paul's guards approaching but a number of officers who were taking part in the conspiracy. As they advanced they called to him excitedly that the escaping *heyduck* had been killed, that the alarm had been a false one and that Paul's body-guard had been arrested by the Colonel of the Semenourki regiment; so the Palace was now in their hands. Joining the group, Roger hurried back with them to the Czar's bedroom.

By the flickering light of the flaming torches a grim sight met their eyes. Paul lay limp across the foot of the bed. His forehead was bleeding from a blow by which he had been struck down. His head lolled back, exposing his neck and the red bruises on it showed that he had been strangled.

Bennigsen hotly disclaimed any part in the murder, and was furiously cursing the Zuboffs. Plato appeared scared by the deed, but Nicholas, a huge brute of a man, only gave a drunken laugh and cried:

'The swine deserved to die. I'll go now to Alexander, hail

132

him as Czar and ask a fair reward for this good night's work—that he restore our estates to us.' Then he staggered from the room.

Hours later Roger learned from Count Pahlen what had followed this terrible scene. Nicholas Zuboff had gone straight to the Grand Duke and told him bluntly that his father was dead. Alexander had been completely shattered, burst into tears and refused all consolation. Pahlen had then learned that the Empress, on being informed that her husband was dead, had claimed the right to succeed and was rallying her friends about her. He had hastened to Alexander, found him still in tears but forced him to pull himself together and, to prevent his mother usurping his throne, allow himself to be proclaimed Emperor. In the murky dawn of March 24th the Brigade of Guards had been paraded and Alexander hailed by them as Czar of all the Russias.

Roger had no means of sending this stupendous news back to London, but he knew that within a month or so it would be known there. Meanwhile he was content to bide his time as Count Pahlen's guest until the new Czar recovered from the shock of his father's murder.

Alexander ordered that his Court should go into the deepest mourning, but that could not prevent matters already set in train from taking their course. Although Paul's declaration of war against Prussia had been promptly withdrawn, before Frederick William received news of it he had reacted to the threat and, on March 29th, opened hostilities against England by invading Hanover. The British too had not been idle and decided to attack the fleets of the Northern Powers piece-meal, before they had time to concentrate. Eighteen ships of the line had been despatched to Copenhagen under Admiral Sir Hyde Parker, with Vice-Admiral Nelson as second in command.

On March 30th the British forced the Sound and on April 2nd daringly destroyed the Danish fleet while under the guns of its capital.

It was not until many weeks later that Roger received a full account of this famous battle. Having forced the Sound

133

Nelson, believing Paul I to be still alive and regarding him as the mainspring of the Northern alliance against Britain, had been in favour of sailing up the Baltic and attacking the Russian fleet. But Sir Hyde Parker had insisted that the Danish fleet should first be dealt with, although he had given Nelson only twelve ships out of his eighteen to engage them and with gross stupidity kept the remaining six under himself out of the battle.

The Danish ships had, in addition to their own armaments, the protection of their shore batteries; so Nelson's squadron had had to face the fire of no fewer than seven hundred guns. A murderous cannonade had ensued and there had come a time when it seemed that the British were receiving such terrible punishment that they must be totally destroyed.

Observing the progress of the action through his telescope, Sir Hyde Parker had signalled Nelson to break off the battle. It was then that Nelson put his telescope to his blind eyes, said he could not see the signal and had one hoisted that his Captains were to engage the enemy more closely. Their personal attachment to him led to their ignoring the senior Admiral's signal and obeying his.

Shortly afterwards the fire from the Danish ships began to waver. Anxious to spare the many wounded in the Danish vessels, and refrain from inflicting further loss on a people that his own policy would have left unharmed, Nelson proposed that firing should cease on condition that the Danes acknowledge him to be the victor. A truce was called, he took possession of the Danish fleet, and on April 9th the Danes agreed to a suspension of hostilities.

By mid-April Alexander had sufficiently recovered from the shock and horror of his father's death to attend to business. Count Pahlen presented Roger to him again, this time as the official envoy of Great Britain. Under the tuition of the Swiss, Colonel le Harpe, the young Czar had acquired a most liberal outlook, and cherished great ideals for the improvement of the condition of the masses. But he believed Bonaparte to be a menace to the peace and well-being of Europe and, headed by Pahlen, Panin and Vorontzoff, the

134

anti-French party was now paramount in his Councils. In consequence he received Roger graciously and informed him that he was agreeable to negotiating a peace with England.

Count Pahlen arranged for a despatch containing this good news to be sent by Roger to Lord Grenville and, by the same vessel, sent instructions to Count Simon Vorontzoff, whom Paul I had suspended on his refusal to return to Russia, to resume his duties and enter into *pour-parlers* with the Court of St. James.

From the time of Paul's death onward Roger had remained as Count Pahlen's guest in his St. Petersburg mansion. During the past few weeks he had made many new friends and had been entertained with lavish Russian hospitality. Spring had come, the snows had melted, the trees were putting out young green leaves and he was thoroughly enjoying himself so, although his mission had been accomplished, and in an unexpectedly horrible manner, he saw no reason to terminate his visit to the Russian capital for some time to come.

In any case he did not plan to go back to England, as it remained his intention to make a career for himself in France. He felt reasonably certain that if Bonaparte's projected expedition to India sailed at all, it would do so in the Spring; so if he returned to Paris in June he would have escaped any danger of being sent with it; and by then he hoped that Bonaparte would have found some other useful employment for him.

Then in mid-May he received one of the worst shocks of his life. He was attending a levee at the palace and conversing gaily with the young Baroness Zukinski, whom he found decidedly attractive, when Muriavieff tapped him on the shoulder and said with a mischievous grin, 'Monsieur, I am sure you will be delighted to make the acquaintance of the French emissary that the First Consul has sent to congratulate His Imperial Majesty on his accession.'

Turning on his heel Roger found himself staring at a stalwart, handsome man, whose jaw dropped with surprise at seeing him. It was his old friend Duroc, whom he had known in Italy, gone duck shooting with in Egypt, shared a tent with in Syria and dined with a score of times in Paris. They knew one another as intimately as though they had been brothers. For Duroc to have found him out to be an Englishman meant the end to all his plans for making a career in France.

CHAPTER X

THE ALIBI

W I T H C O M M E N D A B L E presence of mind Roger made a low bow that enabled him to control his features before again looking Duroc in the face. Having returned his bow, the Frenchman said with a smile, "*Mon cher ami*, what a surprise! You are the last person I should have expected to meet in St. Petersburg.'

Roger's expression remained blank as he replied, 'Monsieur, I fail to understand you, since you are a stranger to me.' Most fortunately, during his stay in the Russian capital he had for much the greater part of the time used German or English; so his having replied in French, but with an atrocious accent, caused no surprise to Muriavieff or the little Baroness.

Duroc stared at him wide-eyed, 'But surely you must be *Le Colonel Breuc*? He . . . you . . . We have been together on a thousand occasions. I could not possibly be mistaken.'

'Unquestionably, Monsieur, that is the case,' Roger smiled, now throwing himself with all the acting ability he could command into playing a part that might save the situation. 'I can, though, account for your error. You have mistaken me for my French cousin who was born in Strasbourg. We are of

137

the same age and in our teens we were said to be as like as two peas. It seems that our close resemblance has continued.'

That explanation had been accepted on several previous occasions; but none of the chance acquaintances who had taken Roger Brook for Colonel Breuc, or vice-versa, had known him as intimately as Bonaparte's A.D.C.-in-Chief. Without calling him a liar, Duroc could not contest his statement; so with another bow the Frenchman said suavely, 'Please accept my apologies, Monsieur, for having addressed you with such familiarity.' But as he turned away Roger saw clearly in his eyes puzzlement and doubt.

Concealing his agitation with an effort, Roger continued his flirtation with the pretty Baroness, but his mind was no longer on persuading her to grant him an assignation. It was ninety per cent engaged in endeavouring to devise a means by which he could allay Duroc's suspicions. Should he fail to do so, it would be highly dangerous for him to return to France. It was certain that Duroc would shortly learn that he was an agent of the British Government, and Duroc was very far from being a fool. There could be little doubt that the extraordinary resemblance between Roger and 'Le brave Breuc' would lead him, on his return to Paris, to set enquiries on foot. Once the secret police had checked up that while Roger was supposed to be at his little château in the south of France he had not, at that time and on numerous previous occasions, been there at all, the fat would be in the fire. The double life he had led would be exposed and if he were caught he would find himself facing a firing squad.

Within a matter of minutes he had decided that either he dare not return to France, or he must provide himself, in the role of Colonel Breuc, with an alibi. To achieve the latter it seemed there was only one way. He must reappear in Paris so soon that no-one there would believe that he could possibly have been in St. Petersburg at the time of Duroc's arrival in the Russian capital.

For another hour or more he moved gracefully among the

138

throng exchanging platitudes or witticisms with a number of his acquaintances but, all the while, keeping an eye on Count Pahlen. When the young Czar had withdrawn and the Minister left the *grand salon* Roger followed him downstairs and asked him to give him a lift in his carriage.

As the carriage moved off Roger said gravely, 'Your Excellency; by secret channels, into which we need not enter, I have tonight received a communication from England. It informs me that my wife has had a serious accident. In the circumstances you will appreciate that I wish to return home with the utmost possible speed; I beg Your Excellency to assist me in so doing.'

The Minister at once expressed his sympathy and willingness to help, and they discussed the swiftest means by which Roger could make his journey. St. Petersburg was now ice-free, so if a ship was shortly about to sail it should carry him down to Copenhagen more swiftly than he could reach a German North Sea port by road. As against that, to take a ship was always to gamble with the weather—unfavourable winds might cause as much as a week's delay, and the roads were no longer deep in snow. Moreover, although Roger could not disclose the fact, Paris was his real goal so he meant to head, not for eastern, but for western Germany.

By the time they reached the Pahlen mansion it had been decided that Roger should travel in a coach, in which he could sleep, and that everything possible should be done to expedite his journey.

Among the numerous offices the Count held was that of Minister of Posts, so he had no need to seek the assistance of a colleague. While Roger packed, all the arrangements were made. Outriders were to be sent ahead of him to ensure relays of horses being in readiness; a *sotnia* of Cossacks was to accompany him as protection against the possibility of his being held up by bandits and, finally, the Count provided him with a document stating that he was travelling on the Czar's business which, as long as he was on Russian soil. would give him priority over all other travellers. Having expressed his heartfelt thanks to the Count, he left St. Petersburg in the early hours of the morning of May 25th on his seventeen-hundred-mile journey.

For travelling fast he had one great thing in his favour. Along two thirds of the way, until he entered Germany, the highway would be almost flat; so there would be no infuriating delays while the horses were walked up hills or down steep declivities. A team of six drew his coach and for long stretches across the boundless steppes and through silent forests of fir and larch they maintained a steady trot.

Even so, the journey seemed endless and was broken only at small towns, to change the horses, renew the stock of cold food with which Count Pahlen had furnished him, and stretch his legs for a quarter of an hour. The Cossacks who formed his escort were hardy, bearded men and their tough little ponies seemed tireless. At times they galloped on for a mile or so ahead of the coach, then dismounted to rest their mounts until it had passed them and covered another mile; but they always kept it in sight and seemed to think nothing of riding a hundred miles or more until they reached a garrison town and were relieved by another troop.

The coach was well sprung and furnished with many cushions, but in spite of that Roger found its swaying and jolting extremely tiring, and the monotony of being driven hour after hour through the cheerless, almost uninhabited landscape became nearly intolerable. Having been up for some twenty hours before he started he would have liked to get to sleep as soon as they were clear of St. Petersburg; but the motion of the coach kept him awake, and it was not until he had been on his way for another eight hours that he dropped off into an uneasy doze. From then on he slept only when nature overcame his discomfort; sometimes during the day, sometimes at night, but never for more than a few hours at a time.

When he reached the city of Paskov, he allowed himself to spend two hours at the best inn having a hot meal. Next day they entered Livonia, but the monotony of the countryside remained unchanged. At Dvinsk he again stopped for a proper meal at an inn. Soon after crossing the Dvina river they were in Lithuania, but the endless steppes occasionally broken by dark forests or a small township appeared no different from those he had passed through on preceding days. At Vilna he could stand the interminable swaying and monotony no longer, so spent a night in a reasonably comfortable bed. There he slept like a log but he had ordered the inn servants to wake him at six the following morning and, still bleary-eyed, stumbled down to the coach which by then he had come to look on as a particularly unpleasant form of prison.

At Grodno he entered Poland, but since its final partition among Russia, Prussia and Austria in '95, it was no longer an independent country and the city now stood just inside German Poland. Count Pahlen had generously made him a present of the coach, but here he had to part with his coachmen and escort.

Prussia, having invaded Hanover at the end of March, was now at war with England and, as Alexander had not yet formally withdrawn from the Northern League, still allied to Russia; so as Roger was travelling as a Russian courier, he had no difficulty, after a few hours, in engaging another coachman and outriders.

Setting off again on his gruelling journey through the still flat lands of Poland he reached Warsaw. There he spent another night in bed, in the morning taking the road to Breslau in Silesia. Two days after passing through it he went to bed to his heartfelt relief in the civilized capital of Saxony. From Dresden onwards there would, at least, be better inns at which to snatch a meal and much greater variety in the scenery. But that had to be paid for by a considerable slowing up of his progress owing to the hilly nature of the country. Maddened by having to get out and walk, at times for a mile or more, while his coach lumbered up steep slopes, when he got to Frankfurt he decided to make the remainder of the journey on horseback.

He had now entered territory held by the French, so he destroyed his Russian passport and drove to the Headquarters. After some enquiries there he ran to earth an officer

141

who knew him as Colonel Breuc. He then had no difficulty in disposing of the coach for a good round sum and securing a military permit to use relays of post horses.

After a good sleep he set off while it was still dark to cover the last two hundred and fifty miles as fast as he possibly could. Breaking his journey only to sleep at Verdun, late on the evening of the second day he rode into Paris. By determination and endurance, and maintaining throughout an average of slightly under five miles an hour, he had performed the amazing feat of covering the immense distance between the Russian and French capitals in fourteen and a half days.

His last *tour de force* on horseback had left him saddle-sore, aching in every limb and terribly exhausted, but he did not mean to lose an hour of the time he had won. At *La Belle Etoile*, while a hot bath was being prepared, he revived himself with a pint of champagne, and after his bath he got Maître Blanchard to massage him vigorously. Then, dressed in his smartest uniform, he had himself carried in a sedan chair to Talleyrand's; for, as Duroc had been sent on a diplomatic mission, it was to the Foreign Minister that he would write any suspicions that he might have about '*Le Colonel Breuc*'.

When the chairman set him down outside the mansion the Rue du Bac, he was on the point of falling asleep. With an effort he pulled himself together, dreading this last hurdle he had to face; for if Talleyrand was disengaged it was possible that he would talk to him for a considerable time, and he feared that in his state of utter weariness he might well refer to some recent happening in Northern Europe that the shrewd statesman would at once realize he could not possibly have learned while rusticating in the south of France. But the luck that had carried him so many hundreds of miles without a serious accident or hold-up still held. It chanced that Talleyrand was holding a reception that evening, so Roger had only to mingle with the crowd until the Foreign Minister noticed and came limping gracefully over to him.

'*Cher ami*, how very pleasant to see you back in Paris,' he

142

said as Roger bowed to him. Then, raising his quizzing glass and studying Roger's worn face through it he added after a moment, 'But *"ventre de St. Gris,"* as the Great Henry used to say, you look as if that wound you received at Marengo has reduced you to a sorry state.'

Roger gave him a pale smile, 'I thank Your Excellency for your concern for me, but 'tis over a year since Marengo and my lung is perfectly recovered. I confess, though, that my powers of endurance are not quite up to what they used to be. As a test of them I've ridden nearly thirty leagues since dawn and have somewhat overdone it. On reaching Paris I should have gone straight to bed; but hearing that Your Excellency was holding a reception this evening I could not forgo the temptation to pay my respects to you.'

In fact Roger had ridden nearly fifty leagues, but he had been given a good chance to establish a limit to his capabilities. Talleyrand shook his powdered head, 'I marvel that any man should so fatigue himself as to ride so far in a day unless he feared for his life. But no matter. Do me the pleasure of breakfasting with me. Let me see—yes, on Friday next. And now get you to bed.'

Unutterably relieved to have come so happily through this last ordeal, Roger bowed his thanks, had himself conveyed back to *La Belle Etoile* and, tumbling into bed in his small-clothes, slept the clock round.

Next day he went to the Tuileries to report his return to Paris, but learned that Bonaparte was somewhere on the Channel coast inspecting garrisons, and was not expected back until the week-end; so he filled in his time by renewing old acquaintances and learning what had been happening in Paris during his absence.

It was now stale news, but on Christmas Eve, only a few days after Roger had left for England, Bonaparte had narrowly escaped assassination. Accompanied by Lannes, Berthier and Lauriston, and followed by another carriage containing Josephine, her daughter Hortense, Caroline Murat anl Bessières, he had been on his way to the Opera to hear the first performance of Haydn's magnificent oratorio of the

'Creation'. While they were passing through the Rue Nicaise a barrel of gunpowder, concealed in a covered wagon at the side of the street, had exploded with a terrific detonation half way between the two carriages. Nearly twenty passers-by had been killed, a great many injured, and the walls of nearby houses had been blown down; but no one in either carriage had been harmed, except that Hortense had received a slight cut on the hand from flying glass as the windows of the carriage she was in were shattered.

Bonaparte had gone on to the Opera and displayed an unruffled calm throughout, but Bessières told Roger that on the First Consul's return to the Tuileries his rage had known no bounds. Without a shadow of evidence he declared that it was the Jacobins who had attempted to blow him up, and that he meant to settle with those old extremists once and for all.

Fouché, who for once had been caught napping, asserted his conviction that it had been a royalist plot. But Bonaparte had shouted him down. Scores of ex-Robespierrists had been arrested and, on January 4th, against considerable opposition, Bonaparte had forced a decree through the Senate that one hundred and thirty of them should be deported. Later, Fouché's investigations proved him right. Two royalists named St. Regent and Carbon had set off the explosion, and were duly executed for their crime. Nevertheless, the innocent Jacobins sent into exile were not reprieved.

Roger was very amused. Knowing Bonaparte so well, he felt certain that the cunning Corsican had seized upon this opportunity to rid himself of the men he had come to consider his worst enemies—the old die-hards of the Revolution who opposed him most violently in his determination to deprive the people of their liberties. For his victims Roger had no sympathy whatever, for they were men such as Rossignol, who had been guilty of some of the most atrocious crimes committed during the Terror.

The bomb plot had led to Bonaparte's most devoted partisans putting about the suggestion that he should be made King of France. They argued that should he be assassinated the Jacobins and Moderates would at once be at one anothers' throats and their struggle for power lead to another period of bloody strife, whereas if the First Consulship had been converted into a hereditary monarchy his successor would be in a position to continue the régime of law and order that he had established.

In support of this contention a pamphlet entitled, 'Parallel between Caesar, Cromwell and Bonaparte,' had appeared and many people believed that it had been inspired by the First Consul himself. But he hotly repudiated the suggestion and, reading between the lines, Roger thought it probable that he had put it up as a *ballon d'essai;* then, when public reaction proved unfavourable, decided that his position was not yet strong enough to attempt such aggrandisement.

The Treaty of Lunéville, forced on Austria in February, had enormously strengthened his position. By it he secured recognition of France's overlordship of all the territory up to the left bank of the Rhine, Belgium, Luxembourg, Holland, Piedmont, the Cisalpine Republic and Liguria; and a month later Naples had been forced to make peace and accept a French garrison.

Meanwhile Tuscany had been turned into the Kingdom of Etruria and given to the young Duke of Parma. In March the newly-made King and his Queen, the Infanta Maria Louisa, had paid a state visit to Paris. Everyone who had met him declared him to be the next thing to an idiot and completely under Bonaparte's thumb.

One piece of news that affected Roger more than all the rest was that, after eighteen years as Prime Minister, Pitt had resigned. In March a new government had been formed by Henry Addington, formerly the Speaker of the House. Roger had met him several times and knew him to be an affable man with long experience of political life, but did not regard him as a strong character. Worn out by his long struggle as Pitt might be, Roger hoped that his retirement would not be permanent, but only for a period of rest, as he felt that no one could replace him as a leader.

It was not until he breakfasted with Talleyrand that he

learned what had led to the fall of Pitt's government. There were present two other guests: Roederer, a politician and economist who had played a leading part in the Liberal Revolution of '89, gone into hiding during the Terror and since become one of Bonaparte's principal advisers, and Cambacérès, the Second Consul. The latter was a famous gourmet and also so great a glutton that out of the head of his own dining table he had had a semi-circle cut to accommodate his huge paunch; so it was, no doubt, on his account that the dishes served at this breakfast would have been more appropriate to a banquet.

The talk was at first of Spain and an expedition that was now being planned to go America. In the time of Louis XIV the French had established settlements in Louisiana but by the Treaty of Paris in 1763 had yielded them to Spain; and twenty years later Spain had recovered from England the province of Florida. Since then the Spaniards had ruled the whole vast territory from Mexico north to California, and across the Mississippi and the Missouri to the Atlantic ocean.

After the break-up of the First Coalition in '95 and the defeat of Spain, France had endeavoured to get back her old territories, but Godoy, King Carlos's Prime Minister and the lover of his Queen, had stoutly resisted. Then, in the previous October, Bonaparte had again raised the matter and brought pressure to bear on the King. This had resulted in a secret deal by which Carlos agreed to cede Louisiana in return for Bonaparte making the King's son-in-law King of Etruria.

Meanwhile it had emerged that it was Lucien who had been the author of the Caesar, Cromwell, Bonaparte pamphlet. He had, from being a rabid King-hater, so altered his views that he now wished to see his brother made King, in the hope that he would be appointed his successor. When the mole-like Fouché had produced evidence that Lucien Bonaparte was the author, Napoleon had been so furious at this premature attempt to promote a monarchy that he had packed him off to Spain to prevent him from making further trouble in France, and with orders to overcome Godoy's continued resistance.

As Ambassador at the Court of Madrid in March, Lucien had forced the Minister to resign. There had followed the Treaty of St. Idlefonso by which Spain not only gave up Louisiana to France but also undertook to make war on Portugal unless she closed her ports to British shipping.

Roger had already learned that the expedition to India had never matured, and as he had never been to America he felt reasonably confident that Bonaparte would not attempt to send him to Louisiana. As soon as he could find an opening he turned the conversation to England.

Talleyrand smiled across at him, 'About affairs there I am now particularly well informed; as, apart from my normal secret sources, I now have an official representative in London. Perhaps you have met him—one Monsieur Otto?'

Shaking his head, Roger replied, 'No, and since we are still at war with England I am much surprised. . . .'

'We may not be for much longer,' Talleyrand cut him short cheerfully. 'Otto, of course, has not the status of an Ambassador; but since the Peace of Lunéville and Mr. Pitt's resignation the English have become much more tractable. They agreed to my sending Otto over to arrange an exchange of prisoners.'

'Since Your Excellency is so well informed and I've not heard the reason for Mr. Pitt's retirement I'd much like to know it.'

' 'Twas due to a disagreement between him and King George on a question of religion. Fearful of another rebellion in Ireland, he has for some years hoped to engender a greater loyalty in the Irish people by incorporating their government with that of Britain and giving them some share in it. Politically he succeeded, by putting through an Act of Union at the opening of this year, but that did not get to the heart of the matter because Catholics were still debarred from becoming Members of Parliament. Although 'tis said that he made no public promise, there can be little doubt that he bought the consent of the Irish leaders to this Union by giving

147

them to believe that he would later put through a Bill emancipating all Catholics from the disabilities they have suffered for so long. His Cabinet was behind him in this wise and humane measure, but the King would have none of it. He maintained that his consent to such a Bill would violate his oath to uphold the Protestant constitution.'

Roederer laughed, 'And so we are rid of our most inveterate enemy through the act of the King he served so well. With him, too, are gone Messieurs Dundas, Grenville, Windham, Spencer, Cornwallis and Castlereagh. The whole pack. That mad monarch deserves that we should put up a statue to him.'

'It is an ill wind . . .' agreed Talleyrand. 'Milord Hawkesbury, who has succeeded Milord Grenville as Foreign Minister, seems much more amenable to reason. I have real hopes now that before many months are past we may agree upon a pacification.'

Cambacérès, who had been eating solidly and who, when at a meal, never spoke on any subject except the food, looked up suddenly and said, 'To do justice to your chef, *Monsieur le Ministre*, I'll take another helping of that lobster pâté. 'Tis excellent, and I must beg of you the recipe.'

Roger would have liked to hear more of events in England, but the chef was sent for and there ensued a discussion on whether the flesh of lobsters or crayfish lent itself better to such dishes. Imbecile as he thought the King's bigoted behaviour and sorry as he was that his old master should have been dismissed for having endeavoured honourably to carry out his understanding with the Catholics, he was extremely pleased to hear that at last there was a prospect of the long and costly war coming to an end.

When Cambacérès had resumed his munching, the talk turned to certain fiscal measures that Roederer was advocating to the First Consul, a subject on which Roger knew nothing; and shortly afterwards the party broke up.

The following day being Saturday, it was to be expected that on his return from the coast the First Consul would go direct to Malmaison for the week-end; so in the afternoon, hoping to re-establish at once his position as one of Bonaparte's intimate circle, Roger rode out there. To his delight the great man was in an excellent temper, pulled his ear, invited him to stay to dinner and, while the meal was being prepared, took him out to walk up and down the splendid avenue.

As usual Bonaparte was full of his own plans, his immediate preoccupation being with the official restoration of religion in France. Pope Pius VI had been most brutally handled by the Republican Commissioners when the French had occupied Rome, but he had died fifteen months before and Bonaparte was in hopes of coming to an agreement with his successor, Pius VII. He had written to him suggesting that he should send a representative to Paris to discuss the reformation of the French National Church, established in the early days of the Revolution, into a body to which the Pope would be willing to give his blessing. Pius had readily responded to the overture and had already despatched Cardinal Consalvi to act as his negotiator.

Dismissing the subject as swiftly as he had entered on it, Bonaparte then confirmed Talleyrand's hopes of an early peace with England. Stalking along with his hands clasped behind his back and his big head thrust forward, he said:

'My position is much stronger than it was eighteen months ago, and theirs is now hopeless. Austria has had her lesson, my hold upon the Netherlands is secure and I am again master of all Italy. Spain is in my pocket and Portugal soon will be. The Danish fleet has taken a beating but the Swedes could yet cause England a lot of trouble in the Northern seas. The murder of the Czar was something of a blow for, mad as he was, I could have made good use of him; and I fear this young man Alexander is likely to be influenced by people about him who wish me no good. But at least, before he died, Paul aided me in pushing the spineless Frederick William into kicking the English out of Hanover, and Prussia is a valuable ally. Taken as a whole the situation is overwhelmingly in my favour.

'Now that stiff-necked fellow, Pitt, is gone we should be

able to talk business. These new men lack both the guts and the ability to continue the struggle for long. And if they refuse to see reason, woe betide them. Now that I've naught to fear from the Austrians behind me I'll invade their damned island and, if need be, raze London to the ground. For such a project I have always counted on your value, Breuc, and with my good Duroc absent in Russia I could again find work for another A.D.C. who has a head on his shoulders. See Berthier on Monday and tell him that you are to be my contact with him in all matters concerning our plans for the invasion of England.'

So, two days later, Roger found himself once again in a position to know all that was going on.

He now took an early opportunity of paying his respects to the Bonaparte family. Madame Letizia had left Joseph's house and had gone to live with her brother Fesch at his equally magnificent mansion in the Rue du Mont Blanc. She spoke sharply to Roger about his master, with whom she had had high words on account of Lucien. She then declared Fouché to be a liar and a scoundrel, devoted to the interests of Josephine. She was convinced that between them they had cooked up the story that Lucien was the author of the Caesar-Cromwell-Bonaparte pamphlet, which had led to Lucien's being sent to Spain. Seething with cold indignation she had gone to the Tuileries, overawed her son and, in his presence, upbraided the hated Josephine, then told her to warn her creature Fouché that the arms of the Mother of the Bonapartes were long enough to make anyone who slandered one of her sons regret it.

Roger had tactfully expressed his sympathy, while secretly of the opinion that Bonaparte had done wisely in ridding himself of his ambitious, truculent and dangerous brother.

He found that Eliza Bacciocchi, the pseudo-bluestocking, shared her mother's anger about Bonaparte's treatment of Lucien. It had ruined for her the happy arrangement by which she had ruled his house since his wife's death the preceding year, and queened it among the literary men who sought her patronage.

Caroline Murat had established herself in the old Hotel de Brionne and was giving magnificent dinners there that won the praise of even Cambacérès.

Brother Joseph had played a most praiseworthy part in the negotiations that had led to the Peace of Lunéville and was now assisting the priest of the family, Uncle Fesch, in the *pourparlers* with Rome.

Pauline had moved to a house of her own and with wild extravagance furnished it magnificently. She received Roger reclining on a day-bed with gold griffon heads and claw feet, looking like a Greek goddess who had just descended from Olympus. Her husband, Leclerc, was still absent with the Army and rumour had it that she was indulging in an *affaire* with Lafon, an actor at the Comédie française. Roger envied him his luck and, in spite of his devotion to Josephine, was so entranced with Pauline's lovely profile that he let her ramble on for half an hour, abusing her brother's wife.

In July Cardinal Consalvi arrived in Paris with a retinue of priests and negotiations for a Concordat began in earnest. Bonaparte, Roger learned, was having an *affaire* with a young, simple and very beautiful actress named Mademoiselle George; and now that he occupied the Palace of St. Cloud, his valet Constant was collecting the lady from the theatre and escorting her out there nearly every night. But, in spite of his own peccadillo, the First Consul had decreed that the laxity of morals current during the Directory must henceforth cease.

To this Talleyrand's conduct, as his most prominent Minister, provided a most lamentable example. For the past two years or more he had had living in his house a Madame Grand. She was very beautiful but an almost incredibly stupid woman and had had so many lovers before him that her immorality was notorious. Not content with keeping her there as his mistress, he treated her as his wife. She acted as hostess at all his receptions and, to the intense resentment of the ladies in the foreign embassies, he expected them to make their curtsies to her.

As Talleyrand had formerly been a Bishop, Bonaparte was

anxious that he should return to the Church and offered to procure him a Cardinal's hat. In the days of the monarchy he had been within an ace of obtaining one but, to his intense annoyance, the high-principled Marie Antoinette had taken steps, on account of his scandalous life, to prevent him from receiving it. Now he told Bonaparte that nothing would induce him again to become a Churchman.

The First Consul then insisted that, in that case, he must marry Madame Grand. But the Pope flatly refused to give him a dispensation to do so. Pius was willing to release him from the vows he had taken as a priest, but said that in no possible circumstances would he countenance an ex-priest taking a wife. In vain Talleyrand hunted up every historical precedent he could think of, including that of Cesare Borgia. The Pope proved adamant. On that Bonaparte had to be content with a half-way house and peremptorily ordered his Foreign Minister to get married to his mistress in a Mayor's Parlour.

Roger's duties were not particularly arduous, but soon after Cardinal Consalvi's arrival in Paris Bonaparte sent him to check the veracity of certain information he had been given about two of the channel ports. He was away for a week and the day following his return he ran into Talleyrand on the grand staircase of the Tuileries. When they had exchanged greetings the statesman said:

'Are you aware that you have an identical twin?'

Having for the past two or three weeks expected such a question from him, Roger smiled and replied, 'So Duroc has written to Your Excellency saying he could swear he ran into me in St. Petersburg?'

Talleyrand's face remained inscrutable, and he was silent for a long moment, then he asked, 'How in the world did you become aware of that?'

A realization of what he had done flashed upon Roger. His heart missed a beat. His glib reply had been an appalling blunder, and by it he had given himself away.

CHAPTER XI

CATASTROPHE

R O G E R ' S heart now began to hammer in his chest. He had managed to keep the smile on his lips but for several heart beats he remained completely nonplussed. His brain had become a whirligig of confused thoughts.

How could he have been such a fool? Was there any possible way out? What had Duroc said? Roger's disappearance from St. Petersburg immediately after their meeting must have increased his suspicions. Still, he could have secured no proof. There was nothing to connect the man seen by Duroc in St. Petersburg with himself. But that was not the point. He had to explain having *known* about that meeting before being told about it. Could he claim second sight? No. Talleyrand would never believe him. And Talleyrand's question could not be left unanswered. It must be though, for there was no answer he could give. What would Talleyrand do when he told him he had no idea why he had said what he had said? Could he have seen the despatch? No, he had no access to Talleyrand's papers, so that was next to impossible. Anyway, he had been absent from Paris for a week.

The last of tnese thoughts streaking like lightning through his agitated brain at least gave him an opportunity to gain a few moments' time, and he asked, 'How long is it since Your Excellency received Duroc's despatch?'

'A week or so ago.'

'And what date does it bear?'

'May 30th, if I remember. Anyhow he had been in St. Petersburg for some days when he wrote it.'

Roger had never felt less like laughing, but he managed a chuckle, 'Then Your Excellency will admit that it could not possibly have been I he saw. I returned to Paris from the South on June 8th, and you may recall that I attended a reception that you gave that evening. I could not have made the journey from Russia in some ten days unless I'd had a magic carpet. His despatch, you may remark, took nearly six weeks.'

'About that there can be no argument. But, *mon cher Colonel*, what I should like to know is how you could possibly have been aware that he had written reporting to me his belief that he had seen you in St. Petersburg?'

Had Roger been confronting anyone other than Talleyrand, or Fouché, he could, in his role of Colonel Breuc, have said that he had heard that his cousin, Roger Brook, had been sent to St. Petersburg and it must have been he that Duroc had seen. But both Talleyrand and Fouché knew that both were one and the same. Now, with a flash of inspiration Roger recalled that, although he rarely used it, he had a third identity.

'You must forgive me,' he gave another smile, 'but I must have been woolgathering when you first addressed me, and answered spontaneously impelled by a subconscious memory of a conversation I had some weeks ago with Senhor Pedro Zarolo of the Portuguese Embassy. As Your Excellency may know, before being transferred here early this year he was *en poste* in London. He mentioned that he had met my cousin Robert McElfic who not long since succeeded his father as Earl of Kildonan, and that he was about to set out on a tour of the northern capitals. McElfic and I are the same age, and said to be as like as two peas. When I last saw him he affected a short curly brown beard, but he may have since

154

shaved it off. However that may be, the moment you said the word 'twins', it flashed into my mind that Duroc must have run into my cousin.'

Actually Roger had no idea where Senhor Zarolo had been *en poste* before being sent to Paris, but as he was only a junior diplomat it was unlikely that Talleyrand would know either. And one thing Roger did know was that, as Bonaparte had pushed Spain into declaring war on Portugal, the Portuguese Embassy had recently been withdrawn from Paris; so there was no danger of the congenitally curious Talleyrand checking up on his story.

' 'Tis strange indeed that Duroc, knowing you so well, should have mistaken him for you,' Talleyrand remarked. 'But that is the only possible explanation.'

His masterly piece of invention having gone over, Roger breathed again. But it had been a most unpleasant episode. After a moment he asked lightly, 'And what news does the good Duroc send out of Russia?'

'None that bodes well for us,' the Foreign Minister replied. 'The young Czar is proving a very different fish from his father. He has lent his ear readily to Pahlen, Panin, Vorontzoff and others of the pro-English party. Russia has already withdrawn from the Northern League and there is even talk of her entering into an alliance with England.'

Roger hid his satisfaction by putting on his glummest face and making a suitable comment. Then they parted.

The Concordat with Rome being well under way, the tireless First Consul soon turned his mind to another major undertaking. Before the Revolution the law had differed greatly in the various Governments of France. In Provence and much of the south, Roman law had, in the main, been adhered to, while in Brittany the old laws of that one-time independent Duchy maintained and in the northern governments the laws were still based on ancient tribal customs.

Throughout the Revolution hundreds of these old laws had been annulled, and hundreds of new ones made, either to bring about equality between all classes or, later, to penalise and persecute the nobility, clergy and rich bourgeoisie.

During the twenty months that Bonaparte had been First Consul he had caused the most vicious measures to be repealed, restabilized the security of property and put an end to the general lawlessness that had become chronic during the Terror and under the Directory. But the laws concerning business contracts, marriages, inheritance and many other matters remained in an appalling hotchpotch. Bonaparte had determined to reduce this chaos to order and establish a system that would be uniform wherever French writ ran.

On August 12th he formed a committee of the ablest lawyers in France and set about his greatest work for posterity. For many weeks he attended a high proportion of the committee's sittings, guiding their deliberations and personally debating points of law with its most learned members. In due course this immense task was completed and the results promulgated as the 'Code Napoleon,' a greater monument to Bonaparte's genius than all his battles.

Yet during the late summer and autumn these labours did not deter him from making a number of visits to the Channel coast. Measures for the invasion of England had been initiated there over a year earlier but only in a very half-hearted fashion. Now they were gradually taking shape. Roger was of the opinion that they still constituted no serious threat but, with England as France's only active enemy, ample forces were available to build them up until they would.

The British Government was well aware of this and of how serious the odds against England had become. The population of Britain was less than eleven million against a manpower controlled by France of forty million. The greater part of the French army was stationed in countries that France had conquered and their people had to pay for the upkeep of these occupying forces; whereas for the British army the British people had to foot the whole bill. The cost of the eight years of war had been enormous, so that the British National Debt now amounted to over five hundred million sterling, and the annual expenditure of the nation had risen from nineteen to sixty-one millions; whereas a great part of France's budget was still being found by indemnities, confiscations and forced loans from the countries she now controlled.

Worst of all perhaps, Bonaparte's policy, which was later to develop into his 'Continental System', was having a disastrous effect on British trade. By bullying and skilful diplomacy he had succeeded in closing every port from Norway down to Cadiz, and in the western Mediterranean, to British shipping. The great wave of prosperity, brought about by the Industrial Revolution, had been halted and was now receding owing to this loss of all European markets for the sale of British goods.

In consequence, Roger was not at all surprised when he learned that overtures from Lord Hawkesbury had led to negotiations for a peace; and that Lord Cornwallis, assisted by Mr. Anthony Merry of the Foreign Office, had entered into conversations with Joseph Bonaparte, behind whom stood Talleyrand.

On October 1st preliminaries for a Peace were signed in London. Roger knew no details of them, as most of the talks had taken place in Amiens, but he assumed that their basis would be similar to those he had taken to London in the last week of '99, although somewhat less favourable to Britain owing to Bonaparte's having since so greatly strengthened his position.

Early in December, winter having set in and the weather become most inclement, he decided that he could now use that as an excuse to take a holiday, and carry out a promise he had made Georgina to spend Christmas again at Stillwaters. Owing to the good progress being made with the peace negotiations Bonaparte had allowed the preparations in the Channel ports to come almost to a standstill; so when Roger told him that his weak lungs were again troubling him, his master made no objection to his request for indefinite leave to spend the worst months in the south of France.

That settled, he took his usual precautions for obscuring his departure from Paris, changed out of uniform into civilian clothes and made his way to a village near Dieppe, from where one of his old smuggler friends, for a good round sum

157

in gold, put him safely across one dark night to Dungeness.

In London he spent several nights with Droopy Ned, and again frequented White's, of which he was a member. As opposed to Brooks', the stronghold of the Foxites just across the road, most of the members of the Club were ardent Tories. Many of them had been among Pitt's staunchest supporters and had been sorry to see him go, but, almost to a man, they were now behind Addison in his conviction that Britain should agree to make peace provided Bonaparte's terms were not too unreasonable.

Two days before Christmas Roger went down to Stillwaters with a load of toys for the children and handsome presents for Georgina, her husband and her father. Again it proved a royally happy festive season. Having seen in the New Year of 1802 there, on January 2nd both Georgina and Roger removed to London. He again occupied his room in Amesbury House, but most nights it was not until the early hours of the morning that he left Georgina's big bed to be carried back from Berkeley Square to Arlington Street in a sedan chair preceded by a running footman holding aloft a smoking flambeau.

By the end of January it was the longest period they had spent together for several years and, far from tiring of one another, they revelled in each other's company. So often the same thoughts came to them at the same time, they laughed hilariously together at the same absurd trifles, and spent such joyous nights in each other's arms that, at the end of the month, both of them were most loath to relinquish their intimate and perfect companionship. In consequence, although it was Georgina's custom to spend the whole of the Spring at Stillwaters, she agreed to come to London again early in March.

Roger spent February in Brighton. The town had not yet become the favourite resort of all England's fashionable world, but the day was not far distant when it would have its Royal Pavilion, the splendid terraces facing the esplanade, and become known as 'London by the Sea'; for the Prince of Wales and his friends already spent much of their time there.

158

The Prince's tutor, Bishop Hurd, had said of him at the age of fifteen that he would be 'either the most polished gentleman or the most accomplished blackguard in Europe —possibly both,' and the Bishop had proved an excellent prophet. In reaction to the cheeseparing economies that his mean mother inflicted on the Royal Households the Prince had early indulged in wild extravagance. Again and again he had got hopelessly into debt and resorted to the meanest shifts to stave off his creditors.

He was by nature profligate, and the Opposition, led by Fox and Sheridan, who were also rakes and inveterate gamblers, had flattered and encouraged him for their political ends. This, together with his morganatic marriage to the talented actress Maria FitzHerbert who was a Roman Catholic, had led to a life-long quarrel with his father. In '87 his creditors had become so pressing that he had had to shut up Carlton House, his London mansion, and go to live with Mrs. FitzHerbert at Brighton.

Then, the following year, King George had been afflicted with his first period of insanity, so, with great reluctance, Pitt had a Bill passed making the Prince temporarily Regent, but the Tory government took steps to restrict his powers as far as possible. In February '89, to the fury of the Foxites, the King's recovery had put an end to the Regency, so the Prince soon found himself in straitened circumstances again. By '94 his debts had become enormous and as the price of paying them his father insisted that he should marry Princess Charlotte of Brunswick. She proved to be a flippant and self-willed young woman and he intensely resented having been forced into marrying her. In consequence they soon ceased to live together and he returned to Mrs. FitzHerbert.

In the eyes of the great hereditary nobles of England the Hanoverian Princes were no more than parvenu upstarts and, since the Prince of Wales's conduct in several cases had been despicable, many of them refused to know him. Roger, too, as a staunch Tory, looked with ill favour on the Prince and his Whig cronies who, during the war, had so frequently hampered and attempted to sabotage measures that were in

159

the best interests of Britain. But a friend of his named Lord Alvanley insisted on presenting him, and he had to admit that the Prince was a most genial companion with great charm of manner.

Although Brighton could not offer the warm sunshine to which Roger was used when in the south of France, its climate in February was infinitely preferable to that of rain-sodden London. While there he rode, walked and, following his custom whenever facilities were available, spent a lot of time at a fencing school and a pistol gallery to keep himself in good practice should he happen to be called on to use his weapons. At the end of the month he returned to London and two days later Georgina arrived at Berkeley Square.

Again for the first three weeks of that month they romped, laughed and loved, interspersing their nights of private delight by attending balls and routs together. But on the 26th Georgina had to leave London to make arrangements for a big party she was giving at Stillwaters on her husband's birthday, the 30th. Roger was, of course, invited and arrived there on the evening of the 29th.

To the surprise of his host and hostess, when he greeted them his face was as black as thunder. When they asked him the reason for his ill humour he replied, 'A peace with France was signed two days ago in Amiens and its terms have just been made public.'

On entering the room Roger had noticed that John Beefy had failed to give him his usual warm smile; but at the announcement Beefy's face instantly brightened and he exclaimed, 'Peace at last! Hurrah for that! We'll get up our best wine this night to celebrate.'

Roger gave him a black look, 'Then I'll not drink it. On the way here I have been mulling over what it means to England, and the more I think on it the more I'm horrified.'

'Nonsense, man!' replied Beefy with a laugh. 'Peace is peace and 'tis that the country needs. To the devil with the terms, say I. With our commerce running at full spate again, whatever they be we'll soon regain our prosperity.'

160

Roger had formed a mild but indifferent liking for John Beefy, because he was such a kind and transparently honest fellow. That apart, he felt for him the faint contempt of a man who had achieved great things in the world, talked familiarly with Princes and defied Prime Ministers, for one who was of mediocre mind, knew nothing of great affairs and had never lifted a finger in the service of his country. Rounding on him, he snapped:

'Does it mean nothing to you that our weak-kneed Prime Minister has given away all our conquests made these last eight years except for Trinidad and Ceylon? That many thousands of British lives have been sacrificed for the declared purpose of restoring to their rights the Bourbon Princes, the King of Sardinia and the Statholder of Holland, and that these monarchs are now not even to receive one penny of compensation for the loss of their realms? That having sent an expedition to reconquer Egypt, we are to recall it? Yes, and that we are even to give up Malta, the key to the Mediterranean?'

'Oh come,' Beefy expostulated mildly. 'Such matters are of small account compared to our having peace and the opportunity again to trade freely. And your criticism of Mr. Addison I count most unjust. In this he has served our country far better than did Mr. Pitt.'

At that Roger's gorge rose and he cried angrily, 'You imbecile! What do you know of such matters? How dare you belittle the greatest Prime Minister that Britain has ever had? The man who has worn himself to a shadow mobilising Europe to resist the hideous octopus arising out of the French Revolution and preserved our liberties. Dam'me. You know nothing and care for nothing apart from the selling of your sugar bags.'

'Roger!' exclaimed Georgina sharply. 'You go too far!'

John Beefy's face had gone a deeper shade of red. At the same moment he burst out, 'Mr. Brook, I resent your imputation. 'Tis more than enough that I should have to put up with the association between you and my wife. Oh, I know about that, and your attentions to her while she is in London

161

are more assiduous than can be justified by however long a friendship. Servants talk, you know. And while I have remained complaisant out of my great affection for her, I'd been of a mind to tell you after tomorrow night that I consider it most unseemly that, as her lover, you should frequent this house.'

Georgina, now very flushed, swiftly intervened, 'John! Before we married it was understood between us that when I went to London I should be free to lead my life as I pleased. I'll neither confirm nor deny your allegations against Roger. But this is not your house; 'tis mine. And I'll have whom I will to stay in it. Even so, I am with you that Roger has behaved most unbecomingly towards you. He will apologize and that is to be the end of the matter.'

Never before had Roger seen John Beefy even approach losing his temper. Realizing now that he had every justification for doing so, he regained control of himself and said quietly, 'I pray you forgive me, John. I had become overwrought by brooding on this terrible peace that has been imposed upon England. As for myself and Georgina, I plan shortly to go abroad again; but if it is your wish I will depart now and send my seconds to you.'

Beefy shrugged his broad shoulders, 'I accept your apology for the slur upon my patriotism. But as an honest merchant unused to handling weapons I'd be out of my senses to engage in a duel with a professional killer. Regarding Georgina's claim that I'd not call into question any associations she might form during her stays in London, she is in the right. But for her to expect me to sit at table with her lover is another matter.' Drawing himself up so stiffly that he looked slightly ridiculous, the injured husband stalked from the room.

Georgina and Roger stared ruefully at one another for a moment, then they both began to laugh and he said, 'How prodigious pompous he was. Head in air and his back as stiff as a ramrod. But there it is, we are caught out.'

'Alas, yes,' she chuckled. 'If only he could have seen himself as the honest merchant looking down his nose at the professional killer. But 'tis no laughing matter. He is a dear

162

fellow and loves me to distraction. One cannot wonder that knowing you now to be my lover he cannot bear having you in the house.'

Roger shrugged, 'In the world to which we have been used a few husbands elect to defend their honour, but most accept such a situation gracefully. Since he'll do neither, what's to be done? Shall I order that my bags be repacked and get me hence?'

'No,' she said firmly. 'I am mistress here, and that I'll not allow. Moreover, while you were quarrelling with him, both your backs were to the hall door, and it was half open. James, the footman, appeared there for a moment and was about to enter then, witnessing the rumpus, quickly withdrew. He cannot have heard much but if you leave tonight the servants will put it down to that and provoke an open scandal. 'Twill be all over the county within a few days. Then, like it or not, John will have to call you out or stand disgraced. I'll tell him so, and that until after tomorrow night he must grin and bear your company.'

On that they parted and went up to their rooms to change for dinner. Fortunately, two couples had been invited; so their presence, together with that of the urbane Colonel Thursby, prevented any further rupture between Beefy and Roger. The former was sullen and morose throughout the evening whereas Roger, being so practised in concealing his feelings when a difficult situation arose, talked with his usual carefree gaiety. And, as none of the other guests had yet heard the peace terms, he deliberatly refrained from bringing up the subject, in order to avoid giving Beefy a new cause to quarrel with him.

As soon as the guests had gone they went up to bed. Half an hour later, Georgina came to his room. Sitting up in bed, he smiled at her and said, 'What a delightful surprise. You have never paid me this compliment since you married your Mr. Beefy.'

With a frown she shook her head, 'I've not come to pleasure you tonight. But I have to talk to you, and we'll

163

have no chance tomorrow. It's chilly here. Move over and make room for me.'

As she got into his bed he gave a laugh and put his arm round her. 'We'll talk later, be it your wish. But how can you think I'd miss such an opportunity? Take off that robe, my dearest love, and all that you may have on beneath it.'

'No, Roger, no!' she exclaimed impatiently and broke his embrace. 'This is a serious matter. I have had a talk with John and must tell you of it.'

'Oh, damn the fellow! Still, if you must. What has the pompous ass to say?'

'He has issued me an ultimatum. Either you go from this house the morning after the party and do not return, or he will leave me.'

'Let him then,' Roger replied angrily. 'Why you should ever have married such an oaf passes my comprehension.'

'He is not an oaf,' she retorted, her black eyes flashing, 'but the dearest, sweetest-natured man that I have ever met in my whole life.'

'Including myself?'

'For me you are a man apart from all others, but had we married it would have been calamitous to our abiding love. I mean as a husband and a father to the children. He has given me a new and happy life with which I am utterly contented.'

'Until you feel the itch to go to London and wanton in your bed with some more civilized and amusing gallant.'

'Nay; there I refresh my mind with intelligent conversation and indulge my love of gaiety. But I'd have you know that since I married Mr. Beefy, excepting with yourself I have been faithful to him.'

'Then the leopardess has certainly changed her spots and I am more honoured than I knew,' Roger commented sarcastically. 'But surely you cannot seriously mean that you will never have me at Stillwaters again?'

'I do. I had hoped to argue him into adopting the complaisancy shown by many husbands; but I failed in that. Like most simple, straightforward persons he is impossible to move when once his mind is made up, and I'm determined not to

164

lose him. To ask me to do so would be to behave like the veriest dog in the manger, Roger. Why should I sacrifice my happy existence while you live abroad, sometimes for years on end? When you do return again to England we can still enjoy ourselves in Berkeley Square.'

'True, true; but never to come to Stillwaters again. . . .'

'Is that so hard?'

'Can you think it otherwise? Many of the happiest hours of my life have been spent here with you. Then there are the children.'

'They can stay with me at times in London and you can see them then.'

' 'Twould not be the same. No lake to take them on; no place for them to ride their ponies safely; no woods in which to ramble with them and find them birds' nests.'

'That I cannot help. My contentment means more to me than the pleasure of having you here for a short time once in a year or two. You are to me each time we meet anew like a draught of rich golden wine, but John is my bread and butter. I'll never find another like him, and nothing will induce me to let him go. That is my final word; and so, good night.'

As she spoke, she slipped out of bed and walked quickly to the door. Sitting up he called after her, 'Georgina! Come back! We cannot leave matters like this. That I must have sounded monstrous selfish, I admit. But returning to Stillwaters has meant so much to me. Each time I love it more. Surely we can find some way to reach a compromise?'

His last words fell on deaf ears, for Georgina had left the room, slamming the door behind her.

Thinking the matter over, he soon admitted to himself that there was everything to be said for Georgina's point of view and nothing for his own. To expect her to part with a husband who suited her so well in order that a lover, whom she could see as often as she liked when he was in London, could pay occasional visits to her country home was utterly unreasonable. Nevertheless, Roger felt extremely sore about the matter. From the age of nineteen, when Georgina was married to her first husband, Sir Humphrey Etheredge, to whom the house had belonged, he had stayed there as a privileged guest, and on most of those occasions they had been free to do as they liked in it; so it was not altogether unnatural that he should look on John Beefy as an interloper.

After a while his agile brain found what he felt could be a way round the difficulty. In the past Beefy had paid fairly regular visits to his estates in the West Indies. Now that he had been married to Georgina for two years it seemed probable that his affairs would demand that he should tear himself from her to go out there again next winter. At times, too, he had to make trips lasting a week or more to Bristol, to inspect his ships and warehouses there. Therefore Roger decided, when he returned to England again next autumn, he should be able to take advantage of Beefy's absence to pay one or more visits to Stillwaters, without upsetting Georgina's marriage.

He meant to speak to her about it next day but no opportunity arose, because she was so busy preparing for the party. Roger was wise enough to refrain from appearing sulky or annoyed with her. On the contrary he made himself very useful, cheerfully helping the footmen arrange the buffet tables, carrying chairs about and fetching cans of water for the big vases in which she was arranging masses of spring flowers; but they were never alone together long enough for him to think it a suitable time to begin a serious conversation.

In due course the violinists arrived, were given a meal and began to tune up at one end of the ballroom. Then carriage after carriage drove up the long drive to set down its load of men in velvet coats, kneebreeches and white stockings, and bare-shouldered women in a gay variety of silks and satins. It was about half way through the reception of the guests that Roger received the second unpleasant shock of his visit. He suddenly caught sight of Colonel George Gunston coming up the stairs.

They had been enemies from their early teens. At Sherborne Gunston had bullied Roger unmercifully, but later

166

Roger, being one of the finest swordsmen in Europe, had inflicted bitter humiliation on George, by making him appear no more than a clumsy lout, in a practice fencing bout witnessed by many of their acquaintances of both sexes. Wherever they had met they had been at loggerheads over policy and quarrelled over women. When in Martinique Roger had deprived Gunston of his command; in India George had been the cause of the death of a girl Roger loved through delaying an attack on the city of a rebellious Rajah.

Naturally, Georgina and her husband were receiving the guests, so Roger and George gave one another only a distant bow. But as soon as he could Roger took Georgina aside for a moment and asked her with a frown, 'What is George Gunston doing here? I didn't know that he lived in the neighbourhood.'

For a moment Georgina did not answer; then, following Roger's glance, she said, 'Do you mean that red-faced, fair-haired Colonel?'

Roger nodded, 'That is he; look at his swagger. The conceited coxcomb.'

'At least he is a fine figure of a man,' Georgina remarked. 'I've not met him before, but he is staying with Lord and Lady Milford at Crossways Hall and Molly Milford asked if she might bring him. She is the tall, gawky, fair-haired woman with the long nose and great doe-like eyes, to whom he is talking at the moment.'

From the cattiness of Georgina's description it was evident that she disliked Lady Milford; so Roger tactfully refrained from saying that he thought her quite a beauty. Instead he said, 'I have known Gunston since my school days. He is a most loathsome cad; but the women seem to like him, and he has quite a reputation as a lady killer.'

'Has he now!' Georgina smiled. 'Then I'll let him try his art on me tonight. Molly Milford must be old enough to be my mother; but when I was young and new at the game she took away from me a beau with whom I was quite smitten. I've a long memory for old scores. It should amuse you to watch me pay her out.'

'Georgina,' Roger said quickly. 'Gunston and I are lifelong enemies. On that count I seek to make no capital with you; yet I beg you to desist from your intent. He is a lecher and a blackguard of the first order. At your dances you have always provided well-screened sitting out places where couples can enjoy a quiet flirtation unobserved. But do you let Gunston lead you to one of them you'll rue it. He is quite capable of pressing his suit so hotly that should you resist your dress will be reduced to such a state that you would be embarrassed to return to the ballroom.'

With a shrug of her fine shoulders, Georgina dismissed Roger's warnings. 'Since when have you found it necessary to talk to me as though I were a school miss? I'm capable of putting in his place any man who, against my will, attempts to maul me.'

At that moment a gentleman came up and asked her to partner him in a quadrille, so Roger stepped aside. Beefy had been in a very touchy mood all day and Roger, feeling that the sight of him dancing with Georgina might lead him to forget himself and make an unseemly scene, had refrained from asking her for a dance; so for the next three hours he had no further word with her.

He danced only twice with other women to whom he felt he owed that courtesy from having known them for several years. For the rest of the time he moved about exchanging small talk with men who were not dancing, and whenever he found himself on his own he went and had a drink at the buffet.

His naturally sunny temperament ensured his suffering from black moods only very occasionally, but that night one of the worst he had ever experienced was upon him. Everyone now had heard about peace having been signed and it was, almost universally, the subject of conversation.

Yet few people to whom he talked seemed to realize its implications. To meet the cost of the war Pitt had had to impose a tax of ten per cent upon all incomes above £200 per annum. No such demand on men of property had ever before been inflicted, and the landed gentry had intensely resented this innovation. Now they were all rejoicing that they would soon be free of it and, knowing little about foreign affairs, cared nothing for the means by which Britain had, to Roger's mind, bought this disastrous peace. To his disgust, with raised glasses they toasted Lord Cornwallis, oblivious of the fact that Joseph Bonaparte and Talleyrand had made rings round the old man and must that night be laughing in Paris, having got everything from him except the clothes he stood up in.

Roger's mood was further soured by the knowledge that next winter, unless Beefy went away, he would be debarred from coming to stay at Stillwaters. His love for Georgina was so fundamental a thing that, faced with a crisis, he would without a second's hesitation have given his life in her defence. But, having had long experience of her forceful character, he intensely resented that she should have refrained from using it in his interests to dominate her mediocre husband and bring him to heel.

Still worse fuel was added to the fire by his seeing, nearly every time he entered the ballroom, that she was either dancing with or talking to Gunston. They were laughing together and showing every sign of getting on famously. Three times Roger turned away, seething with silent rage, to get himself another drink at the buffet.

Justerini's took care of Georgina's cellar, so the champagne was excellent; but, after a time he gave it up for cognac. He had always been capable of heavy drinking, but by midnight was half-seas over and so bloodyminded that if anyone had been in the least offensive to him he would have called him out.

It was about half an hour after midnight that the strange psychic link that existed between him and Georgina suddenly began to function. As clearly as though she had been speaking in his ear, he heard her say, 'Roger, come quickly. I need your aid, lest there be a most horrid scene.'

Pushing unceremoniously aside the people among whom he was standing, guided by an unerring instinct he strode down to the main hall. On either side the great staircase there were

169

deep alcoves with settees in them that Georgina that morning had screened with banks of flowers.

The hall was empty and, as Roger advanced on the nearest alcove, he heard Georgina's half-strangled cry, 'No, no! Desist, I beg! Enough, I say! No, I won't let you.'

Tearing aside the screen of daffodils and hyacinths, Roger stared down at the couple on the well-cushioned sofa. Georgina was lying full length upon it, her feet dangling on the ground. Gunston was on top of her. With one hand he was endeavouring to muffle her protests, the other he had thrust up under her skirts.

Without a thought that someone might come upon them, instead of simply demanding that Gunston should release Georgina and so put a swift end to this unpleasant scene, Roger lurched forward, seized him by the back of his stiff uniform collar, dragged him off her and shouted, 'You lecherous swine! I'll make you pay for this!'

Gunston was much the bigger man. Regaining his balance he squared up to Roger and cried, 'So 'tis you, Brook! My old schooldays' companion, the snivelling little bookworm Brook. How typical of you to come on the scene just as I was about to get to work on our lovely hostess. I've often heard of her as a game filly, and she was making no more than the usual demurs that well-bred women consider necessary as evidence of their modesty.'

'You lie,' snarled Roger. 'You were holding her down and about to force her.'

'Nonsense! 'Tis only your jealousy that makes you see things in that way. All the town knows that she has been your mistress on and off for years. You should not take it ill that she is now tired of you and would welcome a change.'

At one side of the hall stood a long sword rack, in which it was customary for officers to leave their swords on entering a house. In it, besides those of the officers attending the dance, were several rapiers that had belonged to Sir Humphrey Etheredge. Striding two paces, Roger snatched up the nearest. It happened to be only a Court sword with a slender blade and of less than a duelling sword's standard length. But,

swishing it in the air, he advanced on Gunston and cried in a thick, husky voice:

'Arm yourself, you slandering bastard. For having traduced my Lady St. Ermins I intend to kill you here and now.'

'You're drunk,' retorted Gunston. 'Drunk as an owl. Put up that weapon and go douse your head under a cold tap.'

'Drunk I may be,' shouted Roger. 'But I'll not be drunk at dawn tomorrow. You shall face me then and I'll see to it that you never more lay your filthy hands on a decent woman.'

Gunston was sweating under his tight red uniform coat. His normally rubicund face had gone a deep puce and his blue eyes showed fear. Running a finger round his tight high collar to ease it, he shook his head and gasped, 'No, no! I'll not do that. Everyone knows that when sober few men could meet you. I'll not let myself be cut to pieces to make for you a Roman holiday.'

'Poltroon!' Roger sneered at him. 'By refusing to meet me you disgrace the uniform you wear. So be it then. I'll settle your business before you are five minutes older.' Then he made a lunge at Gunston with the fragile rapier.

Georgina had pulled herself to her feet, hurriedly rearranged her disordered dress, and was staring at them wide eyed.

'Stop!' she cried. 'For God's sake, stop! Not here! Not here!'

Ignoring her, Roger made another threatening feint at Gunston, driving him back against the sword rack. His eyes as desperate as those of a trapped animal, Gunston fumbled behind him; his hand fell upon the hilt of a cavalry sabre. Wrenching it from its scabbard he threw himself into a posture of defence.

With a drunken laugh Roger engaged him. The steel clashed but the combat was an uneven one. Gunston's heavy blade far outweighed Roger's slender rapier. Within a minute he found that he needed all his skill to avoid his frail weapon being cut off near the hilt or struck from his hand.

171

Georgina wasted no more breath in pleading with these two life-long enemies to cease from their attempts to kill one another. Gathering up her skirts she ran from the hall into the dining room.

The two antagonists now circled round one another. Roger pinked Gunston's shoulder, but he dared not parry the swipes from the heavy sabre and only by the agility that made him such a formidable swordsman did he succeed in jumping aside in time to save his head from being sliced in half.

Short as their combat was they were both breathing heavily when Georgina came running back with Beefy, whom she had found in the dining room talking to some other men. He shouted to Roger and Gunston to put up their weapons, but they ignored him. Finding his pleas useless, he ran to another rack that held a variety of walking sticks and canes. Grasping a heavy blackthorn, he ran forward brandishing it and attempted to beat down the clashing blades.

Only too glad to see an end to this murderous encounter, Gunston lowered his sabre and gave back. Roger, furious at Beefy's interference, berserk with accumulated rage and determined not to let his old enemy escape without at least a nasty gash that would be a lesson to him, yelled at Beefy to get out of the way, sidestepped and made another thrust.

Beefy was standing between them and sideways on to both, but looking towards Gunston. At Roger's shout he swerved half round and brought up his blackthorn, to strike Roger's rapier down. Roger's thrust had been aimed to pass behind Beefy's back, but the quantity of brandy he had drunk had slightly impaired his timing and, at the same moment, Beefy's swerve had altered his position a little. The slender blade failed to clear him. It ripped through the silk of his coat near the base of his spine.

He suddenly stiffened. His eyes started from their sockets. He gave an awful groan and fell to the ground.

For a moment Roger, Gunston and Georgina all remained as though paralysed, staring with horrified eyes at the squirming figure. Then throwing herself on her knees beside

172

her husband Georgina took his head in her lap. His eyes rolled, froth bubbled from his lips and his body jerked spasmodically, so that she had difficulty in holding him.

Suddenly a prolonged bubbling sound began to issue from Beefy's throat. It was not the first time that Roger had heard a dying man give vent to the death rattle and it confirmed his worst fears. His rapier must have passed through Beefy's liver.

By this time, attracted by the sounds of strife a small crowd of people had come out into the hall. Some of them began to shout, 'Get a doctor!' 'Fetch some water!' 'Give him brandy!', while others violently upbraided Roger and Gunston as being the evident cause of the tragedy.

Ignoring them, Roger threw his rapier on the floor and stared down at Georgina. Letting fall her dead husband's head, she rose and faced him. Then, her black eyes as yet tearless but hard as stones, she said in a low tense voice:

'I always knew you to be unscrupulous towards your enemies. But to have done this thing to me almost passes belief. Seeing an opportunity to gain your ends you put them before all thought of my happiness.' Suddenly her voice rose almost to a scream:

'Go from here! Go! I hate you! I never want to set eyes on you again!'

No more awful thing could have happened to Roger than that Georgina, his life-long love, should drive him from her. Yet even that was not the full price he was to pay for this terrible occurrence. For this was not France, where Napoleon's officers fought one another on the slightest pro- vocation and counted it no more than good practice for using their swords against France's enemies. This was England, where to kill a man was manslaughter—or might be accoun- ted murder.

CHAPTER XII

ON TRIAL FOR HIS LIFE

F O R T H E five weeks that followed Beefy's death Roger felt as though he was living through a nightmare. In deference to Georgina's dismissal of him, and feeling it to be certainly more fitting, he had begged a lift in a carriage, had himself driven in to Ripley and there secured a room at the Talbot Inn.

Next morning he woke with a furred tongue and an aching head. It was not often that he felt the effects on the morning after of what he had drunk the night before; but on this occasion he had punished the cognac very severely—so severely that he had no very clear recollection of what had happened, apart from the salient facts that Georgina had been mauled and insulted by Gunston, with whom he had then fought, Beefy had sought to intervene and, by a misdirected thrust, had then been killed by him. Yet Georgina's last words rang as clear as crystal through his aching head:

'Go from here! Go! I hate you! I never want to set eyes on you again.'

Roger did not for one moment believe that she really meant them. Their lives were so closely interwoven that, whatever he had done, she could not possibly cast him off for good at a moment's notice. That John Beefy should stupidly have got himself in the way of a sword thrust was regrettable. He had been a very decent fellow and it was hard on him that his life should have been cut short when he was only a little over forty. But for a man of his position he had been fortunate—incredibly fortunate—in that for two years he had had Georgina as his wife; and, Roger now recalled, she had read in Beefy's hand before she married him that his life would not be a long one.

Two nights earlier she had made it clear that he meant a lot to her, because he had brought into her life a background of quiet happiness and peaceful regularity; and when a woman had turned thirty she felt a need for a man with whom she could settle down. But Roger felt confident that she would soon get over her loss and forget Beefy in much less time than she had her second husband, Charles St. Ermins, for whom she had cared deeply.

The only thing that really worried him was that she appeared to have thought that he had taken advantage of the mêlée to kill Beefy deliberately, and so rid himself of the prohibition against coming to Stillwaters whenever he wished. But he could not believe that she would long continue to harbour a suspicion that he had acted so basely; and he decided that, for the time being, it would be wiser not to force his presence on her, either to express his sorrow at having killed her husband or to assure her that the tragedy had been an entirely unforeseeable accident.

When he rang for the chambermaid and ordered up a bottle of Madeira, as a tonic to pull himself together, she told him that his things had been sent across from Stillwaters, but no message had come with them. An hour later he dressed with the intention of riding post back to London. But when he went downstairs he found a tipstaff awaiting him. The man touched him with a paper and caused him to stiffen with sudden shock by saying:

'Mister Brook, I 'av horders to take ye into custerdy on o'count o' what 'appened lars night. Ye'll 'ave to answer ter a charge o' manslaughter; so be pleased ter come along o' me.'

Roger's mind had been so occupied with distress at his breach with Georgina that he had not given a thought to other possible consequences of the tragedy. Now, with sudden alarm, he recalled that there were very severe penalties in England for duelling, and it could not be denied that Beefy had met his end as a result of what would certainly be regarded as a duel. Putting the best face he could on the matter, he had his things carried out of the inn and accompanied the tipstaff in a stuffy, closed carriage to Guildford.

There, after having been formally charged, he obtained permission to write to Droopy Ned and, an hour later, had sent off a full account of what had happened the previous night, with a request for his friend's help. The remainder of the day he spent gloomily in a cold and narrow cell.

Next morning he was taken from his cell to a sparsely furnished room in which Droopy, accompanied by an enormously fat man who waddled on two short legs, was awaiting him. The fat man was wearing a lawyer's wig and flowing gown, wheezed badly and had a pair of alarmingly protuberant brown eyes. Droopy introduced him as Sergeant Burnfurze. After a quarter of an hour's conversation the Sergeant said in a deep, sonorous voice:

'Mr. Brook, it cannot be contested that it was by your act that the deceased met his death. My advice to you therefore is to plead guilty, and we will use such arguments as offer themselves in the hope of getting you off with as light a sentence as possible. Today, of course, we shall reserve our defence as the proceedings will be only formal.'

An hour or so later Roger stood in the dock. Georgina was said to be too ill to attend, but Gunston was in Court. Without displaying malice he gave evidence that Roger had forced a fight upon him and of what had then occurred. He was followed by Georgina's doctor who testified that John Beefy had died as a result of a weapon penetrating his liver. The still-bloodstained rapier that Roger had used was produced and the doctor agreed that it tallied with the wound of

176

the deceased. The magistrates did not even withdraw to deliberate. After the Chairman of the Bench had collected nods from his colleagues, he committed Roger for trial at the Guildford Assizes. Sergeant Burnfurze applied for bail and it was granted in two sureties of £2,000 each. Droopy Ned making himself responsible for one and Roger's bond being accepted for the other, Roger was released and, after a gloomy lunch at the Angel Inn, he returned with Droopy and the Sergeant to London.

Next day he wrote a long letter to Georgina telling her what had happened, expressing his deep contrition and assuring her that the thrust with which he had killed Beefy had been entirely an accident.

Two days later, to his amazement and acute distress, he received a brief reply in her round, flowing hand, 'Since you have killed one of the best men who ever lived and by so doing ruined my life you can expect no sympathy from me. Kicking your heels for a few months in prison may cure you of your belligerent ways, which may be suitable when adventuring abroad, but in this country are a menace to decent people.'

Roger could appreciate her distress at having lost Beefy, but he felt it unfair that she should entirely ignore the fact that, had she taken notice of his warning and not encouraged Gunston, she would have had no trouble with him; and that it was owing to her having called him, Roger, to her aid that the tragedy had taken place.

Being in such low spirits, he would have preferred to stay in Amesbury House and spend most of his time attempting to concentrate on the books in the library. But Droopy Ned insisted that shutting himself up and brooding was bad for him; so he allowed himself to be persuaded to join him in leading the normal life of a man-about-town.

On his visits to White's he at least met with congenial company, for the Tories there were as indignant as he about the peace terms. To add insult to injury, only the day after the Peace of Amiens had been signed, the news had come through that the French army in Egypt had surrendered.

Early in 1800, soon after Roger had brought Bonaparte's offer of peace to London, General Kléber, who was then commanding in Egypt, had concluded an armistice with Sir Sidney Smith on the basis of the French being allowed honourably to evacuate the country. But the government in London had delayed so long in ratifying the agreement that, by the time they did, Bonaparte, angered by their rejection of his offer of a general pacification, had refused his consent.

Kléber had been menaced at that time by an army of 70,000 Turks who were advancing from Heliopolis on Cairo. With only 10,000 men at his disposal he had inflicted a crushing defeat on these allies of Britain, so it had then looked as though the French would be able to maintain themselves in Egypt indefinitely.

Two factors had since reduced their chances of doing so. On Kléber's assassination in June he had been succeeded by General Menou, who possessed neither his ability nor determination; and in October Henry Dundas had pushed Pitt into sending an expeditionary force to Egypt under that tough old fighter, General Sir Ralph Abercrombie. Owing to distance, reports of operations were long delayed, and for many months past it had been assumed that the war in Egypt had more or less reached a stalemate. Now this despatch had come in, reporting that on August 15th the French had capitulated.

Within a fortnight it was not only Pitt's old supporters who were denouncing the government; the City, too, and the merchants in all the principal cities of the realm were up in arms. For it now emerged that peace did not, after all, mean a resumption of free trade with the Continent. No stipulation whatever for this had been included in the Treaty, so it had gone by default; and it now became clear that the First Consul intended to reimpose the extortionate tariff on the import of British goods that had existed in the early days of the Revolution.

By the end of April the names of Cornwallis, Merry, Bonaparte and Talleyrand were being cursed on all sides, the first two as fools and the second two as tricksters, as more

178

and more details about the negotiations at Amiens became known. During the preliminaries the British had put forward numerous requirements and matters that would have been to their country's advantage, and the French had agreed to many of them—but only verbally. When the written Treaty was produced it had contained none of them. Cornwallis had vigorously protested, but by then the whole nation was expecting the longed-for peace and, had it failed to mature, the government would have fallen; so Cornwallis had signed and brought home the awful document. But on the last day of April Roger had other things to think about. His trial had been set down for May 20th, and he had held several conferences with Sergeant Burnfurze. Now, the Sergeant, by habit a most jovial man, arrived at Amesbury House looking extremely glum.

After a preliminary cough, he boomed, 'Mr. Brook, I am sorry to say that your affair is going far from well. The agents of the law have been investigating the matter and have recommended that the charge preferred against you should be changed to one of murder.'

'Murder!' exclaimed Roger, aghast.

'Yes, sir. It seems there are certain grounds for supposing that you had reasons for wishing the deceased out of the way; and that the rapier thrust by which he met his death was directed at him, deliberately.'

'This is absurd, fantastic; utter nonsense!'

'I have every confidence that you are right in that, sir. But—er—certain allegations are made that you may find difficult to deny.' Sonorously then the Sergeant gave particulars. In both January and March, Roger had on numerous occasions either accompanied Georgina back to the St. Ermins' mansion in Berkeley Square late at night and had remained with her for several hours before taking his departure, or had spent whole evenings alone with her there. No more positive evidence could be needed that he had been her lover. Further, on the evening preceding John Beefy's death, a footman, one James Trigg, employed at Stillwaters had entered the small drawing room shortly after Roger's arrival

179

and found him quarrelling with his host. Trigg had at once withdrawn, but a natural if reprehensible curiosity had led him to remain outside listening to the exchanges that took place. He had heard Beefy declare that he would not tolerate further visits to the house by his wife's lover and, it was argued, since Roger had been for so many years a favoured guest there, his umbrage had been such that he had seized on the opportunity to remove the impediment to his continuing to enjoy these sessions with his mistress in her country home.

Roger continued to protest his innocence but, when the bulky Sergeant Burnfurze had waddled away on his absurdly short legs, he had to admit to himself with considerable alarm that the case appeared very black against him. Georgina's impetuous nature had often led her to use endearments to him in front of the servants and, owing to their long association, he had allowed himself to become careless about his comings and goings at Berkeley Square. Delightful as had been those little suppers they had enjoyed together in her boudoir in front of a roaring fire, it looked now as though he might have to pay a very heavy price for them.

Greatly perturbed, he consulted Droopy; but that astute, if eccentric, man of the world could give him no comfort. Jenny, Roger knew, would let herself be torn in pieces rather than talk, and many of the other servants at Stillwaters and at Berkeley Square were too attached both to their mistress and to himself to admit to what they must know; but there were others who would have no such scruples and, above all, there was the quarrel that James Trigg, a comparative new-comer to the household, had overheard.

On May 8th Roger was again taken into custody, escorted to Guildford, and charged with murder. The Grand Jury found a true Bill, and it was ordered that, instead of being arraigned for manslaughter, he should stand his trial on the 20th on the capital charge.

His father came up from Hampshire to see him and offered financial support to the limit of his resources. Colonel Thursby came over from Stillwaters and showed the deepest concern. Georgina, he told Roger, had decided that she wished to be quite alone for a while, in order that she might endeavour to forget the tragedy of which Stillwaters constantly reminded her; so she had taken a small house at Weymouth with Jenny to look after her. He added that, since she could not assist in Roger's defence, he hoped to persuade the authorities to refrain from calling her as a witness so that she should be spared the ordeal of appearing in Court and, should he succeed in that, he did not intend to inform her that the charge against Roger had been increased to a degree that now endangered his life. But, should the worst happen, he would, of course, set out at once for Weymouth himself and break the terrible news to her.

Droopy and Sergeant Burnfurze took rooms at the George, other eminent lawyers were sent for and there were numerous consultations, but on considering the weight of evidence none of them could hold out firm hope of an acquittal.

On the morning of the 20th the trial was opened with due solemnity. In a hushed silence the scarlet-robed Judge took his seat. As the crowd subsided with a rustle, Roger was brought in, bowed to the Judge and looked about him. Among the dozen grey-wigged lawyers in the well of the Court he saw his father, Colonel Thursby and Droopy, and smiled at them. Glancing round, he was for a moment surprised to see that the public gallery, instead of being occupied with the usual small, nondescript crowd, was packed to capacity with men and women of fashion, many of whom he knew. He realized then that it was Georgina's name being coupled with his own in such a scandal that had brought them down from London.

The Counsel for the Crown was a small, waspish man who wore his wig slightly awry, had a nose ending in so sharp a point that it quite fascinated Roger, and took snuff with great frequency. Having outlined the case he called his witnesses. George Gunston again told the truth and nothing but the truth. James Trigg stood up well to Sergeant Burnfurze's browbeating and could not be shaken in his story. Several other servants testified, mostly with reluctance, that they had seen their mistress and Roger in compromising situations.

Burnfurze took the only line of defence open to him: namely that Gunston had given Roger great provocation and had refused a challenge to meet him in a duel; that Roger had snatched up a sword only with the intention of driving him from the house; that the deceased's appearance on the scene was entirely fortuitous and that he had become a victim of the brawl only because Roger had been so nearly dead-drunk as to be incapable of directing the thrust of his weapon.

Under cross-examination Gunston, his honour being at stake, flatly denied that he had refused a challenge. He insisted that he had refused only to fight Roger there and then without seconds and the observance of proper formalities.

During the evidence much had been said to show that, although Roger's visits to Stillwaters occurred only at long intervals, he obviously regarded it as his second home, particularly as his little daughter was being brought up there with the young Earl of St. Ermins. It was therefore evident that, having been debarred from visiting the house in future, he had much to lose; whereas with Beefy dead he would be free to continue staying there and making merry in it with his mistress.

In his summing up the Judge stressed this point, and it was clear that on the evidence he believed Roger to be guilty. As Roger was about to be led away he felt it as good as certain that he would be convicted, and he wondered vaguely what the black cap was like that the Judge would put on when sentencing him to be hanged by the neck until dead, after the passing of the next three Sundays.

He had always expected to die from a sword thrust or a bullet, and the thought of being strangled while kicking wildly at the end of a rope both nauseated and frightened him. The Judge had been scrupulously fair, except in one particular for which he could not be blamed, and that could have made no material difference. Gunston's evidence had been truthful and the jury had, if anything, appeared sympathetic. So there were no grounds on which he could lodge an appeal. Thinking again of the horrible death that awaited him, he wished now that the bullet that had hit him at Marengo had done so a few inches lower and proved fatal.

The Judge had already left the dais and the jury had risen, when there was a stir at the back of the Court. Two black-clad women were pushing their way through the press. At the sound of the slight commotion Roger turned, halted, pushed aside the two gaolers who were leading him away and started back towards the dock. He felt certain that he had caught sight of Jenny's face. If so, the other figure, heavily veiled in crêpe, could only be Georgina.

Colonel Thursby had left the well of the Court to meet them. Roger's gaolers tried to make him accompany them out and across the corridor to a cell; but he insisted on remaining where he was, and they were reluctant to make a scene by manhandling him. There were hasty, whispered exchanges between Georgina, her father and Sergeant Burnfurze, then the latter went out to speak to the Judge.

Order was called for. The Judge returned and addressed the Counsel for the Prosecution. 'I am informed that the Countess of St. Ermins is now in Court and has asked to be allowed to give evidence. As this may throw new light on this case I am of the opinion we should hear Her Ladyship.'

Georgina mounted the stand, threw back her veil, took the oath and addressed the Judge in a low voice, 'My Lord, I pray you pardon my belated appearance but it was only yesterday that my maid learned from a news sheet that Mr. Brook is accused of murdering my late husband and was to be brought to trial today. I have been travelling all night to get here, because I was the only independent witness of this terrible affair and felt it my duty to give an account of it to the Court.'

The Judge nodded but made no comment, and she went on in a stronger voice to describe what had taken place. Her account differed from Gunston's on two points. She said that he had refused Roger's challenge to a duel; and that at the fatal moment when Roger had lunged at him, the Colonel, having the much heavier weapon, had knocked Roger's rapier aside; so deflecting the thrust that, with considerable impetus still behind it, the blade had pierced her husband's body.

In the first matter she had told the truth, in the second she had deliberately perjured herself; but if she was believed Roger's life would be saved.

Sergeant Burnfurze put a few questions to her, bringing out that Roger, having been very drunk, could have had little control over his weapon yet, having lurched forward, the whole weight of his body would have been behind it.

Counsel for the Prosecution then rose to cross-examine. He asked if it was true that on the evening preceding the tragedy her husband had said in her presence that he would not tolerate further visits to Stillwaters by the defendant.

'Yes,' Georgina replied. 'He did say something to that effect.'

The little lawyer took a pinch of snuff, gave a self-satisfied smile and said, 'Perhaps Your Ladyship can tell us your husband's reason for being averse to continuing to receive Mr. Brook in his house?'

Looking straight at him, Georgina cried in ringing tones, 'I will; although I doubt not you have already ferreted it out. 'Twas because some rattle-trap servant had told him that Mr. Brook was my lover. And 'twas the truth. I care not who knows it! We have been lovers since we were boy and girl, and no woman ever had a finer, braver man on whom to bestow her favours.'

Georgina's bold declaration caused an excited buzz to run round the Court. The usher called for silence; then Counsel, looking at the jury, said with a slight sneer, 'Her Ladyship's admission is all that was needed to show that she and her lover were so enamoured of one another that they would brook no hindrance to their immoralities. As to my Lady's story of the rapier being struck aside.... I leave you, gentlemen, to judge its worth.'

The moment he sat down, Burnfurze lumbered to his feet. 'M'Lud! I protest! I take great exception to my learned colleague's innuendo. My Lady St. Ermins has testified on

184

oath that the rapier was struck aside. She was in a better position to see what occurred than Colonel Gunston, and he has admitted under cross-examination that this was like no ordinary duel, but an exchange of wild blows the sequence of which neither he nor the defendant can recall exactly.

'As to Her Ladyship's generous admission that she and the defendant had been lovers for many years, nothing could more completely demolish the case for the Prosecution. Had they but just met and become newly engaged in a passionate association, it is perhaps possible that the defendant, seized by violent jealousy while too drunk to control his emotion, might have made a thrust at the hated husband of his mistress. But here we have a couple who have been lovers since their teens. In fact this extra-marital relationship was such that passion must have long since died down and given place to an almost conjugal state. And pray observe, gentlemen of the jury, that there was no question of the association being brought to an abrupt end. Stillwaters alone was to be denied the couple as a place at which to meet. They were perfectly free to see one another wherever and whenever else they would.'

The Judge again summed up. He gave some weight to Georgina's statement that Roger's rapier had been knocked from its intended course by Gunston's heavier weapon, and Burnfurze's argument that as the association between Georgina and Roger had existed for many years it was not reasonable to suppose that a sudden upsurge of jealousy had led him to seize the offered opportunity to kill her husband. But he put it to the jury that, in view of Lady St. Ermins' confessed life-long attachment to the defendant, they might consider the evidence she had given to be very highly prejudiced in his favour.

The Court thereupon rose. The Judge was solemnly escorted from it, the jury retired to consider their verdict and Roger was taken by his warders to a cell across the corridor.

The jury were absent for six hours. During that time the strain on Roger, waiting to hear the verdict they would bring in, was appalling. He was well aware that Georgina had perjured herself in the hope of saving him; for it had been his off-balance stagger that had caused his rapier to pierce Beefy's side—not, as she had sworn, a blow from Gunston's sword that had turned the thrust. But, after her admission that he had been the one man who really counted in her life, would the jury believe that?

At last the summons came for him to be escorted back to the courtroom. It was by then twilight and candles had been lit, throwing queer shadows upon the walls. The jury filed into their box. The foreman rose, bowed to the Judge and said, 'My Lord, we find the accused "Not guilty".'

The relief Roger felt was beyond description. He looked round in vain for Georgina; she and Jenny had left the Court. His father, his friends and many of his acquaintances who had been present during the trial crowded round to congratulate him on the verdict. But he was not allowed to depart a free man.

Within a few minutes he was re-arrested, spent the night in a cell and, the following morning, was arraigned before the same Judge on a charge of manslaughter. The evidence of the manner in which John Beefy had met his death was again given, without Georgina having to be called on. A new jury retired and returned within ten minutes; their verdict being 'Guilty'.

The Judge looked at Roger with a frown and said severely, 'By the statutes of the land duelling is a crime. Armed assault is a still more serious one. That you were drunk is no excuse for having used a weapon, and the public must be protected from persons who resort to violence. Your intemperate act led to the death of a man who was attempting to prevent you from continuing an illegal conflict. For that I sentence you to three years' imprisonment.'

CHAPTER XIII

THE TERRIBLE BETRAYAL

As ROGER had not been convicted of housebreaking, coining or any other felony of that kind he had not been condemned to hard labour, so was to serve his sentence in Guildford Gaol. His cell was on the first floor and contained a bed, table, chair and washstand. The regulations entitled him to see only one visitor, and send and receive only one letter a month; and the only amenity for passing the time was a dog-eared Bible.

But in those days prisoners with money were allowed to have food sent in and nearly all officials, other than Judges, were habitually corrupt. The salaries paid to Prison Governors were so small that, while they would not connive at escapes, they were usually willing to ameliorate the lot of prisoners in return for presents from the prisoners' friends; and during Roger's first week in prison he received visits from his father, Droopy Ned and Colonel Thursby.

The Admiral cheered him greatly by saying that he meant to ask for an audience with the King and, in consideration of his own distinguished service in the Royal Navy, implore him to grant a pardon or, at least, a reduction of Roger's sentence.

The Colonel depressed him by admitting to him with great reluctance that, although Georgina had given evidence that had saved his life at his first trial, she remained adamant in her determination not to forgive him for having killed her husband, and had now returned to Weymouth, where the Colonel was about to join her.

Droopy, combining his foppish charm and his prestige as a wealthy noble with many powerful connections, had made a friend of the Governor. He had brought with him a present of a dozen cases of wine, which it was tacitly understood that the Governor should share with Roger, and had also obtained the concession that he should be supplied with writing materials and allowed to send out for books.

Even with these privileges to solace his confinement the appalling fact remained that, should his father prove unsuccessful with the King, he would have to spend three of the best years of his life in prison; and to that was added the agonising knowledge that, being unable to have a full explanation with Georgina, there seemed little chance of healing the breach between them.

Every morning he was taken out for an hour's exercise in the courtyard, but the remainder of the days dragged interminably. He had always enjoyed reading, but now that he had nothing else to do he lost his pleasure in it. At times he paced his cell restlessly, six paces towards the stout door with its great lock and six paces back towards the heavily-barred window. At others he lay on his bed for hours at a stretch, his thoughts vaguely wandering but returning again and again to what an incredible fool he had been not to have skipped his bail while he had had the chance; for he could easily have got away to France, and the loss of the money involved would have been a small price to pay for retaining his liberty.

In the previous year the question of Catholic Emancipation had had such a disturbing effect on King George's mind that soon after the fall of the Pitt government he had again become temporarily insane. His recovery had been much quicker than it had in '89, but it was still felt that he should be burdened only with a minimum of business. In consequence there were many delays before Admiral Sir Christopher Brook obtained his audience, and it was not until mid-July that the monarch received him at Kew. The following day Sir Christopher came down to see Roger and, as gently as he could, broke to him the ill success of the interview.

The King had received him kindly, exclaiming, 'Admiral Chris! Admiral Chris! What! What! 'Tis good to see you.' But when the Admiral had explained the reason for his visit, the King had taken a very different tone. 'Farmer George', as his subjects called him, was a rigorously moral man and abhorred all forms of violence. His now faulty memory of the case being reawakened he had become angry and flustered; then declared it to be his duty to protect his subjects from dangerous, drunken adulterers, and that Roger, having killed a good honest merchant, deserved to hang for it.

That night Roger felt very low and wrote informing Droopy of his bitter disappointment. In his reply Droopy endeavoured to cheer him by saying that for some time past, apart from his set principles on religious matters, the King's attitude to many other questions often varied from day to day; so he thought it would be worth approaching him again, this time through the Duke of Portland who, after Pitt's retirement, had remained on as Home Secretary. But, Droopy added, the summer recess would soon be taking His Grace out of London and, in any case, it would be unwise to raise the subject again with His Majesty until he had had ample time to forget the Admiral's visit.

Shortly after this Roger received a letter from Colonel Thursby. He said he thought Roger would like to know that Georgina had for the past few weeks again taken up her painting, so was in better spirits, and that he had now persuaded her to accompany him on a visit to Paris. Having for so long been unable to visit the French capital, the English were now flocking there in great numbers and were being received in a most friendly spirit. There everything was now *à l'anglais*, and everything French was the latest mode in London. He was in great hopes that this complete change of

scene would have entirely restored Georgina to her old self by
the time they returned to Stillwaters in September.

Roger also had some talent as an artist, although not
approaching that of Georgina's, who had studied under both
Reynolds and Gainsborough. The letter reminded him of his
long-neglected hobby; and the Governor, who by then was
doing very handsomely out of Droopy Ned, agreed to have
some artists' materials bought for him.

Now being able to occupy himself with sketching and
painting as an alternative to reading, he somehow got through
the remainder of July and the month of August. But having
no model to sit for him, or landscape to copy other than the
view from his window, which consisted of tree tops seen
across the high prison wall, he found his painting from
memory gave him little satisfaction, with the result that when
September came in he was again desperately craving for
freedom.

After brooding on the matter for some days he decided
that if the Duke of Portland failed to secure the King's
clemency for him he must, somehow, escape and make his
way back to France. Food and other things were bought for
him out of a deposit he had arranged to be placed with the
Governor, but he was not allowed to have any money; so it
would not be possible for him to bribe one of his gaolers.
They had, too, treated him decently; so he was very averse to
attacking and attempting to overpower one of them and, even
should he do so, his chances of getting clear of the prison
would be small.

The door of his cell was of stout oak and the lock much
too strong to be forced. There remained only the window
and, after much thought, he decided that he must adopt the
classic method of sawing through a bar then lowering himself
to the ground by a rope made out of his bedclothes. There
remained the problem of getting over the fifteen-foot-high
wall of the gaol; but in that it looked as if luck might favour
him, as some workmen had recently started to renew the
beams and roof of a large one-storey outbuilding that was
just within his view. If they were still working on it when

he made his attempt he would be able to make use of their gear.

That 'if' was the crux of the matter; so he made up his mind to start work on the bar without delay. He had been allowed a penknife to sharpen his pencils for sketching and a small whetstone on which to sharpen the penknife. By breaking the whetstone so that it had a jagged edge he set about serrating the blade of the penknife until he had turned it into a small saw. It was a slow and finicky business and took him the best part of a week; but now he again had a worthwhile project to occupy his mind he felt much more cheerful.

In the door of his cell there was a grill through which, only very occasionally, but at odd times, one of the gaolers looked in at him. While working on the penknife he had no difficulty in concealing what he was doing, by sitting, as usual, at his table with his back to the door. But to cut through one of the inch-thick iron bars to the window without being caught was a very different undertaking. He had now to control his impatience during the day and work during the night, and then only on nights when there was no moon or its light was obscured by cloud.

To dig the ends of one of the bars out of the masonry with the tools at his disposal was clearly impossible, and making two cuts through a bar proved a most laborious task. But by the end of September he had cut both ends so that the bar was held in place only by a remaining eighth of an inch and had protected the cuts from detection by filling them with a mixture of black paint and soap.

Now that Parliament was about to meet again for its autumn session he wrote to Droopy asking if the Duke of Portland had yet returned to London and if he had had any opportunity of approaching him. Droopy replied that he had seen the Duke a fortnight since, but had been so loath to inflict another disappointment on Roger that he had put off letting him know the result of the interview. His Grace, like the King, had been of the opinion that Roger had been lucky to escape a hanging, and had refused to intervene.

To have walked out of the gaol a free man, or even to have had his sentence reduced to twelve months, would have been greatly preferable to taking all the risks that were attendant on an escape; but now that Roger's plans for the attempt were complete he was not unduly depressed by Droopy's reply; and as the builders in the yard were by then nearing the completion of their work he decided to chance his luck that very night.

Soon after it was dark he put out his candles and set to work making a rope out of his sheets and blankets. When he had done he waited impatiently until midnight, by which time it was certain that, except for the gaoler on night duty, the staff of the prison would all be asleep. Exerting all his strength he wrenched at the bar he had sawn almost through until it snapped off at both ends. Having tied one end of his home-made rope to the bar above it and tested the knot by jerking on it as hard as he could, he wriggled painfully through the aperture feet first, clung precariously to the bar for a moment then shinned down to the ground.

The moon was up but, except for brief intervals, its light was eclipsed by scudding clouds. For a few moments, in case anyone was still about, he listened intently. No sound reaching him other than the mewing of a prowling cat, he tiptoed across to the outbuilding that was being re-roofed. It took him half an hour of strenuous effort to assemble against the tall wall enough of the builders' material to surmount it. At the end of that time he was sitting astride its top, nerving himself for the drop down on the far side. Lowering himself cautiously until he was flat against the outer side of the wall, he clung for a moment with both hands to the coping. Hanging in that position he spanned its upper eight feet. There remained seven feet between his feet and the ground.

Praying that he would not break an ankle or hit his head on a stone, he threw himself backwards. He landed with a thud that drove the breath from his body. For a minute he remained dazed then, suffering only from a bruised bottom and shoulders, scrambled to his feet.

As he had stayed at Stillwaters so often he knew the

district well, and had to cover only seven miles to the village of Ripley. Thinking it safer to keep off the road, he took a circuitous route along paths through the woods and, without having seen a soul, reached the silent, lightless mansion soon after three o'clock in the morning.

He had made for it because the one thing he had to have to get to France was money—and a good round sum. Now that Britain and France were at peace anyone could cross by the packet for a few pounds; but he knew that before he could reach the coast the authorities in every port would have been warned to keep a lookout for him; so by far his best chance of getting over without risk of capture lay in being put across by one of his old smuggler friends and, running the risks they did, they expected a handsome payment.

Colonel Thursby would, he felt sure, finance him but he dared not enter the house for fear that one of the servants would betray him; and the Colonel rarely left it except for his morning walk up and down the long terrace or an occasional visit to the hothouses. But Roger was confident that Georgina would not deny him the means to make his escape to France, and he had already thought out a way to make contact with her unseen by anyone else.

She was a splendid horsewoman and at ten o'clock every morning, unless the weather was particularly inclement, she went for a ride of an hour or more. Her mount was always brought round to the front door by the groom who accompanied her, but it was her custom always to ride it back to the stables where lumps of sugar and carrot were put handy for her to give the animal in its loose box.

Walking with cautious tread Roger entered the stable yard. As he expected, the big watch dog kept there came out of its kennel and growled at him. But he knew the animal well and, with a few quiet words, quickly pacified it. Entering the end of the stable where Georgina's own riding horses were stalled, he went up the stairs at the end of the building to the loft above. A good part of it was filled with trusses of hay and straw. As some eight hours would elapse before Georgina was likely to come into the stable, he made himself up a comfortable couch and, well satisfied with his night's achievement, went to sleep there.

He woke soon after dawn and, lest one of the stable hands should come up to the loft, made a hiding place for himself among the bales, then sat down to await events with as much patience as he could muster. An hour later he heard the horses below him being led out to be watered. There was then another long wait until the time approached for Georgina to have her ride. He then took up a position at full length on the floor near an open hatch down which the bales of fodder were lowered when required. By craning his neck he could see into three of the loose boxes. To his great satisfaction, shortly before ten o'clock a liveried groom led out a fine brown mare from one of the boxes.

For another hour and a half he remained where he was, only occasionally easing the contact of his limbs against the hard floor. Then there came the clatter of hooves on the cobbles outside and, a few moments later, Georgina's well-loved voice speaking to her groom as she led her mare into the empty loose box.

The groom had taken his mount to a box further along the stable, so Roger thrust his head out over the opening in the floor and said in a low voice, 'Hist! Georgina!'

Looking up, she recognized him instantly. Her big black eyes widened and she exclaimed, 'Roger! What are you doing here?'

'I've broken prison and I need your help,' he answered quickly. 'Come up, so that we can talk here unseen by others.'

After a moment's hesitation she hitched her mount to the manger, thrust a carrot in the mare's mouth and came up the stairs.

By then Roger was standing and he asked at once, 'Am I forgiven? I swear I never meant to harm him. I beg you say I am.'

She halted well away from him. A frown darkened her lovely face, and her rich red lips took on a sullen expression. ' 'Tis well enough to say that now,' she replied coldly. 'But

194

hard to believe. And all your protestations will not bring him back to me.'

In a swift spate of words he began to plead with her, but she cut him short, 'You behaved like a drunken bully. To seize a sword in my house and force a fight upon Colonel Gunston in my presence was inexcusable. You may count yourself lucky that by perjuring myself I saved your life and you deserved every day of the sentence you received.'

'Georgina, you're devilish hard on me,' he expostulated. 'That I behaved monstrous ill I do admit. But you must believe that my having killed John Beefy was an accident.'

'I wish I could,' she answered, her eyes still fixed upon him stonily. 'But I know well your ruthless nature, and how you'll let nothing stand in the way of getting what you wish. How can you expect me to forget the way you spoke to me the night before you committed your heinous crime? With a selfishness that almost passes belief you urged me to let the man who meant so much to me go out of my life, simply that you might continue to visit Stillwaters when it was convenient to you. Seeing the many years we had been lovers I could do no less than save you from a hanging, but you cannot expect that my feelings for you should ever again be the same.'

'So be it,' Roger shrugged wearily. 'But I stand here penniless. At least you will not deny me the sum I need to get back to France?'

'How much do you require?'

'I must go by subterranean means, else I'll stand a big risk of being caught. But a hundred guineas should see me safely out of the country.'

'I have not anywhere near that sum to hand here in the house.'

'You could send in to your bank in Guildford for it. 'Twould take no more than a couple of hours. Meanwhile I can lie up here and be on my way again tonight.'

Georgina nodded, 'I'll send in to Guildford then. Stay here until I come to you again.' Without the least softening of her expression she turned on her heel and left him.

Sadly he sat down on a bale of straw to wait. Two hours

drifted by. Thinking that time enough for someone to have ridden into Guildford and cashed a draft for her, he began to keep a look-out for her return through one of the low cobwebby windows that overlooked the yard. After a further twenty minutes he caught the sound of hoof-beats in the distance and thought it probable that they were made by her messenger cantering straight up to the house. Expecting that she would soon now come to him with the money he remained near the window, striving to collect all his powers of appeal for another attempt to soften her heart when she returned to him. A few minutes later he could hardly trust his eyes. Through the arched entrance to the stableyard emerged not Georgina, but her groom accompanied by the tipstaff and two constables.

It was unthinkable, unbelievable. Georgina had betrayed him. Instead of sending her groom into Guildford for the money she had sent him to fetch the law. There could be no other explanation. The man was actually pointing to the end of the loft where Roger had talked to her after she had returned from her ride. Still shocked into immobility, he subconsciously took in the fact that the tipstaff was carrying a blunderbuss and that the constables were armed with long-barrelled pistols as well as their truncheons.

Suddenly Roger came to life. To allow himself to be taken and ignominiously escorted back to gaol would be intolerable. Yet he was unarmed, so could not put up a fight, and was trapped there; for there were no entrances to the building other than those giving on to the yard.

Next moment he had dropped through the hole in the floor. As his feet touched the ground he grabbed the mane of the startled mare in the loose box below to steady himself. Georgina's groom having been sent in to Guildford, he had not yet taken away her saddle to clean it. Lifting the saddle from its bracket Roger threw it on the mare's back and swiftly tightened the girths. In frantic haste he adjusted the bit and bridle then, patting the animal's neck, turned her to face the door. When he had called down to Georgina she had left her riding crop lying on the manger. Snatching it up he

196

vaulted into the saddle, then laid his body flat along the mare's back, so that her head screened a good part of him from sight. In the dim light, there was a good chance that anyone entering the stable would not immediately notice him.

He had got himself into position not a moment too soon. The upper half of the stable door was a little open. It was cautiously opened wide. Then the lower half was unbolted and pulled back. Roger caught only a glimpse of the huddle of figures in the doorway about to enter on tiptoe, no doubt hoping to catch him asleep up in the loft. Jabbing his heels into the mare's flanks he gave a loud shout and launched her forward.

With cries of alarm the group in the doorway attempted to throw themselves out of her way but the tipstaff and one of the constables were bowled over by the charge of the frightened mare. The groom, who had been behind the others and furthest from the door, made a grab at her bridle. But Roger had been ready for that. He brought the whiplash of the crop down with all his force right across the man's face. With a scream he crumpled to the ground. The hooves of the mare clattered loudly on the cobbles. There came the bang of a pistol as the other constable fired his weapon, but the bullet whizzed harmlessly over Roger's shoulder. Thirty seconds later he was through the arch and away.

As he galloped across the lawn towards the cover of the woods on the far side of the lake he considered the best course to take. He was still penniless so must get hold of money somehow. London was only twenty-five miles away and on such a fine mount he felt certain he could outdistance his pursuers. Droopy would help him without question. There was a certain risk in going to him because the Governor of Guildford Gaol, knowing Droopy to be his friend, might anticipate that he would do so and that morning have sent a message to London for the Bow Street Runners to lie in wait for him at Amesbury House. But that risk must be taken.

It had been just before midday when Georgina left him, so it was now getting on towards three in the afternoon. By five o'clock he was in Arlington Street and he felt there was less risk in going straight to the house than waiting until darkness fell. He was confident that he had a lead on his pursuers, but he would lose it within an hour; and if the Runners had not already been alerted to waylay him there, it seemed certain that a message would be sent asking them to do so as soon as the authorities in Guildford learned that he had got away from Stillwaters.

Dismounting in front of the door, he kept the mare's reins over his arm in case he had to remount in a hurry and again make a dash for liberty. The footman who answered the door said that Lord Edward was out, but expected back at about six o'clock. Roger knew the man well and had often given him a good tip; so when he replied to Roger's low-voiced enquiry whether anyone had asked for him and replied, 'No, sir,' Roger had good grounds for believing him. Roger then said that he had called to see Lord Edward on a highly confidential matter so if anyone asked for him he was to be told he was not there. Then he handed the horse over to be taken round to the stable and went upstairs to Droopy's private apartments.

Until nearly seven o'clock he waited there in considerable apprehension for, however loyal the footman on the door might prove, if Bow Street Runners arrived and produced a warrant, he could not prevent them from searching the house.

At last Droopy appeared. He was slightly drunk after spending four hours dining at the Beefsteak Club and afterwards consuming the best part of a decanter of Port. But he exclaimed, 'Roger! Makes me old heart beat better at the sight of you. But, dam'me! I didn't expect to see you before tomorrow at the earliest.'

'Tomorrow!' Roger repeated, much surprised. 'And why, pray, should you have expected to see me then?'

'Then, or within the next few days,' Droopy lowered himself with some care into an elbow chair. 'But meseems they've been prodigious swift to act upon their orders.'

I don't understand!' Roger frowned. 'To what orders do you refer?'

'Why to those for your pardon, of course.'

'Pardon! Dear God, you cannot mean it.'

'I . . . I do indeed. After your father's failure and His Grace of Portland's refusal to approach His Majesty I was loath to raise your hopes again, lest they be once more disappointed. But I . . . I went down to see Billy Pitt. He's no power now . . . more's the pity. But he agreed that something must be done for you, and . . . and the King could not refuse him an audience. He told our poor addle-brained monarch that even had you blown up the Houses of Parliament which, as things are would be no bad thing,' Droopy broke off and tittered, 'you . . . you still deserved a pardon for the immense services you have in these past ten years rendered to the State. Whatever may be said against "Farmer George," he . . . he has ever put what he believes to be the interests of our country before all else. Billy Pitt is no fool. He'd had the forethought to bring a parchment with him in his pocket. Before the old dunderhead could have second thoughts, he had him sign it.'

Roger took a deep breath. 'So I'm free! Oh, Ned, dear Ned, bless you for that. I'll go pay my respects to Mr. Pitt tomorrow and thank him for his share in this. But 'tis to you I owe it.'

'Think naught of that. You look, though, in a sadly bedraggled state. Order yourself a bath brought up and a change of raiment. Meanwhile I . . . I'll stretch myself for two hours on my bed. Then we'll sally forth together and go to old Kate's place behind the Haymarket. Sup there, have her pretty wenches disport themselves for us, eh? And . . . and make a night of it.'

Hardly able to believe in his good fortune, Roger rested and refreshed himself. Later old Kate received them with many curtsies. Droopy threw handsful of golden guineas on the floor and laughed uproariously as the girls scrambled for them, then fought to sit on his and Roger's knees and show their appreciation of this generous patronage.

In the small hours the two friends returned to Amesbury House, decidedly the worse for wear and, arm in arm, supported one another up the stairs. It was eleven o'clock next morning when Roger woke, but over a late breakfast they knocked back a couple of bottles of Florence wine and felt the better for it.

Roger then rode down to Beckenham; but his thoughts were the saddest he had had for many a day, as he could not get over Georgina's betrayal of him. At Holwell House Mr. Pitt received him kindly and said:

'Mr. Brook, we have had many differences of opinion, but that does not alter the fact that you have served England far better than many more eminent men of your generation. Owing to the secret nature of your work, I was unable to recommend you for a knighthood; thus there was all the more reason for coming to your assistance when you fell into grievous trouble. Naturally I deprecate the crime of violence for which you were condemned, but the life you have led must have forced upon you many dangerous and desperate situations; so, to some extent, the habit you have acquired of resorting on the instant to weapons must be accounted a mitigation of your act. Let us now forget it.'

Mr. Pitt was alone that day and invited Roger to stay to dinner. Roger accepted as both a command and a pleasure. Over the meal Pitt talked freely of the situation.

He had been such a close friend of Addington's that when ill the previous year he had stayed in his house and been treated as one of the family; so most men would have taken it hard that such an intimate friend, when sent for behind his back by the King, should have consented to supplant him. But Pitt bore Addington no malice and as a private Member was giving him his support.

About the King's attitude to Catholic Emancipation he was caustic, declaring that His Majesty's ostrich-like policy was both dangerous and unjust towards many thousands of his loyal subjects; that the days when 'Popery' was a danger to the realm were long since gone, and that it was now entirely unreasonable that many patriotic and intelligent men should remain debarred from holding office because they were either Dissenters or Romans.

200

Since Roger's return from Russia he had not seen his host, so he gave him an eye-witness account of Paul I's murder. When he had done Pitt commented, ' 'Twas a terrible business and shocked all Europe. Why they could not simply have put him under restraint, as we have our King in the past, I cannot think. But his removal proved invaluable to us at that time. The pity of it is that the present government is rapidly losing the advantage gained thereby. Young Alexander greatly favoured an alliance with us, and with his help we might have crushed Bonaparte. Instead they signed the Peace, although eighteen days after my retirement Admiral Nelson had smashed the nucleus of the Northern Fleet at Copenhagen. Since then Russia and France have been drawing together on the Eastern question, as both have designs on Turkey. And now we are again at loggerheads with the Czar over Malta.'

'As I have been incarcerated for above four months, sir,' Roger remarked, 'I know little of what has been going on.'

'Indeed yes; that I had momentarily forgotten. By this disastrous Peace it was agreed that we should return all our maritime conquests made during the war, with the exception of Ceylon and Trinidad, to France and her allies Holland and Spain. Those, of course, included the Cape and Malta. Should we give up the Cape our route to India could be cut at any time and our mercantile interests in the sub-continent become gravely imperilled. This has raised such an outcry that, I gather, the Government is considering going back upon its word lest it be kicked out of office.

'As regards Malta, under the treaty it should be returned to its former owners, the Knights. But the Order has become so effete that it is now quite incapable of protecting shipping in the Mediterranean from the Barbary pirates. Within six months the Corsairs would have the island and soon be using it as a base to raid the coast towns of southern Italy. It was, therefore, decided that it should be governed by a Protecting Power, to be neither France nor Britain. The obvious choice is Russia and the Czar insists that he should take it over. But

201

again our government is having second thoughts and is resisting his claim, whereas the French are backing it. Hence the Czar's annoyance with us, and his new inclination to enter into a pact with the French.'

When they had talked of numerous other subjects, Pitt asked 'What now do you plan to do; settle in England or return to France?'

'Recently, sir,' Roger replied, 'apart from my spell in prison, I have met with a private misfortune which makes me disinclined to remain here, where I am likely to be reminded of it.'

Mr. Pitt made a slight grimace. 'If 'tis your own country-men that you wish to avoid you'll be hard put to it in Paris. I'm told the capital now swarms with them, and many of them are touring the provinces. Charles Fox spent September there, and his speeches praising the Revolution having been reprinted in the French journals, he was given a royal welcome in every city through which he passed. Bonaparte received him with special honours, and he was shown his own bust at St. Cloud, among a collection including Brutus, Cicero, Hampden, Washington and other champions of Liberty.'

Roger gave a cynical laugh, 'Then, since it pays so well, if there is another war I'll play the part of a traitor.'

'Nay, Charles Fox is no traitor. At least, not intentionally so; although it must be admitted that he caused grievous harm by encouraging discontent among the masses in this country while we were at war, and often seriously hampered my measures for the prosecution of it.'

Two days later Roger said good-bye to Droopy Ned and the members of his family who lived at Amesbury House; then he went down to Lymington to see his father, whom he found sadly crippled by the gout.

Having thought matters over he had decided not to return to Paris. It was nine months since he had left there and during that time the whole European scene had changed. Now that the war was over, even if Bonaparte was prepared to forgive his long, unexplained absence, it seemed that the

202

First Consul would have little use for him; and as Paris was full of English people he might run into several whom he knew. To reply in broken English to one or two who might claim his acquaintance that they had mistaken him for his English cousin would cause him no worry; but should he have to tell the same story to a number of them, and they compared notes, that could result in the resemblance arousing a most undesirable interest in his past activities.

In consequence, after staying for three nights at Walhampton House he boarded a brig in which he had arranged a passage from Southampton to Bordeaux. On landing in France he hired a coach and made a leisurely progress through Agen, Toulouse, Carcassone, Nîmes, Arles and Aix-en-Provence, spending a night or two in each of these cities to enjoy the remains of their ancient or mediaeval glories, before arriving at St. Maxime on November 14th.

The morning after his arrival he took a walk to his vineyard and enquired of a labourer working in the neighbouring one after the health of Madame Meuralt. With a grin the man replied, 'She lives here no longer, Monsieur, although she still comes to stay at times. In the summer she married a Monsieur Tarbout who, I'm told, has a prosperous mercer's business in Nice.'

Roger was glad for her, but could not make up his mind whether he was glad or sorry for himself. To have renewed his liaison with pretty, plump, passionate little Jeanne would have given him something to occupy his mind; but he was still so sick at heart about Georgina that he felt no real inclination to philander with any member of her sex.

He had been at his château for about ten days and one afternoon returned from a long, solitary walk on the seashore. As he was passing the room he used most frequently, in which he had collected a small library, he happened to glance through one of the tall windows. To his surprise he caught sight of a man sitting at his desk going through his papers. Imagining the intruder to be a thief, he was about to tiptoe round to the hall and collect his pistols. Then the man turned his head slightly, exposing his profile to view. Roger's surprise turned to amazement, then wonder and sudden apprehension. He found himself staring at his old enemy Joseph Fouché, the Minister of Police.

CHAPTER XIV

BONAPARTE BECOMES NAPOLEON

R o g e r and Fouché had buried the hatchet shortly before the *coup d'état* of *Brumaire*, because Fouché had foreseen that Bonaparte would most probably succeed in seizing power and Roger had provided the bridge between them. For many years Fouché, like Talleyrand, had known that *'Monsieur,' 'Chevalier,' 'Citoyen'* and now *'le Colonel'* Breuc were, in fact, Roger Brook, the son of an English Admiral. But neither had ever caught him out while spying for Mr. Pitt and, since '99, both had accepted it that, as a protégé of Bonaparte's, all his interests lay in regarding France as his adopted country that might hold a fine future for him.

What, then, was Fouché doing here, going through his papers in his absence? Had he, in his amazingly widespread intelligence net, picked up some little happening out of the past that had led him to believe that for all these years Roger had been acting as a British secret agent, and had come to the château in the hope of finding corroborative proof?

Swiftly Roger ran through in his mind the papers that were in his desk. Almost at once he was able to reassure himself that there was nothing among them which could be associated with his secret missions. Breathing more easily he walked softly on, entered the house, tiptoed to his little library and quietly opened the door.

At the faint noise it made, Fouché looked up; but he made no effort to conceal what he had been doing. Shuffling the papers before him into a pile, he pushed them away and came to his feet. With a faint smile on his lean, cadaverous face, but without looking directly at Roger, he bowed and said:

'Ah, here you are at last. You have a very pleasant place of retirement here, *Monsieur le Colonel.*'

Roger returned the bow. 'I am happy that it meets with your approval, *Monsieur le Ministre.* May I enquire to what I owe the pleasure of this visit?'

' 'Tis very simple. It may not be known to you, but before the Revolution my family owned a plantation in San Domingo and ships that plied thence and back to my native town of Nantes. In recent times I have been fortunate enough to make a modest sum out of contracting to supply the requirements of our armies. But now we are at peace, such transactions may no longer prove very lucrative; so I am again interesting myself in shipping and have just spent some days in Marseilles. The port being not far distant from your—er—hideout, it occurred to me that it would be pleasant to renew our acquaintance. That—er—is if you happened to be here and not—er—perhaps away engaged in other activities.'

To Roger the implication was clear. Fouché suspected that his long sojourns on sick leave in the south of France might be, as indeed they often had been, cover for secret trips to England. But he had his answer ready, and said smoothly:

'I am most fortunate in being here to receive you, for had you looked in to see me above ten days ago you would have found me absent—as you have no doubt already informed yourself by enquiries made of my servants or in the village.'

Fouché held up a long, bony hand in protest, '*Mon cher*

Colonel, how can you think that I would seek to ferret out particulars of the doings of my friends?'

'Yet I came upon you going through my papers,' Roger replied a trifle tartly.

'Oh, that!' Fouché waved the matter aside then smoothed down his long, grey frock coat. 'Alas, I have never been able to acquire the habit of idleness that our friend Talleyrand is so fortunate in possessing. Your man said you were to be expected back shortly and showed me in here. Such journals as I found on the table were hopelessly out of date, and I had to employ my accursedly active mind in some way, so it occurred to me to look through your desk.'

A cynical little smile twisted Roger's lips, 'I suppose such a manner of passing the time must be second nature to a Police Chief. But I fear you were unfortunate if you hoped to come upon any secrets.'

'No, no. You wrong me. I had no such thought. But I have always been fascinated by the way others live, and how much their households cost them. I did no more than look through your bills.'

Confident that Fouché could have come upon nothing that could injure him, Roger said, 'But I forget myself. You must be in sad need of a glass of wine and I trust you will stay to dinner.'

'You are most kind. I might even stay here overnight if that would not be trespassing too greatly on your hospitality; for I should much like the opportunity of discussing various matters with you at some length.'

'About that there will be no difficulty. Indeed, I am honoured to have *Monsieur le Ministre* as my guest.'

Fouché bowed, 'I thank you; but there is one—er—small point upon which I must put you right. The First Consul has recently dispensed with my services. I am no longer Minister of Police.'

'You astound me,' Roger replied, raising his eyebrows. 'Have you then quarrelled with Bonaparte?'

'No, no; I would not say that,' Fouché replied, looking away and blowing his nose. 'It is only that he thinks that he

207

can now do without me. He is, of course, mistaken—that is, if he wishes to retain both his life and his power; but let us talk of such matters later.'

Roger left the room to order a somewhat better dinner, and a bottle of wine to be brought to the library.

Over dinner they talked of many things, and there were few about which Fouché did not have inside information.

Roger had been absent from France for close on a year and a few weeks after he had left for England Hortense de Beauharnais had been married to Louis Bonaparte. She had been in love with the handsome Duroc, but he had not cared for her and had refused Bonaparte's offer of her hand. Josephine, meanwhile, perpetually harassed by the hatred of her Bonaparte relations, had been seeking some way to sow dissension among them. If she could marry off her daughter to Louis Bonaparte that should detach him from his family and make him her ally. With the arts she knew so well how to use she had persuaded her husband that it would be a most suitable match. Hortense had been very averse to it; but her mother had overruled her protests. Louis, too, had greatly disliked the idea, but he was a weakling and had tamely submitted to his brother's orders. So on January 7th these two young people, although hating one another, had been united in wedlock.

In January, too, the renewal of the Legislative Bodies had become due. No provision for this had been laid down in the hastily composed Constitution; so Bonaparte had decreed that the Senate should name the Tribunes and Legislators who were to go or remain. As might have been expected, no member was left in either Assembly who had the courage to oppose him violently.

Another innovation the First Consul had introduced was the splitting of the principal Ministries, so that their functions were divided under two equally responsible Chiefs. By this means he had cunningly deprived any single Minister of the power to thwart him and could check the activities of one Minister by the reports of another employed on more or less the same type of work. Fouché had found himself the opposite number to Savary, formerly one of Desaix's A.D.C.s, whom Bonaparte had found to be a useful man and had now made Chief of the Security Police. All this, Fouché declared, was a clear indication of Bonaparte's intention to make himself Dictator. On May 8th another step had been taken by his succeeding in getting passed a measure that extended his First Consulship for a further ten years. Two months later he had followed that up by having a referendum put to the people, and such was his immense popularity that the voting had been only eight thousand odd against the three million five hundred thousand in favour of his becoming First Consul for life. He had at once introduced a new Constitution, that he had ready in his pocket, which curtailed still further the liberties of the people who were so besotted about him, and from August 1st had decreed that henceforth he should be known as 'Napoleon'.

Meanwhile he had forced through reform after reform, all aimed at restoring France to a monarchy in all but name. In April he had ratified the Concordat with Rome and, to celebrate it, had a spectacular *Te Deum* sung in Notre Dame, which he had compelled all the notables to attenc. Those old die-hard Revolutionary Generals Augereau and Lannes had had to be virtually arrested and conveyed to the Cathedral under escort in a carriage. Throughout the service they had talked without restraint, using their habitual oaths. Augereau had spat on the floor and Lannes declared loudly, 'Just to think that a million Frenchmen gave their lives to get rid of all this nonsense, and now we are forced to submit to it again.'

In an endeavour to win the allegiance of the Generals, Bonaparte had ignored the abolition during the Revolution of Orders of Chivalry and proposed to introduce a new one to be called the 'Legion of Honour'.

This was announced in May and was to have several grades so that persons of all classes should receive the distinction as a reward for their services to the State, and the highest rank of the Order was to be awarded both to the leading Generals and learned men of the Academy.

209

Against considerable opposition Bonaparte had forced his project through the Senate and a great outcry from the old *sans-culottes* had resulted. Many of the Generals, too, had declared it contrary to the principles of the Revolution.

Lafayette, whom Bonaparte had compelled the Austrians to give up after having been for many years a prisoner of war, flatly refused to accept the new honour. Moreau, revolting at this desecration of Revolutionary ideology, declared that he would hang the Cross of the Order he had been awarded to the collar of his dog.

Fouché went on to say that, having crushed the Jacobins, Bonaparte had found a new threat to his ambitions in many of the Generals and the rank and file of the Army, which was still strongly Republican. Augereau, Brune, St. Cyr, Jourdan, Lannes, Oudinot, Macdonald, Masséna, Moreau and Bernadotte all intensely resented his assumption of virtually monarchical powers.

They had actually conspired against him and introduced a proposal to the Senate that his power should be curtailed by dividing France into a number of Military Governments. Bonaparte, of all people, had promptly assumed the role of the defender of the 'Liberties of the People' and, declaring Military Governments to be a most tyrannical form of rule, had the measure thrown out.

Bernadotte, who positively hated him, had then had his Chief of Staff, General Simon, despatch in secret thousands of pamphlets for distribution among the troops, that began, 'Soldiers! You no longer have a country; the Republic has ceased to exist. A tyrant has seized upon power; and that tyrant is Bonaparte....'

Fouché had, of course, known all about this and had Simon and a number of officers arrested. Bonaparte had again shown extreme astuteness. Instead of ordering a purge that might have set half the army by the ears, he had had the arrested officers released without trial; one by one, quietly, got the recalcitrant Generals out of France to distant commands where they could do him no harm, and despatched all the most revolutionary-minded regiments on an expedition to San Domingo.

This, the largest island in the West Indies, had been a source of enormous wealth to France in the days of the Monarchy but, early in the Revolution, fiery agitators had been despatched there to preach the doctrine of equality, with the result that the slaves had risen and massacred thousands of the white population.

Out of this imbroglio a Negro General named Toussaint l'Ouverture had arisen. He was a man of remarkable gifts and had succeeded in restoring a state approaching order in the island. In May 1801, following Bonaparte's example, he had given San Domingo a Constitution and appointed himself Governor for life. He had then written to the First Consul requesting that France should take the island under her protection and defend it from the English. As at that time Bonaparte was already putting out peace feelers towards Britain he acted with extreme duplicity. Replying to Toussaint in the most flattering terms, he said that he would send an army to protect San Domingo, while his real intention was to reconquer it.

The expedition had sailed the previous December under the command of Pauline's husband, General Leclerc. Fouché, who rarely laughed, sniggered into his handkerchief as he told Roger of Pauline's fury when her brother had ordered her to accompany her husband. She adored the gaieties of Paris, visualized life in the West Indies as exile among savages, and believed it to be a plot hatched by her enemy, Josephine, to get her out of the way. But Bonaparte had proved adamant, so she had had to pack her many dresses and Paris had lost the most beautiful of all her beautiful girls.

In May Bonaparte had shown his complete contempt for the doctrine that 'All men are equal' by a decree that slavery should be re-introduced in San Domingo. In June the unlucky Toussaint had been lured aboard a French ship, treacherously arrested and sent back to France as a prisoner.

In European affairs the First Consul had been equally active. Having drafted a new Constitution for the Cisalpine

Republic, early in the year he had summoned four hundred and fifty representatives from it to meet him in Lyons and there settle which of them should be appointed to the most important offices. Count Melzi was proposed for President and, as he was both the most important person in Lombardy and strongly pro-French, the Deputies naturally expected that this choice would please their overlord. To their surprise he had angrily refused to sanction the appointment. Thereupon, before the next session of the conference, Talleyrand had dropped a hint to a few of the right people that the First Consul was very hurt that no one had thought of proposing him for this honour. In consequence, next day he had been elected unanimously and with acclaim, President of the Republic, now to be styled that of Italy.

In the summer, the British having withdrawn from Elba, he had promptly put a French garrison on the island, with the excuse that France was the Protecting Power of Italy. He had then annexed Piedmont and the Duchy of Parma.

During the autumn he had busied himself mightily in negotiations for the redistribution of the German territories to various petty Princes who had been dispossessed during the war. And here he had been able to offset the annoyance of the Czar about his annexation of Piedmont and Parma by favouring several Princes who were relatives of Alexander's through his German wife and mother.

He had, however, run into trouble over Switzerland. Although the independence of that country was supposed to be restored by the provisions of the Peace, he had demanded of the Swiss the cession of the Valais so that he could carry out one of his pet schemes; the building of a military road across the Simplon Pass. The Swiss had refused him the Canton and the English were encouraging them to stand firm.

In fact, from Bonaparte's point of view the English were behaving altogether badly. They were seeking to wriggle out of numerous clauses in the Peace Treaty they had signed because, they now declared, they had been tricked over them. They had refused to restore Pondicherry, the sphere of French influence in India, and were delaying the withdrawal of their garrisons from both the Cape and Malta on the pretext that Bonaparte had broken his word by interfering in the affairs of Switzerland.

Roger knew well enough that Cornwallis had been made a complete fool of at Amiens but, however idiotic the concessions made there, it seemed that, affairs in Switzerland apart, the British Government had ample grounds for the attitude they were taking as retaliation for Bonaparte's seizure of Elba, Piedmont and Parma. But Fouché, his long bony fingers picking at a bunch of grapes, was going on:

'So there, *mon cher Colonel,* matters rest at the moment. It has been another wonderful year for France and 'tis my opinion that "Napoleon" will go even further than has "Bonaparte". But now that I have put you *au courant* with great affairs, pray tell me about yourself, and how you have spent these past many months?'

Roger was ready for the question and replied quietly, 'I spent a good part of them in prison.'

'Prison!' Fouché exclaimed, his fish-like eyes for once meeting Roger's. 'You astound me. What can possibly have so bemused your mind that you failed to call on my good offices? Whatever you had done, I would have found a pretext to get you out.'

'I thank you for your good intent,' Roger smiled, 'but it was beyond even your powers to do so, for 'twas in England that I was in gaol. On the signing of the peace I decided that I would go over there and visit some of my less unpleasant relatives.'

Fouché nodded his long, thin, skull-like head, 'I recall now that you long since quarrelled bitterly with your immediate family. But what was the trouble in which you landed yourself?'

'A duel was forced upon me, and in regard to such affairs the attitude of the English is still barbarous. Here in France, from time to time, the monarchs issued Edicts forbidding duelling, but they were sufficiently civilized to appreciate that there are occasions on which a man has no alternative but to defend his honour. Provided the accepted code of duelling was observed, no serious action was ever taken. The treatment I received in the country of my forebears made me more than ever disgusted with it; so as soon as I was freed I returned to France.'

'And what do you plan to do now?'

'Remain here, I think, at least for some months. Now that France is at peace Bonaparte, or Napoleon as we must now call him, can have little use for me. And I'm told that Paris swarms with Englishmen. So incensed am I about their having imprisoned me, did I get into an argument with one of them I'd like as not have another duel on my hands.'

With a shrug of his lean shoulders Fouché remarked, ' 'Tis true that throughout the summer and autumn there were thousands of them in Paris, but now the winter has come all but a few are gone home. As for remaining here, this is a charming retreat you have but, if you would permit me to advise, I would advocate your return to Paris.'

'Why so?' Roger asked.

'Upon two counts. With Peace France is prospering as never before, so 'tis my view that everything possible should be done to maintain this happy state of things. But there is a grave danger that it will not last. Napoleon is so disgusted with the English that he is already contemplating again making war on them. Should he do so, now that Italy is completely ours and we have naught to fear from Austria, Prussia or Russia, 'tis certain that he will revive his long-cherished plan for invading England. I am of the opinion that such a venture would prove a great disaster. You are one of the few people who might persuade him of that, and so stay his hand.'

'He may well refuse to give me back my place,' Roger demurred. 'I should have reported to him again last Spring, or at least have asked his leave before proceeding to England. My failure to do so may have angered him exceedingly and cost me his good will.'

Fouché shook his narrow head, 'Nay. He has ever a soft spot for his old friends and will forgive them much. In spite of your long, unauthorized absence I feel confident that he will take you back into his good graces. Then, if you regained his ear, your knowledge of England and the dangers involved in a cross-Channel expedition might prove the fly on the chariot wheel.'

Putting his bloodless lips to his glass Fouché drank a little wine, then went on, 'The other side of the picture is that, should his ambition overrule sane judgment, you would again be one of his immediate entourage and so be in a position to promote the career that you told me, upon our settling our old differences, you meant to make for yourself in France.'

For a moment Roger studied the lean, corpse-like man seated opposite him. He could see no trap in the advice offered and recalled Fouché's having once said to him that his policy was, whenever possible, to have friends rather than enemies. It could, therefore, be assumed that his present object was to induce Roger to return to Paris for their mutual good, in the belief that Roger would himself benefit and, at the same time, prove a friend for him near Napoleon.

'I thank you,' he replied gravely. 'I agree that everything possible should be done to preserve the peace. Should I decide to go to Paris, my reception by Napoleon would depend much on the mood in which he happened to be, but were it good I'd not forget the generous interest that you have shown in my affairs. I'll think the matter over and let you know my decision tomorrow morning.'

That night both his sense of duty and his inclination prompted him to take Fouché's advice. However bad the bargain Britain might have made at Amiens, there was no reason whatever to suppose that, should the war be renewed, she would get a better one a year or two hence; in fact, since she had no single ally left on the Continent, it might prove very much worse. Talleyrand, Roger felt sure, would do everything possible to hold Napoleon back, and some occasion might arise in which he could be of help in that. It would mean denying himself the winter sunshine, the azure skies, the mimosa and carnations, the oranges and tangerines of the South of France, that he had been looking forward to in January and February; but little Jeanne Meuralt was no

215

longer there to give him her companionship, along that part of the coast there was no society and the longer he remained outside Napoleon's orbit the less chance he would have of regaining his old position as a confidant of secrets that might change the destinies of nations.

So next day he packed such things as he needed, while Fouché walked down to the village and drove back in the travelling coach that he had had stabled there. Roger left money with the Dufour couple and told them and the other servants that he might not be returning for some months; then, that afternoon, he and Fouché set off in the coach for Paris.

They arrived on December 2nd, and Roger was made as welcome as ever at *La Belle Etoile* by the Blanchards. They had wonderful things to say about the happenings in Paris since he had last been there. The peace had brought not only scores of English '*milors*' to France but also many Russian and German nobles. The *Place du Carousel* had been a sight to see on review days when they all went there in their splendid equipages. The parties at the Tuileries were becoming ever more brilliant. Now, like a King and Queen, Napoleon and Josephine received at their Court all the Foreign Ambassadors who presented to them the visiting aristocracy from their countries: Lord Whitworth for England, M. Markoff for Russia and the Marquis de Lucchesini for Prussia; and the Ambassadors in turn gave magnificent receptions for the First Consul and his wife. Never since the fall of the Bastille, thirteen years ago, had the theatres been so packed or the fêtes been attended by so many thousands of well-dressed people.

Business was booming, not only in the capital but throughout the whole country, for the Industrial Revolution had come to France. Napoleon's remaking of the roads and canals and his suppression of brigandage now made commerce between cities swift and profitable. The bad old days of the almost worthless paper *assignats* were gone and the funds, which at the time of *Brumaire* had been down to seven francs, now stood at fifty two.

216

In the Autumn Napoleon had organized an Exhibition of Industry in the Louvre and converted many of its splendid apartments into an art gallery, where could be seen the great collection of Old Masters looted out of Italy and such masterpieces as the Venus de Medici. It had again become fashionable to go to Mass. In return for the Concordat the Vatican had led the way in recognizing the new Kingdom of Etruria and the Helvetii and Batavian Republics as French Protectorates. Food was plentiful and cheap. New buildings were going up everywhere. The projects of Napoleon for the betterment of France seemed endless and he was looked on by the majority of the people as the giver of all good things.

Next day, dressed again as a Colonel and wearing the sash of an A.D.C., Roger was received by the great man. Napoleon stared at him for a moment then snapped, 'How dare you present yourself to me in uniform! You forfeited the right to it months ago. Owing to your weak chest I gave you leave to spend the worst of last winter in the south. Your failure to report to me in the Spring amounts to desertion and I mean to have you court-martialled for it.'

Roger had known this to be a risk that he would have to run, but felt fairly confident that he could surmount it. Making a pretence of beginning to take off his A.D.C.'s sash, he gave a shrug and replied, 'As you will. If my old friend and master has become an unjust tyrant in my absence there is naught that I can do about it. Strip me of my uniform. Have me drummed out, if it pleases you. Order your Court to condemn me; but I'd be unfortunate indeed if I were thrown into a French prison after having spent a good part of the year in an English one.'

'An English prison?'

'Yes. Before reporting to you in the Spring I thought I'd take advantage of the peace and spend a few weeks in England, so as to be able to inform you on my return how things were going there. A duel was forced upon me and for fighting it I was clapped into gaol. As soon as I was free I returned via Bordeaux, then went to St. Maxime for only long enough to see that all was well with my small property there. Then, although it is mid-winter, giving no thought to my chest, I came with all speed to Paris, so that I might with the least possible delay congratulate you on having become First Consul for life.'

Napoleon grunted, 'I see! I see! That certainly puts a different complexion on matters. But now there is peace I have no use for *beaux sabreurs*. At least not at present.'

'No; not at present, First Consul,' Roger smiled. 'But I have a feeling that you will before we are much older.'

'What the devil do you mean?'

'I travelled north with Joseph Fouché. He gave me the impression that you are by no means satisfied with the conduct of the English.'

'Fouché, eh! That intriguing Jacobin! He has a finger in every pie and although I got rid of him he still catches news of everything in his spider's web.'

Beginning to pace up and down with his hands clasped behind his back, Napoleon went on. 'But he's right, of course. They are thwarting me in India. They are still sitting at the Cape and refuse to evacuate Malta. Their journals, too! No doubt you saw them. Article after article, maligning me most shamefully. 'Tis disgraceful that they should allow their scribblers to write filth about a friendly Head of State. But I've no wish for war. Under me France has become prosperous as never before. I intend to keep it so. Yet this haggling with them infuriates me. They agreed the peace terms so they should keep them; but I suppose one can expect no better from a nation of shopkeepers.'

'In view of their recent treatment of me I'd like nothing better than to have at them again,' Roger remarked. 'But since you are set on maintaining the peace, why not let me resume my old duties as assistant to Bourrienne?'

'Bourrienne!' Napoleon stopped pacing and frowned again. 'He is here no longer. I got rid of him last October.'

'Got rid of Bourrienne!' Roger exclaimed. '*Mon Général,* I can scarce believe it. Why, he was your oldest friend and invaluable to you. What frightful crime did he commit?'

' 'Tis naught to do with you. And no man is indispensable.

218

Méneval now serves me just as well and has all the help he needs. No, for the moment I have no use for you, so you had best return to the sunshine of the south.'

Although Roger was well aware of Napoleon's duplicity, he had formed the opinion that he really meant what he had said about not wanting a renewal of the war, which was a considerable relief; but he had been so taken aback at the dismissal of Bourrienne that for a moment he was at a loss to think of any other suggestion which might lead to his employment. He had just made up his mind to bow himself out and see Talleyrand, who might find a use for him, when Napoleon suddenly snapped his fingers and cried:

'I have it. You will have heard of our misfortunes in San Domingo?'

Roger's heart gave a lurch and seemed to descend to his boots. The last thing he wanted was to be ordered off to the West Indies, and if he was but did not go it would almost certainly mean Napoleon's finishing with him for good.

'No, First Consul,' he replied, striving to keep the anxiety out of his voice. 'Since my return to Paris yesterday I have seen no one of importance before waiting on you; and Fouché made no mention of the island except that the Negro general Toussaint l'Ouverture had been sent back to France a prisoner.'

Napoleon made an impatient gesture. 'Oh, Leclerc did well enough on his arrival on the island. He found Cap Haïtien in possession of the Negro General, Christophe. But he had sailed from France in thirty-two ships carrying twenty thousand men; so, although he had to land his troops on the beach a few miles from the town, the very sight of our force was enough to scare the blacks into abandoning it. After that he soon had the island under control and he dealt with l'Ouverture as I had directed.

'But that was in the winter, when those fevers that apparently rise from the lowland swamps lie dormant. Since then, alas, the situation has become very different. With the warmer weather our men began to go down with the fatal sickness. By high summer they were dying like flies. That encouraged the Negroes to revolt. Seeing our increasing weakness, whole battalions of them that we had trained and armed for our service deserted and went over to the enemy. By October this accursed yellow fever had reduced Leclerc's effectives from twenty thousand to two thousand; and against the black hordes he was hard put to it even to hang on in Cap Haïtien. Now that he is dead, unless courage and intelligent leadership save the day for us we may be forced to abandon the island altogether.'

'Leclerc dead!' Roger exclaimed.

'He was stricken with the pestilence and died early in November.'

'I am most distressed to hear it. He was a charming and intelligent as well as a brave man.'

'Yes,' Napoleon nodded glumly, 'he was a good man and I am sorry now that I chose him for that command. I did so only because he was up to his ears in debt. Like all my family, with the exception of my mother, Madame Leclerc has no idea of the value of money. She is appallingly extravagant and poor Leclerc was half out of his wits wondering how to pay her bills. My idea was that, after a few years as Captain General on that great island, he would have returned rich enough to live like a millionaire for the rest of his life.'

As Napoleon spoke, Roger was wondering anxiously what was coming next. Never having commanded a formation he thought it unlikely that he was to be sent out to take Leclerc's place; but with Napoleon one could never tell. He had sent Duroc, who had no diplomatic experience, as his Ambassador to St. Petersburg and had recently made Savary, another soldier, Chief of Police. Roger thought it more likely that he was to be despatched to this devilish island as A.D.C. to some other General, or as the First Consul's personal representative, to send him an on-the-spot report of the situation.

Pausing at one of the tall windows Napoleon stood staring out for a full minute. Roger, silently regarding the back of the short, stalwart figure, continued to wait for the blow to fall.

CHAPTER XV

WHITE MAGIC

SUDDENLY the First Consul swung round, his expression changed to brisk geniality. 'We must do what we can to console Pauline. I had intelligence yesterday by a fast sloop that she is on her way home. Her ship should dock at Bordeaux in a week or ten days' time. Someone must meet her, tell her of my grief for her, and act as her escort. She prefers well-born men to rough soldiers. You, Breuc, are the very man for this task. Take one of my coaches, proceed to Bordeaux with all speed and, when Madame Leclerc lands, do all you can to bring the smiles back to those bright eyes of hers.'

Roger could hardly believe his ears. To be given this intriguing mission instead of being packed off probably to die of yellow fever in the jungles of San Domingo seemed too good to be true. Jerking to attention, he cried, '*Mon Général,* you can rely on me.' Then with a laugh he uttered one of those 'Gasconades' that at times he used to support his rôle as a Frenchman. ' 'Twill be a sad day when the master whose thousand activities have again made France great cannot find a use for a man with the qualities of his servant, "*le brave Breuc*".'

'You impudent fellow,' Napoleon replied. But he loved flattery, so he smiled and pulled Roger's ear as he added, 'You are almost as conceited as that gallant who commands the Hussars of Conflans. What is his name? Yes, Brigadier Gerrard. Very well; keep your sash, and take good care of my favourite sister.'

After visiting the stables and arranging for a comfortable coach with a team of six horses and outriders to take him on his way to Bordeaux next morning, Roger went to the Rue du Bac. There Talleyrand received him, but could give him only a few minutes as he was about to leave to attend a reception at the Prussian Embassy. Roger gave him a somewhat edited account of his misfortunes in England, then enquired the reason for Bourrienne's dismissal.

Having taken snuff, the Foreign Minister replied, 'Poor fellow, he lost his place through a mere peccadillo, but unfortunately one that is a heinous crime in Napoleon's eyes. He takes no exception to his Generals looting the territories over which they are sent to rule, or to me in maintaining myself in reasonable comfort by accepting, now and then, a few francs from the Ambassadors whose business I choose to expedite; because that is foreign money. But for some reason I have never understood poor Bourrienne was paid no salary. He was permitted to draw such money as he needed from the First Consul's private purse. Such an arrangement was well enough in its way, but not one by which one could put aside a comfortable fortune. In consequence, Bourrienne entered on a speculation with one of these army contractors. Extraordinary to relate it did not turn out well, so he endeavoured to recoup himself by drawing on the Public Funds. Savary got wind of this and reported it to the First Consul. To rob the French Exchequer is the one thing that he will not permit even his family to do; so Bourrienne was sent packing, and without even a gratuity, after his many years of faithful service.'

'Indeed! It is unlike Napoleon to show ingratitude; and I am most sorry for our old friend.'

'And I.' Talleyrand took another pinch of snuff, then

222

flicked the grains from his lapels with a lace handkerchief. 'Méneval is highly competent, but Bourrienne was the finest personal assistant any monarch could have. He had a marvellous memory, could speak and write many languages, and take down dictation as fast as anyone could speak. He knew how all the departments worked, was well versed in international law and had known Napoleon from the days when they were cadets together at Brienne. To retain his services for a million francs would have been cheap at the price. But our little man has at times these queer quirks of moral rectitude which, I must confess, I find surprising in anyone almost as unprincipled as myself.'

Roger then told Talleyrand about his new mission. The diplomat raised an eyebrow. '*Mon cher ami*, I at the same time congratulate you and deplore your fortune in being charged with acting as the official protector of this lady. She has been well named *la belle des belles* and you would not be human did you not swiftly become a prey to a desire to sleep with her. I think that as far as she was capable of being in love she loved Leclerc; so you may find her still chilled by his death and unresponsive to any man's attentions. But the Bonapartes are a lecherous breed, and Pauline is the most libidinous of them all. Did you know that not long after Leclerc was despatched to serve with the Army of the Rhine she entered on *affaires* with three Generals simultaneously; Moreau, Macdonald and Beurnonville? On comparing notes they found her out, but that gives you the measure of her amorous propensities.'

'Then after six weeks aboard ship she must be ripe for some masculine entertainment,' Roger smiled.

'Perhaps; unless she seduced the Captain of the ship on the way over, and has formed a passion for him, as such hot-blooded women are apt to do. I wish you luck with her but, should you succeed, I advise you not to become deeply involved, for I am convinced that to set your affections on such a woman could lead only to unhappiness.'

Still pondering this sage counsel, Roger set out for Bordeaux. His coach covered the three hundred and forty miles in six days. On reaching the port he engaged the best suite of rooms in the most comfortable hostelry, pending Madame Leclerc's arrival.

Pauline's ship docked four days later and Roger went aboard at once. Her Captain, a fine handsome man in his early thirties, received him in his stern cabin and together they drank some excellent triple-distilled Rum termed Sugarcane Cognac. Over this warming tipple the Captain gave him an account of the way in which things had gone wrong in San Domingo.

That a great number of the troops had fallen victim to yellow fever was only half the story. The real cause of the disaster had been Napoleon's decree that the estates of the French planters should be restored to them and the Negroes be reduced once more to a state of slavery. Leclerc, realizing the danger of promulgating such a decree, had refrained from doing so, but General Richpanse, the Governor of Guadeloupe had, and the news had spread like wildfire to the other islands. With Toussaint a prisoner and Christophe defeated the great majority of the Negroes had been quite willing to accept the Government of France and to regard themselves as French citizens; but when they learned that they were again to become slaves, the whole black population of the island rose in revolt.

Had a state of peace been maintained many of the troops stricken with the fever might have been nursed back to health. As it was, French detachments up-country, already weakened by the ravages of the disease, had been either massacred or driven into the forts along the coast. Cap Haïtien had been besieged by a rabble of Negroes many thousands strong led by their witch doctors and screaming for French blood. The situation had become so threatening that Leclerc had feared he would have to evacuate the island and had sent a company of troops to escort Pauline and her ladies down to the beach.

Despite her frivolous nature, she had played her part as a Governor's wife in a way that did her the greatest credit. During the early months of the occupation she had enormously enjoyed being the First Lady of the land, designed a special costume for her staff and an orchestra, received all the notables most graciously and given a constant succession of concerts, dances and expeditions to beauty spots.

Then, as the Spring advanced, a number of unknown infections had broken out. She had been inflicted with sores on her hands and arms and several of her household had gone down with yellow fever, which was already spreading as a serious epidemic among the troops. But Pauline had refused to be intimidated and go into isolation with her little son and immediate entourage. Instead she had insisted on continuing to hold her receptions and concerts to maintain morale, and could not be prevented from visiting the stricken soldiers in the hospitals.

When the crisis came and Leclerc had determined on a last sortie against the great horde of Negroes, he had sent a party of Grenadiers to bring Pauline and her household down to the beach but she had refused to accompany them, proudly declaring to the other women, 'You may go if you wish, but I shall not. I am the sister of Bonaparte.'

Ignoring her defiance, four soldiers had picked her up, put her in a chair and carried her off toward the waiting ships. But she had never gone aboard. News had arrived that Leclerc's sortie had succeeded, the blacks had broken and temporarily fled; so she had had herself carried back to the Residence, yawned gracefully and said, 'How I despise these stupid panics.'

By then Leclerc had already been infected by the pestilence. Although desperately ill he continued to conduct the defence in person, but the fever proved too much for him and he had had to take to his bed. Regardless of the danger of catching the fell disease, Pauline had nursed him devotedly but in vain. On November 8th, weakened by his exertions, he died.

Her grief for 'her little Leclerc', as she always called him, had been terrible to witness. Adhering to the old Corsican custom, she had cut off her beautiful golden hair and laid it at her husband's feet in his coffin. She had then draped herself in funeral black and refused all consolation.

When Roger enquired how she had supported the voyage, the Captain replied, 'I have hardly seen her. Except for rare occasions she has kept to her cabin. Her maid, Mademoiselle Aimée, has taken her such little food as she could be persuaded to eat, and reports that for whole days she has sat as though in a stupor. Her health, too, has never been good and the summer heats in San Domingo thinned her blood and sallowed her wonderful complexion. No doubt these weeks at sea will have restored her beauty; but, seeing the mental state she is in, it has been a relief to me that as her host while aboard my ship I have not had to attempt to entertain her. And I do not envy you, *mon Colonel*, in having to be her companion in a coach for a week while escorting her back to Paris.'

Quietly and efficiently Roger then made his wishes known. Leclerc's coffin was to be taken ashore without his widow's knowledge, so that she should be spared the sight of it, and sent independently to Paris in the splendid catafalque, drawn by six white horses with black trappings, that he had had prepared while waiting for her in Bordeaux. Her child, whom she had sent for only twice on the voyage, and his nurse, were also to be taken ashore in advance, and would travel in a separate coach. He would escort Madame Leclerc that evening to the hostelry where he had engaged lodgings for her.

These arrangements were duly carried out. At five o'clock he went with the Captain to the small state-room that Pauline occupied in the day-time. Gravely he conveyed to her the compliments of the First Consul and his deep sympathy, then said that he had been charged with the honour of escorting her wherever she wished to go.

She showed no sign of recognizing him and acknowledged what he had said only with an inclination of her head, which was so heavily draped in black veils that he could hardly discern her features. After murmuring a few words of thanks to the Captain she took Roger's proferred arm and allowed him to lead her to the coach that stood waiting on the dock.

226

In complete silence they covered the half-mile journey to the inn. There, Roger escorted her and her maid up to their rooms, then left them.

Downstairs he ordered a bottle of Château Filhot and, while drinking it, considered the situation. Pauline was clearly in a far worse state than he had expected. Mercurial by temperament, she could be the gayest of the gay; but, as she was now, a prey to heartbreaking grief, it would prove difficult to rouse her from it. However, she was barely twenty-two and had a nature that demanded love and laughter; so it could be only a question of time before she emerged from her black depression. How long that would be was the imponderable that he had to endeavour to assess.

Her dead-black garments had not concealed her superb figure and her sombre veils had not so entirely hidden her lovely face that he could not recall it in all its beauty. In the past she had always accorded him something a little more than just friendly interest, regarding him with the eyes of an experienced woman who was weighing up what sort of lover he might make. Should he now dare to count on that to re-arouse her passions? If he did, and failed, she would report his unseemly conduct to her brother, and that could be the end of any prospect of his continuing in the great man's service. That was the devil of a risk to take. But it was now or never; and Roger knew that if he did not take it, he would regret to the end of his life having forgone this chance to make the most beautiful woman in France his mistress.

He sent for the chef and ordered supper. Meat tended to make people feel heavy, whereas shell fish were light and their properties stimulated desire; so he ordered lobsters lightly simmered in fresh butter and then flambé in cognac, sweetbreads with mushrooms and, as a final course, white truffles cooked in champagne; another natural aphrodisiac. Then he talked with the *sommelier* and they decided on a glass of *pinaud* new-made from the last vintage and only procurable in the Bordeaux district, a bottle of Château Cheval Blanc, as the nearest approach to Burgundy which, for this occasion, Roger would have preferred, then a magnum of champagne that had lain in bin for twenty years. For two covers was Roger's injunction; and to be served at eight o'clock.

Newly shaved, powdered and immaculate he entered Pauline's sitting room at that hour. The waiter had already laid the places at the table. She was still wearing a light veil. Through it, mistily, with large sad eyes she looked up at him and said:

'*Monsieur le Colonel*, you must excuse me, but I prefer to eat alone.'

Roger bowed. 'Madame, that I appreciate. But I am under orders from that great man who has remade France anew—your brother. He charged me not only to act as your escort but to do my poor best to persuade you that, despite your tragic loss, life can still hold much happiness for you. I dare not disobey his commands, therefore I pray you at least to permit me to sup with you.'

'As you will, Monsieur,' she replied dully. 'I have both affection and a great respect for my brother, and have never questioned his judgment. But you must forgive me if I am in no mood to converse.'

Handing her a glass of the apéritif, he said, 'If you have not drunk this before, you will find it quite an experience. It is a kind of wine, but does not travel; so is obtainable only in these parts.'

She drank it down without comment, then they took their places at the table. Roger did the talking and he was extremely able at it. To begin with he spoke gravely of serious things, that he knew perfectly well would not interest her, then went on to talk about the change in Paris that had taken place during the past year: the fêtes, the receptions, the foreign nobility and the new fashions in women's clothes. At that a faint flicker of interest showed in her lovely eyes and, breaking her long silence, she began to ask him questions. By the time they got to the truffles served covered with a napkin, she was smiling. Then as the champagne was produced her depression descended on her again, and she said:

'I have had enough wine, and you must excuse me if I now go to bed.'

'No, Madame,' replied Roger firmly. 'Not yet, I pray you. Join me in just one glass while I talk to you about a matter of real importance.'

She shrugged, 'Very well then; but I cannot think what it will be.'

Roger sat back and said with the greatest gravity, 'Madame; your august brother, your family and all your friends are greatly concerned for you. It is only natural that a feeling of loss and desolation should now hang like a dark cloud over your mind, but it will not continue there indefinitely. You are still so young and time is the healer of every sorrow. Sooner or later you will emerge from your widow's weeds to become again your old gay self.'

She shook her head and tears welled up into her big eyes, 'You may be right, Monsieur; but I loved Leclerc dearly and not for a long time yet will I be consoled for his loss.'

Roger made her a little bow, 'Understandably, Madame, you think that now. But I cannot believe that you wish to continue in this state of despair. Your own well-being and the consideration you owe your friends both demand that you should take any step that will shorten your period of bereavement and enable you to enter fully into the joy of life again.'

'What step could I take?' she asked sadly.

'There is one, the potency of which has been proved many times in cases similar to your own.' Roger paused a moment, then added, 'But it would mean resorting to magic.'

Her eyes widened. As a descendant of Corsican peasants she had an inbred belief in every sort of superstition and in the powers of witchcraft. A little fearfully she said, 'I would give much to regain my former happy state; but I'll have no dealings with the Devil.'

'The Devil plays no part in this,' Roger assured her earnestly. 'It is of White Magic that I speak: the performance of a simple ceremony in which no sacrifice is made. It is a remedy of great antiquity based on the laws of nature and handed down through countless generations. You have only to imbibe a potion in certain given conditions and when you wake you will think on your tragedy as no more than an event that happened many years ago.'

She leaned forward a little, 'Where can I procure this wondrous draught that will make me forget poor Leclerc and become my happy self again?'

Roger smiled at her, 'You will recall, Madame, my telling you that your brother charged me to do everything that lay in my power to dissipate your sorrow. So I have this potent medicine with me. Do you consent to participate in this ceremony with me you shall receive it.'

'What are the conditions of which you spoke?' she asked.

'Have you a white garment?' he enquired. 'If not we must procure one for you.'

'My night robes are white.'

'That will serve, but it must be a clean one; and you must wear naught else, even jewellery, so that you must take off your rings and remove those earrings from your ears. We shall need the light of three candles, no more and no fewer. And a bright fire should be burning in your room. A little before midnight I will come to you and, on the hour, administer the potion.'

She gave him an uneasy look, 'Monsieur, I gather that it is to my bedroom that you propose to come. My maid will be sleeping in the adjacent room. Our voices might rouse her, and thinking someone had broken in upon me she would alarm the house. Were you found with me that could provoke a most terrible scandal.'

'Then you must speak to her beforehand and tell her that you are expecting someone. You could say that a courier with a letter from the First Consul is expected to reach Bordeaux tonight, and you have given me instructions that at whatever hour he may arrive I am to bring the letter straight up to you.'

'That would suffice,' Pauline agreed thoughtfully. Then she looked down at her plate and went on in a low voice, 'But, Monsieur; although I assume your intentions to be honourable, is it essential to the magic that I should appear

230

before you near-naked in a night shift? I'd find that most embarrassing.'

Roger smiled across at her, 'Madame, I appreciate the delicacy of your feelings and am happy to reassure you on that point. You can remain in bed and receive the potion there. Should you feel that modesty demands it, draw the sheets up to your chin. The position you are in will make no difference to the efficacy of what I shall give you.'

For a long moment Pauline hesitated, then she said, 'I would give much to be free of my memories of San Domingo. Will you swear on your heart that this potion of which you speak owes nothing to the Devil?'

Roger crossed his heart. 'Madame, I swear it.'

'Will I find taking it very unpleasant?'

'On the contrary, you will at first find it so stimulating that you may beg of me a second draught; but later you will feel deliciously relaxed and fall into a sound sleep.'

'So be it then,' she nodded, and beneath the light black veil she was wearing the candle light caught the gold of the short crisp curls with which her head was covered. Rising from the table she went on, 'I'll speak to my maid as we agreed, see to it that there is a good fire burning and no more than three candles alight. Then I'll expect you a little before midnight and take this magic potion which you promise will work such wonders. Meantime I thank you, *Monsieur le Colonel,* for this excellent supper and your kindness to me. Talking with you while we ate has made me feel almost human again.'

Well satisfied, Roger kissed the hand, still showing scars from the sores that had marred it in San Domingo, that she held out to him and bowed her out through the door that led to her bedroom.

Returning to his own room he spent the best part of two hours there. At first he tried to concentrate on a book, but after he had read several pages twice over, found that he had absorbed hardly any of their contents. His brain refused to function except in forming mental images of the beautiful Pauline in scores of different circumstances and positions.

At last the time of waiting was over. By then the inn had

231

fallen completely silent. Quietly he made his way along to Pauline's sitting room. His heart was beating furiously and he knew that he was taking a wild gamble with his future. Another few moments would decide. Either he would be holding her divine form in his arms and she would be returning his kisses, or she would rouse the house, bring people running and declare he had assaulted her. Then he would have to run for it himself and somehow escape to England; for it was certain that when Napoleon was told of this attempt to ravish his favourite sister, he would have every police agent in France hunting for *le Colonel Breuc* to throw him into prison.

Crossing the sitting room he knocked gently at the bedroom door. For a moment there was silence, then, in a low voice, Pauline called, '*Entrez, Monsieur.*'

In the bedroom a bright fire was burning, its flames flickering on the ceiling. Three lighted candles were set on the dressing table. Pauline was sitting up in bed leaning against her pillows, no longer enveloped in her black robes and the veil that had half hidden her features. Her face was thinner than when he had last seen it fully and the light of the candles caught the gold in the short, crisp, boyish curls that now covered her head. At the sight of her loveliness he drew in a sharp breath.

As he advanced to her bedside her eyes held his. They were wide with anticipation and excitement at the thought of the magic potion he had promised to bring her.

He was wearing a chamber robe and had nothing on beneath it. Suddenly he threw it off and stood naked and erect within two feet of her. She gave a gasp, but before she could speak he smiled and said:

'I have not lied to you. I have within me the magic potion that you need.'

CHAPTER XVI

THE STOLEN HONEYMOON

I T W A S not long after midnight when Pauline gave a happy sigh and exclaimed, 'Oh God, how good it is to be possessed again by a man!'

Pulling her towards him, Roger buried his face in her neck for a moment then gave a laugh, ''Twas that you needed, most beautiful of all the beauties. And when you wake tomorrow you'll find all your joy in life restored.'

Clutching him closer she said quickly, 'I'll not sleep yet. Remember you promised me a second draught of your magic potion; though I little thought then how you meant me to receive it.'

'You shall have it, sweet, and a third; and yet another as dawn breaks over Bordeaux. I wonder, though, that you did not suspect my intent; for though I spoke a riddle I had in fairness to give you the chance to read it aright.'

She laughed. 'You fooled me utterly. 'Twas your talk of magic, three candles only, a bright fire, a deep sleep and to awake relaxed. Then when I saw you standing beside my bed! Such a fine figure of a man, so handsome and so—so virile, how could I resist?'

It was that upon which Roger had counted, and it had

been his only card. Had she rejected him he would not have attempted even to kiss her, let alone force himself upon her. Knowing by repute her passionate nature and that for two months at least she had not been made love to he had gambled on the sight of him naked being alone sufficient instantly to stir her hot southern blood. And her reaction had been that for which he had hoped.

She had suddenly stretched out a hand to grasp him. Next moment his mouth had been glued to hers. There had been no amorous dalliance, not a word spoken between them. Both she and he had been seized with a brainstorm that resulted in a wild scramble. He remembered tearing aside the bedclothes and her great eyes moist and gleaming in the light from the candles as she threw herself back then pulled him down upon her. Next moment they had been locked in a fierce embrace ending several minutes later in sweet oblivion as they together died the 'little death'.

Turning slightly in his arms, she whispered, 'You are prodigious brave, *mon Colonel*. Do you realize the risk you ran? Had I not felt on the instant a desperate urge for you, I might have screamed for help. Then, even had I later had the wish to pardon you, your outrageous conduct would have come to the ears of Napoleon; and he has had people shot for less.'

'I know it; but having counted the cost of failure my yearning for you overcame my fears. The very sight of you has sent me half crazy with desire ever since I first set eyes on you at Montebello.'

'Can that be true? I was then but a chit and getting over my schoolgirl infatuation for Fréron.'

'You were the loveliest baggage for your age in all Italy; or Europe for that matter.'

She leaned over and gave him a long kiss, then said, 'How truly delightful it is to hear you say that you have been in love with me for years. It makes me far less shamed to think that I gave myself to you without even the demurs demanded of my sex by convention. And I'll confess now that more than once when you have paid your respects to me in Paris

234

I've caught myself thinking that I'd enjoy going to bed with you.'

'Then this night was decreed by Heaven. Though I'm mightily flattered that you should have had such thoughts of me.'

'I'm not alone in that. When women are together the subject is always men and I've heard several confess that they would welcome your attentions. But in Paris you are looked on as a prude.'

'Indeed!' Roger laughed. 'I'm far from that. But I find little pleasure in casual romps with ladies only passably good-looking, and there are few who are perfect enough to rouse in me ardent desire.'

'Another compliment. If words were all, you would make a gallant any woman would dote on. But if we are to enter on an *affaire* I need to judge you by your deeds, and our first joust was too fierce and swiftly over for me to assess your mettle by it.'

Pushing her from him, Roger slipped out of bed. Startled, she sat up and cried anxiously, 'Don't leave me. What is it? Have I offended you?'

'Not in the least,' he assured her gaily. 'I was but teasing you; and unless other ladies have misled me you'll find naught to complain of in my staying powers. Before we make a test of that though, I crave a boon of you.'

'What is it?' she asked, smiling at him.

'That you, love, get out of bed, let me remove that white night robe you are wearing and feast my eyes upon your loveliness.'

Without a moment's hesitation Pauline pulled her shift off over her head and jumped down on to the floor. She was extremely proud of her magnificent figure; so much so that she scandalized her family by acting as a model in the near-nude for the sculptor Canova's masterpiece 'Venus Victrix'.

To Roger's delight she displayed her charms to him with the utmost freedom, standing in front of him with her hands clasped behind her neck so that her breasts stood out in

235

perfect symmetry, then walking up and down the room, dancing a few steps and assuming provocative attitudes. She drew him like a magnet and, his joy in watching her overcome, he took her in his arms, picked her up and carried her back to the bed.

Later he collected from the sitting room the magnum of champagne of which they had drunk only a quarter at supper. Over the wine they talked, laughed and caressed one another for two hours that seemed to pass like twenty minutes. They then made love again, put out the candles and curled up together in dreamy bliss. But there was no dawn party for, in his excitement, Roger had forgotten that it was December so the sun would not rise until late; and he did not want Pauline's maid to catch him in bed with her mistress.

At about four o'clock, finding that Pauline had fallen into a heavy sleep, he gently disengaged himself from her, slipped on his robe and tiptoed from the room.

When his man woke him at seven, although he had slept for only a few hours, he felt like a giant refreshed and, looking back on the past night, decided that he was the luckiest fellow in the whole world.

He had just finished a hearty breakfast when Pauline's maid, Aimée, came to tell him that her mistress had passed a very bad night, so she did not feel like setting out for Paris that day, and wished him to cancel the arrangements for her departure.

Knowing very well how Pauline had passed the night, Roger was not at all surprised and was delighted at the thought that this meant for him another night with his ravishing new mistress in their present comfortable quarters; but he gravely asked Aimée to convey his respects and sympathy to 'Madame'.

The maid was a pretty young person with dark hair and a fresh complexion bronzed by the tropical sun. After a moment she said, 'I have been with Madame since her marriage to the General and his loss was a great blow to her. Despite her bad night I found her more cheerful this morning than I have seen her for a long time and *Monsieur le Colonel* will perhaps permit me to remark that I attribute that to his having entertained her so charmingly at supper. Such company is excellent for her and if I can be of any service in encouraging her to spend longer in the company of *Monsieur le Colonel*, I should be happy to do so.'

To Roger a wink was as good as a nod and he guessed at once that Aimée was aware that he had spent the night with her mistress. With a smile he replied, 'As Madame will be spending most of the day in bed, no doubt she will allow you a few hours off to do some shopping, and there must be quite a number of things you would like to buy after your years in the Indies.' Then he fished out of his waistcoat pocket four gold twenty-five franc pieces and slipped them into her hand.

Bobbing him a curtsey she returned his smile. '*Monsieur le Colonel* is most kind, and anyone can see that he is not one of those jumped-up officers but a real gentleman. I feel sure that Madame will be sufficiently recovered to get up this afternoon, and I will suggest to her that she should dine with you.'

Well pleased by this happy understanding with Aimée, which would lessen the necessity for subterfuge in his *affaire* with Pauline, Roger went out into the town to buy her a mass of flowers.

Before escorting Pauline to the inn, Roger had seen her son, Dermid, but had not spoken to him. That afternoon he found the boy with her. He was a pretty, fair-haired child and would be five in April, but he was far from strong. She had borne him when she was only seventeen, and such an early pregnancy had harmed the health of them both. Roger had, that morning, thought of the boy; so was able to produce for him both sweets and toys, which soon made them good friends. When his nurse had taken him away, Pauline threw off her black weeds and the lovers eagerly embraced to exchange passionate kisses.

Over dinner Pauline was as gay as a lark, but towards the end of the meal, when Roger broached the subject of their journey, her face clouded over and she said, 'I have been thinking about us this morning. In Paris I no longer have a

237

house so, for some weeks at least, I'll have to live with my mother, or my brother Joseph, which will make our being together difficult. Besides, I'd have to continue to wear mourning, and I've always hated black. It does not suit me. Why should we not go incognito to some place where we can live for a while openly as husband and wife?'

Roger considered for a moment. Her idea held out to him a temptation to spend several weeks in Paradise; but it could prove extremely dangerous, and he said, 'My love, it would be heaven; you must remember, though, that you are now a person of great importance—a member of an almost Royal family. If we disappeared 'tis certain that your brother would set his police to search for us, and when they ran us to earth the fat would be in the fire with a vengeance.'

She pouted, 'But I do not want to go to Paris. My poor little Leclerc was weak and ill for a long time before he died, so I have been starved of love for an age. When one is only twenty-two that is a terrible state to be in. Somehow we must arrange matters so that you can continue to sleep with me.'

Smiling at her, Roger replied, 'I think it could be done if you will write to the First Consul. Tell him that you dread having to see again in Paris scores of people who will condole with you and constantly remind you of your loss; that you must have more time to get over it before facing such an ordeal, so you wish to make a tour incognito through some parts of France that you have not yet seen. Happily he charged me with the care of you and to do my best to alleviate your sorrow; and I'd be failing in my duty did I not act as your escort.'

Pauline's brown eyes with their golden glints lit up as she returned his smile. 'You are clever, *cher Colonel*, as well as strong. I will do that. Now, whither shall we go?'

'I have a small château at St. Maxime that I occupy occasionally. There is no society in the neighbourhood, nor anyone likely to recognize you. To get there we should have to pass through several towns of interest, about which you could later tell your brother, and give him the impression that

238

you had stayed longer in each of them than would actually be the case. How does that idea appeal to you?'

Clapping her hands, she cried with delight, 'Bravo! What a man I have found! You have everything. Even a château in the southern sunshine by the sea where we can enjoy together a pastoral life. We'll set out tomorrow.'

'What of young Dermid and his nurse?' Roger asked.

She shrugged, 'Oh, I'll send them on to Paris. My mother will take good care of the child.'

'Then they can go in the coach I brought for you, escorted by my sergeant and his troop. In any case we'd have to rid ourselves of the men; otherwise in every place we lay for the night it would be all round the town in no time that you were the First Consul's sister. I'll hire another coach privately, and we must choose a name for ourselves.'

For some minutes they discussed possibilities, then Pauline said, 'I have it! Spring is in my heart again. Let us be known as Monsieur and Madame Printemps.'

'Excellent,' he laughed. 'Now, what of Aimée? I take it you would not wish to go without her, but if she comes there'll be no preventing her knowing that we are lovers.'

'She knows it already. Even if she slept like the dead and failed to hear our gambols through the partition wall, the state of my room when she entered it this morning would have told her everything. 'Twas considerate of you to creep away without waking me, but you left half the sheets and one pillow on the floor, and the empty champagne magnum on my bedside table.'

With a contrite grimace, Roger said, 'For that I greatly blame myself. But it was still pitch dark when I tiptoed away and I was so drunk with happiness that my mind was quite bemused.'

'No matter. The little baggage is entirely to be trusted. She even had the impudence to congratulate me on you.'

Roger grinned, 'When she brought me your message this morning about having passed a sleepless night, I felt sure she knew the reason. All, then, is well. And now loath as I am to leave you, sweet, I must beg to be excused. Since we're to

239

start tomorrow, and secretly, I have much to do between now and supper time. Meanwhile, I suggest that you write that letter to your brother, and I'll give it to my sergeant in the morning.'

After a further session of long kisses, he tore himself away and went out into the town. At a military outfitters' he bought the shako and sabretache of an officer in a regiment of Curassiers and the rank badges of a Captain. Then, his Colonel's rank badges hidden under the long cloak he was wearing against the cold, he went to a hostelry some distance from that in which he was staying and, as Captain Printemps, hired a comfortable coach to be ready for him at one o'clock the following day, giving his destination as Toulon.

Returning to his own inn he went in search of Aimée and when he found her learned that her mistress had already informed her that they were to set out next day on a secret journey. He told her to pack only the clothes that 'Madame' insisted on taking and have them ready by midday. The rest, and the mass of impedimenta she had brought with her from San Domingo, were to go in the coach to Paris. He then took Aimée up to his room, gave her his spare uniform coat and asked her to change the Colonel's badges on it for the Captain's.

Next, he sat down to write two letters. The first was a brief despatch to Napoleon, reporting Pauline's safe arrival and that, being in a sad state of depression, she desired to spend a few weeks before returning to Paris among people who did not know her, and of her tragic loss, and that, anticipating it to be the wish of the First Consul, he had agreed to remain with her until she felt capable of facing the world again.

His second letter was to the Defours at the château, informing them that he had recently married and, soon after the arrival of the letter, would be bringing his wife to St. Maxime. There were to be flowers in every room, and no expense was to be spared on local purchases that would make the house more pleasant as a residence for 'Madame'.

Having finished his letters he had time only to clean himself up before joining Pauline for supper.

Tonight she had cast aside not only her veil but all her black garments and was wearing a blue velvet dress embroidered with gold flowers, that set off to perfection her tanned arms, neck and face. It was another gay meal and afterwards there was no question of his leaving her. Carrying a magnum of champagne he accompanied her into her bedroom and there undressed her. Neither did he creep away in the small hours. When Aimée came in she found them still together in bed sound asleep.

An hour and a half later Pauline gave her orders to Dermid's nurse, and a letter for her mother. Roger gave the two letters for Napoleon to his sergeant and told his servant to return to Paris in the coach with the nurse. The good-byes were said and at eleven o'clock the little cavalcade moved away on the road to the capital.

When paying the bill, Roger told the landlord of the inn that Madame Leclerc had decided to stay for a few days at the little seaside village of Arcachon, but first wished to drive down to the port and thank again the Captain of the frigate that had brought her from San Domingo. He then asked for a coach and a carriage to be summoned.

When they arrived at the door he had the luggage put into the coach and, when Aimeé had settled herself in it, told the coachman to drive her to Arcachon. Returning upstairs he escorted Pauline, now again draped in black from top to toe, down to the carriage and handed her in.

Outside the dock gates he called on the driver to halt, told him that Madame wished to take a little exercise by walking along the quay to the ship, and paid him off. After half an hour's stroll round the docks they came out, picked up another carriage and drove to the inn at which Roger, in the name of Captain Printemps, had ordered a travelling coach to be ready for him. Leaving the carriage for the coach, they drove the forty miles to Arcachon, arriving there soon after dark. Aimée had reached the village half an hour earlier and had taken the best rooms at the only inn for Captain and Madame Printemps. Hungry from having missed their dinner they made an excellent early supper off freshly caught lobsters and the local cheese, then went happily to bed as man and wife.

Next morning, with Roger wearing his Curassier shako and uniform with a Captain's badges, they took the road south to Dax, Madame Leclerc and *le brave Breuc* having disappeared into the blue.

By way of Pau and Tabres they drove through the lovely scenery of Navarre, then on through Toulouse, Béziers and Montpellier to Nîmes with its fascinating Roman ruins, Avignon with the Palace of the Popes, and charming Aix-en-Provence, to Toulon. They travelled by easy stages because, owing to her early pregnancy, Pauline was afflicted with an internal trouble that plagued her if she rode for too long over bumpy roads. But, like many women who suffer from ill health, when she was happy minor ailments never seemed to bother her.

At Toulon Roger paid off the coach and, next day, hired another at an inn some way from that in which they had passed the night. With him once more a Colonel wearing his A.D.C. sash, they covered the last stage of their journey to St. Maxime.

On the morning after their arrival, touched by the compliment but considerably perturbed, he learned that the villagers intended that afternoon to present an address of welcome to Madame, his wife. He had brought this on himself owing to his generosity to local charities and there was no escaping it. With considerable anxiety he and Pauline awaited the ceremony.

To their relief it passed off without incident. The Mayor and the Curé both made fulsome speeches, there were cheers and everyone was given plenty of wine in which to drink the health of the newly-weds. To account for Pauline's golden-bronze skin, Roger had given out that she was the daughter of a wealthy plantation owner in Guadeloupe and had only recently arrived in France. No one recognized her and she enjoyed enormously assuming her new role as the lady of the manor.

The last days of December and the first week in January

1803 had been occupied by their journey from Bordeaux. For a month they revelled in being alone together in the winter sunshine by the sea.

Roger found that Pauline had only a very small knowledge of great affairs and little interest in them. She was extremely self-centred, concerning herself only with love, her personal appearance and frivolous amusements. But she was straightforward, generous, easily pleased and spontaneously gay.

At times he still thought with bitterness of the terrible ending to his life-long bond with Georgina, but Pauline's ardent passion for him and his delight in her loveliness had restored his zest for life, just as his unflagging desire for her had restored hers. With no single duty or commitment to observe they lived entirely as they pleased, sometimes lying in bed until well on in the afternoon, at others getting up at dawn to go fishing. On some nights they went on moonlight rambles and made love in the woods or on the beach. They never saw a journal and cared nothing for what might be happening in the world outside their own little Paradise. Like Venus and Adonis, they thought only of their love and of pleasing one another.

Yet, as with all mortals, there had to come an end to this dispensation from all care that the kind gods had granted them. One night towards the middle of February Roger said to the radiant goddess who faced him across the supper table:

'Beloved, my heart is heavy with the thought, but soon now we must return to Paris. It is more than seven weeks since we disappeared from Bordeaux. However great the preoccupations of your brilliant brother, he must at times wonder what has become of his favourite sister. If he has not already done so it cannot be long now before he sets his police on to discover your whereabouts. Should they find you here living as Madame Breuc, that would be disastrous. It would mean for me at least several years' imprisonment for having abused his confidence, and for you, with your husband only four months dead, a scandal that would besmirch your name through France.'

'Oh, must we go!' she cried in protest. 'I have been

happier here with you, Rojé, than ever in my life before. I cannot bear the thought of returning to that dreary round of behaving like a great lady and being pleasant to scores of people, most of whom are atrocious bores. Can we not stay stay here for another month, or a fortnight at the least?'

He shook his head, 'No, dear goddess. I dare not risk it, for your sake even more than my own. We will have one more week here but not a day longer. On that my mind is set, and with all your wondrous wiles you will not move it.'

So, one week later, their stolen honeymoon ended. On February 20th, sad but resigned, they took the road to Paris.

CHAPTER XVII

OF LOVE AND WAR

NAPOLEON'S face was black with anger, his broad jaw stuck out and his eyebrows were drawn down. In his harsh, Italian-accented voice, he rasped, 'Two months! Two whole months and not one word from you!'

Roger raised his eyebrows, 'I would have thought, First Consul, that you had enough anxieties to occupy you without worrying about your family.'

'My family! *Sacré Nom!* They are the cause of half my worries. My brothers do me more harm than I can do them good. And now Madame Leclerc must get herself lost in southern France for eight weeks.'

'But, *mon Général*, you knew that I was with her, so could be certain that she would come to no harm.'

'You, and who else? No one but a serving wench! And Leclerc but four months dead! If this gets out, 'twill be the scandal of the year.'

'It will not get out, unless you let it; for she travelled under a false name. You have but to endorse the statement she has already agreed to—that she spent seven weeks in a convent hearing Masses for the repose of her husband's soul. No one has cause to suspect she spent her time otherwise, and did some scribbler ferret out the truth he'd never dare publish it.'

'My sister, running round France under a false name with a man like yourself. What a way to behave!'

'Since she was determined to preserve her incognito, what else could she do? Had she travelled in your coach with a full escort she would have been harrowed by having to listen to addresses of condolence from the Mayors of every town through which she passed. On the other hand, had she not taken me with her she would have been pestered day and night by the unwelcome attentions of a score of gallants.'

'True! True! But she should at least have taken a chaperone. A month ago I ordered Savary to use his police to locate her. What a story would have been made of it had they come upon the two of you unchaperoned.'

'Where was she to find a chaperone, pray, at short notice in Bordeaux? I mean one who, entrusted with such an honour, would not have been so puffed up by her appointment as to blab about it to all and sundry?'

'You are so glib of tongue, Breuc, that you have an answer for everything. But I regard your conduct as most reprehensible.'

'Then, First Consul, you do me a great injustice. You charged me with the care of Madame Leclerc, but you gave me no order that I should bring her direct to Paris. Your actual words to me were, "Do all you can to bring the smiles back to those bright eyes of hers". Well, I have done it.'

'That, at least, I am glad to hear,' Napoleon grudgingly admitted.

'Indeed, our tour of the ancient cities in the south worked wonders. Knowing something of their history I was not badly qualified to be her guide. She showed the greatest interest in many places that we visited, particularly in the ruins of the Roman amphitheatre at Nîmes.'

'Ruins!' Napoleon gave a harsh laugh. 'Pauline has never cared a fig for ruins! The sight of them wrought no change in her, I'll vow. 'Twas yourself and your sleeping with her.'

Drawing himself up, Roger cried, 'First Consul, I protest! You have no right so to malign Madame Leclerc.'

'Nonsense, man! I know Pauline better than you will ever do, however many times you've tossed her between the sheets. She gave horns to Leclerc before they had been married three months, and during his absence on the Rhine I had to post a dozen officers to the provinces to prevent her scandalous *affaires* with them becoming the talk of Paris.'

Roger was furious. Being in love with Pauline and having witnessed her terrible distress at Leclerc's death, he had gradually formed the belief that the tales of her immorality were untrue, and that she had done no more than flirt with her many admirers. Seething with anger, he snapped:

'Were you not who you are I would call you out for that. You should be ashamed to believe such slanders about your sister.'

With one of his amazing changes of mood, Napoleon suddenly laughed, then pulled Roger's ear, 'My poor Breuc, you have completely given yourself away. No man issues a challenge in defence of a woman's honour unless he is in love with her. For that I cannot blame you. She is so dazzling a creature that many times when she has entered a room a sudden silence has fallen and I've heard a dozen men catch their breath. But she is as licentious as she is beautiful, and if you did not seduce her I'd stake my life that she seduced you: I'll not now insist that you admit it; but I'll have to send you to the provinces.'

Relieved as Roger was to have got through his ordeal, his heart sank, and he said, '*Mon Général*, as Madame Leclerc has gone to live with her brother Joseph and his wife, we will have no opportunity to see one another except in public, and as no one but yourself knows of the journey we made together no scandal will link our names. It is above fourteen months since I had the honour to serve on your personal staff, and see something of Paris. Can you not possibly find some use for me that will allow me to remain here?'

Napoleon, his big head bowed, took a few paces up and down before replying, 'Perhaps, yes. Now I think on it I may need you in a few months' time. The accursed English are playing me up most damnably. They have agreed to evacuate

247

the Cape and Egypt, but most dishonourably refuse to carry out the terms of the Treaty by which our territories in India were to be restored to us, and they remain adamant about Malta. Not content with that, they continue to slander me in their journals; yes, even to the vile extent of asserting that I seduced my step-daughter Hortense then, having got her with child, quickly married her off to my brother Louis.'

'How infamous!' Roger exclaimed with genuine indignation, for he felt convinced that there was not an atom of truth in such an accusation.

'Yes. What minds they must have! But in that, at least, I proved them to be liars. I had a poet write some verses praising Hortense's dancing, then gave a ball at Malmaison. There, to her great annoyance, and much as I dislike the sight of pregnant women, I made her do a few pirouettes in front of me. She was then seven months gone and her state plain for all to see. As she had been married to Louis for over nine months that made it as clear as crystal to everyone that she could not have conceived by me before her marriage.'

For a moment he was silent, then changed the subject, 'But about yourself. Although I wish the peace to continue and am being very patient with the English, their attitude is so unfriendly that I can only regard the present state of things as a short armistice. I am convinced, too, that to make war upon them again would be ultimately to our advantage. Therefore I am already preparing to resume hostilities. When the peace was made I allowed our activities on the coast to be slowed down, but recently I've given orders that they are to be increased. You can report to Berthier and take up again with him your previous rôle as my liaison officer in all matters concerning the invasion of England.'

Having expressed his gratitude Roger withdrew, marvelling now at the narrowness of his escape. After he and Pauline had left Arcachon no one could have had any idea whether they had gone north, south or east and France had many cities, but as Savary's police had been on the lookout for them during the past month, they were lucky not to have been identified as Captain and Madame Printemps in one of the towns where they had passed a night on their way up from St. Maxime to Paris. Still luckier, he felt, was the fact that Savary had replaced the astute Fouché as Chief of Police; for the latter, with his unerring instinct for assessing possibilities, would have sent one of his agents straight to St. Maxime, and God alone knew what would have happened when the First Consul learned that his A.D.C. had taken his sister there to live openly as Madame Breuc.

As Roger descended the grand staircase he saw Duroc coming up. After Duroc's mission to Russia he had been transferred as Ambassador to Prussia and was still in Berlin when, some fifteen months earlier, Roger left Paris to go secretly to England. Since then Roger had spent only two days in the capital early in December, during which they had not chanced to run into one another; so this was the first time they had met since they had come face to face in St. Petersburg.

As old friends they exchanged hearty greetings and swapped news of their more recent doings. Duroc, it transpired, was no longer being used as a diplomat and for over a year past had re-occupied his old post as Comptroller of the Palace. After they had talked for some minutes he said:

'You know, Breuc, I would have taken an oath that I saw you in St. Petersburg at a reception given by the new Czar. Those blue eyes, straight nose and firm chin of yours seemed to me unmistakable. The man I took for you turned out to be an Englishman who spoke the most atrocious French; but the two of you were as alike as two peas.'

Roger laughed, 'Yes, Talleyrand told me that you had written to him about the encounter. But at that time I was at my château in the south of France, and a week later here in Paris. There's no great mystery to the matter though. It was my Scottish cousin, Robert McElfic, now Lord Kildonan, whom you met. We are much of an age and when young were often taken for twins.'

After another few minutes of lively talk, they agreed on an evening to dine together and parted. As Roger made his way back to *La Belle Etoile*, he again had good reason to thank his stars that, when Count Muriavieff had introduced Duroc to him, he had addressed him only as 'Monsieur' and omitted to mention his name.

When Roger reported to Berthier next morning they naturally discussed the worsening of Anglo-French relations, and the ugly little Chief-of-Staff was of the opinion that if the First Consul really wanted to keep the peace he was going the wrong way about it. In the autumn he had sent a Colonel Sabastiani on a tour to Algiers, Egypt, Syria and the Ionian Isles. The Colonel had returned to France late in January and, to everyone's amazement, the First Consul had ordered his report to be printed in *Le Moniteur* on the 30th.

It had been undisguisedly an intelligence appreciation of France's prospects in the Mediterranean and Near East should she again go to war with Britain. The report described the British Army in Egypt as being in a very poor state and that of the Turks as beyond contempt, so that an army of six thousand French should have little difficulty in re-conquering the country. It barely disguised the fact that Sabastiani had gone there for the purpose of contacting Ibrahim Bey and inducing him to lead his Mamelukes in a revolt against the English. It also stated that the people of Corfu would declare themselves for France immediately they received French support.

Naturally the English had been greatly incensed and now flatly declined even to discuss withdrawing their troops from Malta. They had gone further and brought a measure before Parliament for an increase in the armed forces. But the Government was weak, with Pitt still in retirement and Grenville and Dundas now in opposition. Fox, too, had attacked the measure furiously in one of his great orations and this violent dissension in Parliament had led Napoleon to believe that Britain had become so impotent that he could ignore any protests she might make about his doing what he liked on the Continent.

So confident was he of this that on February 18th he had had a violent scene with the British Ambassador, Lord Whitworth, using the old trick of carrying the war into the enemy's camp by declaring that Britain had been guilty of the basest perfidy, while he was doing no more than assist countries adjacent to France in maintaining stable governments.

His assistance to the Swiss had consisted in sending in his two German-speaking Generals, Ney and Rapp, with an army at their backs to make known his wishes about Switzerland and to insist on the Valais being handed over to France. This also had led to heated protests by the British, but he had brushed them contemptuously aside and declared his intention of becoming the sole arbitrator between the Federals and the Unionists who had long been disputing the way in which Switzerland should be governed.

Roger was sufficiently broadminded to appreciate that there were faults on both sides. The British had failed to honour numerous clauses in the miserable treaty they had signed, while Napoleon had ignored the limitations it had set to the aggrandisement of France on the Continent; so there was justification for the re-opening of hostilities by either. Berthier's view was that, recognizing the immense power now at the disposal of France, the British would accede to the First Consul's demands without a fight. But Roger was not so certain. Although the weakness of Addington's government was deplorable and the nation evidently divided, he knew the streak of obstinacy in his countrymen that had led to their defying the might of Spain and wresting the control of the seas from the Dutch; so that if pressed too far they might yet sink their differences and, weak though they were by comparison, again challenge France.

Among Berthier's activities, Roger learned, was the sending over to Britain of Consuls and Vice-Consuls who were in fact military engineers with orders to make plans of the harbours and coasts; but there was nothing he could do about that.

For the moment he was much more concerned with his private affairs. His eight weeks with Pauline, far from having decreased their desire for one another, had made its satisfaction nearly a necessity. After their first hectic weeks together there had naturally followed a decline in their amorous propensities. But it had not lasted. There had followed a more temperate intimacy that had soon become a habit to which they both looked forward with unflagging delight. Both of them were highly experienced in the art of love and physically each was the perfect counterpart of the other. Pauline had declared frankly that never in a life-time would she find a lover who satisfied her more fully, while Roger remained entranced by the perfection of her beauty and thought himself the luckiest man in the world every time he took her.

Now she was living in Joseph's new house, the splendid Hôtel Marbeuf in the Rue du Faubourg St. Honoré, and it was impossible for them to continue spending their nights together but, fortunately, they had the willing Aimée as a go-between; so on every afternoon that Pauline had no commitment she changed into clothes belonging to her maid, slipped out from the garden door of her brother's house and came to *La Belle Etoile*, there to make love with Roger in his bedroom.

Hating her black garments as she did, they served as an excuse for her to refuse to participate in her sister-in-law Julie's charitable or social activities; but there were afternoons when a visit from her mother, or an old friend such as Laure Permon, now the wife of General Junot, prevented her from leaving the house, so that Roger waited for her at *La Belle Etoile* in vain. And there were others when she arrived at the inn to find that he had not been able to keep their rendezvous owing to some call of duty. Thus, to their intense annoyance, their plans to be together were quite frequently frustrated.

Meanwhile, Roger had been back in Paris for ten days before he had a chance to talk alone with his old friend Talleyrand. He found the Foreign Minister far from happy about the way things were going. Talleyrand agreed that, if driven too far, the English would again resort to war; and, in spite of all his endeavours, France's relations with Russia had steadily deteriorated. Napoleon had refused to compen-

sate the King of Sardinia for the loss of his kingdom of
Piedmont by more than offering him the small territory of
Siena, or a slice of Greece, should France and Russia continue to dismember the Turkish Empire. The Czar, as a
fervent upholder of the rights of hereditary monarchs, had
been greatly incensed by this and once again it looked as
though armies might clash and thousands of soldiers die on
account of the claims of King Victor Emanuel. Roger considered such a cause for going to war utterly unreasonable,
but consoled himself with the thought that in this case it
would at least lead to Russia becoming the ally of England.

Another matter that had given Talleyrand grave concern
was the French claim to Louisiana. The previous autumn
Napoleon had organized an expedition which, under General
Victor, was to cross the Atlantic and take over this territory
from the Spaniards. The plan had been for it to be sent out
on the pretext that it was a reinforcement for General Leclerc
in San Domingo. But two factors had led to its sailing orders
being postponed. Firstly, the French forces in San Domingo
had been reduced by casualties and yellow fever from twenty
thousand to two thousand effectives and these appalling
losses had caused Napoleon to hesitate to send more troops
to a country in which they would be exposed to the same
disease. Secondly, the ex-British Colonists in the northern
states of America had declared that they would oppose any
nation that claimed suzerainty of the territories that lay to the
south of those of the Union.

Jefferson had instructed Monroe, the Ambassador of the
States in Paris, to make a deal if he could. Talleyrand had
foreseen that to refuse it would be to throw the new Power,
with its considerable number of warships, into the arms of the
British, whereas a reasonable settlement with the Americans
could make them the ally of France. In consequence, he had
wisely negotiated a treaty with them by which France ceded
her rights to Louisiana for a payment of fifty million dollars.

As March advanced, relations between Britain and France
grew still more strained. On the 13th there occurred a most
unseemly scene during a reception at the Tuileries, of which

253

Roger was a witness. In front of the assembled Ambassadors Napoleon, without warning, violently attacked Lord Whitworth.

'It is you,' he rasped, 'who are determined to make war upon us. If, for the sake of preserving peace, I should yield on a single point, the English would become more treacherous and insolent. Were we to yield now, England would next prohibit our navigation in certain parts of the world, and I am not the man to brook such indignities. Your government wishes to drive me to war, but France will lose nothing by it. In a very short time I can have two million men at my disposal. You will be the first to draw the sword; I shall be the last to sheath it. Woe to those who show no respect for treaties.'

Lord Whitworth was a cold, hard man and an aristocrat who had difficulty in concealing his dislike for the upstart Corsican. Later he told his friends, 'The fellow is beyond the pale. Before the assembled *Corps Diplomatique* he abused me in the language of the barrack square. From the glare in his eyes I thought he was about to hit me. Had he done so I would have knocked him down without regard to the consequences.' As it was, with true British phlegm he had merely raised his eyebrows, turned on his heel and walked quietly from the room.

His report of the episode to the British government led, after considerable hesitation, to their sending him orders on April 23rd that, if Napoleon continued to refuse to satisfy their requirements about Switzerland and on other matters, the Ambassador was to demand his passports.

On May 11th a conference was held at St. Cloud. The three Consuls, Talleyrand, Joseph Bonaparte, the Secretary of State Maret and numerous other dignitaries were present. Roger, with several other A.D.C.s and secretaries, was in attendance and later learned what had taken place. Joseph had pleaded hard that *his* Peace of Amiens should be kept and Talleyrand had supported him. The others, fearing to displease the First Consul, cautiously hedged when giving their opinions.

254

Napoleon admitted that he had not wanted to engage the English again until the autumn of the following year, by which time his ship-building programme should ensure France a fleet of equal power to that of the British. But he declared that he would not give way over Switzerland or Malta, and that if the English wanted war they should have it. When a vote was taken all but Joseph and Talleyrand voted for the rejection of the British demands.

In consequence, Lord Whitworth left Paris next day and, on May 18th, Britain declared war on France.

For some months both countries had been preparing for a renewal of the struggle and their Navies took immediate action, first blood going to the British by the capture of two merchantmen off the coast of Brittany. On the 22nd this was announced in Paris, together with an order that all Englishmen between the ages of eighteen and sixty still in France were to be arrested and held prisoner for the duration of the war, as a reprisal for the merchantmen having been seized before the declaration of hostilities. This was not the case, as the vessels had been taken on the day war was declared and three days after Napoleon had laid an embargo on all British vessels in French ports, thus himself being the first to commit a hostile act.

No such order for the internment of enemy civilians on the outbreak of war had ever before been issued in any country. To penalise non-combatants in this fashion was an innovation that horrified all Europe. Even in France it was regarded as a most barbarous act; but Napoleon refused to rescind the order and as a result over ten thousand British subjects were condemned to languish in concentration camps, many of them for as long as eleven years.

Although war had been declared, Talleyrand determined to make an effort to arrange a suspension of hostilities; and Napoleon, no doubt owing to his concern over the weakness of the French fleet, agreed that he should do so. The Russian Ambassador, Markoff, also attempted to mediate through his colleague, Vorontzoff, in London. But Napoleon remained

255

adamant on the question of Malta; so these negotiations broke down.

Britain, for her part, made an endeavour to limit the sphere of conflict by offering to respect the neutrality of Holland; but Napoleon would not hear of it. He needed the Dutch Navy and the closure of the Dutch ports as an essential part of his 'Continental System' which he hoped, by excluding all British goods from Europe, would ruin the commerce of Britain; so the unfortunate Hollanders were forced to take up arms on behalf of France.

By the peace of Amiens, Hanover had been returned to Britain and King Ferdinand restored to the throne of Naples. But General Mortier swiftly overran Hanover, compelling the hopelessly incompetent Duke of Cambridge to surrender, and General St. Cyr promptly re-occupied Southern Italy. Napoleon, meanwhile, was working with his usual intensity, organizing with Berthier the withdrawal of French forces from the Rhine to the Channel coast for his projected invasion of England.

To Roger it was now clear that this new war that had been entered upon would be fought to a finish. Napoleon was not content to be only the master of a great part of Europe. His ambitions extended to an Empire that would stretch from the Americas right across North Africa and through Egypt to include India; and in whichever direction he cast his covetous gaze his way was blocked by England. Only by completely crushing the stubborn British could he succeed in his vast designs. On the other hand, defeat for Britain must mean bankruptcy and near-slavery, so it was certain that she would fight to the last ditch. It was possible, too, that she might again persuade other nations that Napoleon was a menace to them all, use her great wealth to subsidize their armies, and form another combination of powers which would succeed in defeating France. But the struggle could end only in one or other of the great protagonists being utterly broken.

For Roger, personally, the war meant a great increase of work. Throughout May and June he was often closeted with Berthier or members of his staff far into the night, and on four occasions he was sent by Napoleon on missions to the coast that took him from Paris for several days.

Meanwhile, Pauline had ceased to be dependent on her relatives. Now that Napoleon was the undisputed master of France he could allocate funds as he wished, and in April he had granted her a pension of sixty thousand francs per annum. Overjoyed at having the money to make the best of her almost royal position in the new society, she had rushed out and bought herself a fine gilded carriage, more splendid even than that of her sister, Caroline Murat. Then she had acquired as a home of her own the magnificent Hôtel of the Ducs de Charost[1] only a few doors away from Joseph, in the Rue du Faubourg St. Honoré. Regardless of expense she had furnished it in the latest Greco-Egyptian fashion; so that the salons and her bedroom, with its great canopied state bed surmounted by a gilded eagle and supported by sphinxes, had become one of the sights of Paris.

But being the sole mistress of this luxurious mansion made it no easier for her and Roger to pursue their secret love affair, since he dared not go there, except when she held receptions, from fear that Napoleon would soon be informed of it and send him permanently away from Paris. Moreover, many afternoons when they could otherwise have met she had had to give to furnishing and installing herself in the Hôtel de Charost, while the increase in his duties occasioned by the renewal of the war more often than formerly prevented him from taking advantage of the afternoons when she was free. In consequence as summer advanced their meetings became less and less frequent and, when they did manage to meet at *La Belle Etoile,* instead of being able to spend a long afternoon together he usually had to rush off back to the War Office after only an hour with her.

The lengthening of the periods between their meetings added fuel to the fire of their desire, and they both became a prey to terrible frustrations; yet there seemed no way in which they could surmount the barriers that kept them so much apart until, one afternoon towards the end of June,

1. Historical Note. Now the British Embassy.

after twelve days had elapsed since they had seen one another, Pauline said:

'*Rojé, mon coeur*, I cannot support this state of things much longer. It is now close on four months since we have spent a night together, or even enjoyed a meal in one another's company. Our meetings are confined to this one room. We dare not go for a drive in this lovely summer weather nor picnic in the Bois. Even on the few occasions when I see you in public we may not exchange more than a few conventional platitudes, then must quickly separate lest Napoleon's argus eye detects us and he sends you to Italy or the Rhine. But of late I have been giving much thought to this atrocious restraint placed upon our love and have thought of a way to overcome it. We must get married.'

It was a lovely sunny afternoon and she was lying naked on the bed, her hands clasped behind her head. He was already hurrying into his breeches. Balanced uncertainly on one foot, he stared at her for a moment with his mouth open, then repeated, 'Married!'

'Yes; why should we not?'

'Do you mean secretly?' he asked.

'No. What good would that do us? We'd be no wit better off. But as my husband you could come to live with me and share my huge bed. We could go about together and have a marvellous time.'

'Of that I've not a doubt,' he agreed quickly. 'But 'tis not yet eight months since Leclerc died, and you are still in mourning. 'Twould outrage convention did you marry before the year is out.'

She rolled over on her stomach, kissed the pillow on which his head had rested while he had lain beside her, and murmured, 'I care nothing for that. A few stuffy old ladies will say catty things of me, but they always have. 'Twould be the topic of the week and then forgotten.'

'Maybe. But what of your brother? I do not see him readily giving his sister's hand to a simple Colonel like myself.'

'Why should he not? Eliza is married to Bacciocchi, who is

258

a nobody, and Caroline to that handsome blockhead Murat. He had only just been made a General when they married and Leclerc was no more than a Colonel when he first courted me. You are a better man than any of them.'

'I thank you, sweet, for the compliment,' Roger smiled. 'But Eliza's marriage was arranged by your mother without Napoleon's knowledge and, even then, he was furious that she had not made a better match. Since the marriages of all three of you he has enormously increased in stature and now looks on himself almost as a monarch. He'd never . . .'

Suddenly she turned over again, swung her legs off the bed and sat up facing him, 'Not if you are afraid to ask him,' she cried with tears in her voice. Then she hurried on, 'Are you called *le brave Breuc* for nothing? I've heard it said you are one of the few men who on occasion dare defy him. He cannot kill you because you wish to marry me. And, whatever people say of him, he has a noble nature. Whatever cause his old friends give him for anger he never bears umbrage against them for long. We cannot go on like this! We cannot! There are times when I lie in bed half out of my mind from wanting you. Get his consent and our whole lives will become a joy to us. Does my love mean so little to you that to retain it you'll not risk incurring his displeasure?'

Roger had never tired of looking at her; and there she sat, as beautiful as Venus descended from Olympus, splendid in her nakedness, her body perfection, her lovely face alight with love. There could be only one answer to her challenge. Taking a step forward he seized her in his arms, glued his mouth to hers for a long moment, then gave a laugh.

'It will be all or nothing, but in my life I've gambled oft enough for a far smaller reward.'

That night, no longer hypnotized by her presence he thought the matter over in cooler blood. To secure Napoleon's consent would be to take the biggest fence he had ever attempted in his life. Passionately in love with Pauline as he was, he asked himself if he really wanted her as his wife. She was light-minded and irresponsible and he was well

259

aware that their present desperate craving for one another could not last indefinitely. Even so, it seemed that it could be a long time before they tired of each other physically. And the advantages to himself of such a marriage could be immense. Having never been trained as a professional soldier, he thought it unlikely that Napoleon would make him a General of Division, as he had Leclerc. Neither did he wish it. But such a marriage could well lead to his being made an Ambassador, or the Pro-Consul of some State subservient to France, and in such a post he would not only wield great power but be in a position to influence events in favour of his own country.

For years past he had endeavoured to persuade Georgina to marry him, but his hopes in that direction had, alas, been finally shattered by her betrayal of him. So why should he not make a bid to become the husband of the sweet-natured and dazzling Pauline, the most beautiful woman in France?

Carefully he thought over the strategy he must adopt. He felt sure that to approach Napoleon direct could only result in a peremptory refusal. The fortress must be mined before he attacked it.

Josephine had always been his good friend. Although Napoleon was not faithful to her she retained great influence over him. At times he still slept with her and quite frequently she read him to sleep. The violent hostility of his family to her had failed to undermine her position, because as First Lady of France she did him great credit. The fact that she had never been presented at the Court of Versailles did not detract from her ability to assume the role of a great lady in a way that none of the Bonaparte women could ever have done. Her taste was admirable, the new décor of the Palaces in which they held court had been designed by her and was faultless, the clothes she wore were beyond reproach and, with great charm and tact, she had gained for her husband the goodwill of ex-Revolutionaries, returned émigrés and foreign Ambassadors alike.

Having decided that in securing Josephine's aid lay his best hope of succeeding in this hazardous but tremendous *coup*,

260

the following afternoon Roger secured a private audience with her. For a while they talked of times past and the extraordinary rise to supreme power that Napoleon had achieved in so short a time. Then Roger divulged his personal problem.

Josephine reacted as he had hoped she would. As she considered the matter, he could almost see her mind working. She had pushed her own daughter Hortense, against the girl's will, into marrying Louis Bonaparte solely with the object of detaching him from the hostile camp. Of all the Bonaparte sisters Pauline was the bitterest enemy because, in spite of her dazzling beauty, at great receptions Josephine's *savoir faire* always showed up the Corsican girl's gaucheries and put her in the second place. But Roger had long been a devoted friend. Had it not been for him her contemplated marriage to Napoleon would never have taken place. It was, too, owing to his advice to her children that they should appeal to Napoleon's affection for them that he had refrained from casting her off when, on his return from Egypt, he had received proof of her infidelity to him. If, therefore, Roger married Pauline, he would become another friend in the enemy camp and could be counted on to induce his wife to adopt a less hostile attitude.

After a few minutes' thought, Josephine nodded gravely and, although she did not disguise her feeling that it would be a far from easy task to persuade Napoleon to agree to the match, she promised to do her best.

Two days later Roger was summoned to the presence. Napoleon was not only a stickler for personal cleanliness; he so enjoyed his morning bath that quite often he lay in it for two hours or more, meanwhile dictating to his secretary or transacting business. This happened to be such an occasion. Méneval brought Roger into the bathroom, poured a can of hot water into the bath to keep up the temperature, then left them together.

Napoleon, having sat up for a moment, without the least embarrassment lay down again at full length in the big marble bath. Looking down on him Roger observed that his

261

once spare body had filled out and, unless he took much more exercise, might soon become fat.

'You wished to see me, First Consul,' he asked, in a voice that betrayed no emotion. But he knew that in the next few minutes his whole future would be decided. It was possible that he would become the brother-in-law of the most powerful man in Europe, with a wife that every man would envy him. On the other hand, Napoleon might place him under temporary arrest as a precaution against his marrying Pauline in secret then, on some trumped-up charge, get him out of the way for good by shipping him off to a fever-ridden French penal settlement, such as Devil's Island.

CHAPTER XVIII

SOLD DOWN THE RIVER

TO ROGER'S relief Napoleon said quite quietly, 'Madame Bonaparte tells me that you wish to marry Madame Leclerc.'

'That is so, First Consul,' Roger replied. Then, having given a slight cough he added, 'You—er—may recall that early this year circumstances provided Madame Leclerc and myself with an exceptional opportunity to get to know one another, and . . .'

'Circumstances!' chuckled Napoleon. 'What a way to put it. You mean that Pauline, having tired of playing the widow, the two of you planned to go off on this jaunt together. As for "getting to know one another," I'd take a wager that by now she knows the exact number of hairs on your chest.'

Anxious to encourage the mood of good humour that his master was in, Roger smiled and said quickly, 'She might; for it happens that I have very few.' Then, realizing the admission he had made, he added hurriedly, 'That is, if she has a good memory. We picnicked once, outside Aix I think it was, and on a lovely day. That I might enjoy the sun she permitted me to take off my shirt.'

'How gracious of her. And is that all you take off when she visits you in your room at *La Belle Etoile*?'

263

As Roger's jaw dropped, Napoleon laughed, 'My dear Breuc, for what do you think I pay my police if not to know what goes on in the city? But you have conducted your *affaire* with admirable discretion, so I let you be. Had she not been whoring with you it would have been with some other muscular young gallant.'

Roger reddened, 'First Consul, I protest.'

'Don't be a fool, man. As I told you before, I know my sister better than you will ever do. And though my word is now law to some forty million people, I cannot stop her from jumping into bed with any man she fancies. But her marrying again is quite another thing. How do you propose to keep her?'

'I have my pay and, owing to your generosity in allowing it to continue during my long absences on account of ill health and other matters, I have spent little while away from Paris; so I have quite a tidy sum put by.'

'Bah! It would not keep Pauline in the nightshifts that she is always taking off. She has no sense of money whatever, and is the most extravagant woman in France with only one exception—my wife. *Mon Dieu*, you should see the bills I am called on to pay for Madame Bonaparte. Dressmakers, silk merchants, modistes, jewellers form a queue here every morning, and her ante-chamber is piled as high as a haystack with their wares. She can resist buying nothing that they show her; and as she cannot remember from day to day what she has bought, they fail to deliver half the goods then charge her double the price they have asked on the rest. I've found a way, though, to deal with these rogues. When, every few months, she finds herself in difficulties and comes to me for a million francs or more, I take her bills, send these vultures a quarter of the amount they claim and scrawl "In full settlement" across them. But Madame Josephine is the First Lady of half Europe and may yet be of the whole. Madame Leclerc is but a widow with a pension, and when she marries again her pension will cease.'

Roger smiled, '*Mon Général*, in spite of your known generosity to all the members of your family, I had not counted on its continuing. Neither do I ask that you should dower her; only that you should appoint me to a post in which I can earn enough money to make her happy.'

'I did that for poor Leclerc, and see what became of him. Rochambeau now commands in San Domingo. Would you like me to send you out to relieve him?'

In spite of the money that might be made as Captain-General there, it was a far from pleasant prospect; but Roger replied, 'I am ready to go wherever you may decide, provided only that Pauline is willing to accompany me.'

Napoleon sat up and rang a handbell, upon which his valet appeared with another can of hot water. When he had poured it into the bath Napoleon lay back and shook his head, 'No. Pauline's courage while she was in danger there warmed my heart; but 'twould not be right to expose her to it again, and I've no wish that either of you should die of yellow fever. Besides, although you wear a Colonel's uniform you are no soldier in the true sense.'

Roger shrugged, 'You must admit that I have never failed you yet in any task you have set me.'

'That I admit.'

'Then why not appoint me Ambassador to some country, or make me your Pro-Consul in one of the territories under your rule?'

'There you certainly have an idea. But where? Yes, I have it. You speak English like a native and know the habits of those barbarous people well. When I have conquered their fog-ridden country I could make you Pro-Consul there.'

It was Roger's belief that Napoleon would never succeed in conquering Britain but, if Fate decreed that he should, whoever he appointed Pro-Consul there would have enormous powers for good or ill. Hateful as was the thought of ruling one's fellow countrymen in the name of a foreign power, Roger realized that in such a situation he could greatly alleviate the suffering of the people and might, by skilful planning, even succeed in restoring their freedom.

As the proferred appointment would be a princely one, he

said at once, '*Mon Général*, I am overwhelmed by your generosity. In such a situation I could give of my very best in serving you. But we have not conquered England yet. In the meantime, what are your wishes with regard to myself?'

'Madame Leclerc is only recently a widow. It would be most indecorous for her to marry again before her year of mourning is up, and that will not be until November.'

'That I appreciate,' Roger replied. 'I assume then for the next few months you will desire me to continue as your liaison officer with Berthier on the invasion project?'

Napoleon considered for a moment, then he said, 'No. If you are to act as Pro-Consul you will have command of all the forces that I may decide to leave in Britain to garrison the island and keep down its population. For that you should have knowledge of many matters of which you have so far had no experience—the strategic placing of units, the allocation of quarters, the distribution of supplies and rations, the state of health of your men and so on. You should, therefore, qualify for at least the rank of General of Division. I think I will send you to Davoust. He is an extremely conscientious and competent General. With your quick mind, you will learn under him in a comparatively short time how to become a real soldier. Go now, and send Méneval in to me, so that I can dictate a letter informing Davoust of my wishes concerning you.'

In a state of high elation Roger bowed himself out of the steamy bathroom. Contrary to his expectations his master had not roared with rage and put him under arrest. Instead he had raised no objection to his A.D.C. marrying his beautiful sister. True, it meant a four-month separation, which Pauline would take hard, but that was a small price to pay for such a great reward.

Presently Méneval emerged from the bathroom, sat down at a desk outside, penned the letter from the notes he had taken, sanded and sealed it, then handed it to Roger with a formal bow. 'The First Consul's orders are that you are to horse at once and deliver this personally into the hand of General Davoust.'

Roger returned the bow and marched off down the corridor. He thought it a little inconsiderate of Napoleon not to give him at least twenty four hours in which to have a last meeting with Pauline and tell her the splendid news; but he was used to his master considering a matter, deciding upon it, issuing his orders, expecting them to be obeyed immediately and dismissing the matter from his mind.

Back at *La Belle Etoile*, while his servant was packing his things and their horses were being saddled, he wrote Pauline a note. Being by long habit cautious, just in case his letter fell into the wrong hands, he did not like to put in writing that, although they must keep it secret, they were now virtually engaged, then go into rhapsodies about what the future held for them. Instead he wrote:

'I have seen him. All has gone beyond belief well. But I must qualify myself to hold a post that will give me a big income. At the least I'll be a General of Division by November. This means that I must spend the next four months with the Army. You will know what a terrible wrench it is for me to leave Paris; but think what this means on my return. Think, too, of Bordeaux, Pau, Nîmes and a little place by the sea. During my absence such scenes and the future will occupy all my thoughts. R.'

Having left it with Maître Blanchard to be given to Aimée when she made her daily call to pick up any note from Roger asking for a rendezvous with her mistress, he had a quick meal and set out, followed by his servant leading a third horse carrying the baggage.

Few people knew better than Roger the dispositions of the Army of the Coast of the Ocean, as it was now called. Its cantonments were spread over a vast area stretching from Antwerp right down to Le Havre. Flanders, Artois and Picardy swarmed with troops, while huge reserve formations were assembled at Utrecht, Ghent, St. Omer, Montreuil, Compiègne and St. Malo. At Boulogne alone there were fifty thousand men under the command of Soult, at Etaples thirty thousand under Ney and at Bruges another thirty thousand under Davoust; so it was to the ancient Flemish town, with

267

its old gabled houses, canals and grassy ramparts, that Roger rode in the summer sunshine.

General Davoust, to whom he reported, was a strange character. A Burgundian aristocrat by birth, he had been a junior lieutenant in the Royal Champagne Regiment at the outbreak of the Revolution. Unsociable by nature and holding Republican views, he had led a mutiny, been cashiered for it and imprisoned for six weeks. The triumph of the Third Estate had soon led to his reinstatement as an officer and his rising to the rank of Lieutenant-Colonel; but later he had again been deprived of his commission, this time by the Jacobins on account of his aristocratic birth. Then, under the Directory, he had emerged once more, as a Brigadier in Moreau's Army of the Rhine.

In '98 he had been sent to Egypt. As a 'Moreau man' and a staunch Republican, he had regarded Bonaparte with dislike and distrust, and consorted with the little clique of senior officers who were always criticizing their General-in-Chief. Then had come the Battle of Aboukir. There, Davoust had been given a reserve formation, of which Bonaparte made no use during the battle. Afterwards Davoust had demanded an interview with the object of making a bitter complaint that he and his men had been slighted. The interview was a long one and no one ever learned what had been said between the two. But Davoust had emerged from it a changed man.

Previously he had been uncouth in manner and slovenly in his dress; from that day he became a stickler for courtesy and smartness. Henceforth he took Bonaparte as his model in everything, gave him absolute devotion and studied his methods of waging war with such assiduity that, having a fine brain, he later became the ablest of all Napoleon's Marshals.

But he was a dour, hard man, with few friends and many enemies—particularly Bernadotte, whom he hated for his intrigues against Napoleon. He loved no one except his wife, to whom he showed the most tender feelings, and he had no interests outside his duties. He took great care of his men, but was the harshest disciplinarian of all the Generals, being

268

especially severe with his senior officers, all of whom loathed him. Roger knew him only slightly, but enough of his reputation to wish himself posted elsewhere.

Having read Napoleon's letter, Davoust gave Roger a cold smile and said, 'The First Consul has ordered me to instil into you the rudiments of soldiering. These are usually acquired by having served for a period in the ranks; but he does not desire that I should temporarily deprive you of your commission. He feels that the desired end can be achieved by your joining my Endurance Course for junior officers who show promise. You will appreciate that for you to do so with your present rank would be most unsuitable; so while you are under my command you will revert to that of Lieutenant and, of course, you will not use your A.D.C.'s sash.'

With every word the General uttered Roger's heart sank further into his boots. Going pale with rage, he burst out:

'General, I am confident that the First Consul never . . .'

'Silence!' snapped Davoust. 'And if I do not have a good report of you, Lieutenant, you will have cause to rue it. You may go.'

Roger had seen summary discipline exercised in the French army too often to become defiant. Almost choking with fury, he saluted, turned sharply on his heel and went.

An adjutant took charge of him. Half an hour later the Headquarters tailor had changed his Colonel's rank badges for those of a Lieutenant and he had been deprived of his servant, who was put on general fatigues. He was then conducted across the town to a big building that had formerly been a school. There he was handed over to a short, gimlet-eyed Major of Infantry, named Gaudin, who was the Chief Instructor of the Course.

Gaudin asked him a few questions about himself. Feeling it to be pointless and even dangerous to disclose the reason for his having been sent to Bruges, Roger said only that he had served on the Staff in Egypt and more recently with the Paris Headquarters of the Army of the Coast.

Under the Major's black, upturned moustache his mouth

269

took on a sneer, 'I see. Then you have put a foot wrong somewhere and been sent here to be disciplined. As we poor fellows have to fight the wars, most of the time half-starved, while you Staff people loll about at Headquarters stuffing yourselves with the fat of the land, it will give me special pleasure to have you on my Course. Go through that door on your left and report to Captain Adott, the instructor in charge of B Company. I can trust him to put you through the hoop.'

Captain Adott proved to be a huge Dragoon with a manner and vocabulary which made it obvious that he had been an N.C.O. in the old Republican Army. He, too, asked a few questions, then clearly thought it a grand joke to have anyone like Roger in his Company.

The classrooms in the building had been converted into dormitories and the unhappy Roger got his first glimpse of what was meant by 'Endurance Course' when he saw that the close-ranged beds consisted of three planks apiece with no bedding and only a single blanket.

Soon after he had been allotted one, his new companions swarmed into the room. A few of them showed a vague interest in him as a newcomer; but the rest were too tired to do anything but lie at full length on their planks, and he was in no mood to talk. Half an hour later a bugle sounded and, pulling themselves together, they trooped down a corridor to the Company dining hall. Supper consisted of Army biscuits and an ill-cooked stew of vegetables.

When Roger commented sourly on this sparse fare, the young man next to him replied, 'It is as much as one can expect to get while living off the land during a campaign, and I don't suppose we'll do any better when we land in England.'

He passed a hideous night, turning restlessly on his plank bed, with only his uniform for a pillow. Had Napoleon been at hand Roger would cheerfully have killed him for having played him this scurvy trick. For a while he contemplated creeping out, finding a horse and making his escape; but the thought of Pauline restrained him. Napoleon had as good as promised her to him so, for her sake, he must somehow put up with this martyrdom.

A bugle call roused them at five o'clock. Hastily pulling on their outer garments, they ran out into the big yard and lined up for their first parade of the day. There followed half an hour's violent exercise during which they were required to throw themselves down, heave themselves up, then jump high in the air. Next came early morning stables and, while Roger was an excellent horseman, he loathed having to groom a horse himself. Before breakfast, another meal of biscuits and vegetable stew, they were given half an hour to shave in a crowded washroom and clean themselves up. There was then an inspection by the gimlet-eyed Major and Roger was awarded seven days' fatigues for no apparent reason.

Instead of the technical instruction about supplying and administering large bodies of troops, that Roger had expected to receive, he found himself for fifteen hours a day being drilled on a barrack square, ordered off on twenty-five-mile route marches without water, and sent for cross-country runs from which the last ten men in were penalized by having to get up at four in the morning and clean out the latrines. In the riding school they had to trot without stirrups and jump hurdles bareback, while cynical N.C.O.s flicked their mounts with long whips until they became almost unmanageable. There were sessions of bayonet fighting, wrestling and swimming in the noisome canals until half of them were sick from the stench of the sewage with which houses on the banks fouled the water. Grimly, Roger stuck it, now falling asleep exhausted each night on his plank bed. And in one way he earned the respect of his fellow sufferers. He was a superb swordsman and soon found that in the fencing school no one could touch him. So, after he had been in Bruges a week he challenged the giant Captain Adott to a bout. The tough ex-sergeant was a fine blade and his strength made him a formidable opponent, but Roger got the better of him and he handsomely admitted it. After that, life for Roger became a little easier; but there was no escaping the daily drills, the constant exertions and the monotonous, unsatisfying food.

271

His rancour against Napoleon gradually subsided, for he had come to the conclusion that the First Consul's idea had been that, before he commanded troops, he should learn to appreciate the hardships they suffered during an arduous campaign. And the thought of his beautiful Pauline waiting for him in Paris enabled him to endure these weeks of physical fatigue and acute discomfort.

The officers on the course came and went, usually rejoining their units after a period of a month. None of those engaged on it had a moment to read a journal, so the only news they received from the outside world was from newcomers. It was early in September that one of these remarked one evening to Roger, 'That Prince Borghese is a lucky fellow. Just think what a night one could have going to bed with Pauline Bonaparte.'

Roger stiffened as though a ramrod had been thrust down his gullet and demanded, 'What the devil do you mean?'

'Why, don't you know,' replied his companion with a smile. 'Although she is only ten months a widow, she married this Italian Prince towards the end of August. On the 23rd, I think.'

Utterly staggered by this casual statement, Roger remained absolutely still for a moment. He felt sure that it could not possibly be true; but he had to make certain. Without a word he stood up, went along to the Instructors' Mess and asked to be allowed to look through some of the journals. By that time he had come to be regarded as quite a good fellow who had been kicked off the Staff only because he had antagonized some General; so permission was readily accorded him.

Shuffling swiftly through the numbers of *Le Moniteur* for the last week in August, he soon came upon an announcement that he could still hardly believe but had half feared to find. There it was in black and white; 'Marriage of the First Consul's sister, Madame Leclerc, to the millionaire Italian Prince, Camillo Borghese.'

Almost physically sick at the thought of the way in which Pauline had betrayed him after all he had endured for her sake, he left the Mess and stood for a few minutes outside in the passage. Rage welled up in him, taking the place of disgust, then sudden determination.

Davoust was completely merciless, and even took pleasure in signing death warrants for wrongdoers. He spent half his time having British spies, with whom the coast swarmed, hunted down and hanged; and any deserter from his army who was caught could be certain of facing a firing squad. Regardless of the fact he was risking his life, Roger walked out to the stables, went straight to the stall in which stood the best officer's charger and saddled, bridled and mounted her. He could stand no more. Come hell or high water he meant to confront in Paris the brother and sister who had used him so ill and call them to account.

CHAPTER XIX

BLACKMAIL

THE OFFICERS on the course were allowed only one pass a week to spend an evening in the town; so as Roger rode through the gate the picket on duty shouted at him, asking where he was going on horseback. With the resource that had become second nature to him, he forced a grin and replied:

'To Paris, of course. I've a young woman there who is expecting me. 'Twill make a pleasant evening's ride.'

Paris being some hundred and eighty miles distant, the young officer doing picket duty that night thought it a huge joke, gave a loud guffaw and waved him on.

By midnight Roger was in Lille, where he slept, and next night at Estreés-St Denis. On the second afternoon after leaving Bruges he entered Paris. At *La Belle Etoile* he enjoyed his first bath for two months and rid himself of the lice and bedbugs that had been a torment to him.

Dressed in civilian clothes he went out that evening and, regardless of consequences, called at the Hôtel de Charost, where he enquired for Aimée. The footman on the door fetched a haughty major-domo who regarded Roger with surprise but, judging from his clothes and manner that he was a man to be obeyed, he despatched the footman to the rear of the house. A few minutes later he returned with Pauline's plump, pretty little maid.

At the sight of Roger her eyes went round with apprehension and she gave a little gasp. But he smiled at her, led her to the far end of the great empty hall, where they were well out of earshot of the footman and slipped two gold pieces into her hand. Then he said in a low voice:

'Aimée, I am anxious to congratulate your mistress on having become a Princess; but you will understand that I would prefer to do so in private. Can you suggest a time that would be suitable for you to take me to her?'

For a moment Aimée hesitated, then she replied, 'There'll be no better opportunity than the present, *Monsieur le Colonel*, as His Highness is out dining with some gentlemen. But I dare not. I dare not. 'Twould lose me my place.'

Roger first pressed into her now unwilling palm two more gold pieces, then he produced from the top of his breeches a short, sharp knife, and said with a smile, 'Be not afraid. You have been a good friend and I would not harm you for the world. But you can tell your mistress that I threatened to cut your throat with this, if you refused to take me to her.'

The girl gave a sudden half-hysterical laugh, '*Grâce Dieu*, you are the very devil of a man. I've always thought so, and that you'd stick at nothing to gain your ends. I'll do it then; but first you must swear to me that you will not harm her.'

'No, I mean to do no more than lash her with my tongue for her infidelity to me.'

Aimée shook her head, 'She has deserved that, and to my mind has made herself a poor bargain. I suppose it means a lot to her to be called "Your Highness," but I wouldn't let her weakling of a Prince share my bed, however much he offered me. Come then, *mon Colonel*, I'll take you to her; but point your dagger at my back as we go into her room.'

She led him up the broad pillared staircase, across a lofty landing and into a blue and gold boudoir. Pauline was sitting at the far end clothed in filmy draperies. The only light in the room came from a wall bracket holding candles beneath which she was sitting reading.

Turning her head she asked, 'What is it, Aimée?' Then in the dim light she recognized Roger, dropped her book and came to her feet.

At the same moment Roger flashed his knife, so that Pauline caught the glint of steel, and snapped at Aimée, 'You may leave us now. Should you rouse the house I'll seek you out, and I've told you what will happen to you.'

Aimée backed away and swiftly closed the door behind her. Most women in Pauline's situation would have been seized with fear that Roger, having forced his way in, intended to inflict a bloody vengeance on them. But a smile suddenly dawned on her lovely face and she cried, 'Oh, Rojé, what a joy it is to see you.'

Taken aback by her greeting, he put up his dagger, frowned and replied, 'I am surprised to hear you say so, after your treatment of me.'

She shrugged, 'You mean my marriage. But you abandoned me; so you cannot blame me for that.'

'Abandoned you! *Nom d'un nom*! I've served two months in prison and was ready to serve two more, so that we might be permanently reunited in November. And what do I find? In August, before even your twelve months of mourning were up, you have married another.'

'I heard only that you had left Paris, and that without a word to me. I assure you that for some weeks I was utterly disconsolate.'

'Did you not get my letter?'

'No; to whom did you give it?'

'To my landlord at *La Belle Etoile*, for Aimée. I wrote to let you know that Napoleon had as good as promised me your hand, but decreed that I must spend the time of waiting experiencing what the troops go through; so that when I had married you I should be fitted for a post as Governor-General.'

She shrugged. 'I never received your letter. And you must be aware of the duplicity of which Napoleon is capable at

276

times. Clearly he never intended us to marry and adopted these means of getting rid of you. It seems, too, that he had you watched and, somehow, intercepted your letter to me.'

Roger could not believe that either Maître Blanchard or Aimée had betrayed him; but the landlord was a busy man, so it was possible that he had given the note to a potman to hand to Aimée and that, before Aimée had come to the inn, some police spy had bought it from the potman.

'Whether or not you received my note,' he cried angrily, 'you could have gone to your brother, enquired my whereabouts and communicated with me.'

Pauline stamped her foot, 'Rojé, you are unjust. You left me stranded and with the impression that you had run away because you were too frightened of Napoleon to ask him for my hand. I am not made to live like a nun and Borghese pressed his suit with all the ardour of an Italian.'

'So you fell in love with him?'

'No, oh no! It was the emeralds he offered me. They are the finest in Europe. I must show them to you. I simply could not resist them. But that bitch Josephine! Would you believe it, she had the walls of a room specially repainted turquoise in which to receive me on the first occasion that she knew I would wear them on going to Court. The colour killed that of the stones utterly. I was so furious that I could have scratched her eyes out.'

Roger sighed. What was he to do with this magnificently-beautiful but utterly inconsequent creature? After a moment he asked, 'And Borghese? What sort of a husband does he make?'

'Oh, terrible! I've been an utter fool. I don't think he is attracted by men, but he is practically a neuter. I am as starved of love as when we first met in Bordeaux.'

Suddenly she advanced on Roger and threw her arms round his neck. As he felt her warm, thinly clad body pressed against his own he was conscious of a swift upsurge of passion and clasped her to him.

With a low laugh she murmured in his ear, 'Borghese will not be back for hours yet; and when he does return it is certain that he'll go straight to his own room. Oh Rojé, how good it is to feel your strong arms about me again. I want you, Rojé. I want you desperately.'

Two minutes later he was in her bedroom with the door locked behind them.

In the early hours of the morning Aimée smuggled him downstairs and out into the street through a door in the garden wall that led into the Champs Elysées.

That day Roger lay long abed contemplating his position with very mixed feelings. All prospect of marrying Pauline was now gone, and with it that of some well-endowed post as a member of the Bonaparte family. On consideration he decided that the latter was more to be regretted than the former. He had never been afraid of work or of taking responsibility, so he would have enjoyed using his talents as the Viceroy of some French-dominated territory; whereas Pauline's light-mindedness and instability of character might have caused him many irritations if he had married her; and she was now, once again, his mistress.

It was as clear as crystal that she had married the Roman Prince only for his title, his family jewels and because he was so rich she could indulge to her heart's content in every kind of extravagance.

She had told Roger that, on the rare occasions Borghese did come to her, it was always before midnight; so at that hour Aimée could safely let Roger in by the door in the garden wall and bring him to her. If at any time there was a risk of his being caught in her room, he could go out on to the balcony and clamber down into the garden. With his happy memories of their tour through Navarre and Provence, and stay at St. Maxime, this opened a prospect that half the men in France would have envied him. But there was another side to his return to Paris which was far from being so satisfactory.

Napoleon had evidently never had the least intention of letting him marry Pauline and, instead of saying so frankly, had used his guile both to break up the *affaire* and to prevent it from developing into a scandal. No doubt his ambition had been gratified by his sister marrying a millionaire Prince and he had derived considerable amusement at having rid himself of his troublesome A.D.C. in a way that should teach him not to be presumptuous. But what was he going to say when he learned not only that Roger had returned to Paris but had also, as his police would soon find out, again become Pauline's lover? Added to which there was the most unpleasant fact that by this time Davoust would have had 'Lieutenant' Breuc posted as absent without leave.

After much thought, Roger dressed in civilian clothes, called a sedan chair and had himself carried round to the Rue du Bec. Having waited for well over an hour in an ante-room, he was received by Talleyrand. Gracious as ever, the Minister rose from his big desk, extended a perfectly-manicured hand and said:

'*Cher ami,* you must forgive me for keeping you waiting but, try as I will, I simply cannot avoid sometimes having to attend to affairs of State. Where have you been all this time, and why are you not wearing your beautiful uniform?'

Sitting down in a gilt Louis Quinze elbow chair, Roger crossed his long legs, gave a rueful smile and replied, 'The First Consul decided that I should be taught the rudiments of soldiering, so sent me to Davoust's school for young officers at Bruges.'

Talleyrand raised his eyebrows, 'So that is where you were. Not a very pleasant experience, I imagine. But I did hear a rumour that he had sent you out of Paris because he was annoyed by your attentions to a certain lady.'

Roger grinned, 'So you know about that. I might have guessed it.'

'The lady happens to be one of a dozen or so about whose—er—activities I find it useful to keep myself informed. Her marriage must, I fear, have been something of a blow to you. But she was so set on it that she refused even to wait until her period of mourning was over; and Napoleon, fancying himself as the brother-in-law of a Prince, was persuaded to give way to her.'

'Well, it is a *fait accompli*; and on account of it I've

landed myself in a fine mess. When I learned of her marriage I was so infuriated that I took horse and rode straight to Paris; so I am a deserter or, at least, absent without leave.'

'The devil you are! That is no laughing matter. What stupid things we do on account of women. Really there are times when I feel it would be wiser to become a Trappist monk and be done with them for good. But I simply could not live without these silly creatures.'

'Nor I,' Roger agreed. 'Of course, what I ought to have done was to write to Napoleon and say that now the cause for his sending me out of Paris was removed, would he give me leave to return here? As things are, when he is informed by that awful man Davoust that I've deserted he will be furious.'

'You must see him and endeavour to put yourself right with him before he hears from Davoust.'

'I should have done so yesterday but I missed my chance. As he charged Davoust in a personal letter to put me through the mill, I count it certain that by this morning a despatch from the General reporting my disappearance will have reached him. If I present myself, the odds are that his Captain of the Guard already has an order to arrest me and send me back to Bruges.'

'That would mean a court-martial and your complete ruin. Your only chance is somehow to persuade Napoleon to see you, complain of his harsh treatment of you, declare that he has punished you enough, and plead your past services to induce him to call off Davoust.'

'I entirely agree. And that is why I am here. Would it be asking too much that you should speak to him on my behalf and induce him to give me a hearing?'

Talleyrand considered for a moment, 'Out of friendship alone I will do that; and in any case I consider you too valuable a man to be deprived for good of a place near him, if that can be prevented. I think, too, that you had best send for some things and remain here for the night. If Davoust's courier has arrived in Paris this morning, an order for your arrest may already have been issued. If so, the odds are that the Provost Marshal will go straight to *La Belle Etoile* as the first place to look for you. I will take you with me to the Tuileries tomorrow. But, should Napoleon consent to see you, I would not count on his restoring you to his good graces. Desertion is a crime that you may be sure he will not look upon leniently.'

Roger made a grimace, 'I know it; but if I can see him at least I will have some chance of mitigating his anger.' He then thanked his friend most gratefully for the help he had promised to give him and, a few minutes later, Talleyrand sent for his steward to tell him that Roger would be staying there that night.

That evening the Foreign Minister had first to attend a reception then a ball; so Roger dined alone and spent the time browsing through some of the beautifully-bound books in the library. Next morning there was a breakfast for eight at which many of the topics of the day were eagerly debated; but Roger's mind was so taken up with wondering whether he would be free or a prisoner by dinner time that, though he smiled automatically at the witticisms uttered by the others, he hardly took in what they were talking about.

At midday he accompanied Talleyrand in his coach to the Tuileries. In Napoleon's antechamber there was the usual crowd of Ministers, Generals and functionaries waiting to be received in audience. Several of them smiled at Roger and asked him where he had been. Anxious to avoid being drawn into conversation, he only returned their bows and replied that he had just come back from the coast.

The twenty-minute wait seemed to him interminable; but at last an usher, with a list in his hand, called out Talleyrand's name. Roger had expected the Minister to go in and plead his cause while he went through another ten minutes or more of agonizing suspense. But Talleyrand transferred his cane to his other hand, smiled at him and said, '*Mon cher Colonel*, be kind enough to give me your arm.' And next minute they were walking towards the great double doors.

Instantly Roger realized how skilfully the great diplomat was handling this difficult situation. If Napoleon was in one of his black moods the very mention of Roger's name might result in a peremptory refusal to see him, and lead to an order for his immediate arrest; but he was not going to be given a chance to refuse. For at least a moment Roger would be face to face with him—but, possibly, only for a moment.

The big doors were thrown open. There fell a sudden silence in the ante-room. In a loud voice the usher announced, 'Monsieur de Talleyrand-Perigord, Minister of State for Foreign Affairs,' then his mouth opened again to call out Roger's name; but with a swift, imperious gesture Talleyrand motioned him to silence.

Napoleon was standing with his hands clasped behind his back looking out of a window. The doors closed with a gentle swish. In his beautifully-modulated voice, Talleyrand said:

'First Consul, I am fortunate this morning. I bring you an old friend of ours whom I chanced to see outside the Palace on the bank of the Seine. He told me that he was in such despair that he intended to throw himself into the river. Knowing that his loss would grieve you deeply I insisted that he should give you the opportunity of restoring his faith in humanity.'

At Talleyrand's first words Napoleon had swung round. He stared at Roger for a moment then opened his mouth to speak, but before he could do so the Minister added smoothly, 'Colonel Breuc has refused to confide his troubles to me, so it would embarrass him if I remained. My business can wait until you have comforted him.' He already had a hand behind him on the door knob. Giving it a twist and a quick push, he bowed himself backwards out of the room.

It was a brilliant *démarche* and Roger took swift advantage of it. Looking angrily at Napoleon he asked in a bitter voice, 'Seeing the way you have treated me since last we met, can you be surprised that I was about to take my life?'

'Psst!' Napoleon made an angry gesture. 'What nonsense! Surely you did not expect that I meant to give you my sister?'

'You led me to suppose so. Then having got rid of me,

pushed her into marrying this Italian Prince. What a way to behave!'

'I did nothing of the sort! I even tried to dissuade her from marrying him until the end of the year. But she forced me to give my consent by telling me that the ardour of this Italian had led to her letting him get her with child.'

Roger suppressed a gasp; for if Pauline had been in the family way it must have been he who was responsible. But she had made no mention of that, so had evidently since got herself out of that trouble. After a moment he said:

'Nevertheless you gave your consent to her marriage, and so spoiled for good our chances of happiness. And you prepared the way most skilfully, leading her to believe that I had deserted her by stealing the letter I wrote her after I last saw you.'

'Letter! What letter! I have more important things to do than steal other people's *billets doux*!'

'Your police intercepted it. They must have, as it never reached her. You'll not deny that you set them to spy on me and make certain I left Paris.'

'Of course. I gave orders that in no circumstances were you to be allowed to enter the Hôtel de Charost. Had you openly appeared there to take leave of Pauline it would have been certain to end in a lovers' parting that would have set the servants' tongues wagging. You might even have declared yourself her fiancé. I should have been mad not to take precautions against your doing something of the kind.'

'I might have. I loved her desperately, and had the right to. But out of respect for you, I refrained. And what was my reward for behaving honourably towards you? You had me reduced to the rank of Lieutenant and put through a more brutal course of training than is inflicted on any raw, rebellious conscript.'

Napoleon gave a short, harsh laugh, 'That was no more than you deserved for holding your head too high. And it is still too high! I'll not have you attempt to browbeat me in this fashion. Such leave as General Davoust gave you is cancelled from this minute. You will return to Bruges immediately.'

'Have you not then received a despatch from the General this morning?' Roger asked with a pale smile.

'No. Why should I have? What had he urgent to communicate to me?'

'Only that I never asked for leave, but had simply taken it.'

'What!' Napoleon's eyes grew black with anger. 'D'you mean you actually dared to leave Bruges without permission?'

Roger's dark blue eyes blazed back into those of his master, 'Dare!' he cried. 'Surely you know me well enough to realize that having risked my life for you a dozen times I'd not hesitate to dare anything on my own account? On learning of Pauline's marriage I took horse at once for Paris. And how can you blame me? Since you'd gained your end and married her off to this Italian, how could it longer serve you to keep me in slavery at Bruges? Naturally, I returned expecting you to reinstate me; but this morning I was seized with a morbid fit and decided that you were a master not worth serving, so I would make an end of myself.'

'Do you realize that you have laid yourself open to a court martial?'

'Of course. But whatever you may do to me, I now have at least the consolation of knowing that Pauline still loves me.'

'And how do you know that?'

'Because on arriving in Paris I at once sought an explanation with her, and we spent last night together.'

'You ... you!' Napoleon stammered, his eyes bulging. 'You actually had the audacity to ... to ....'

'Why not? She loves me, and I had the right to.'

'*Mon Dieu*, your insolence knows no bounds. I'll have you court martialled for desertion and that will be the end of you.'

'Do, if it pleases you,' Roger sneered. 'First you plan to wreck the happiness of your favourite sister and a man who would have made her an excellent husband, then you decide to ruin the career of one of your most faithful servants. People will not think so well of you when they learn how you have treated your poor brother-in-law.'

'Brother ... brother-in-law,' Napoleon stared at him. 'What the devil do you mean?'

Roger shrugged, 'You will admit that when faced with an unexpected situation you are apt to be hasty in your judgments?'

'What of it?'

'Well; when Pauline and I returned from our little, er—journey, we thought it wiser not to spring it upon you, but to ask your consent to our marriage and go through another ceremony later here in Paris.'

'Another ceremony!' Napoleon gasped, having gone white to the lips.

'Yes. Of course we were commendably discreet and purposely selected the Mayor of a tiny Commune to marry us, so that news of it should not get about.'

'I ... I don't believe it.'

Again Roger shrugged. 'You have only to tell that idiot Savary, whom you have made Chief of Police, to send one of his agents down to St. Maxime. He will then report to you that for a month Pauline lived with me openly at my château as Madame Breuc. Somewhat to our embarrassment the villagers, headed by the Mayor and Curé, came to present us with an address of welcome. Of course they did not know Pauline was whom she was; but they soon will if you start to stir up trouble.'

'But ... but this means that Pauline's marriage to Prince Borghese is null and void. She has committed bigamy.'

Now really beginning to enjoy himself, Roger nodded, 'I fear that is the case. Unfortunately Pauline is not gifted with your brains. Greatly as I adore her one must admit that she takes life very lightly. Owing to your machinations she thought that I had gone out of her life for good, and I had great difficulty last night in convincing her that by her hasty marriage to Borghese she had committed a form of crime. Of course, in the bad old days of the Revolution it would not have been of much consequence and you could somehow have wriggled her out of it. But I fear you have cooked your own goose by arranging the Concordat with Rome. The Pope would have given you a dispensation for her before she married again, but he cannot do that afterwards. So if I claim my wife publicly, as I now feel inclined to, there seems little that you can do about it, and poor Pauline will have to pay for her stupidity by burying herself with me somewhere in the country.'

'You ... you devil!' Napoleon stormed, froth beginning to appear on his lips. 'But there is a remedy for this. I'll have you taken in a closed carriage to Vincennes and thrown into a dungeon. There you may talk as you will; the gaolers will suppose you only to be a madman.'

'And what of the glorious Revolution?' Roger gave a bitter laugh. 'Do I see in you another Louis XV about to sign a *lettre de cachet*? How unfortunate for you that the mob pulled down the Bastille in '89; so that you cannot follow tradition fully and send me to it.'

'Vincennes will serve well enough,' gasped Napoleon.

'To hold me prisoner,' Roger sneered, 'but not to ensure your peace of mind. How can you suppose that I did not resent the treatment meted out to me at Bruges on your orders? I spent this morning writing letters to men, several of whom are your worst enemies, telling the truth about myself and Pauline. I have made arrangements that should I not be reinstated on your personal staff within a week, those letters are to be despatched to their destinations, which include the Russian, Prussian and Austrian Ambassadors, and His Holiness the Pope. Now, arrest me if you dare!'

The froth from Napoleon's mouth dribbled down his chin. His eyes bulged, he gulped for air. Suddenly he lurched forward.

He would have measured his length on the floor had not Roger caught him just in time. Lifting his rigid body into a chair, Roger stepped back a pace and stared at him in near panic. He felt sure that his master's intense rage had resulted in an epileptic fit. The clenched teeth, open, turned-up eyes and purple face were all evidence of it. But what to do?

His immediate impulse was to call for help. But that would bring the crowd in the anteroom streaming in, and all France getting to know that the First Consul was an epileptic. On the other hand, to remain there alone with him could have appalling consequences. If, in the next few moments, he died Roger would be held responsible for his death. The quarrel between them was certain to come to light, then public indignation would demand a trial and an execution. But to prevent his weakness from becoming generally known would be a sure way to earn his gratitude. Taking one of the biggest gambles of his life, Roger sloshed some water from a carafe into a glass and threw it in Napoleon's face, then slapped him hard.

After a few moments Napoleon's limbs began to jerk, his features lost their rigidity and he struggled into a sitting position in the chair. Regarding him anxiously, Roger asked, 'Shall I send for your doctor?'

Feebly the stricken man shook his head, 'No, no! ... You ... you did right to restore me yourself. No one must know that I ... I occasionally suffer from these fits.'

For a full minute they remained silent, then Napoleon drew a long breath and said, 'Breuc, I have treated you ill. I admit it. For me to give you Pauline was too much to ask. But ... but you have proved that you can be a terrible enemy as well as a good friend. That we have been at loggerheads is as much your fault as mine. You should have told me of this secret marriage. I love my sister, so I would go to great lengths to protect her from the results of her folly. For her to be adjudged a bigamist would be a terrible thing. Can I rely on you to keep this secret?'

Roger nodded, 'Yes, *mon Général*. For I love her too. And what is done is done. There'd be no sense in bringing grief to all of us on account of it.'

'Then you may resume your place here as one of my A.D.C.s and, well ... I'll think of some way of compensating you for what you went through at Bruges.'

'It has done me no harm and I have learned now what

287

your soldiers suffer when on a campaign; so I need no compensation other than one thing.'

'What is it?'

'That you will not allow your police to interfere between myself and Pauline. We love one another, and we have already arranged a way in which we can assuage our desire to be together without Borghese coming to know of it.'

'Very well then. I gather that in spite of the Prince's fine appearance he is little good to a woman; so it's certain that if it were not you Pauline would soon take some other lover. Since you have proved yourself to be discreet, I'd as lief it was you than some new fancy of hers who might prove boastful and make trouble between her and her husband.'

For the first time during their interview Roger smiled with real pleasure. He had lied like a trooper about his having married Pauline; but their having lived at St. Maxime for a month as man and wife provided a sound basis for his story. He intended to tell Pauline that, should Napoleon question her about her marriage, she was to tell him that she had forgotten the name of the little Commune in which the ceremony was supposed to have taken place; so he thought it most unlikely that his lie would ever be found out.

Napoleon came unsteadily to his feet, extended his hand and said, 'Then let us regard bygones as bygones.'

Roger took it and replied, '*Mon Général*, I thank you. You know well that at any time I would cheerfully die for you.'

Returning his smile, Napoleon lifted his hand in the familiar gesture as though to pull Roger's ear; then it dropped to his side and he said wearily, 'Yes. I believe you would. Go now. I do not feel equal to receiving anyone else this morning. Tell all those people outside that I have just received a despatch that needs my immediate consideration, and get rid of them.'

As Roger was not in uniform he did not salute. Drawing himself up, he cried, '*Mon Général*, to hear is to obey.' Then, swinging on his heel, he marched triumphant from the room.

That evening he thanked Talleyrand for his brilliant intervention, and when he had told the whole story they laughed together over the way Napoleon had been fooled and blackmailed.

Soon after midnight Roger was outside the gate in the wall of the garden behind the Borghese mansion. Aimée let him in and took him up to her mistress.

After they had been nearly eating one another with voracious kisses he told Pauline about his interview with her terrible brother. At first she was horrified that he should have been told that she had committed bigamy. But Roger pointed out that she could be certain that he would never mention it to anyone; so the lie would go no further. She then held him away from her at arm's length, smiled at him, gave a sigh and said:

'Rojé, what a man you are! What other would have dared first to defy him, then have so skilfully brought him to heel? And he'll not now seek to interfere between us. What a triumph. Oh, I am so proud of you.'

Next day, once more wearing his Colonel's uniform, Roger reported at the Tuileries. Napoleon showed no signs at all of the epileptic fit that had struck him down the day before, and was as usual displaying his dynamic energy in dealing with innumerable problems.

The following week Roger accompanied him on a tour of inspection of several of the seven Army Corps that had been assembled for the invasion of England. They did not go as far north as Hanover, where Bernadotte commanded the First Corps, or Utrecht, where Marmont had the Second, or as far south as Brest, where Augereau was stationed with the Seventh. But at the Headquarters of the Third at Bruges, Roger had the satisfaction of enquiring politely of the sour Davoust whether he had had any deserters shot lately. At Boulogne, Soult had the Fourth Corps and, being a great devotee of music, entertained them to a fine concert. The many times wounded but apparently unkillable Lannes had, the previous year, been packed off as Ambassador to Lisbon, because of the intense irritation he had caused Napoleon by continuing to 'thee' and 'thou' him familiarly—a habit now forbidden to even the oldest friends of the First Consul. But he was too fine a soldier to be left out of the invasion plans, so had been recalled to take command of the Fifth Corps at Calais, where they found him as bluff and foul-mouthed as ever. Red-headed Ney had the Sixth at Montreuil, Murat the Cavalry Corps and Bessiéres the Consular Guard.

They also toured long stretches of the Scheldt, Somme and Seine, for in every town and village along their banks—and those of the rivers Elbe and Weser as well—shipwrights brought from all parts of France were labouring night and day building the vast fleet of invasion barges that was to carry the 'Army of the Coast of the Ocean' across the Channel.

On their return to Paris there were other matters to be gone into that had already been put in train earlier that autumn. An American inventor named Fulton, a man of undoubted genius but uncertain sympathies—at one time he claimed that he would 'Deliver France and the world from British oppression' and a little later that Napoleon was 'A wild beast who ought to be hunted down'—had been busying himself on two projects. One was an adaptation of the steam vessel with which Henry Bell had filled all beholders with wonder and terror on the Clyde in 1800. The other was a forerunner of the modern submarine.

Fulton's first paddle steamer had been so ill constructed that during a gale it rid itself of the weight of its engine by breaking in half, but he had since made another that astonished the scientists of the Institute by chugging very slowly down the Seine. The submarine, or 'plunging boat' as it was termed, suffered the disability that, being a sailing vessel, as soon as it disappeared under water it lost all power to move forward. Admittedly it succeeded in discharging a form of torpedo into another small vessel and sinking it, but it certainly would have been blown to pieces before it could have done so had its victim been armed with a cannon.

Napoleon, like most wise military commanders, was extremely chary of changing any main type of armament while his country was at war because, although the new type might be an improvement on the old, the change-over involved great organisational difficulties and the troops had to be trained in handling it before it could be used effectively. So he could not be brought even to consider building a fleet of Fulton's steamboats for the invasion.

By that time his building programme of flat-bottomed barges was well advanced, and during the autumn Roger saw a letter of his to Admiral Gantheaume in which he said that he would soon have one thousand three hundred barges on the northern coast capable of carrying over one hundred thousand men, and another flotilla based on the Dutch ports that would transport a follow-up of a further sixty thousand.

The menace of an invading army of such a size would have made Roger tremble for the safety of his country had he believed that any great part of it would succeed in getting ashore. But Napoleon and his generals knew nothing of the tides, cross-currents and uncertainties of the English Channel, whereas Roger had spent countless days of his boyhood sailing from Lymington on yachts large and small up and down the coast; so he knew a great deal. It was, therefore, his firm opinion that even a moderate choppiness of the sea would make most of the troops in the cumbersome barges terribly seasick, that many of the barges would sink and all be extremely vulnerable to both the guns of the Royal Navy and those of the shore batteries.

During the autumn, whenever Roger was not on duty with his master, or being despatched on brief missions by him, he continued his delightful liaison with the unfailingly amorous Pauline, to the great pleasure and satisfaction of them both.

On several occasions he encountered her husband, Camillo Borghese, when attending receptions at the Tuileries, the Hôtel de Charost and other private mansions, and soon knew all about the Prince. He was twenty eight and an attractive man with large dark eyes. His estates in Italy were vast, but his education left much to be desired. He spoke French with a heavy accent and was incapable of writing even his own language correctly. Five years earlier, with the enthusiasm of youth for new ideas, he had espoused the Republican cause

291

in Rome. Accepting the doctrine of 'Liberty, Equality and Fraternity' without reserve he had, with other like-minded young nobles, thrown his coat of arms into a public bonfire, wherein Cardinals' hats were already blazing, and danced round it.

These antics had since been discreetly overlooked, and older members of his family had seen to it that he retained his vast possessions. His courtship of Pauline had been warmly approved by her mother, whose natural language and sympathies were Italian; and it was Madame Letizia who had pushed Napoleon into agreeing that Pauline should be allowed to marry Borghese before her twelve months of mourning had expired.

When in society Roger tactfully refrained from paying more attention to Pauline than to the other Bonaparte ladies and, secure in her passionate attachment to him, he could afford to make himself pleasant to the Prince. Meanwhile a furious strife was raging among the members of the Bonaparte family.

The idea had long been canvassed that to protect himself from assassination Napoleon should become an hereditary monarch and thus, having appointed a successor, ensure that his death would not lead to rival factions plunging France into civil war. As Napoleon had no son, all the Bonapartes were already at loggerheads over their claims to become his heir. Joseph, as the eldest, naturally asserted it to be his right. Lucien, the ex-Robespierreist, was now more eager to become an heir apparent than any of them and argued that, had it not been for the part he had played during the *coup-d'état* of *Brumaire*, Napoleon would never have become consul at all. The two younger brothers, Louis and Jerome, both put in bids. Then there were the children. Eliza had only a daughter, but both the ambitious Caroline and Pauline had sons. Louis, too, had a boy and Josephine did her utmost to persuade Napoleon to adopt him, because he was her grandson by Hortense. Last but not least there was her own son, Eugène de Beauharnais, who could not altogether be ignored owing to his having become a good soldier and because Napoleon was fonder of him than he was of any of his own brothers.

During the autumn, however, two of the claimants ruled themselves out. Jerome, now aged nineteen, had been put into the Navy and sailed to the West Indies. France, since the Louisiana settlement, having most friendly relations with the United States, young Jerome had had himself landed there and, as the First Consul's brother, been most handsomely received. In Baltimore he had met and married a Miss Elizabeth Patterson.

When Napoleon had learned of this he had become berserk with rage. Pauline having married a Prince had impressed upon him the heights to which he could raise his family now that, in all but title, he was a monarch; so he had intended that Jerome's wife should be nothing less than a Princess, and the wretched boy had spoilt this gratifying prospect by getting himself tied up to the daughter of an American merchant.

The case of Lucien, by far the cleverest but also the most pig-headed and troublesome of Napoleon's brothers, was even more deplorable. An habitual lecher, while Ambassador in Madrid, he had tried but failed to seduce a Spanish Infanta, and had then acquired the beautiful Marquesa de Santa Cruz as his mistress. On his return from Spain, to the fury of his sister Eliza who, after the death of his first wife, had enormously enjoyed acting as hostess for him, he had brought the Marquesa back with him and installed her as châtelaine in a château that he had taken just outside Paris.

Napoleon, regarding this as a temporary *affaire*, made no objection to it and, ever forgiving of the ungrateful way in which his family abused his generosity, endeavoured to make friends again with Lucien, then evolved a fine plan to further his fortunes. The young and incredibly stupid King of the newly created Kingdom of Etruria had died the previous May; why should not Lucien marry the widowed Queen and so become the son-in-law of the King of Spain, which would bind Spain still more firmly to the interests of France?

Meanwhile Lucien had got rid of the Marquesa and acquired a mistress with a most dubious reputation, named

293

Alexandrine Jouberton, the wife of a defaulting stock-jobber, and had installed her in a house in the Rue du Palais Bourbon. Then, at the end of October, when Napoleon approached him about marrying the Queen of Etruria he had calmly revealed that he had already been married for six months to Alexandrine; giving, of all things for such a man, as his reason that he had felt in honour bound to marry her because he had put her in the family way.

Napoleon's anger knew no bounds and he declared that as Jouberton was still alive the marriage could not be legal; but fate was against him because the defaulting broker had fled to San Domingo and, soon afterwards, it was learned that he had died there of yellow fever. Pleas and threats alike failed to induce Lucien to divorce the undesirable wife he had acquired and, supported by his mother, who always took his side, he declared that he would have no more to do with his autocratic brother and departed with his wife to live in Italy.

Napoleon, meanwhile, was taking, with the ladies of the theatre, such relaxation as he could snatch from his endless commitments. Little Mademoiselle George, honest, sweet-natured, unambitious, devoted, the perfect companion for a tired man, remained his favourite. But from time to time others were summoned, among them the superb actress Mademoiselle Mars and the pert, mentally agile Thérèse Bourgoin. The latter he took from his Minister of Finance, Chaptal, who had long kept her, to that elderly gentleman's fury and, not long afterwards, Thérèse's disgust; because she had given up a rich permanent lover for the mercurial Napoleon who, tiring of her rapacity, soon threw her aside.

The usual procedure was for Constant, Napoleon's valet, to collect these ladies from the theatre at which they were playing and conduct them in a coach, driven by the First Consul's faithful but notoriously drunken coachman, to St. Cloud. There Rustem, Napoleon's Mameluke bodyguard, took over, escorted them to a vast room with a bed in one corner and reported their arrival to his master; after which these delectable young ladies might wait for anything from ten minutes to four hours before being received by their host, according to what other matters might be occupying his immediate attention.

Josephine, of course, knew all about these goings-on and, occasionally, threw jealous scenes during which she wept copiously; but in the main she accepted them with resignation, on other nights reading Napoleon to sleep and consoling herself with his abiding affection for her.

Early in November Roger suffered a severe blow to his self-esteem. On the nights when he was able to visit Pauline in secret, which averaged about twice a week, it had become customary for him to undress in a small closet on the far side of Pauline's boudoir from her bedroom. On this occasion he had spent some two hours with her and returned to the closet to dress. The little room held only a marble basin, in which Aimée always left a covered jug of hot water for him, hooks on which to hang clothes and a shelf holding a few toilet things.

He was just about to blow out the candle and leave the room when he noticed among the scent bottles and powder jars a round pocket mirror. His attention was caught by the elaborate gold cipher on the leather back, and he recognized it at once as that which the flamboyant Murat had emblazoned a foot high on the doors of his coaches and carriages.

To come upon the little mirror in that particular place gave Roger furiously to think. But it was possible that on some occasion Pauline, finding that she had neglected to put her mirror in her reticule, had borrowed it from her vain brother-in-law and had forgotten to return it. Picking it up he walked across the boudoir into Pauline's bedroom and, as she sat up in bed for him to kiss her goodnight, he held it out to her and asked:

'How did you come by this pretty thing?'

Smothering a yawn, she replied sleepily, 'Oh, that is Joachim Murat's. He is always looking at himself in it and must have left it on the table in the boudoir when he was taking coffee with me this afternoon.'

By admitting that Murat had been there that day she had

given herself away; as there was no lavatory in the closet nor water, except that brought up by Aimée at night in a can. If he had wanted to wash he would have done so downstairs; so he could have used the closet only to undress in.

After a moment, Roger said, 'Drinking coffee was not the only thing you did together, was it? You see, I found this in the closet.'

'Oh dear!' Pauline sighed. 'How very careless of him to leave it there. He . . . he went in to . . . to, yes, fetch me some scent.'

'Stop lying.' he told her sharply. 'You keep all the scents you use yourself in your own bathroom. You went to bed with him, didn't you?'

Now wide awake and very flushed, she stammered, 'I . . . well . . . if you must know the truth, yes.'

'And he your sister's husband! '

'What has that to do with it?' she asked peevishly. 'Caroline goes to bed with lots of men, and would have with Leclerc if she had had half a chance. Camillo had ridden out to Chantilly to see a race horse he wants to buy; so was out of the way and . . . well, Joachim and I just felt like it.'

'I don't doubt he did. I remember hearing Napoleon once say of him, "Apparently Murat has to sleep with a woman every night but any woman does for him". But you! Damn it! And knowing that I was coming to you tonight! '

'Oh, Rojé, please don't be unreasonable. How could I refuse an old friend?'

'So this wasn't the first time?'

'No, oh no. The first time was years ago, when I was a girl at Montebello.'

'And how many other old friends have you?' Roger demanded angrily.

Becoming angry too, she snapped at him, 'Since you insist on prying into my affairs, quite a number. And I don't see what you have to complain about.'

'Don't you, indeed! I thought you loved me.'

'But I do. I put you before all others. I let you come to me any night you choose.'

296

'D'you mean that on the nights I don't, you have other men here?'

'Well, now and then. After all, when you have to go to the coast you are sometimes away for a week or more. You can't expect me not to have a little fun with someone else occasionally.' Suddenly she flung her arms round his neck and burst into tears.

Angry as he was, he could not bring himself to upbraid her further, and she clung to him until he said he would forgive her.

While walking back down the Champs Elysées across the Place de la Concord, then through the dark, older streets of Paris to *La Belle Etoile,* he sadly took stock of this new situation. Scandalous stories had come back from San Domingo about Pauline's immoralities while she was there—even that she had participated in orgies and had had a giant Negro as a lover. Those he still did not believe, but it was now beyond doubt that she was a nymphomaniac and so unable to control her sexual urges. He then admitted to himself that her attraction for him was solely a physical one, and that his distress was not really because he had a deep love for her but because his pride was hurt. There remained the question of whether he should break off the *affaire* or continue it knowing that she had other lovers.

Having slept upon it, he decided that since going to bed with her gave him so much pleasure, and he apparently held first place in her affections, to break with her would only be to cut off his nose to spite his face; so during the next week he went to her again on two occasions, both of them tacitly ignoring the scene they had had after her revelation that he was not her only lover.

Yet fate decreed that their liaison should shortly be brought to an abrupt termination. One night near the middle of November, when Aimée took him up to Pauline's room he found her in the depths of depression. Borghese had for some time tired of Paris and wanted to return to his own palace in Rome. Pauline had told him to go if he wished but that she had no intention of accompanying him. Loath to leave her behind, Borghese had spoken to Napoleon and he had written to her from Boulogne. In his letter he said that she must go with her husband and at once, as otherwise snow would make the Alps impassable. There had followed injunctions to 'love her husband, be respectful to his relatives, conform to the customs of the country, admire everything, never say "in Paris we have better than that", show attachment to the Holy Father, receive only people of unblemished reputation and never the English, etc., etc., and above all not to be wanton or capricious.' The lecture ended by pointing out that she was twenty-four so ought now to be mature and sensible. In fact she was barely twenty-three, but that did not make the letter any less an order that must be obeyed.

Packing had started, the house was already upside down and arrangements had been made for the Borgheses to set out for Italy in three days' time. Roger did his best to console Pauline, but he was able to make her forget that she was being driven into exile only for the duration of a last long passionate embrace. Then they took a sad farewell of one another.

Had Roger not learned of Pauline's infidelity he would have felt their parting much more grievously; but his love affair with her had lasted, with only the two-month interval he had spent at Bruges, for very nearly a year, so the edge had already been taken off their physical desire. Even so, her going left a sad gap in his life and he continued to think of her with longing. Then, early in December, he was given a far more serious matter to think about.

Somewhat to his surprise he received a politely worded letter from Talleyrand, not inviting him to supper but requesting him to come the following evening to St. Cloud to discuss a certain matter. Having ridden out through the Bois to the Palace in its well-wooded grounds on the far bank of the Seine, Roger enquired for the Foreign Minister and was shown up to a magnificent apartment.

The tall windows were now screened by curtains of blue satin embroidered with the golden eagles and bees that Napoleon had already taken as his emblems. The furniture was of gilt and marble embellished with sphinx's heads and winged griffons which was to become known to posterity as 'Empire'. Talleyrand was seated there behind a vast desk, as impeccably dressed and smiling as ever. As Roger bowed to him, he said:

'*Cher ami,* I must apologize for having brought you all the way from Paris, but our little man has now insisted that I should spend a certain amount of my time here. At least he has had the decency to provide me with a pleasant setting for me to take my naps between attending to tiresome business. Do you approve it?'

Roger glanced round and smiled, 'Your Excellency was born of a princely family and even a Prince could not complain about having to work in such luxurious surroundings.'

'True, true, *cher Colonel*. But alas, work I must to justify these trappings. And I need your advice. Your mother, I recall, was a Scottish lady.'

'Yes,' replied Roger, somewhat surprised. 'She was a McElfic and a daughter of the then Earl of Kildonan.'

'Then my memory has not failed me. And he was a Jacobite, was he not?'

'Yes. He led his clan in the rising of '45, which sought to place Prince Charles Edward on the throne of his Stuart ancestors. After its failure the Earl was heavily penalized and all but a small part of his lands were confiscated. Naturally he became embittered on that account and remained a staunch Jacobite. He would have followed the Pretender to Rome had his health permitted. As things were, you can imagine the antagonism with which he would have regarded a match between his daughter and my father, Admiral Sir Christopher Brook, who was a staunch Hanoverian. In consequence, they eloped and married without his consent; so my contact with my Scottish relatives has always been exceedingly slender.'

Talleyrand nodded, 'That is unfortunate, because it was information on the present feeling of Jacobites in Scotland that I sought from you. Ireland, of course, has long been a thorn in Britain's side, and by stirring up trouble there we

299

have several times made good use of it. But it has now occurred to our master that when the invasion of England takes place we might also create a valuable diversion by making a landing in Scotland and rousing the Jacobites there against their Hanoverian King. What think you of the prospects of such a project?'

Roger shook his head, 'Far from good. The rebellion of '45 took place nearly sixty years ago. The Hanoverian Kings have since then ruled Scotland wisely, on a light rein, and won over the greater part of the country's inhabitants. Only a few die-hards would again take up arms against King George and most of those, like my cousin the present Earl, are powerless to raise their clans because they have for long lived abroad, to begin with as exiles at the Court of the Pretender in Rome and since his death either there or at other places on the Continent.'

With a quiet smile Talleyrand said, 'That is much as I supposed. It seems though that you are not aware that your cousin died above a year ago.'

Suddenly an alarm bell began to ring in Roger's brain. After a slight hesitation he said, 'No. I did not know that. And I am sorry to hear it, for he was the last of his line and the peerage has become extinct upon his death.'

Talleyrand took snuff, flicked the fallen grains from his lace cravat and remarked with, for him, unusual gravity, 'Enquiries through our Ambassador in Rome about these Jacobite nobles has led to my receiving certain authentic information about them. Over three years ago your cousin was knocked down by a runaway horse. The injuries he sustained were so serious that he was never afterwards able to do more than limp about the apartment that he occupied. He met his death when his crutch slipped on a polished floor-board and he fell down the stairs, breaking his neck. It is therefore, obvious that it could not have been he whom Duroc mistook for you when in St. Petersburg. What have you to say about that?'

300

CHAPTER XX

POISED ON THE PRECIPICE

THE ALARM bell that had begun to tinkle in Roger's brain a few minutes earlier suddenly increased to a shrill clangour. He knew Talleyrand far too well not to realize now why he had been sent for. It was not to get his opinion on the chances of stirring up a Jacobite rising in Scotland. That had been only his devious lead in—the sort of cat and mouse game that he loved—before resurrecting this dangerous question of the identity of the man Duroc had met in Moscow.

Masking his perturbation with a shrug, Roger replied, 'Then since it could not have been my cousin it must have been some other person who closely resembles me.'

Talleyrand had ceased to smile as he asked, 'And who could be so near a twin to yourself as that English Admiral's son, Mr. Roger Brook?'

Roger had rarely felt less like laughing; but he threw back his head, chuckled and said, 'Oh, come, *Excellence*! To you it has been no secret since we first met that he and I are one and the same person. But you will recall that within a fort-night of Duroc's having imagined that he saw me in St. Petersburg I attended a reception you gave in the Rue du Bac. For me to have made such a journey in so short a time would have been utterly impossible.'

'I wonder,' the Minister picked up an ivory paper-knife and began to twirl it between his elegant hands. 'Impossible I grant you to all but a very few exceptionally determined men capable of great endurance . . . such as yourself.'

'You flatter me mightily by the comparison.' Roger made a little bow. 'But I do protest. After being wounded at Marengo I could not possibly have travelled at such speed over a distance of seventeen hundred miles.'

Still unsmiling, Talleyrand returned the bow, 'I congratulate you on your knowledge of geography. It must be considerable to be able to give the distance between the two capitals without reference to a map.'

Silently Roger cursed himself for having made such a slip, while the deep melodious voice went on, 'As to your wound, a year had elapsed since Marengo; ample time for your health to have been fully restored. Yet, I recall, you arrived at my reception so exhausted that you could hardly stand and I sent you off to bed. Your explanation was that you had just returned from recuperating at your château in the south of France, that to test your recovery you had ridden thirty leagues that day, and it had proved too much for you. Might the fact not have been that you had fully recovered and were exhausted from having ridden fifty leagues?'

That was indeed the distance Roger had ridden. Intensely anxious now about the outcome of this interview, he could only hope that Talleyrand was simply fishing and had no definite information to support his evident suspicions. Raising a smile, he said in as light a tone as he could manage:

'That is a hundred and fifty English miles; and even before Marengo I could ne'er have done it. For the life of me I cannot imagine what could have put such an idea into Your Excellency's head.'

Talleyrand ceased toying with the paper-knife, laid it down and said with cold deliberation, 'Then I will tell you. Reluctant as I have ever been to give my mind to business, I much enjoy allowing it to roam in idle speculation. From the first Duroc's report intrigued me and, knowing your antecedents, I wondered if it could possibly have been you

302

that he met in St. Petersburg. The alibi you produced appeared indestructible; but when some weeks ago I received a report about the Jacobite nobles living in exile in Rome and learned that it could not possibly have been the Lord Kildonan that Duroc saw, I once more began to speculate upon the matter. So intrigued was I that I went further. I instructed my agents to make certain enquiries.'

Pausing, the Minister continued to hold Roger's gaze steadily while taking a pinch of snuff. Roger, meanwhile, felt his heart beginning to pound so that he had difficulty in keeping his breathing even. He knew now that the cat and mouse game was over and the cat was coming in for the kill.

Flicking away the grains of snuff from the satin lapels of his coat the elegant human cat went on, 'Having been given the relevant dates my agents reported to me that during the first half of 1801 you did not at any time occupy your château at St. Maxime and that the register of post services chargeable to the Army shows that on June 6th a Colonel Breuc was furnished with a mount in Frankfurt, lay in Verdun for a few hours the following night and arrived in Paris on the 8th, the evening of my reception.' Suddenly Talleyrand leaned forward and pointed an accusing finger:

'*Touché, Mistair Brook; et touché encore.*'

With a sigh Roger put up both his hands palms outward, 'I admit it. I might have known that although I could fool Duroc I could not fool you. That is if it occurred to you to go into the matter; but I saw no reason why you should.'

Talleyrand smiled but his smile had no humour in it, 'The gamble you took was a good one. It would have come off had I not learned of Lord Kildonan's accident and its having made it impossible for him to leave Rome during the last years of his life. 'Tis upon just such slender chances that the fate of empires hang. In this case it is your own. Now, Mr. Brook, be good enough to inform me of your reason for going to St. Petersburg.'

'I spent some time there in '87 and, having become bored by my long convalescence after Marengo, I thought it would be interesting to pay another visit to the city.'

303

'Indeed!' The Minister's mobile mouth curved into a sneer. 'And, no doubt, you found a swift cure for your boredom in plotting the murder of the Czar?'

'You wrong me, *Excellence,*' Roger protested with a frown. 'I would never make myself a party to assassination.'

'In that I believe you. I should have said in plotting his removal from power. I have much information on that affair and it seems that the original intention was only to place the Czar under restraint. I also know that an Englishman was among those who forced their way into Paul's room. From the description I have had of him I've now not a doubt that he was yourself. Can you deny it?'

Roger shrugged, 'Since Your Excellency is convinced of that I have no means by which I can alter your opinion.'

'I would have wagered a fortune that you could not.' Talleyrand's deep voice had taken on a harsh note. 'And so we have the true picture. Long since I suspected you of being an English secret agent. In '98 I charged you with it, but you assured me that you were no longer working for Mr. Pitt and intended to carve out for yourself a career in France. Still only half-convinced of your sincerity I nullified your prospects of sending information back from Paris to London by insisting that your duty lay in accompanying Bonaparte on his expedition to Egypt. On his return you played a valuable part in the *coup d'état* of *Brumaire* and, your prospects of advancement being so good, it seemed to me that you had everything to gain by remaining loyal to France. With a skill that one can but admire you have since led me to believe that my suspicions of you were entirely groundless. Napoleon, myself and many others have made you privy to our most secret intentions and you deceived us all. Now, it is revealed that for all these years we have been nurturing a viper in our bosoms.

'For your activities while in Russia there can be only one explanation. Mad as the Czar Paul may have been, we had made him the friend of France, so it was in our interest that he should retain his throne; whereas the interests of England lay in his removal from it. Taking advantage of the indefinite

304

leave granted you to recover from your wound, I haven't a doubt that you went to London and that there your real master discussed with you the situation in Russia. He would have told you that the Czar had many enemies but that they were a cowardly, woolly-minded, irresolute lot. You are the very antithesis of that, and he sent you to persuade, urge, bully, bribe them into taking action. History will not record the part you played but it will the result of your mission. You temporarily altered the balance of power in favour of your country. That was a great achievement, Mr. Brook. But it is your last. You have deceived us far too long and will deceive us no more. You must know, too, the penalty for a spy who has been found out. It is death.'

Never before had Roger seen Talleyrand in such a mood, nor thought him even capable of displaying such harshness. Gone was the urbane, charming friend and another personality had emerged; a ruthless intriguer who had had his cherished plans brought to naught and for that meant to exact vengeance.

Roger had gone slightly pale. The knuckles of his hands showed white as, with rising tension, he clasped them on his knee. He had always thought that if he ever slipped up badly he could count on Talleyrand to get him out; but such a hope was now obviously vain. The very fact that they had been such close friends was, he realized, the clue to the Minister's rancour; for he prided himself on his astuteness, and to learn that he had been fooled by a man with whom he had been intimate for years must have roused in him intense resentment. In a low voice Roger said:

'Your Excellency has made a case and I am in no position to refute your charges. I have performed many services for France but my first loyalty has always been to England, and will be so until I die.'

'That is a brave declaration. Many men in your present position would have sought to save themselves by offering to use their contacts in England to work in future for France.'

'*Monsieur le Ministre*, if you mean that as a suggestion I can take it only as an insult.'

Talleyrand raised an eyebrow, 'Spies form a class apart. As their profession largely consists of betraying confidences they are regarded as persons without honour, so cannot be insulted. But let that pass. We have worked together so often and for so long that I would have liked to find a means by which you could escape the fate you have brought upon yourself. Can you suggest one?'

'No, I fear not,' Roger shook his head. 'What alternative is there? Only an appeal to you that you should allow me to go free and return to England. But, being as well informed as I am of French affairs, that would be too much to expect. Our countries are at war. You know me now to be a danger to yours; so you could not with a clear conscience allow me to continue to give assistance to France's enemies. My only regret is that it should be you who has found me out, and so be inflicted with what must be the unpleasant duty of sending me to face a firing squad.'

Regarding him curiously, Talleyrand said, 'I admire your scruples in refraining from appealing to my personal feelings for you; although in your circumstances I would not have them. However, there remain the services you have rendered France, and they are considerable. I can at least ensure that they are given full prominence at your trial with a strong recommendation to mercy.'

Roger gave a pale smile. 'I thank Your Excellency for your good intentions; but I'd as lief you allowed matters to take their course. Mercy in this case could mean retaining my life only at the price of spending many years imprisoned in a fortress. I have had a wonderful life and a long run for my money. But I've always anticipated that, sooner or later, I would be called on to pay for that and I'd much prefer to settle the bill in one lump sum.'

'Are you not then afraid to die?'

'I am of being executed. Contrary to popular belief I am, physically, the veriest coward. But I've no fear of death itself, nor any great regret at being deprived of a continuance of my present existence. Pauline Borghese is the most lovely creature; but she has gone to Rome and, to be honest, drawn though I was to her like an iron filing to a magnet, at rock bottom I had no deep feeling for her—nor she for me, else she would not have married Borghese while I was in Bruges. So that is finished. From my teens onwards until some fifteen months ago I had an abiding passion for an English lady who returned my love. But that, too, alas, is over, and for good. So I have nothing much now to live for.'

'Yet you would surely rather live than die?'

'Naturally. Even with no special inducement to survive, life still holds many pleasures and interests. Not least to learn how the war between our countries will end.'

Opening a drawer in his desk, Talleyrand took from it a dog-eared piece of thin pasteboard on which the writing was almost illegible. Pushing it across to Roger he asked, 'Do you recognize this?'

Picking it up, Roger looked at it for a moment then exclaimed, 'Why, yes! It is the passport that I fooled Danton into giving me for you, so that you could escape from France to England at the height of the Terror.'

Talleyrand nodded, 'It saved me from the guillotine. And, although people rate me guilty of many things, no one has ever accused me of not having a good memory.'

From the drawer he then produced a clean, new oblong of pasteboard and added, 'Here is another. It will take you via the Netherlands into Germany, and from a port there you should have no difficulty in finding a ship that will carry you to England.'

Roger had needed all his fortitude both to remain calm and resist the temptation to plead for his life. What he had said of Pauline and Georgina was true but, in spite of that, he was far from ready to die. He had made a pretence of resignation only because he felt that by doing so he would stand a better chance of taking Talleyrand by surprise, snatching up a heavy candle-stick from the desk, rendering him unconscious by a blow over the head and walking calmly out of the Palace before he could be arrested.

Now tears started to his eyes, and he stammered, 'You ... you really mean that . . . that despite all I know of French

307

affairs you did not mean even to put me in prison, but . . . but allow me to leave the country? That is indeed generous and I thank you from my heart.'

Talleyrand was now smiling, 'Can you suppose that if I had ever had any other intention I would have been quite so big a fool as to remain here alone with such a resourceful and desperate fellow as Mr. Roger Brook?'

For the first time in years Roger found himself blushing, 'Well,' he laughed. 'I do confess that I had it in mind to hit you over the head, then make with all speed for the coast.'

'A very natural reaction, *cher ami*. But I could not resist this temptation to enjoy your discomfiture at my having found you out. I have, of course, given that very serious consideration and it is my opinion that, even if I allowed you to remain here as a free citizen, the ill you could do to France would, except in some quite exceptional circumstance which is unlikely to arise, be outweighed by your usefulness to me here. You and I have always been at one in believing that no permanent peace and prosperity can be maintained in Europe unless our two great countries sink their differences. You have considerable influence with many important people here, and a quick and subtle mind; so for my secret endeavours to bring about a lasting settlement I could have no better lieutenant than yourself.'

After taking snuff again, the Minister added, 'But now it is my intention to use you as my secret emissary to England.'

Roger stiffened slightly, 'I thought I had made it clear that . . .'

Talleyrand made an impatient gesture, 'You did. And when giving you that passport I made no conditions. Do you wish it you may proceed freely to England and never return. But I have hopes that you will agree to give me your help in a matter that will in no way conflict with your conscience. A while back you said that you would never become a party to an assassination. May I take it that implies that you would prevent any attempt at assassination if you could?'

'Certainly. However much one may hate an enemy, to kill

308

him in fair fight is one thing, but to take him off his guard and stab him in the back is quite another.'

'I agree; yet across the Channel there is a plot to assassinate Napoleon.'

'You imply that the English are engaged in such a plot. Greatly as they loathe him, I do not believe it.'

'No. I do not believe that the King's Ministers would lend themselves to such despicable measures, but I have evidence that several of their subordinates are encouraging the designs of the embittered Royalist refugees. For one, a Mr. Hammond who is the Permanent Under Secretary at the Foreign Office. And there are others of whom I will tell you. One, Hyde de Neuville, is the Royalist leader and it has come to my knowledge that he and his right-hand man, Méhée de la Touche, have been several times recently in Paris spying out the land. These extremists believe that if only they could put Napoleon out of the way, rather than be plunged again into civil strife, the French people would prefer to receive back the Comte de Provence as King Louis XVIII. But these out-at-elbows plotters are a cowardly lot and, instead of risking their own skins, they plan to use Georges Cadoudal, the Breton peasant leader.'

'You surprise me,' Roger put in, 'Cadoudal is a brave fellow, and by his skilful resistance has won the admiration even of his enemies. I would not have thought him the type of man to agree to become an assassin.'

'Nor I. But one must remember that he is a fanatic. In August last he landed secretly at Biville, near Dieppe, and proceeded to Munich, where he conferred with Méhée de la Touche and Mr. Drake, the British agent. Do you perchance know Drake?

'No,' Roger shook his head, 'I have heard of but never met him. I owe my long immunity to the fact that, as far as circumstances permitted, I have held no communication with any other British agent.'

'How wise of you,' Talleyrand smiled. 'However, there it is. I have particulars of the conversations they held. It was agreed that some time during this Winter Cadoudal should enter France again with a band of resolute adherents and make an attempt to eliminate Napoleon. You know as well as I do that, as things stand, the people of France would never accept the restoration of a Bourbon to the throne. It follows that the death of Napoleon could lead only to anarchy and a renewal of the Terror. While I believe Drake to be acting on his own initiative, and that the British Government plays no part in this, they must have knowledge of the centres in which Royalist plots are bred. You have the entrée to highly placed persons in England so could find out where those centres are and, perhaps, penetrate them. Should you succeed in that you could then return here and furnish me with particulars of the plotters' intentions. Then I would be able to take due precautions. Let us be clear. I do not ask your aid in anything that would be harmful to England; only your help in preventing an assassination which would further embitter the relations between our countries. Now; what say you?'

'I agree,' Roger replied without hesitation. 'We have many times worked together for what we believed to be good ends. Should Napoleon be assassinated it would be attributed to the English, and since he has become the idol of the French people, there would then be no hope of seeing peace in our life-time. This vile conspiracy must be thwarted at all costs, and I'll spare no effort to aid you in nipping it in the bud.'

'Well said!' Talleyrand stood up and clasped his hand 'But the matter has become urgent; so I will tell Napoleon that I have temporarily deprived him of you for a special service in which his own safety is concerned, in order that you can leave France without delay.'

The following day Roger set out for England.

CHAPTER XXI

THE DOUBLE AGENT

R O G E R had no need of the passport with which Talleyrand had provided him and did not proceed via Holland into Germany; neither, in view of the war situation, did he go to Calais. Instead he took the road to Dieppe and, in a fishing village not far from it, sought out a smuggler who on two previous occasions had put him across the Channel. There, to his distress, he learned that his old friend had, a few months earlier, been killed in an affray with the English. Having made the man's widow a present of a sum of money, he rode the thirty-five miles down the coast to Fécamp and there he proved luckier. Another smuggler, to whom the widow had sent him, intended to sail two days later and agreed to run him over; although he had to pay twice the sum that he had when he had last crossed two years earlier.

This was owing to the threat of invasion that now menaced England. While Napoleon had been mustering his vast army the British had been far from idle. Lord Keith commanded a squadron in the North Sea covering the Dutch ports and Lord Cornwallis another blockading Brest, while the narrows between Kent and the Pas de Calais swarmed with sloops and

311

gunboats, the latter largely manned by the Sea Fencibles, as volunteers for local sea services were called.

In consequence, as Roger had assumed, smuggling from either side across the narrows had become such a hazardous venture that it had almost ceased. But the demand in Britain for French wines and cognac was as great as ever, while the French, despite Napoleon's interdicts, were still eager to secure English cloth and Nottingham lace; so the illicit traffic continued but had to be by longer sea passages to the west, and even on the Dorset and Devonshire coasts the risk of capture had increased considerably.

Early in the morning of December 12th, the wind being favourable, they set sail; but, instead of running out into the open sea, they spent the whole day crossing the Bay of the Seine until, late at night, they reached the tip of the Cherbourg peninsula. There they lay to until the following afternoon and only then again set sail on a northerly course across the Channel.

Towards evening the weather worsened and it was Roger's misfortune that when about half way across they were hit by a sou'wester. Stripped of her canvas the little ship bucked most horribly and he was dreadfully sick. When morning came she was many miles off her course and that day went in getting her back to a position from which she could make her run in; so it was not until an hour before dawn on the 15th that, still pale and ill, he was put ashore a few miles west of Christchurch at the foot of a deserted gorse-covered chine which many years later, was to form part of Bournemouth.

Carrying his valise he trudged unhappily to Christchurch; but the walk did him good and, as he had not eaten for the past two days, restored his appetite. After breakfasting at the best inn, feeling more his own man, he hired a postchaise and drove through Lymington to Walhampton Park with the intention of visiting his father before proceeding to London.

There he was received by Sir William Burrard, with whom his father had gone to live in the Spring of 1800. After greeting him cordially but a little awkwardly the Baronet broke it to him that his father had died the previous winter.

312

Roger was not greatly surprised as, after his retirement from the Navy, the Admiral's health had deteriorated and when Roger had last seen him he had been far from well. Neither did he feel any great sense of loss, as during his youth fear of his father had brought him near to hating him and it was not until later years, during which they had seen one another only at long intervals, that they had become good friends.

Sir William pressed him to stay as long as he wished at Walhampton and Roger gladly accepted for a few nights; then, tired out from his journey, went straight up to bed. That night over supper his host gave him particulars of his father and told him that Mr. Drummond to whom the Admiral had let Grove Place was still occupying it pending some arrangement with the Admiral's heir; although the three-year tenancy had come to an end in the previous March.

Next day Roger rode into Lymington, spent a few minutes standing silently at the foot of his parents' grave, then went to see the family solicitor, a Mr. Blatch. As he expected, his father had left everything to him except for an annuity to his faithful servant Jim Button and a few personal possessions to old friends. The solicitor estimated the inheritance to amount to something over forty thousand pounds, mainly acquired in prize money from ships taken by the Admiral while serving in the Navy. As an executor and trustee he had invested it in the Funds, and Roger was content to leave it there for the time being. With the carefulness inherited from his Scottish mother he had, during the past fifteen years, put by the greater part of the money he had made while occupying several lucrative posts and, invested with the shrewd advice of Droopy Ned, his own small fortune amounted to a considerably greater sum; so he now reckoned himself to be worth well over a hundred thousand pounds.

That evening he called upon the Drummonds, to find that his old home had not only been well looked after but in many respects improved, as the banker had spent a considerable amount of money on it. The young couple now had a girl of two and a boy of nine months and Mrs. Drummond was again 'expecting'. They were very happy in the house and wished to stay on there; so Roger willingly agreed to renew their tenancy for a further three years. They then pressed him to stay on to supper and he enjoyed a merry meal with them.

Jim Button, he learned, had gone to live with a niece and her husband in their cottage at Pennington; so the next afternoon Roger rode over there. Jim was now in his middle sixties but still hale and hearty. While Roger talked to him of old times the buxom niece bustled about to provide a bumper English tea, the like of which their guest had not enjoyed for years. But she had four young children and the cottage seemed to Roger too small for such a family to live in in comfort. So instead of doubling Jim's annuity as he had intended, Roger told him that he meant to give him a thousand pounds out of which he could buy a much larger place and still have a good nest egg over. In those days to such people a sum of that kind was a fortune and, full to the gills with home-made bread, jam and cake, he rode away with the blessings they called down on him still ringing in his ears.

On the 18th, having been assured that he would always be a welcome guest at Walhampton, Roger said good-bye to the hospitable Sir William and took coach to London. When he reached Amesbury House he learned that Droopy Ned was in residence but had left an hour before and was not expected back until the early hours of the following morning, as he had driven down to Sion House at Isleworth, the residence of the Duke and Duchess of Northumberland who were giving a ball there that night. Droopy's father, the Earl, as was his custom all through the shooting season, was at his seat, Normanrood in Wiltshire, and the only person staying in the house was an elderly cousin whom Roger had always found a bore. So, having been installed in his usual room and freshened himself up after his journey, he decided to sup out at his Club.

As he had an hour or more to spare and the evening, although cold, was fine, he went out to stretch his legs in a stroll round the heart of fashionable London. Piccadilly was

314

brightly lit as the shops then stayed open late, the roadway was packed with coaches, carriages and horsemen, the pavements crowded with a motley throng of homeward bound pedestrians, hucksters and ladies of the town dressed in tawdry finery. Roger was always polite when rebuffing these young painted harpies but, finding himself accosted at every twenty paces or so when he paused to look into a shop window, he tired of saying, 'No, thank you, m'dear,' or 'Not tonight, my pretty,' and turned out of Piccadilly into Berkeley Street.

On his left lay Devonshire House and as he walked at a good pace alongside the tall wall behind which lay the Duke's big garden he suddenly realized that he was heading towards Berkeley Square. Immediately his thoughts turned to Georgina. Although her betrayal of him had caused him more bitterness than any other event in his whole life, time had at least healed the wound sufficiently for him to dwell now and then on some of the many happy hours they had spent together.

While riding from Paris to Dieppe he had even hoped that when she learned that he was again in England she might seek a meeting with a view to expressing her contrition for her abominable act, and he had decided that should she do so he would readily forgive her. In any case he meant to get in touch with her to arrange to see his daughter and, if she was agreeable, her boy Charles. But that was a thing apart from healing the breach between them and he felt that after having put the Sheriff's officers on to him the first move must come from her.

Yet now, as he was approaching Berkeley Square, he realized more fully than he had ever done before what an appalling gap their quarrel had left in his life. Although from the age of fifteen he had lived for much the greater part of the time abroad, whenever he had come back to England Georgina had always been there to give him a tempestuous welcome. They had had no single secret of any kind from one another, talked and laughed the hours away and, regarding themselves as two beings bound by a tie that transcended all

accepted standards of conduct, made passionate love regardless of marriage vows or any other commitment.

It had long been clear to him that John Beefy had repre-
sented something entirely different in her life from her two
previous husbands and the many gallants with whom she had
had passing affairs; so he had come to condone the fury and
distress she had displayed on the assumption that he had
killed Beefy in a fit of drunken jealousy. But what he did not
understand was her refusal to believe his word that it had
been an accident and, in any case, in view of their very
special relationship, to forgive him. Even more puzzling was
the fact that, although she had appeared as a witness when he
had been tried for murder and had saved him from hanging
she should, four months later, have still felt so bitterly
towards him that she had deliberately betrayed him.

But all that had happened well over a year before, and
surely by now she too would at times think with regret of the
shattered love that had meant so much to them. Why not, he
thought to himself, be generous and make the first approach?
At this time of year it was as good as certain that Georgina
would be in London and, at this hour, unless she too had
gone down to the ball at Sion House, be dressing either to go
out or to receive guests.

Roger's heart leapt at the thought. They had only to come
face to face for all to be forgiven and forgotten. Whatever her
commitments for that night, she would ignore them, pleading
a sudden attack of the vapours. They would sup as of old
before a roaring fire in her boudoir and later, fortified by
good wine and drunk with the joy of their reunion, lie
clasped in one another's arms between the sheets until
morning.

When he reached the St. Ermins' mansion, his new-found
elation subsided as though a bucket of icy water had been
sloshed into his face. The house was dark and shuttered, so
evidently Georgina was not in London.

Recovering slightly at the thought that, now he had decided
to call bygones bygones, he could go down to Stillwaters next
day, he rang the front door bell. After waiting for a few

316

minutes he rang again then, as it still was not answered, he grabbed the bell pull and jerked it up and down until at last an elderly servitor, mumbling apologies for his delay, opened to him.

To his enquiry the man replied, 'Nay, sir; Her Ladyship is not at Stillwaters. She sailed last month for the West Indies to arrange for the disposal of her late husband's estates there. But the children are at Stillwaters in the care of Mrs. Marsham.'

Bitterly disappointed, Roger thanked him and turned away. Gone now was all prospect of restoring his erstwhile happy relationship with Georgina, anyhow for many months to come; for within a few weeks Talleyrand would expect him back in France with a report on all he could pick up about the plot to assassinate Napoleon, and it was impossible even to make a guess at when he would again be able to come to England.

His spirits now very low, he walked back to White's. There he found several old acquaintances, supped with four of them, drank fairly heavily then, although he was not normally a gambler, sat for four hours playing faro. Morosely, as he walked across to Arlington Street at half past two in the morning, he recalled the saying 'lucky at cards, unlucky in love', and the fact that he had come away from the club with three hundred and fifteen golden guineas in his breeches' pockets did not console him.

With the sleepy footman on night duty at Amesbury House he left a message that he was not to be called until Lord Edward roused, and would join him for breakfast. Both of them slept late and it was not until midday that Roger, still in his chamber robe, went along to his old friend's suite. Over eels in aspic, kidneys and bacon, a cold game pie and other trifles, washed down with copious draughts of fine Bordeaux, they lingered for two hours.

Roger, as always when with Droopy, made no secret of the reason for his return to England and consulted him on how best to set about his mission. Droopy peered with his shortsighted eyes across the table at Roger and said:

317

'Meseems that in this matter you are become a police spy. Hardly a role I would have expected you to play; but no doubt you have squared it with your conscience.'

'I have,' replied Roger firmly. 'Were the French Royalists alone concerned in this I'd have naught to do with it. Only by destroying Napoleon can they have any hope of placing a Bourbon Prince again on the throne of France. After ten years of exile and penury certain among them may have become so desperate that they would even stoop to murder to gain their ends. That they should have sunk so low is lamentable but, in view of their fanatical hatred of the usurper, at least understandable; and their bitter enmity towards him none of our affair.

'What is our concern is that the British Government are, at least to some extent, assisting in the plot. The French espionage system is extremely good and Talleyrand gave me chapter and verse for our government's participation. In August last the Chouan leader, Georges Cadoudal, was landed at Biville from a ship commanded by Captain Wright on the instructions of one E. Nepean, an assistant to Admiral Montagu in our Admiralty. It is also known that towards the end of that month, at the instigation of the royalist Baron de Roll, our Permanent Under Secretary for Foreign Affairs called on His Highness the Comte d'Artois who was then living at No. 46 Baker Street. This resulted in the Prince producing a memorandum naming those Generals and others in France who could be counted on to help in overthrowing Napoleon. Meanwhile Cadoudal, together with Méhée de la Touche, had proceeded to Munich and there, with or without the authority of the Government, our official representative, Mr. Francis Drake, furnished them with funds to further the conspiracy. Méhée then went to Vienna and enlisted the support of the Honourable Charles Stuart, our Chargé d'Affaires there; but the French got wind of that, seized the go-between and took his papers from him. So, you see, should this plot to assassinate Napoleon succeed, the French will be able to produce evidence that the British Government was at the bottom of it.'

Droopy nodded his narrow head. 'I appreciate now why you are deeply concerned. From all you have told me Napoleon's popularity in France is immense; so were he assassinated and the deed laid squarely at our door, the rage of the French people would be such that there'd be no prospect of their agreeing a peace with us for another generation. You are right, Roger; even if it means that a number of Frenchmen who are only pawns in the game must lose their lives, the attempt must be stopped.'

After a moment Droopy went on, 'The state of things here is pitiful. On the renewal of the war last May, the British people became united as never before. As you well know, during the Revolution a great part of the masses and the Whig nobility, led by Charles Fox, was undisguisedly pro-French. Although we were at war with that nation, carried away by the new doctrine of "Liberty, Equality and Fraternity" they would have created a revolution here had not firm measures been taken to suppress them. They hailed the conquests by the Revolutionary Generals of Belgium, Holland, the Rhineland States and, later, Bonaparte's of Italy, as triumphs against ancient tyrannies which must benefit mankind.

'But now, matters are very different. By the Peace of Amiens we came near to licking the boots of the French. We gave them back all the conquests that during eleven years of war many thousands of British lives had been sacrificed to make, agreed to their retaining territories that made France a mightier nation than ever before and, in fact, did everything possible to ensure a lasting peace. And with what result? After barely a year Bonaparte's grandiose pretensions forced us into war with him again.

'Before, it was felt by at least half the nation that the French were Crusaders, fighting at first desperately to protect their newly-won liberties, then to benefit the people of neighbouring lands by releasing them, too, from serfdom. But now it has become clear to all. The French are not liberators but despoilers of the lands they overrun; and this new war has but one object; the aggrandisement of Bonaparte. 'Tis that

319

which has united the British people against him; so that he is
known here now as the Corsican Ogre, but our tragedy at the
moment is that all this patriotic fervour is being so hopelessly
misdirected.'

'From what little I have been able to gather of the matter,'
Roger remarked, 'our trouble lies in having a near-mad King
who cannot fully grasp the situation, and so will suffer only
Ministers subservient to him, instead of ones capable of
directing the war against the French.'

'You are right in that. King George's poor bemused brain
revolves round one subject only; to resist being pressed into
breaking, as he believes, his Coronation oath, which forbids
Roman Catholics to hold office. Seeing that Mr. Pitt was set
on putting through his Catholic Emancipation Bill, the King
fell back upon the hopeless mediocrity Addington and
allowed him to choose that imbecile my Lord Hawkesbury as
his Foreign Secretary. In such feeble hands now lies the fate
of our poor country.'

'Hawkesbury must receive all reports from our Secret
Service,' Roger said, 'so must be aware of the activities of the
French exiles. Think you he would be disposed to disclose
such matters to me did I wait upon him?'

Droopy looked dubious, ' 'Tis possible; but the man is an
utter fool. So much so that those acquainted with him oft
refer to his "vacuous grin". The odds are he'd hum and haw
and you'd get no further. You'd do better, I think, by
approaching your old master. Although he has been out of
office for some time, he was Prime Minister for so long that
his knowledge of our intelligence system must be unrivalled.
Moreover, that quick, clear brain of his would grasp at once
the importance of thwarting this conspiracy, so you could
count upon his doing his utmost to aid you.'

'Tomorrow then, I'll ride out to Bromley.'

'No, no!' Droopy shook his head. 'Mr. Pitt is no longer at
Holwood. As you know he has no private fortune, and
having given all his thought for so long to the welfare of the
nation he allowed his own finances to fall into the most ill
condition. Even before he left Downing Street and was still

320

receiving his stipend as First Lord of the Treasury the bailiffs threatened to remove his furniture against debts of a few hundred that he could not immediately meet.'

'What a shocking thing!' Roger exclaimed. ' 'Tis disgraceful that a man to whom the country owes so much should be harassed by private debts.'

'I'm with you there, and his integrity is such that he'd not take advantage of his high office, as did his predecessors, to make himself a single guinea. From time to time his friends have come to his assistance but, even so, over a year ago he was forced to sell Holwood House and acquire a smaller residence; Bowling Green House on Putney Hill. But you'll not find him there either. On the outbreak of war, although only a private member, he appeared in the House and made the speech of his life, thereby carrying the miserable Addington's motion, against the opposition of Fox and his cronies who would have had us kow-tow to Bonaparte. Then, since he is still Lord Warden of the Cinque Ports, he went straight to Walmer Castle and raised a battalion of militia, of which he is now Colonel.'

'What! Billy Pitt become a soldier?' Roger exclaimed. 'He, so frail and ill a man, so unsuited to being exposed to the elements at all hours, and long night marches. I would ne'er have believed it.'

Droopy smiled, ' 'Tis the fact, though. And 'tis said that his Fencibles are the best trained and disciplined on all the Kent coast.'

'If Napoleon does invade, they will need to be,' Roger rejoined. 'For it will be on the Kent coast that the brunt of the attack will fall. I'll go down to Walmer then, as you advise, and seek the help of Britain's greatest patriot.'

'What of Christmas?' Droopy asked. 'Three days hence I set out for Normanrood to spend it with my family. You should be back by then and would be made most welcome if you'd accompany me.'

'I thank you, Ned. No prospect could be more pleasant. But my mission is urgent and on my return from Walmer I ought not to go so far afield from London as Wiltshire. I learned last night that Georgina is gone to the West Indies to dispose of Mr Beefy's estates there; but the children are at Stillwaters and, if it be possible, I'd like to spend at least Christmas Day with them.'

'I see no bar to that. I'm told Georgina left them in the care of her father and your late wife's aunt, Mrs. Marsham.'

Roger nodded, 'Colonel Thursby was ever my good friend and Aunt Marsham is a pleasant woman. I'll send a note asking if they will have me for a night or two. A reply should reach here by the time I get back from Walmer and I doubt not 'twill be in the affirmative. Meanwhile, so as to lose no time I'll book myself a seat on the night coach for Dover.'

At Dover next morning he freshened himself up then hired a postchaise to take him on to Walmer, arriving there shortly before midday. Outside the castle he found a great concourse of people watching a parade that was in progress and soon learned that General John Moore, who commanded in East Kent from his headquarters at Shorncliffe, was inspecting Mr. Pitt's two battalions, each a thousand strong, of Cinque Port Volunteers.

Using his postchaise as a grandstand, Roger watched the review, marvelling to see the tall, stooping figure of the Prime Minister that he had seen so often behind a desk now stumping up and down and shouting orders as sharply as a sergeant major. The stumping was caused by one of his boots being much larger than the other; so Roger knew that he must be suffering from an attack of the gout which sadly plagued him, and admired him all the more for his devotion to his country.

When the parade was finally dismissed Colonel Pitt and his officers escorted the General into the castle. Roger realized then that he would stand little chance of a private conversation with his old master that afternoon, and would have to stay overnight in Walmer; so he sent his driver with his valise along to the inn with orders to book him a room. But he felt that there was no point in delaying making known his presence and, entering the castle, had his name sent up. Five minutes later Mr. Pitt was shaking him warmly by the hand

322

and presenting him first to his niece, Lady Hester Stanhope, who was keeping house for him, then to the assembled company.

Lady Hester was dressed in a scarlet habit and had a gold-laced cocked hat perched on her ash-blonde curls. Roger had seen her on the parade and wondered who she could be. He soon learned that she accompanied her uncle on all military exercises and was a most gay and charming young woman who had brought sunshine into his monastic bachelor existence.

When it emerged that Roger had recently arrived from France everyone wanted to hear the latest news about the Corsican Ogre and his plans for invasion; but that had to wait, as General Moore was about to give the officers a short talk.

The future hero of Corunna was then forty-two years of age. He had served in Corsica, the West Indies, Holland and Egypt and so distinguished himself that, although by British standards young for a General, he had now been charged with the defence of the coast upon which it was expected that the invasion would take place. He had a fine presence, a most striking personality, a clear melodious voice and a pretty sense of humour.

He aired it by his opening remark, 'Well, gentlemen, I congratulate you on your turn out and the performance of your men; but when General Lannes lands here one morning I shall have you drawn up in close order on the top of a hill, as I am sure your appearance will strike fear into him. Meanwhile my own men will fight his Grenadiers on the beach.'

Seeing their downcast looks he laughed, and went on to explain. Experience had shown that volunteers who had never seen active service could be used only in large formations; otherwise, if heavily attacked, they swiftly went to pieces. Moreover, up to that time the same principle had been adhered to in all regular armies, so that the men should remain under the immediate control of their officers and N.C.O.s and take courage from their example. But with his

323

Light Infantry he was developing a revolutionary form of training, by which he sought to take advantage of the difference between the British soldier and that of the Continental Powers.

The latter, he said, were for the most part peasants who had only recently emerged from serfdom, and the majority of them were automatons, good fighters in a body no doubt, but incapable of thinking and acting for themselves. Whereas the common people of Britain had for centuries been free to lead their lives as they would and use such brains as God had given them to make a living. This had given them a much stronger individuality and a sense of responsibility, and his object was to give every man under him the chance to show it. His ideal rifleman should have the mentality of a poacher and not feel lost and bewildered if he found himself cut off behind the enemy lines, but have the initiative and confidence to make his way back to his unit under cover of darkness. During an advance such troops would not have to be marched into battle in solid formations, and so form a fine target for the enemy cannon, but could be sent forward in open order, each man using his common sense when to make a rush and when to lie down.

Roger listened fascinated to this exposition of the infantry tactics of the future, and much else that this inspiring General had to say about the desirability of officers attending not an occasional drill but every drill, and getting to know each one of their men personally—doctrines unheard of in those days.

Dinner was served at half past three and during it Roger learned much about the preparations that had been made to resist an invasion. From all over England great numbers of horses and carts had been brought into the coastal area to be used in what was termed 'the driving'. This was the evacuation inland of not only all non-combatants but cattle, poultry, fodder, the contents of shops and household stores so that if the invader did get a foothold he would find the land barren of all sustenance.

But General Moore was of the opinion that although Bonaparte was causing them by his threats to expend a great deal of effort he was not such a fool as to undertake the mad gamble of a cross-Channel operation, and that if he did he would rue it. Both the regular troops and the volunteers were in splendid heart. There were now three hundred and eighty thousand of the latter, plus thirty-one thousand Sea Fencibles. As Lord Warden, Pitt alone had under him one hundred and seventy gun boats, in addition to his two battalions of militia, and every man among them was eager to have a crack at the enemy.

Roger, with his personal knowledge of Napoleon's vast preparations, was not so confident that he was only bluffing. But he did think it unlikely that many of the French would reach land.

In his view that was the one question upon which the success or failure of an invasion hung. He gathered that General Moore had under him only some three thousand eight hundred regulars. If on a foggy day the protecting flotillas could be evaded and ten thousand French get ashòre, General Moore's men must be overwhelmed. Then, once a beach-head had been secured, the volunteers, brave though they might be, would be scattered like chaff before the massed veteran troops of Soult, Ney, Davoust and the iron Guard of Bessiéres.

A little before six o'clock General Moore was cheered away into the winter darkness and soon afterwards the other officers followed. Mr. Pitt then expressed his surprise that so old a friend as Roger had not taken it for granted that he would lie that night at the castle—as indeed he had been expected to be invited to do—and had his valise sent for. Soon afterwards they were settled before a roaring log fire in Mr. Pitt's untidy but comfortable study and an hour slipped past while Roger answered innumerable questions about the state of things in France; then he disclosed the reason for his return to England.

Having heard him out Mr. Pitt looked very grave and, after a moment's thought, said, ' 'Tis now close on three years since I left office and although my friends keep me informed of events they are in no situation to know the mind of Ministers. Henry Addington has proved a sad disappointment to us all but I'd stake my own life that he would not lend himself to such a crime, and my Lord Hawkesbury, though a fool, is no knave. If you are right that Drake, Hammond and others are involved, they must have acted through an excess of misplaced zeal and I am confident that their participation in this plot cannot be known to their superiors. But, however that may be, you are right, Mr. Brook—one hundred times right. This dastardly attempt must be prevented at all costs. Did it succeed and were laid squarely at the door of England 'twould be an indelible blot upon the fair name of our nation, and the righteous rancour of the French be such that they'd hold it against us for a lifetime.'

It being one thing to seek to penetrate the military intentions of an enemy nation and quite another to pry into the secrets of individuals with intent to betray them, Roger had all along been very conscious of this most unpleasant aspect of his new mission; so it heartened him greatly that so upright a man as Mr. Pitt should unhesitatingly endorse Droopy's opinion that he must proceed with it as an affair of State upon which great issues hung. But when it came to practical help he found that there was little Mr. Pitt could give him. While Prime Minister he had always avoided going into society, so had met very few of the French émigrés; and, since his retirement, he had devoted himself first to his garden then, since the renewal of the war, to his military duties.

Later they supped with the gay Lady Hester, no other guests having been invited for that night owing to the big dinner party that had been given earlier in the day. During the meal Roger was greatly struck by the change that had taken place in his old master. By nature a shy, aloof patrician, he had become Prime Minister at the age of twenty-four and for nearly eighteen consecutive years given his whole mind to the well-being of his country. He had never married or had a mistress and under constant attack from his political enemies he had become ever more irritably abrupt in his manner, unbending and dictatorial.

326

But now he was relaxed and cheerful, responding wittily to Lady Hester's banter and, Roger was amazed to learn, he even chaperoned her to local dances, staying up till all hours of the morning to bring her home.

When she had left them and they were sitting over their port this new human warmth of character he displayed emboldened Roger to ask him frankly why, the government having fallen into such feeble hands, he did not return to politics and pull the country out of the mess it was in.

With a smile he replied, 'For the past year many of my friends have been urging me to do that. But there are certain difficulties. If not in so many words, by implication I promised our friends in Ireland to put through the Catholic Emancipation Bill. But His Majesty would have none of it, and, behind my back, sent for Addington. Without my support he could not have formed a Ministry. Had I refused it the King would willy-nilly have had to accept the Opposition with Charles Fox, who is anathema to him, as his Prime Minister.

'I was desperate tired and in half a mind to wash my hands of the whole business. Had His Majesty not been afflicted as he is, I would have. But he began again to suffer brief periods of insanity, and 'twas said to be my fault for holding him in a cleft stick and endeavouring to force him to agree to Catholic Emancipation against his conscience. In consequence I went to him, promised that I would not again raise the question of emancipation in his lifetime and that I would give Addington my support.

'That I did to the best of my ability. Grenville, Dundas, Spencer, Wyndham. Cornwallis and Castlereagh in Ireland, all refused their help and resigned. But I persuaded Rose, my brother Chatham and others to enter the new Cabinet and myself spoke in its favour in the House. Having done so, how can I now retract and form a Cabal to unseat Addington?'

Roger nodded. 'I appreciate your scruples, sir. But surely the welfare of the nation should be put before personal

327

feelings. Had those fine brains you gathered about you—Dundas, Greville, Castlereagh and the rest—remained in office the country would not have fallen into quite so evil a pass. But I gather that most of them, as well as the Foxites, are now in opposition, although from a different angle, and the Cabinet, being filled with mediocrities incapable of rebutting their criticisms, staggers from side to side like a drunken man, so that the nation's affairs are becoming chaotic. Should such a state of things continue we'll stand no chance at all of checking Bonaparte's ambitions. Still worse, we may be forced into making another peace, more disastrous than the last. Yet did you but take the helm again, with the patriotic fervour that now animates the nation we might still emerge from the war triumphant.'

Mr. Pitt shrugged, 'Maybe you are right, Mr. Brook. My old friends Bishop Tomlin, Wilberforce and others all use the same arguments and urge it upon me as a duty. But to get the best results I'd have to take into my administration men of all parties—the Portland Whigs and perhaps even Charles Fox—and so form a Ministry of all the talents. That would need much delicate negotiation, and I'm not yet willing to undertake it. But we'll see.'

After pausing a moment he went on, 'In the meantime I believe that Britain can continue to hold her own. We are faced with only one danger, and that a great one. Bonaparte, I understand, is now building ships of war in every port he controls from Holland right down to Bordeaux. Should he in a year or two be able to muster a Fleet superior in strength to our Navy, then we shall indeed be undone. Should we lose control of the seas we will lose everything and be at his mercy. I pray you, when you return to France, bear that in mind, and that the greatest service you can render your country in the months to come will be timely intelligence to our Admiralty about movements of the French squadrons, so that we may hope to defeat them piecemeal before they become too strong for us.'

Pushing back his chair, Mr. Pitt stood up and added, 'And now, old friend, to bed. It has been good to talk with you

328

again; but I have to set an example to my officers and be on parade with my men at six o'clock tomorrow morning.'

On the night of December 21st Roger was back in London but it was not until the afternoon of the 22nd that he received a brief letter from Mrs. Marsham. In it she said that some trouble in working the Manchester Ship Canal, in which Colonel Thursby held a big interest, had led to his leaving for the north two days previously, and that he had accepted an invitation from his partner in that venture, the Duke of Bridgwater, to spend Christmas with him. But she would be most happy to have Roger at Stillwaters and the children were greatly looking forward to seeing him.

Intent now on buying presents, on the 23rd Roger went to his bankers, Messrs. Hoare in the Strand, to draw some ready money. As he was coming down the steps from the entrance a dark, foreign-looking man, who appeared to be in his late twenties, raised a square-crowned hat from his head and accosted him.

'Mr. McElfic,' he said with a smile and a heavy German accent, 'some years it is since we haf met. But you recall me, yes? I am Nathan, the son of Maier Amshel of Frankfurt, although now we haf family name Rothschild.'

Roger's mind instantly switched back to '95. In the Autumn of that year Mr. Pitt had sent him on a mission to the Rhine. After Robespierre's death in the previous year the Directory had come to power and was hard put to it to suppress an upsurge of reactionary feeling. There had seemed a good hope that if the right Republican General could be suborned he might play the role of Monk, march his army on Paris and restore the monarchy.

General Pichegru had been selected as the most promising man to take this part. Roger had first gone to the Prince de Condé, who commanded the army of Royalist exiles then in Baden, and persuaded him, on behalf of his King, to sign a promise that if Pichegru put Louis XVIII on the throne he should be made a Duke and Constable of France, be given the Château of Chambord and become the second man in the kingdom. Roger had then gone to Pichegru, who had been

329

inclined to accept this huge bribe but feared that on his army
approaching Paris it would be infiltrated by old *sans culottes*
who would cause it to mutiny and so wreck their plan. In
consequence he had required that, before he committed
himself, Roger should go to Paris and organize the pro-
monarchist elements there to rise against the Directory
simultaneously with his advance on the capital.

To that Roger had agreed, but one problem remained.
Pichegru's army was poised for a swift move to join up with
that of Moreau, and once their armies were united the defeat
of the Austrian army was inevitable. For Austria to be forced
out of the war before the proposed *coup d'état* would have
greatly weakened the Allies' power to insist that the restored
King of France should grant his people a democratic Constitution; so to gain time, Roger, having Pitt's open draft on the
British Treasury in his pocket, had offered Pichegru a bribe
of a million francs in gold so to arrange matters that his
army failed to make junction with Moreau's. Pichegru had
accepted, and it was the Jewish bankers in the Frankfurt
ghetto at the sign of the Red Shield who, at short notice, had
honoured the draft and provided this huge sum in gold.

Pichegru had kept his bargain and sent only two divisions
into the attack, so it had been repulsed. It was in Paris that
this great plan for a restoration had broken down. Shortly
after Roger arrived there the reactionaries had made a premature rising. Barras had appointed the untried young
General Bonaparte as Military Commandant of the City.
Overnight he had sent Captain Murat galloping off to bring
the guns up from the suburb of Sablons and, next day,
quelled the revolt with his famous 'whiff of grapeshot.' By
that the pro-monarchist fervour had been dissipated and the
Directory again had the situation so firmly in hand that
Pichegru dared not march his army on Paris. Later he had
been accused of treachery and had fled to England.

While Roger was recalling all this the young Jew said,
'You p'haps remember, sir, that at time we meet I tell you I
believed there to be good future in England our financial
deals to make. My honoured father in '98 say yes to my

330

request, and gif me for to operate here sum of twenty thousand pounds. I settle first in Manchester. Soon my capital is turn into sixty thousand. Now I come very frequent to London. Presently I have own establishment here. A Rothschild do not forget those who aid to make a fortune for his house. Discounting the bill you give on British Treasury for a million francs make us profit very handsome. You wish loan at any time, Mr. McElfic sir, I am honoured to oblige. Hoare's Bank here tell you address to write to me.'

Roger smiled at him, 'Yes, of course, I remember you now; and I thank you for your offer. I am glad, too, that your ventures here have proved so successful. But I am surprised that you should have recognized me; for when we met before I had side whiskers and, but for a shaven chin, a beard.'

'Your eyes, sir. So very blue, and the long lashes. I recognize at once.'

Suddenly an idea came to Roger and he asked, 'General Pichegru. He was denounced by the Directory and escaped to England. Presumably he is still here. Do you happen to know where he dwells?'

The squat little Jew nodded, 'Yes, sir. Some part of his money he invested with us. For him we get it out, and I his man of business am. He has lodging now at 22 Rupert Street.'

Roger thanked the dark, keen-eyed young man, shook hands with him and went his way, much pleased with the result of this chance encounter.

Next day, Christmas Eve, Roger went down to Stillwaters. Apart from the nursery quarters and a few of the smaller rooms he found the great house shut up, which sadly depressed him. His late wife's aunt, Mrs Marsham, received him joyfully, and the children, to whom he had, after his two years' absence, become almost a stranger, soon accepted him again as a half-forgotten friend who brought them intriguing presents and played jolly games with them.

But the memories of the many happy hours he had spent there with Georgina weighed heavily upon him. He could not get her out of his thoughts. Every feature of the place reminded him of one occasion or another when they had laughed and loved together. More than ever he regretted that she was not in England so that he was deprived of the chance of making his peace with her. Grimly, he forced himself to act the part of a jolly uncle with the children on Christmas and Boxing Days then, on the 27th, much relieved, and intent on his mission, he returned to London.

The more he had thought of the matter the more convinced he became that General Pichegru could prove the lead into the conspiracy that was brewing against Bonaparte. During the wars of the Revolution Pichegru had ranked with Dumouriez, Kellermann and Moreau as one of France's most brilliant Generals. Therefore, to have had his career cut short; to be, although a patriot, unemployed and in exile he must be bitterly antagonistic to Napoleon. In '95 he had been willing to gamble his high command for Royalist honours if he could bring about a Restoration. How much greater now was the inducement of the prospect of returning to France as a Duke and Commander in Chief of the Army as a reward for eliminating the Corsican upstart.

On the 28th Roger sent one of the footmen from Amesbury House to make discreet enquiries at No. 22 Rupert Street. From them he learned that Pichegru had gone to friends in the country before Christmas and was not expected back until after the New Year. For the next few days Roger controlled his impatience as well as he could, frequenting White's, Almack's and other clubs to pick up such information as might prove useful to him.

As far as the French exiles were concerned he drew a blank. The majority of the great nobles had foreseen the coming troubles and sent large sums abroad previous to '89, then left France well before the Terror. Those who had settled in England had either long since been accepted into society and had no desire to return to France or, if stirred by ambition, had made their peace with Napoleon and had become welcome members of his Court. The lesser fry, desperate and nearly penniless, had by now surrendered their pretensions as aristocrats and had sunk to the level of bourgeoisie, becoming language teachers, dancing masters and even barbers; so they were no longer in a position to frequent expensive clubs.

On January 3rd, learning that General Pichegru had returned to his lodging, at two o'clock that afternoon Roger took up a position on the corner of Rupert Street. After an hour's wait he recognized the tall figure that sallied forth from No. 22. The General walked only a hundred yards then turned into a chop house on the far corner. A few minutes later Roger followed, went in and saw to his satisfaction that Pichegru was seated alone in one of the high-backed booths made to accommodate four people. Making him a formal bow, Roger sat down on the opposite side of the table.

Having ordered a portion of steak and kidney pudding he looked across at the General and said in his perfect French, 'Can I be mistaken? Surely, Monsieur, you are General Pichegru?'

The General looked up from his plate, gave Roger a sharp glance and replied, 'Indeed I am, Monsieur. But I cannot recall our having met before.'

'I can,' Roger said with a smile. 'You were then commanding an army on the Rhine, and I arranged for you to receive a payment of one million francs in gold.'

'Mon Dieu!' the General exclaimed. 'I recall you now, though at that time you had whiskers and a short curly beard.'

' 'Tis true,' Roger agreed. 'I favoured that fashion in those days. What a tragedy it was that the well-conceived plan we made together never came to fruition.'

'Alas, alas!' Pichegru sighed. 'The accursed Corsican spiked our guns by putting down that premature pro-monarchist rising with such firmness. But for that, the state of things in Europe would be very different now.'

'Indeed yes. There would be peace and you, *mon Général*, would be the right hand of the King of France. Still, fortune did not treat you too badly; assuming, that is, that you have not lost the million that we paid you.'

333

'I still have a part of it that luckily I left with those honest Jews in Frankfurt; so I am at least better off than many of my poor friends, and do not have to labour at some dreary employment for a living. But that is no great consolation to a soldier who has been active all his life.'

Roger nodded, 'I sympathize; for time must hang heavy on your hands. Let us hope, though, that another turn in the wheel of fortune may again open to you opportunities worthy of your talents. As long as Bonaparte rules the roost in France there's little chance of that. But, like ourselves, he's only mortal and did aught befall him the situation in France would change overnight.'

'In that I agree. He has made himself as near as makes no difference a monarch, and the French people have ever been monarchists at heart. Were he removed from the scene no other General could replace him and the nation would demand the return of the King.'

'So far he has been lucky in escaping assassination,' Roger remarked quietly, 'but he has many enemies and his luck may not hold. It needs only skilful planning and a few resolute men to put him out of the way.'

Pichegru frowned. 'Greatly as I detest the man, as a soldier I am most strongly opposed to such methods. However, there are others. It might be possible to kidnap him and bring him as a prisoner to England. But to succeed in that would require an extensive and very costly organization.'

'Think you that really could be done?' Roger hazarded 'If so it would restore peace to Europe, and for such a venture I doubt not that I could provide another million from the secret funds.'

For a moment the General remained silent, then he said, 'When last we met I recall that you were acting as the personal emissary of Mr. Pitt. May I ask what is your position now?'

'Mr. Pitt's retirement made no difference to my status,' Roger lied blandly, 'but our present Prime Minister leaves all such matters to my Lord Hawkesbury at the Foreign Office.' Then, to draw Pichegru out, he added, 'But for the past year my master has employed me mainly in affairs concerning Russia, so I am ill informed on what is passing in Royalist circles here in England.'

Even an astuter man than the simple soldier, having already received from Roger a huge bribe to assist in an attempt to restore the French monarchy, could not have been blamed for trusting him completely; and Pichegru replied at once:

'We already have a plan for kidnapping Bonaparte, but lack of funds has so far prevented us from putting it into execution. Since you are prepared to aid us I would like you to come to the *Cercle Français* in Soho Square on Friday next at six o'clock. I and my friends who are concerned in this meet there every Friday, and a room in the club is set apart in which we pretend to play cards but actually hold our conferences.'

Hiding his elation, Roger willingly agreed, and over the remainder of their meal they talked of general matters. As they were about to part Pichegru said, 'You must pardon me, Monsieur, but I have forgotten your name.'

Roger smiled, 'When we met I was using that of Robert McElfic and in this affair 'twill serve as well as any other.'

On Friday 6th, he duly went to the *Cercle Français* and found it had previously been a large private mansion. On enquiring for General Pichegru he was taken up a broad staircase and into the principal salon on the first floor at the back of the house, in which a score or more of Frenchmen were either reading news-sheets or talking. Pichegru greeted him warmly and after some minutes of casual conversation, led him back across the landing to a lofty but much smaller room on one side of the staircase with a single tall window looking out on to the street.

Six other Frenchmen were seated round a table at cards, and when the General introduced Roger to them the only names that Roger recognized were those of Baron de Roll and Méhée de la Touche. The latter was a tall gawky man with, Roger decided, a decidedly shifty look. After a few polite exchanges they pushed the cards aside and got down to business.

It emerged that the brave Chouan leader, Georges Cadoudal, was already in Paris and, with a small company of his Breton patriots, was prepared to undertake the kidnapping of Napoleon one dark Saturday night when he was on his way from the Palace of St. Cloud to spend Sunday at Malmaison. Other Chouans in relays would rush the prisoner to the coast, but for that many horses would have to be purchased and tended in secret stables, for perhaps several weeks, and a ship would have to be held in readiness to transport the captive across the Channel.

Roger conceded in his own mind that Pichegru, and perhaps several of the others, honestly believed this to be possible; but his own conviction was that it was not. Too many people would have to be involved in it for the plot not to be betrayed or go wrong somewhere; so all the odds were that to make certain of the success of their *coup* some of the more unscrupulous of the conspirators intended to murder Napoleon soon after he had been kidnapped.

The next stage in the plan was to seize power before one of the other Consuls, or perhaps Bernadotte, could do so. For this a man was required who had the confidence and respect of the French people. As a general who had been denounced and sought refuge in England, Pichegru could not fill the bill; but Moreau could. So it was intended that Pichegru should go secretly to Paris, and persuade his old comrade-in-arms, on a given signal that Bonaparte had been got out of the way, to raise the troops of the Paris garrison, who adored him, and declare for the King. At the same time a Bourbon Prince was to enter France and take over from Moreau as Regent until Louis XVIII could be brought from Mittau on the distant Baltic.

A long discussion followed during which Roger learned that an Abbé David, General Lajolais and a man named Querelle were the principal Royalist agents then in Paris and that one of them would arrange the meeting between Pichegru and Moreau. But when he pressed for further information about these people and the identity of the Prince who was to act as Regent the conspirators refused it. They declared that they could not disclose such matters without the consent of their chief, Monsieur Hyde de Neuville, who had recently been in Paris and caught such a severe cold while recrossing the Channel that he was in bed, which had prevented him from attending the conference that evening.

At that, in order to learn further details of the plot Roger dug his toes in. He said that if he was to finance the operation he must be able to give his master full particulars of it, and especially the name of the Prince, as there were several and the British Government would have greater confidence in some than in others.

In consequence it was agreed that, as by Monday Hyde de Neuville should be sufficiently recovered, they would meet again with him present. Roger then spent the remainder of the evening drinking and talking with his new friends and left them greatly pleased with the progress he was making.

On the evening of Monday 9th Roger again went to the *Cercle Français* and, this time, on giving his name was shown straight up to the front room on the first floor. As he was a little early only four of the conspirators—de la Touche, the Baron de Roll, the Chevalier de Brie and a Colonel Lafont—had assembled, but they greeted him cordially and poured him a glass of wine. A few minutes later Pichegru came in followed by a thick-set middle-aged man. After smiling at Roger the General turned to his companion and said:

'De Neuville, this is Mr. McElfic who, as I have told you, has promised . . .'

The rest of his sentence was drowned in a roar from de Neuville. His eyes starting from his head, he thrust out an accusing finger at Roger and shouted, 'Are you gone mad that you have betrayed our secrets to this man? He is *le Colonel Breuc*, one of the Corsican's Aides-de-Camp.'

CHAPTER XXII

THE GRIM AFFAIR OF THE
DUC D'ENGHIEN

ROGER drew a quick breath. He had never before to his knowledge seen de Neuville, so was taken completely by surprise.

Pichegru's jaw dropped and for a moment he looked dumbfounded. Then, turning on de Neuville he said sharply, 'You must be mistaken. This is the man who in '95 signed an order for a million francs on the British Treasury with the object of bringing about a Restoration. I'd stake my life on that.'

'In '95,' de Neuville sneered. 'Many a man has changed his coat since then.'

'But damn it man!' protested the General. 'He is prepared to do the same again. To suggest that he is one of Bonaparte's people does not make sense. He was then Mr. Pitt's personal emissary, and now represents my Lord Hawkesbury.'

'Have you proof of that?'

'No,' Pichegru hesitated. 'I've naught but his word.'

'Then you have been fooled. I tell you I know him to be *le Colonel Breuc*. In Paris, less than a month ago, I stood within fifteen feet of him. It was at the entrance to the

Tuileries and he held Bonaparte's horse as the Corsican dismounted.'

De la Touche, de Roll and the other two men had come to their feet and were staring at Roger threateningly. For a moment he considered attempting to play his old gambit of mistaken identity. But he was seized with a sudden conviction that they would never believe him if he now protested that he was the English Admiral's son and Colonel Breuc a cousin who had often been mistaken for him.

It was de la Touche who clinched the matter by exclaiming, 'De Neuville is right! On Friday evening I thought I knew his face. Now I recall where I saw him. It was last September. He was sitting at a table drinking with General Bessiéres outside a café in the Palais Royal gardens. I was at the next table trying to catch what I could of their conversation.'

'*Mort Dieu*!' de Roll muttered. 'And he knows our plan. If he gets back to France our friends there will be ruined.'

'Not necessarily,' put in the Chevalier de Brie. 'He got from us only general particulars and a few names, but no details or addresses.'

'He knows too much,' said de Neuville grimly. 'We must see to it that he does not return, or pass on what he has learned to some traitor here.'

'That is easier said than done,' remarked Pichegru with a frown.

'Then you have become squeamish for a soldier, General,' de la Touche declared. 'There is but one penalty for a spy who is caught, and he has earned it.'

During these swift exchanges Roger's mind had been working furiously, and he had no illusions about the imminent peril in which he stood. He did not think they would dare murder him in the club, but the six of them could overpower him and force brandy down his throat until he was dead drunk. Drunkenness was so common that the other members of the club and the servants would think nothing of seeing a man who had passed out being carried downstairs by a party of apparently half-drunk friends and being driven off

339

with them in a coach. They could then finish him off with a knock on the head and leave his body in some back alley where, when it was found in the morning, it would be assumed that he had been attacked and killed by a footpad.

The six of them were standing on the far side of the table with the door behind them, so he stood no possible chance of getting past them to it. Had he had a sword he could have held them off long enough for his shouts for help to bring other people to his assistance; but he was unarmed. And if he did shout, that would drive them into rushing him and knocking him out at once, then telling whoever arrived on the scene that he had gone down in a fight following a quarrel over cards. His only asset lay in his extreme fitness and agility; but he rated his chances of getting away as slender.

Nonetheless he had made up his mind what to do when the attack came, and the moment de Neuville opened his mouth to cry 'Come; get him!' he acted.

Springing forward, he grasped the edge of the heavy table with both hands, gave a violent heave and overturned it. To his right, only two paces away, lay the fireplace. Even before the glasses and decanter had crashed on the floor, by a sideways dive he had grabbed the poker. The far edge of the table struck Pichegru and the Baron de Roll hard above the knees, knocked them both backwards and temporarily pinned them beneath it. Assuming that Roger meant to make a rush for the door, de Neuville jumped back and planted himself firmly in front of it. De Brie, who had been beside him, leapt round that end of the overturned table towards Roger, while Lafont, followed by de la Touche, ran at him round the other.

Lafont was a pace ahead of the others, so Roger turned to face him, swung the poker high and aimed a blow at his head. Just in time he jerked his head aside; but the poker slashed down across his ear, tearing it half off. Clapping his hand to it, the Colonel gave a screech of pain, reeled backwards, tripped on the edge of the hearth and fell backward upon it.

340

Before Roger had time to recover from the stroke, de Brie was upon him and had grabbed him by the back of his coat collar. As he twisted round they were at too close quarters for Roger to strike at his assailant's head. Instead he drew the poker back and drove its point hard into the plump Chevalier's stomach. De Brie gave a gasp and his eyes popped from their sockets. Letting go Roger's collar he, too, staggered back then doubled up in agony.

Knowing that de la Touche must now be immediately behind him, Roger swivelled on his heel. As he turned his head he thought that he was finished. De la Touche had drawn a poniard from beneath his coat and had it raised high to plunge into him. It was too late for him to spring away or bring up the poker to guard against the blow. But he was saved from it most unexpectedly. Still standing in the doorway de Neuville gave a sudden shout.

'Stop, you imbecile! No bloodshed! No bloodshed here or we'll hang for it.'

With an effort de la Touche checked the stab in mid-air. Glowering with hatred he stepped back. Now facing him, Roger brought up his right foot and kicked him hard on the shin. He gave a grunt, swore foully and, as Roger swung at him with the poker, swiftly retreated.

Panting from his exertions but still unharmed, Roger was now free from attack; but he knew that he would remain so only for a matter of moments. Pichegru and de Roll had come out from beneath the table, de la Touche had received only a minor injury, de Brie was getting back his wind and de Neuville might, at any moment, decide to enter the fray. To fight his way through them to the door was still out of the question. Grimly he realized that there was only one way in which he might perhaps save himself. Turning his back on them, he brought the poker with all his force against the lower half of the tall window.

It shattered, but great jagged pieces of the glass still adhered to the sides and bottom of the frame. Three more swift blows sent the largest of them crashing into the street below. Pounding feet on the floor behind him told him that

341

he would never get through the window before his enemies had seized and overcome him.

Turning, he faced them once more. Clenching his teeth he slashed at them right, left and centre. His first blow caught Pichegru on his outstretched arm; his second felled the Baron with a cracked skull; his third missed the Chevalier but, throwing Roger off balance, saved him from a brandy bottle that de la Touche had picked up from the floor and hurled at his head. Recovering from his lurch he lunged with the poker at de Brie's face, smashing in his front teeth. Pichegru, in spite of his disabled arm, came at him again but got a jab from the poker right over his heart that rendered him temporarily *hors de combat*.

Colonel Lafont still sat moaning on the hearth with his hand over his torn ear. De Neuville had not entered the fray but remained guarding the door. De la Touche now hung back, evidently unwilling to risk serious injury. It was Roger's chance and he took it.

The bottom of the tall window was only a foot from the floor. Thrusting one leg over he dropped the poker, grasped the sill with both hands and swung himself out. Giving a swift glance down he was appalled. To the pavement below was a drop of fifteen feet. If he let go it seemed certain that he would either break his neck or a leg.

Then he saw that only a yard to the right of the window and a few feet below it there projected from the wall an iron bracket holding a lantern that lit the entrance to the club. For a second he wondered whether it would bear his weight, then decided that he must chance that. Shifting his grip on the sill, he swung himself sideways, grasped the bracket and lowered himself to it. But he was still twelve feet above the street level. Yet worse—another quick look downward showed him that he was now hanging immediately over a row of spiked railings on one side of the steps that led up to the door of the club. If he let go his hold he would be impaled upon them.

His breath coming in gasps he hung there, his mind fraught with terrible indecision. He could still climb back and surrender to his enemies. He had no doubt they meant to kill him, but to let himself drop might also mean death; or, at least, terrible injuries.

A moment later he was given no option. De la Touche was leaning out of the window, an evil grin on his shifty countenance and his dagger in his hand. He made a slash at Roger's fingers. Instinctively Roger let go of the iron bracket.

As he plunged downward terror seized him. In his vivid imagination he could already feel the iron spikes piercing his flesh and smashing his bones. Ten seconds later he was brought up with a violent jerk. He had missed being impaled by a fraction of an inch. The spikes had penetrated under his flying coat tails, ripped through the back of his coat and left him suspended by its thick collar.

For a moment he hung there. Then he realized that his feet, beneath bent legs, were resting on the steps up to the club. From inside it there came the sound of excited shouts. Although every minute of the desperate encounter he had just survived had seemed like five to him, he knew that it could have occupied only a very short time; so the shouts and crash of glass in the room above had not drawn attention to the fact that there was trouble there until it was almost over. But by now the other occupants of the club must be up there seeking an explanation.

To accuse his attackers of an attempt to kidnap and later murder him could serve no useful purpose, and to lend himself to an enquiry into the affair by their compatriots might even prove dangerous. So, bracing his legs, he wrenched at his coat until he had torn himself free of the railings, then staggered off round the square until he came upon an unoccupied sedan chair that carried him back to Amesbury House.

Next morning, knowing himself to be now a marked man, and that as long as he remained in London the conspirators would do their utmost to trace him, then stick at nothing to prevent his return to France, he said good-bye to Droopy and set out for Walmer.

That evening he informed Mr. Pitt of all that had taken

place and, as he had hoped, his old master agreed to place at his disposal one of his cutters manned by Sea Fencibles, as the quickest way for him to get back to France. He sailed in it that night and shortly before dawn on the 12th the cutter put him ashore in a quiet cove some miles south of Boulogne. Soon after he had landed he had a narrow escape from being caught by a beach patrol, but he succeeded in evading it and on the morning of the 14th was back in Paris.

After sleeping through most of the day at *La Belle Etoile*, he rode out that night to St. Cloud and made his report to Talleyrand. His old friend listened with much concern to his account of the danger to which by an ill chance he had been exposed, then congratulated him warmly on having penetrated the conspiracy.

Over a tête-à-tête supper, worthy of them both, they discussed the matter at length and agreed that, as Roger had not secured sufficient details of the plot to nip it in the bud, the probability was that it would be proceeded with. Although Fouché was still out of office Talleyrand was of the opinion that he, and the agents he continued to employ, were much more likely to get to the bottom of the affair than were Savary's regular police. He said he would seek the co-operation of that subtle master-mind the following day and ask its unprepossessing owner to endeavour to discover the whereabouts of Cadoudal, the Abbé David and M. Querelle and to have a close watch kept on General Lajolais.

They then speculated on which of the Bourbon Princes had been selected to make a dash for Paris, take over from General Moreau and act as Regent until the Comte de Provence could reach the capital and be proclaimed as Louis XVIII.

The legitimate choice was his younger brother, the Comte d'Artois; and it was known that he had spent long periods on the Isle of Yeu, off the Brittany coast, under the protection of the English, so that he could be swiftly landed in France in the event of a successful counter-revolution. But Charles d'Artois was a lazy, pleasure-loving man and Talleyrand, who had known him well in pre-Revolution days, thought it unlikely that he would risk putting his head into a noose if there was the least possibility of it closing on him.

The Prince de Condé seemed a better bet, as it was he who had commanded the army of Royalist exiles on the Rhine and done all he could to aid the Austrians in their war against Revolutionary France. But in recent years his army had withered away, many of the exiled nobles having made their peace with Napoleon, and others having left it to settle as civilians in the German cities. So the Prince had become dispirited and was no longer looked on by the Monarchists as a leader of promise. It might, however, be the Prince's son, the Duc d'Enghien. He was a handsome and vigorous young man in his early thirties with a dashing personality and likely to have a strong appeal to the French people.

Another possibility was d'Artois' son, the twenty-six-year-old Duc de Berri; but he was living in Italy, so it would not be possible for him to enter France overnight, and for a *coup d'état* to prove successful swift action was essential.

Lastly there was Louis Philippe, Duc d'Orleans, who was living at Twickenham near London. But his side of the Bourbon family had ever been a thorn in the side of the senior branch. His father had even gone to the length of siding with the Revolutionaries, laying down his title and calling himself, 'Philippe Egalité' then, as a member of the Convention, voting for the death of his cousin, Louis XVI. Roger had later taken considerable pleasure in being instrumental in getting him sent to the guillotine. They decided that for the Monarchists to choose a prince with such antecedents was very unlikely.

The next day Roger reported back to Napoleon, who abruptly enquired the reason for Talleyrand's having requested the loan of him. Not feeling that he could refuse, Roger gave an account of his mission, but he did so with reluctance as he felt sure that Napoleon would instruct Savary to go into the affair, and feared that the heavy-handed Minister of Police might ruin the investigation of the infinitely more skilful Fouché.

When he had done Napoleon laughed, tweaked Roger's ear

and said, 'What a man you are, Breuc. You are worth half a dozen of my other *beaux sabreurs.*' Then, with a sudden change of mood, he added, 'Moreau is a fine soldier but a fool politically; and as he hates me it is quite likely that he will be idiot enough to allow himself to be drawn into this conspiracy. As for this Prince who is to play the part of Viceroy until the Comte de Provence can be brought from Mittau, if we catch him I'll make such an example of him as no other Bourbon will ever forget.'

During the month that followed Roger saw both Talleyrand and Fouché several times and they kept him informed of the progress of the conspiracy which, as he had expected, was going forward. Cadoudal, it was learned, had again been landed at Biville on January 14th and was believed to be in Paris but could not be traced. On the 24th, by having the Abbé David shadowed, Pichegru was found to have arrived in the capital, and on the evening of the 27th he was seen to meet Moreau, accompanied by General Lajolais, apparently by accident, in the Boulevard de la Madeleine; but after only a few minutes' conversation they went their respective ways. There followed four lengthy secret conferences for which they met in private houses; so it was now clear that the victor of Hohenlinden had been drawn into the conspiracy. Then, on the 15th February Savary jeopardized all prospect of allowing the affair to ripen until all the conspirators could be caught in the net by arresting Monsieur Querelle.

In an attempt to save himself Querelle gave away the addresses at which Cadoudal and Pichegru were in hiding. But, taking alarm at Querelle's arrest, both had swiftly vacated their lodgings. However, on the 29th Pichegru, given away by a treacherous friend, was seized while in bed in his house. Ten days later a series of domiciliary visits to suspects led to the finding of Cadoudal and, after a desperate resistance, he was carried off to prison. There followed the arrest of the Duc de Polignac, the Marquis de Riviére, who had come over with Pichegru. Lajolais and a number of the lesser conspirators.

Moreau had continued to reside openly at his house out-

side Paris so could be picked up at any time; but there
remained the problem of the unidentified Bourbon Prince.
Napoleon was anxious that he, above all, should be caught
and, believing him to be the Comte d'Artois, had despatched
Savary to Biville to lie in wait for him when he landed.
Captain Wright's vessel was lying off the coast and appropriate messages purporting to come from the conspirators
were sent off to her. But either the Prince was not on board
or had already had intelligence that things had gone wrong in
Paris.

Meanwhile numerous agents had been keeping a close
watch on the other Princes. During Savary's absence, some of
those acting for his opposite number Réal, Fouché's old
lieutenant, had sent in a report that the young Duc d'Enghien
was engaged in highly suspicious activities. He had chosen
Baden as his place of exile and lived at Ettenheim, not far
from the Rhine, and was said in recent months to have made
frequent secret trips across it to Strassburg, which was in
French territory.

The failure of d'Artois to appear led at once to the sup-
position that he was not, after all, the selected nominal head
of the conspiracy, and that d'Enghien's visits to Strassburg
were to make preparations for a dash to Paris. As a further
indication that he was their man it was reported that he had
staying with him at Ettenheim a Colonel Smith, who had just
come from London, and General Dumouriez. This last was a
particularly damning piece of information, for Dumouriez,
before becoming disgusted with the excesses of the Revolution
and going over to the English, had been a brilliant and
popular General; so he was just the man to rally the troops in
north-eastern France to the Monarchist cause.

Napoleon, assuming that from that quarter he might now
expect really serious trouble, flew into one of his great rages,
summoned a Privy Council and declared his intention of
cutting the ground from beneath the conspirators' feet by
striking first: he would send a raiding force into Baden to
seize the Duke.

Both his fellow Consuls opposed the plan, pointing out

that this violation of neutral territory would arouse a shocking outcry among the nations and, possibly, embroil France with both Germany and Russia. But Talleyrand said he was confident that he could appease the Margrave and Fouché, who was also present, expressed the opinion that they ought to take this opportunity of crushing the hopes of the monarchists once and for all. In consequence, as usual, the First Consul got his way.

After the conference Napoleon sent for General Ordener, told him what was required and ordered him to proceed at once with a small force to the Rhine opposite Ettenheim. Roger happened to be on duty in the anteroom to the Cabinet and was standing just outside the door as Ordener emerged from it. Catching sight of him, Napoleon beckoned him and called to Ordener to come back. Then he said to Roger:

'Breuc, you were among the first to secure for us information about the Royalist conspiracy. As a reward you shall witness the end of it. You may go with Ordener on the mission I have just given him. He will tell you about it.'

Much intrigued and having thanked his master, Roger left the Palace with the General, was told what was afoot, and arranged to set out from Paris with him that afternoon. Shortly before midday on March 14th they reached Strassburg and held a conference with Réal's agents, who knew the exact location of d'Enghien's house and would accompany them on their kidnapping expedition. After having dined they slept for some hours then, at ten o'clock in the evening, started on their twenty-mile ride along the left bank of the Rhine.

On arriving at the village of Rhinau they rested their horses and ate a snack they had brought with them. At about two in the morning, they were put across the river in relays by the village ferry. They had only a further seven miles to go and found Ettenheim dark and deserted. The agents led them to the small château in which d'Enghien resided. Ordener had his troopers surround it, then ordered two of his N.C.O.s to break in the door.

The noise they made roused the household and when

Ordener and Roger went inside they were met by the young Duke, partially dressed, coming downstairs with a drawn sword in his hand. The General told him that he had orders from the First Consul to arrest him for having as an exile made illegal entries into French territory.

D'Enghien now broke into violent protests and claimed immunity from arrest by virtue of his being on foreign soil. Ordener refused to listen, upon which the Duke put himself on guard and declared his intention of defending himself. But by this time there were half a dozen troopers standing in the hall and the shocked friends with whom d'Enghien was living persuaded him that resistance was useless.

While, under supervision, he dressed and packed a small valise, Réal's agents searched the house and confiscated all the papers they could find. The Duke was then led out and mounted on a spare horse; but he insisted on taking his dog with him, so the animal was handed up to be carried by him on his saddle bow. Shortly before dawn the cavalcade recrossed the Rhine and by eight o'clock on the 15th they were back in Strassburg.

Réal had arrived and that afternoon, in the presence of Ordener and Roger, set about questioning their prisoner. Accused of conspiracy to assassinate the First Consul he showed amazement and indignantly denied even knowing that such a plot was afoot. At the suggestion that General Dumouriez and Colonel Smith had come over to join him he laughed and replied:

'What nonsense. The Colonel who was staying with me was not named Smith but Schmidt, and lives in Frankfurt. As to Dumouriez, I can only suppose that some stupid agent has reported that I often spend an hour or two with the old Marquis de Thumery, who lives in Ettenheim, as when pronounced with a heavy German accent that name sounds rather like Dumouriez.'

Réal had also received information from a servant at the de Polignac's that a mysterious stranger had paid several visits to their house and that both his master and the Marquis de Rivière had risen to receive him and paid him the sort of respect that they would have shown to a Prince of the Blood; but d'Enghien stoutly denied having ever been in Paris since the Revolution, when he was still in his teens.

Questioned about his visits to Strassburg, he did not deny having made them but disclosed their reason only with reluctance when impressed with the seriousness of his situation. It then emerged that he was in love with the Princesse Charlotte de Rohan who lived in that city. His visits had been to see her and, occasionally, to take her to the theatre.

Roger was greatly impressed by the young Duke's open countenance and frank manner; so he formed the opinion that Réal's agents had stumbled on a mare's nest and that d'Enghien was in danger of becoming their innocent victim. After the interrogation he said so to Réal, but the Police Chief and Ordener replied that it was not their business to act as judges in the matter. They had orders to convey the Duke to Paris and consign him to the fortress of Vincennes; so must carry them out.

Much troubled, when the cavalcade set off next morning for the capital, Roger decided to remain behind and carry out a further investigation. First he waited upon the Princess de Rohan whom, having heard of her lover's arrest, he found in great distress. Crossing herself, she assured him on oath that, to the best of her belief, the Duke was not the least interested in politics, that his visits to Strassburg had been only to see her and she felt certain that within recent months he had never been to Paris.

That night Roger again crossed the Rhine. His German was sufficiently good to pass muster in that area that had so often changed Sovereigns and a great part of the population was of mixed Franco-German descent. During the following day he made cautious enquiries which confirmed d'Enghien's statement that the friend who had stayed with him was a Colonel Schmidt and that a Marquis de Thumery had a small property near the little town.

Convinced now that the young Prince was innocent, he returned to Strassburg, secured a fresh mount and rode all out for Paris, arriving on the morning of March 20th. At the

Tuileries he learned that Napoleon was at Malmaison so, after a meal and freshening himself up, he went on there.

To his request for an audience the reply was returned that the First Consul was heavily engaged, but was leaving for St. Cloud that evening and would receive him there the following day. An instinct telling him that the matter was urgent, he asked for Josephine and she had him brought to her in a small closet where she often spent an hour or more arranging the flowers in which she so greatly delighted.

Swiftly, Roger informed her of the matter that was worrying him so much. Putting down the loose flowers she held, she turned to him and he saw that her big brown eyes were gravely troubled as she said:

'I believe you right. Even Réal now admits that his agents may have been mistaken. But the First Consul is adamant. He insists that d'Enghien must be tried; and by a court martial in secret. Yesterday he ordered Murat, as Governor of Paris, to convene a Court. I am told Murat was furious and declared that to bring the Duke to trial on such slender evidence would be a stain upon his uniform. Napoleon replied that he would do as he was ordered or forfeit his post. In the park here I pleaded with him myself to give up this wicked idea of making d'Enghien a scapegoat for the malice of the other Bourbon Princes; but he would not listen to me. He brushed my appeal aside, replying only, "Go away. You are a child; you do not understand public duties."'

After another futile attempt to get a hearing from the First Consul, Roger rode to St. Cloud with the object of getting Talleyrand to intervene; but the Foreign Minister was not there. He was spending the night at his mansion in the Rue du Bac. There, in the evening, Roger saw him and told him of his absolute conviction that d'Enghien was innocent.

Rising from his chair, the elegant, impeccably-dressed aristocrat laid a hand gently on Roger's shoulder and said in his deep voice, '*Cher ami*, I pray you concern yourself no further in this matter. It is no business of yours.'

'But it is!' Roger protested hotly. 'It was I who found out

for you when in London that a Bourbon Prince was to enter France and act as Regent until Louis XVIII could be brought to Paris. How can I now stand by and see an innocent young man condemned to spend years of his life in prison? For I've no doubt that, if he is court-martialled, Napoleon will have given orders that he is to be found guilty.'

Talleyrand sighed, 'Of course. And guilt in this case, as he will be charged with treason, would result in a sentence of death.'

'Death!' cried Roger. 'No! You cannot mean it. 'Twould be the most atrocious crime.'

'True,' the Minister nodded. 'Yet I pray you remember that during the past ten years several million people have had their lives brought to a premature end for no good reason at all. That this young man should lose his is unfortunate; but the interests of the State must override all other considerations. Forfeiting his life may preserve civil peace and save many other people from losing theirs in abortive attempts to overthrow our present government.'

To execute a handful of trouble-makers, even if one or two of them had become involved by accident, rather than allow them to continue at liberty until a movement developed leading to riots in which scores of innocent people lost their lives, were wounded or had their property destroyed, was a policy to which Roger had always subscribed; but he would not accept it in this instance. For a further ten minutes he pleaded with Talleyrand to intervene; then, finding him firmly resolved to take no action, took his leave.

His next resolve was to ride to Vincennes and learn what was actually happening there. He arrived a little before eleven o'clock to find Savary in charge and that the Duke had just been put through a preliminary examination. To his horror he learned that the trial was to take place at one o'clock that morning and that d'Enghien's grave had already been dug in the dry moat of the castle.

Old General Hulin, a veteran revolutionary who had been one of the leaders in the mob's attack on the Bastille in '89,

352

had been nominated as President of the Court; so there could be little doubt that against a Bourbon Prince a verdict of 'Guilty' would be brought in.

Savary was an old acquaintance of Roger's. It was he and Rapp, Desaix's other A.D.C., who had found him naked and wounded on the field of Marengo while searching for the body of their dead General; so, in a sense, Roger owed his life to him. But that was the only bond between them; for Roger had found him a hard, unfeeling man. That, he supposed, was the reason why Napoleon had made him Chief of Police. Nevertheless Roger now did his utmost to persuade Savary, in the event of the verdict being 'guilty,' to postpone d'Enghien's execution till the following day. But Savary refused to depart from normal procedure, which was that after a sentence had been passed it should be carried out within a few hours.

Tired as Roger was, in desperation he remounted his horse and rode back to St. Cloud. The fact that he was an A.D.C. enabled him to enter the Palace unchallenged. Although it was well after midnight he thought it probable that Napoleon would still be at work, so went straight to the Orangery, that the First Consul had made his office. There he found Rustem, the faithful Mameluke that Napoleon had brought back from Egypt. He was sitting on the stairs that led to an upper room with his scimitar across his knees and obviously on guard.

Assuming that the First Consul was up there Roger demanded to see him. Rustem shook his turbaned head. 'That is not possible, *Monsieur le Colonel*. He is amusing himself upstairs with a lady, and has given imperative orders that he is not to be disturbed.'

At that moment Constant, Napoleon's confidential valet, entered the room to collect Napoleon's hat, cloak and sword. Turning to him Roger asked quickly, 'Who has the First Consul upstairs with him?'

Constant, who knew Roger well, replied with a grin, 'A new one: Madame Duchâtel. She is Madame Bonaparte's reader, and a real beauty. She is only twenty but as clever as they make them, and very discreet. No doubt she does not want to upset her old husband who is no use to her. But she has been skilfully angling for our master ever since she has been here.'

'I have got to see him,' Roger said tersely. 'It is a matter of life and death: a matter that may seriously affect his own future.'

For a moment Constant hesitated, then he shrugged, 'In that case ... but God help you if he does not regard the matter as so serious as you seem to think.' Then he waved Rustem aside.

Roger ran up the stairs, knocked twice hard on the door, waited a moment then, although no reply came, threw it open and marched in.

Napoleon, wearing only a shirt, stood near the hearth on which there was a blazing fire that gave the only light in the room. Obviously he had only just jumped out of bed. Lying there was a beautiful girl with golden hair, cornflower blue eyes, a perfectly shaped aquiline nose. Her mouth, half open in surprise, showed too that she had lovely teeth. After one glance at Roger she hurriedly turned over so that her back was to him. Meanwhile, Napoleon, scowling like thunder, snarled:

'What is the meaning of this? How dare you force your way in here? Who gave you permission to disturb me? This abuse of your position is unforgivable! Here and now I deprive you of your appointment as an A.D.C.; and of your rank of Colonel. Get out! Get out! D'you hear me?'

Roger did not attempt to check the flow of vituperation that followed, but stood his ground. When it had ceased he said in a tired, hoarse voice, 'Consul, I come upon the matter of d'Enghien. Unless you intervene before dawn they mean to shoot him. He is innocent. I know it. I swear it.' Then, in a spate of words he gave his reasons for his belief.

'Damn you!' roared Napoleon before he had finished. 'I have heard all this before, and I don't give a hoot for it. This is no affair of yours but a matter of State, and to preserve the peace the Prince must die.'

354

'A few hours back Monsieur de Talleyrand said the same to me,' Roger retorted. 'Yet if it is not my affair it certainly is yours. Do you permit this to happen 'twill be murder! Murder! Murder! And your name will stink in the nostrils of all Europe as a result of it. For your own sake you have got to give me a reprieve that I can carry to Vincennes before it is too late. You must. If you refuse you will never live this down. For the rest of your life you will regret it.'

For a moment Napoleon considered; then, his mood completely changed, he shook his head and said quickly, 'No, Breuc. You have ever advised me soundly and I appreciate that you have broken in on me only on account of what you believe to be my best interests. But it cannot be. I am determined to make an example of this Bourbon Prince as a deterrent to others.'

From the way he spoke Roger knew that further argument was useless; so he replied, 'Very well then. I will return to Vincennes, tell Savary that I have seen you and that by word of mouth you have sent me to order a stay of the Prince's execution. There is still a chance that by doing so I may save you from your own folly.' Then he turned on his heel and left the room.

Outside the Palace he wearily mounted his tired horse and again set out on the ten-mile ride through the southern suburbs of Paris to Vincennes, which lay right on the other side of the city. He had covered no more than a quarter of the distance and was already reeling with fatigue in the saddle when, while trotting along a dark, tree-lined road, the faint light that lit the scene grew dimmer until he found himself staring ahead into impenetrable darkness.

For a moment he thought that, for the first time in his life, he must have fainted. But almost immediately a new light dawned about him. It was not bright but clear and he found himself looking down on a wide expanse of sea upon which the sun was setting. He knew immediately that it was in the tropics for, in the distance, he could see a palm-fringed island. Close in to it there was a ship from which a cloud of smoke was ascending. She was on fire and sinking. Nearer, but some way off, there was a longboat in which the seamen were rowing desperately. Still nearer several men were swimming and one man held a slender sword clenched between his teeth.

Suddenly, immediately beneath him he saw Georgina struggling in the water. As clearly as if she had in fact been only a few feet from him he heard her shout, 'Save me, Roger! Oh, save me!'

The strange psychic link that several times before, when one or other of them was faced with an emergency, had enabled them to communicate although hundreds of miles apart, had functioned once again. He felt as certain as he had ever felt of anything that the intangible spirit that gave him being and purpose had been transported to the West Indies and that at that moment Georgina was actually on the point of drowning.

In his deep consciousness he knew that physically he could not aid her, but that by joining the power of his will to hers he might give her the additional strength to keep herself afloat until she was rescued. No thought of their quarrel or her betrayal of him entered his mind. He was conscious only of his life-long love for her. Calling silently on God to help him, he threw out the very essence of himself to buoy her up in her struggle to survive.

Next moment he found himself diving right on to her. He felt no impact but in some miraculous way they seemed to have become one. She had gone under but swiftly surfaced. Her arms flailed the water with new strength. Turning, she struck out vigorously for the shore. While still some distance from it his sight began to blur. Swiftly the vision faded. In earthly time it had lasted only for a few seconds. During that time he had lost control of his horse and plunged headlong from the saddle. In rapid succession he felt blows on his head, shoulder and ankle. The horse trotted on leaving him lying in the road unconscious.

CHAPTER XXIII

OVERWHELMED

WHEN ROGER came to, he dimly realized that he was in bed and that strangers were grouped round him. As his mind cleared his gaze focused on the face of a youngish man who was hurting him abominably by doing something to his head, then on a portly woman holding a basin of water. At the end of the bed stood an older man and with him a rather plain young woman.

Several hours later he learned that he had lain in the road unconscious for a long time, been found by two workmen in the dawn and carried into the house of a couple named Boutheron. They had called in their doctor to dress his wounds and the girl was their daughter Héloise. Still later he learned the full extent of his injuries. The back of his skull had been cracked, it was thought by a blow from a rear hoof of his horse as he fell from it; he had dislocated his left shoulder and sprained his left ankle.

The doctor declared that he ought not to be moved for some time and the Boutherons, who were prosperous bourgeois, said they were perfectly willing to look after him until he was out of danger. In due course, when he was able to tell them about himself, they declared themselves delighted and honoured to have as their guest an A.D.C. of the idolized First Consul.

His memory of the vision he had had of Georgina returned to him in his first spell of full consciousness, and as he lay there through the following days he spent many hours thinking about it, hoping that she had survived but tortured by the thought that she might be dead and that he would never see her again.

At first his head pained him too much for him to think coherently for long, but as he grew stronger he spent an hour each night attempting to solve the question by the only means which offered a chance that he might do so. Long since, they had solemnly promised one another that if one of them died he or she would appear to the other. Although fearing the result he forced himself to concentrate on willing her to come to him if she was dead; and when, after a week, his efforts proved abortive, he felt more hope that she was still alive. But he could feel no real certainty that she was, as, although he was a convinced believer in survival, he could not dismiss the possibility that others, who did not believe in it, might be right.

Either Madame Boutheron or Héloïse sat with him for a good part of each day and, when he grew strong enough, either talked or read to him, often from the news sheets. From them he learned that Savary had had d'Enghien executed in the moat at Vincennes at half past two on that fatal morning, and also learned the results of this terrible affair.

In spite of the Government's attempts to suppress the facts the truth had leaked out and all Europe had denounced Napoleon as a murderer. Even several of Roger's friends who, when they learned where he was, came to see him, spoke of the affair with horror and said that it had stained the First Consul's reputation in a way that would long be remembered.

Then in mid-April Pichegru was found one morning strangled in his cell. It was given out that he had committed suicide but, after the d'Enghien affair, many people were of

the opinion that Napoleon had given orders that the General, too, should be murdered.

Nevertheless Napoleon did not intend such adverse speculations to interfere with the designs he had formed for making use of the conspiracy, as Fouché told Roger when paying him a visit.

Keeping his fish-like eyes well away from Roger's, the cadaverous ex-Minister sniffed and said, 'Although Napoleon has been made Consul for life, as long as he remains an elected ruler his death would mean a struggle for power between half a dozen people ambitious to step into his shoes, and in the resulting turmoil the Monarchists would stand a very good chance of putting a Bourbon on the throne. In consequence, as soon as they have recovered from their recent setback they'll start planning another attempt to assassinate him. But if he became an hereditary monarch, whoever he had appointed as his successor would take over at once. Knowing that would put a real damper on Royalist hopes. None of them would then be willing to risk his neck on the chance of being rewarded with a dukedom.'

Roger nodded, 'That, I remember, was the argument used after the attempt to blow him up on his way to the Opera in December 1800. But he was not then firm enough in the saddle to risk the violent opposition of the Old Guard Republicans, like yourself.'

'Oh. I. . .' Fouché snuffled into his handkerchief. 'I have always been in favour of his wearing a crown. As long as the régime started by him continues I shall retain my modest fortune and have nothing to fear; whereas a return of the Bourbons would be the end of me. But it's true that many of my old colleagues who are in the same boat would then have been fools enough to cut off their noses to spite their faces by raising the mobs against him. Now though, matters are very different. There is not a Jacobin left with enough stomach to raise a pea-shooter, and this recent conspiracy has given him just the chance he was seeking to get himself made a monarch. He has as good as given an order to everyone dependent on him to canvass the project at every oppor-

THE WANTON PRINCESS

tunity, and any day now you will see the measures he is
taking in secret produce results.'

As usual in such matters Fouché proved right. On April
23rd an obscure member of the Tribunate named Curée
proposed the adoption of the 'hereditary principle', and so
well had most of the members been primed that Carnot, who
had saved the Republic from being overwhelmed in its
infancy by his brilliant organization of the Armies, alone had
the courage to speak against it. A commission was appointed
to debate the proposal and obsequiously reported in its
favour. On May 18th the Senate decreed that Napoleon
should henceforth be styled 'Emperor of the French'.

A spate of resounding titles then gushed forth from the
Napoleonic cornucopia. The two junior Consuls became the
Arch-Chancellor and the Arch-Treasurer of the Empire, Tal-
leyrand Grand Chamberlain, Duroc Grand Marshal of the
Palace, Berthier Grand Master of the Hounds, Caulaincourt
Grand Master of the Horse. The most loyal among the
Generals—Mortier, Berthier, Murat, Davoust, Ney, Soult,
Moncey and Bessières—were all made Marshals of the
Empire; but so, too, in order to reconcile them to the new
state of things, were the potential trouble-makers—Berna-
dotte, Augereau, Masséna, Jourdan, Brune and Lannes—and
four old heroes of the Republican wars were also brought to
heel by being given the honour of this supreme rank.

Best of all fared the Bonapartes. Honest old Letizia flatly
refused to accept any title, so Napoleon had to content
himself by having her styled 'Madame Mère'; but Fesch,
already 'His Eminence the Cardinal', became Grand
Almoner, the brothers Joseph and Louis Their Imperial
Highnesses the Grand Elector and the Constable of the
Empire. The three sisters were also given the rank of Imperial
Highnesses. Thus, to heights equalled only by the Hapsburgs
and the Romanoffs, was raised a poor Corsican family that
ten short years before had been dependent on the charity of
the Republic so ironically termed, 'One and Indivisible.'

Roger could well imagine the unfeigned delight with which
Pauline would display the second coronet which, in her own

right, she was now entitled to have embroidered on her lingerie. That was, if she had the chance to do so to any man other than her semi-impotent husband.

Since she had been forced to leave Paris he had received occasional scrawled and ill-spelt letters from her; in each she had described her situation as ever more deplorable. Roman society was rigidly conventional as far as women were concerned and both her own mother, who had gone to join Lucien in his voluntary exile, and her horrid old mother-in-law kept an eagle eye on her to ensure that she remained, like Caesar's wife, a paragon of virtue.

Added to that, an unidentified infection she had contracted while in San Domingo had recurred. It caused sores to break out on her hands and arms and, so far, no doctor had been able to produce a cure. In vain she had taken courses of the waters at Pisa and Florence, but without their doing her any good, and she complained bitterly at the frustration she felt at being the wife of a millionaire, yet unable to enjoy life owing to ill health and being denied the excitement of continuing to have lovers.

Roger felt deeply sorry for her, but it now amused him to speculate upon what glorified appointment he would have received had they married. Murat, although he knew nothing whatever about war at sea, had been made High Admiral, so Roger, as another of Napoleon's brothers-in-law, could have counted on becoming Grand Something or Other of the Empire, with a huge income to support the dignity. Even so, now he was no longer subject to Pauline's extraordinary sexual attraction he felt that he had had a lucky escape; for no honours, however great, could have compensated him for enduring an empty-minded, nymphomaniac wife.

Meanwhile, towards the end of April he had been able to get up for an hour or two each day and by mid-May to come downstairs for gentle exercise and fresh air in the garden. At the end of that month, although the kindly Boutherons pressed him to stay on, he insisted that he no longer had any excuse for accepting their generous hospitality. To show his gratitude for their care of him he spent a considerable sum in buying mother, father and daughter extravagant presents that amazed and delighted them; then he returned to his old quarters at *La Belle Etoile.*

As he continued to suffer now and then from splitting headaches he still felt unequal to resuming his duties, so he whiled away the best part of June, whenever he felt up to it, by dining with many of his numerous friends and attending the most famous salons to hear the news and rumours of the day.

The chief topic was Moreau who, with the other conspirators, had been put on trial on May 28th. A special law had been passed depriving all persons of trial by jury who had plotted against the First Consul's life; so the accused were subjected to a form of court martial which meant that pressure could be exerted on the judges to secure convictions.

As the victor of Hohenlinden, Moreau still enjoyed a considerable degree of popularity with the masses; so his trial had to be conducted with ostensible fairness. In consequence, Napoleon could not prevent it from emerging that, although Moreau had met Pichegru in secret, he had persistently refused to lend himself to the plot and could be convicted of no more than desiring Napoleon's overthrow.

The result was that, on June 20th, the judges sentenced him only to two years' imprisonment. Napoleon was furious at this, as he had wished Moreau to be condemned to death, so that he could receive credit for the gracious act of pardoning him. As things were, all he could do was to grant Moreau his release on condition that he emigrated to the United States.

Of the real conspirators who had been tried with him, twenty were sentenced to death. Owing to the intercession of Josephine and *Madame Mère,* Napoleon commuted the sentence of the Polignacs and de Rivère to a term of imprisonment; but Georges Cadoudal, his brave Bretons and the other commoners suffered the extreme penalty.

A few days after the conclusion of the trial Roger reported for duty to his master. Napoleon was the last man ever to admit having made a mistake but, with a sharp glance at Roger, he said, 'In Fouché's opinion, my having ordered the execution of d'Enghien was not a crime but worse, a blunder. No doubt you think that too, but I have no regrets that your accident prevented you from interfering with my plans. I always know what I am doing and the Duke's death served its purpose.'

Nothing now was to be gained by arguing the matter, so Roger said suavely, 'The fact that I may now address you as "Sire" is proof of it; and now that I am well again I hope once more to be of service to Your Majesty. May I take it that you are still contemplating the invasion of England?'

'Certainly,' Napoleon replied abruptly. 'But I have suffered certain most annoying setbacks. My building programme for big ships is a long way behind schedule and the smaller ones are far from satisfactory. In April some forty of them were caught in a storm while on an exercise off Boulogne and driven on to the coast at Etaples mostly as wrecks.'

After a moment he went on, 'However, I have good hopes for this summer. In the Spring Latouche-Tréville succeeded Gantheaume as Commander of our Mediterranean Fleet. I have ordered him to put to sea from Toulon and elude Admiral Nelson's squadron by heading for Egypt, then to turn back in the night and pass the Straits of Gibraltar. He is next to drive off in turn the English squadrons blockading Cadiz and Rochefort, thus freeing our ships lying in those ports. With these reinforcements he will sail far out into the Atlantic, as though making for the West Indies, turn back again, elude Cornwallis by a dash up the Channel and join our fleet in Cherbourg. Should he succeed in this we'll have a fleet massed there large enough to take on the English at any time the weather becomes favourable for transporting an army to the coast of Kent.'

Apart from the fact that the plan under-rated British alertness, it was sound strategy and Roger showed no hesitation in congratulating his master upon it.

Recently he had learned that, in the middle of the previous month, Mr. Pitt had again become Prime Minister. How that had come about, and of the composition of the new Cabinet, he as yet knew nothing; but he recalled Mr. Pitt's saying when they were last together at Walmer that he thought Britain had little to fear as long as the French fleet could be prevented from dominating the Channel. Roger wished now that he had some way of conveying Napoleon's intentions to Downing Street; but for a long time past he had had no channels by which he could send secret information back to England and, having again only just reported for duty, he saw no prospect of getting across himself for some time to come.

Napoleon then added, 'I am setting out on another inspection of the Army of the Coast early in July. You will come with me.'

Realizing that the interview was over, Roger made a deeper than usual bow to the newly-created Emperor, said 'As ever, it will be a privilege to accompany Your Majesty,' and withdrew.

Three days later there was a magnificent ceremony at *Les Invalides*. The Comte de Segur, a returned émigré who had once been a Chamberlain at the Court of Versailles, was put in charge of the arrangements and produced a splendid spectacle. It was over four years since Bonaparte had announced his intention of creating a Legion of Honour, but so great had been the opposition to it by the old Republicans that he had shelved the idea. Now, as Napoleon I, Emperor of the French, no one could dispute his right to do so.

Members of the Imperial family, the newly-made Marshals, the members of the Council of State and the Senate, scores of Generals, Brigadiers and Colonels, all in brilliant uniforms or rich robes, were assembled there, together with Josephine and the ladies of her Court dressed in bright silks, satins, velvets and brocades and decked with dazzling jewels. The assembly also included scientists, men of letters, doctors and lawyers; the best brains in France, for distinguished civilians were also eligible for the Order.

Everyone among the soldiers who had received a Sword of Honour, which included Roger, was automatically to become a member of the Legion. But, under Napoleon himself, as

Grand Master, it was to consist of four grades, Grand Officer, Commander, Officer and Legionary. To Roger's surprise and delight, when his turn came to be decorated he was given the cross of a Commander; a great honour, as only three other Colonels in the whole army were given that rank and even some of the Generals were not. As *le brave Breuc* none of his companions grudged it to him, but when Napoleon pinned the cross on his chest he said:

'For your devotion to duty at Toulon, Venice, in Egypt and at Marengo.' Then he bent forward to whisper, and Roger thought he was going to say something about the conspiracy; but, with sly humour, he added 'and as a Lieutenant at Bruges'.

The following day a great cavalcade of coaches and horsemen set off with the Emperor, accompanied by Josephine, for the coast. But there a horrible disaster was to take place. On arriving at Boulogne Napoleon ordered Admiral Bruix to send his flotilla to sea next morning to perform an exercise that could be witnessed from the shore. When morning came the vessels were still in harbour. Bruix was sent for and said that the exercises could not take place as a storm was expected to blow up.

Napoleon was furious and curtly told the Admiral to have the flotilla put to sea at once. Bruix retired, but an hour later the vessels were still in port; so he was sent for again. In vain he protested that the weather was worsening and that to carry out the exercise would endanger the lives of his men. On receiving a further imperative order to proceed, he flatly refused to obey.

The Emperor roared with rage, threw his hat on the floor and raised his riding whip. His staff stood by petrified by this awful scene, for the Admiral took a quick step back and laid his hand on his sword. Napoleon did not strike him but, with a torrent of foul language, dismissed him from his post and exiled him to Holland. Then, with blazing eyes, in a voice of thunder he turned to Bruix's second in command, Rear Admiral Magon, and charged him instantly to carry out the order.

The flotilla put to sea. The sky grew dark and an hour later a violent storm was sending great waves crashing on the shore. The low-built, heavily laden invasion craft proved incapable of weathering it. One after the other they were swamped and overturned. The Emperor and his staff, watching from the beach, were horrified.

Appalled by the result of having enforced his order, Napoleon set an example by running to a small boat with the intention of attempting to rescue some of the men who were being tossed towards the shore by the huge breakers. Fearing he would be drowned, some of his officers dashed after him and endeavoured to hold him back. But yelling, 'Let me go! Let me go! They must be saved!' he broke away from them and jumped into the boat. A minute later a wave broke over it, filling it with foaming water. As it sank under him he was dragged back, soaked and blaspheming, to the shore. Nothing could be done. They could only stand there, drenched with spray, while the seamen and soldiers drowned before their eyes. Next morning over two hundred bodies were washed up.

Undeterred by this terrible event, Napoleon held the great review that had been planned. In the huge natural amphitheatre, not far from Caesar's Tower, the eighty thousand men who formed Soult's army were drawn up. Seated in an ancient iron chair that was said to have been the throne of King Dagobert, Napoleon received the acclamations of his troops, then administered to them *en masse* the same oath of allegiance as had been taken by the brilliant company at *Les Invalides*. There followed another distribution of crosses of the Legion. Finally, with a dramatic gesture, he pointed across the sea to the white cliffs of Dover and cried to those about him, 'We need only to be masters of the Channel for six hours to be masters of the world.'

Roger cheered as loudly as the others; while thinking to himself how extraordinary it was that a man who could grasp the essentials of not only military problems, but also social, legal and administrative ones, with such swiftness, should continue to be so blind to those that concerned the sea.

366

Now that he was taking a special interest in all matters to do with the French Navy, he had recently gone to some pains to get a sight of a confidential report from the Admiralty. So as not to give umbrage to the Emperor one fact had been sugared over with 'ifs' and 'buts'. Yet when denuded of those it was a statement that, owing to the vast number of invasion craft that had been built, it would take six days to get them out of their ports. And after the tragedy that had befallen the local flotilla Roger was of the opinion that, even if the British fleet was decoyed away from the Channel for a week, Napoleon would still not succeed in landing any considerable body of troops on the English beaches.

As it transpired Latouche-Tréville, who was due to sail from Toulon on the 13th of that month, in the attempt to fox Nelson and Cornwallis, never reached the Channel. On August 20th he died suddenly and this led to the operation being postponed.

Meanwhile the Imperial cortège moved up the coast for a further series of inspections, in due course arriving at Aix-la-Chapelle where Charlemagne's remains were entombed. A solemn Mass was held in the Cathedral and afterwards Josephine was offered the arm-bone of the mighty King. Proudly she declared that she would not deprive the city of this precious relic as she had the support of an arm as great as that of Charlemagne. But Napoleon made off with the insignia and sword of the Frankish Emperor so that he could use them at his own coming Coronation.

The sight of the white cliffs of Dover and the progress of the cortège up the Channel coast had caused Roger to think more frequently than ever of Georgina, until he became obsessed with the idea that he must find out for certain if she was alive or dead. By now it was certain that she would either have returned to England or her fate would be known; but the only way to find out was to go there.

Having made his plan he pretended loss of appetite and for ten days half-starved himself until he had lost a stone in weight, become pale and looked obviously ill. Josephine drew Napoleon's attention to his state, which gave him the opportunity he was seeking. With apparent reluctance he admitted that something was radically wrong with him and said that he feared he must ask for sick leave.

The Emperor granted it at once but, before dismissing him, said kindly, 'Get well quickly, *mon brave Breuc*. Unless your state does not permit it I insist that you rejoin me before the beginning of December. I wish all my old friends to be present at my Coronation. I have sent for the Pope to crown me and it will be a magnificent affair.'

In consequence, while Napoleon and his entourage made their way up the Rhine on a long tour of the defences there, Roger rode back to Paris then down to Bordeaux. After two days of discreet enquiries he found a Captain who was about to run a cargo of claret over to the Devon coast, and on September 10th he landed in a secluded cove near Sidmouth. Two days later he was in London.

As usual, he went straight to Amesbury House and, the moment he came face to face with Droopy Ned, enquired about Georgina. His old friend sadly shook his head and said:

'Alas, dear Roger, I fear we will see her no more. As you know, she sailed last autumn to the Indies, in part for the pleasure of getting away from our atrocious climate during the winter months, but also with a view to supervising personally the disposal of John Beefy's plantations there. That, I am told, she carried out to good advantage, for she was far nimbler witted than most women, and 'twas in order to guard against being rooked by some unscrupulous land agent that she journeyed there herself. About mid-March she sailed for home in a well-found merchantman out of Bristol named "Enterprise." 'Tis known that the ship took the usual north-eastern course through the "Windward Passage" between Cuba and San Domingo, but after that she disappeared. No hurricane was reported at about that period but in those waters there are many uncharted rocks and shoals, so the ship may have struck one in the night and gone down. On the other hand she may have been attacked. . . .'

'She was,' Roger cut him short, 'by a Sea Rover, a

Frenchman or some other privateer. I know not which, but I am certain of it. On the evening of March 20th, which fits well with what you say, I saw the ship burning and about to sink.' He then gave an account of the vision he had had.

Droopy did not question his having had this psychic experience, but said, 'Then we must account her dead. This happened nearly six months ago. Had she become the captive of some buccaneer he would have demanded a ransom for her, and by this time we'd know of it.'

Roger bowed his head, 'Somehow I cannot believe her dead. Yet the facts as known appear to prove it to be so. In time, perhaps, I'll get used to the thought. But she was the love of my life, and 'tis a blow from which I'll ne'er recover.'

That night, to take Roger's mind off his sorrow, Droopy brought him up-to-date with the political situation. Soon after he had last left England dissatisfaction with Addington's government had become almost universal. In February the King had been afflicted with another spell of madness and was extremely ill. Fox had seized the opportunity to initiate another intrigue with the object of getting his patron, the Prince of Wales, made Regent. The Tories had succeeded in thwarting it temporarily but when, in May, the King had recovered he could no longer ignore the popular outcry that Addington must go. So he had sent for Pitt.

During his long administration Pitt had fought the French with dogged determination; but he was a man of peace, detested war and had no gift for directing it. His real genius lay in the field of finance, and in his early years as Prime Minister he had performed a miracle by bringing Britain to a marvellous prosperity after the terrible depression into which the loss of her American colonies had dragged her. On becoming Prime Minister Addington had scrapped Pitt's taxation policy and introduced one that was proving disastrous to commerce. And it was in the hope of saving Britain from bankruptcy, more than on any other count, that Pitt had agreed to accept office again.

During the three years Addington had been Prime Minister the House had become divided into several parties, each bitterly opposed to the others. He had had the support of the die-hard Tories who were determined to keep the Whigs out, but many of the ablest ex-Ministers who had served under Pitt were determined to bring him back and criticized Addington at every opportunity. Fox, as the leader of the die-hard Whigs, had gained strength owing to this dissension; yet the Portland Whigs refused him their full support. Grenville, who hated and despised Addington, had, meanwhile, quarrelled with Pitt and was leading a splinter group of Tories.

In consequence, that Spring Pitt had been faced with the awful problem of reconciling these factions and inducing their leaders to combine in an administration that would be truly national, so that it should have the confidence of the country.

To achieve this, he had attempted to bring Fox into his Cabinet, which had cost him a renewal of Grenville's allegiance, then the King had refused to accept Fox as a Minister. The Portland Whigs supported Pitt but, to keep a balance, he had to include in his Cabinet Hawkesbury and several other incompetents from Addington's old followers, with the result that, on average, his new colleagues were much inferior to those who had worked with him in his former administration.

Soon after he had again become Prime Minister there had occurred another split in the Tory party. Pitt had always favoured the Abolition of the Slave Trade and, owing to the untiring efforts of his friend Wilberforce, the national conscience had at last been aroused to the inhumanity of the traffic; so Pitt had felt the time ripe to bring in an Act of Abolition. Its opponents, who had always argued that Britain could not afford to give up this lucrative commerce, particularly in time of war, immediately raised a tremendous outcry. Addington bitterly attacked the Bill, but Fox gave Pitt his support, so it was carried, although only at the price of alienating many of Pitt's old supporters.

When Roger called on the Prime Minister he was received by him after a long wait. He looked tired and harassed and

370

spoke with some bitterness of the difficulties he was having in getting his measures through the House. Then, when Roger had given him such particulars as he could about the dispositions of the French Navy, he said:

'I am even more convinced than when I spoke to you of the matter at Walmer that our one hope is to maintain our superiority over the French at sea. With that in mind, soon after I returned to office I put in hand an increased ship-building programme. The French émigré General Dumouriez sent me a long memoir upon the subject and he argued wisely that nothing is so perilous as remaining perpetually on the defensive; that our Navy should be made strong enough to go over to the attack, and that if we could make it so we would stand a much better chance of drawing other nations into a new alliance against Bonaparte.'

'What, sir,' Roger asked, 'are our present prospects of doing so?'

'Encouraging, to say the least. The foul murder of the Duc d'Enghien has helped us there. Before that the Czar was inclined to admire Bonaparte for the new internal peace and prosperity he has brought to France; but since then he has declared him to be a monster in human form who will stick at nothing for his own aggrandisement, and so must be checked. Can we but persuade him to come in with us, we may then count upon Gustavus of Sweden also to take up arms against the French. Given those two we would have good hopes of also drawing Austria into a new Coalition; and I am now in friendly correspondence with all three monarchs to that end. I am, though, much concerned about the attitude of Spain. Not only has she blackmailed our old ally Portugal into closing her ports against us but she is paying Bonaparte a huge subsidy which is of great assistance to him. That, she can continue to do only so long as her treasure ships from America are freely allowed to enter Cadiz. Since she continues to ignore our protests that she is infringing her neutrality by providing Bonaparte with the sinews of war, I have recently given orders that her ports are to be blockaded.'

Roger raised his eyebrows, 'Is that wise, sir? Surely it would be sounder policy to let Napoleon continue to receive these supplies of Spanish gold, rather than risk Spain entering the war actively against us.'

'She will not fight,' Mr. Pitt asserted with conviction. 'It is not without reason that her Prime Minister, Godoy, has been christened "Prince of Peace," and he is as slippery as an eel. Should we take any of their ships we'll not rob them of their bullion; only hold it for them, and thus give him an excuse to resist any pressure Bonaparte may exert upon him to act against us.'

While Roger had a poor opinion of Mr. Pitt's capabilities as a strategist, he had a great admiration for his financial genius, and it was obvious that holding up the Spanish treasure ships would make it difficult for the French Treasury to find the vast sums needed to pay Napoleon's army; so he said no more. For a further half hour they talked of other matters, then he took his leave.

Next morning he bought a variety of toys and in the afternoon drove down to Stillwaters to see the children. On arriving he found Colonel Thursby there and at once enquired about Georgina, but the Colonel could tell him little more than he had learned from Droopy Ned and, with tears in his eyes, the old gentleman said that as no news of her or the 'Enterprise' had been received by midsummer he had since reconciled himself to the thought that she must be dead.

Previously the Colonel had made only frequent visits to Stillwaters, spending the rest of the year either at his old home near Lymington or at his house in Bedford Square, but Roger was greatly pleased to learn that, in order to help Aunt Marsham bring up the children, he had now decided to make Stillwaters his permanent home.

That night after dinner, when Aunt Marsham had left them to their port, they talked again of Georgina. She had taken to the Indies with her a Mr. and Mrs. Skiffington, who were old friends, and the handsome young Lord Rockhurst who, knowing her so well, Roger assumed to have been her lover at that time. No news had been received of them, nor of any of the crew of 'Enterprise', so it seemed that the ship must have gone down with all hands.

Legally, Georgina's death could not be presumed for some years, but the family solicitors had shown her father her Will. She had left Stillwaters to little Charles, a legacy of £50,000 and most of her jewels to Susan, the contents of her library to her father should he be living at the date of her death, £5,000 each to her faithful Jenny and Aunt Marsham and numerous smaller legacies to other friends and servants. To Roger she had left her paintings, her horses, any of her personal possessions he chose to select and her hair.

By her last bequest Roger was deeply touched and, as the Will was a recent one made shortly before she sailed, it was clear that by then she must have regretted her betrayal of him and again thought of him with great tenderness. As the Colonel made no mention of that dark day when she had nearly caused Roger to be re-arrested, he refrained from speaking of it.

He remained at Stillwaters for a week, spending most of each day playing with the children. While doing so, or talking with the Colonel, his mind was occupied; but every room, the hothouses, the stables and every corner of the gardens held memories of Georgina and these saddened him so much that, although the Colonel pressed him to stay longer, he excused himself as having business to attend to and was glad to get away.

But in London he had no business; the weather had turned cold and rainy and the more he heard of the way in which Mr. Pitt was being hampered by his political enemies in his endeavours to conduct the war, the more depressed he became. So, after a few days spent with Droopy Ned, he decided to return to France and enjoy some weeks of sunshine at St. Maxime.

On September 23rd he caught the night coach to Exeter and two evenings later was in Sidmouth, tactfully sounding the landlord of the local inn about the prospects of getting a passage to France. He had to kick his heels there for six days, then the French smuggler who had put him over came in with another cargo and on October 1st landed him back at Bordeaux.

From there, by diligence, he followed the same route as he had on his stolen honeymoon with the gay and wanton Pauline, and passing again through the towns on that route he was frequently reminded of that happy journey. On reaching Aix-en-Provence it chanced that he got news of her as a result of reading a copy of *Le Moniteur*. It was reported that she had recently lost her son Dermid. Continued poor health had caused her to move from spa to spa in the hope of a cure, and she had been at Bagni di Lucca, when she learned that the frail little boy had been carried off by a sudden fever.

Roger felt deep sympathy for her; but she now meant no more to him than any of the other lovely women he had enjoyed for a brief season, and he thought of her only as an old friend. Georgina had been the only abiding love of his life and, although there had been times when they had been separated for years at a stretch, the thought that he could never more return to her continued to cause him a grief that he felt he would never overcome.

On October 8th he reached St. Maxime and spent the next seven weeks there idling in the autumn sunshine. Daily he went for long rides or walks but only because it had been his habit of a lifetime to keep himself in perfect physical condition. Since Droopy had confirmed his fears about Georgina he had become a prey to a curious lassitude and lacked the urge to interest himself in anything; so it was only with an effort that he forced himself on November 20th to set out for Paris in order to keep his promise to be present at Napoleon's coronation.

When he reached the capital he learned that the Emperor was at Fontainebleau, so next day he rode out there and found the little town swarming with busy people. Two days earlier Pope Pius VII, lured by promises of concessions to the Roman Catholic Church in France, which Napoleon had no intention of fulfilling, had arrived there. To avoid any ceremonial reception in which he might appear to be taking second place, Napoleon had arranged a hunt in the forest then, apparently by chance, intercepted the Pontiff's carriage a few miles from the Palace.

The last time Roger had been at Fontainebleau King Louis and Queen Marie Antoinette had been in residence; but gracious and colourful as their Court had been, it paled beside the splendour of that of the new monarch. Having lodged his baggage in an attic room already occupied by two other A.D.C.s, Roger had to exercise all his patience that evening in worming his way through the press of dignitaries, Marshals, Ambassadors and prelates to present himself.

Not long after the Imperial couple had withdrawn, Madame de Remuset, Josephine's First lady in Waiting, managed to find him and told him that her mistress wished to see him. She then took him down to a small boudoir on the ground floor where Josephine was reclining on a day bed.

As soon as they were alone, she said, 'I am so glad you have returned to us, *mon cher Colonel*. You have ever been my friend and I sadly need the advice of someone I can trust.'

Smiling, he assured her of his devotion, then she made him sit down and went on, 'You were largely instrumental in bringing about my marriage to Bonaparte and you will recall that it was a civil marriage. Moreover, although I blush to confess it, I falsified my age, so that I should not appear to be older than the Emperor. On either count he could, if he wished, put me from him.'

'But why should he, Your Majesty?' Roger asked. 'Between us it is no secret that he has his peccadilloes, but they never last, and he is devoted to you.'

She sighed, 'It is this awful question of the succession. As you have been absent for so long you may not be aware of the situation. My hateful in-laws have fought for months like a pack of wolves over it, but at last it has been settled. Joseph, Lucien, Louis and Jerome have all been passed over, and it has now been vested in the natural or adopted son of Napoleon.'

375

'I see. And you are troubled because you have not yet provided him with an heir.'

'Alas, yes. And I fear now that I shall never do so. I have tried every nostrum that the doctors can propose but they have proved of no avail.'

'It can be no fault of yours, Madame, for you have had two fine children by your previous marriage, Eugene and Hortense. Since he has proved incapable of begetting a child. . . .'

'There is no proof of that,' she put in quickly. 'You may perhaps recall my reader Madame Duchâtel. His *affaire* with her has caused me more tears than any of his others. I was even fool enough to break in upon them one evening when they were together in the room over the Orangery at St. Cloud. His rage was terrible. He declared that he was a man apart and a law unto himself; so that afterwards I almost felt that I was the guilty party. 'Tis rumoured that she is with child. Since she entered my service she lives apart from her old husband and, before she set her cap at Napoleon she was such a paragon of virtue that if she does have a child he will certainly believe it to be his.'

Her mention of Madame Duchâtel swiftly recalled to Roger the fateful night on which d'Enghien had been executed. It was she who had been in Napoleon's bed when he had forced his way into the room above the Orangery. After a moment he said:

'But, Madame, even if she does give the Emperor a natural son he would never put you aside in order to take one of your ladies as his wife.'

'No, no,' replied Josephine hastily. 'I have no fear of that. And as a mistress for him she is certainly to be preferred to that horrid, grasping de Vaudry woman with whom he started an *affaire* while we were at Aix-la-Chapelle. My danger lies in the possibility of his proving to his own satisfaction that he is, after all, capable of becoming a father. Since my marriage to him is not valid in the eyes of the Church, he might repudiate me so that he could take to wife some young woman of Royal blood, thereby both elevating himself in the eyes of other monarchs and with the hope of getting a legitimate son by her.'

'Has he . . . er . . . given you any indication that he might take such a step?' Roger enquired diffidently.

'Praise be to God, no. But his horrid family are urging him to do so.'

For a moment Roger remained thoughtful, then he said, 'Since you have sought my advice, Madame, it is that you should spare no effort to persuade him to legalize the bond between you. And now is the time. Once this question is raised His Holiness could not possibly ignore it. Should it be brought to his attention that you are not man and wife in the eyes of the Church it is certain that he could not square it with his conscience to bless you both at the Coronation ceremony. And the Emperor cannot possibly afford to risk the Pope's now refusing to officiate at it.'

'You are right. Yes, you are right. But, circumscribed as I am, how can I bring such a situation about?'

After considering again Roger replied, 'I suggest, Madame, that you should make use of Fesch. Although he is a Bonaparte he is not a bad man, and as a priest he is under an obligation to shepherd you back into the bosom of the Church. Although he must be aware that you married without its blessing he cannot refuse to hear your formal confession and aid you, as a penitent, to regularize your position. Should he refuse, you could, as a last resort, tell him that you intend to speak to His Holiness himself. But I do not think that will be necessary.'

Josephine stood up. Roger rose too. With tears in her eyes she put her hands on his shoulders, kissed him on both cheeks and murmured, 'I will do as you suggest. For your wise counsel I can never thank you enough.'

Four nights later, at the final pre-Coronation reception on December 1st, Madame Remusat again sought out Roger in the crowded ballroom where Henri II had had the monogram of his beautiful mistress Diane de Poitiers made the motif of the inlaid floor and ceiling, and slipped a note into his hand. It was from Josephine and read:

377

'Bless you a thousand times. Napoleon made no difficulties and this afternoon we were privately married by Cardinal Fesch.'

Early next morning the whole Court repaired to Paris. As Master of the Ceremonies, the Comte de Segur again excelled himself. The assembly in Notre Dame exceeded in brilliance any gathering there in the days of the *anciene régime*: a horde of soldiers in brilliant uniforms, Senators, Ambassadors, dignitaries and bejewelled women packed the great Cathedral. Napoleon, wearing a laurel wreath on his broad brow, clad in a gorgeous velvet robe embroidered with golden bees and wearing the sword of Charlemagne, led Josephine up to the altar.

There was only one unpleasant incident. The Bonaparte sisters, furious at having been ordered to carry Josephine's train, maliciously pulled on it as she ascended the shallow steps to the chancel and she nearly fell over backwards. But she managed to retain her balance.

Among the train bearers Roger was a little surprised to see the beautiful Pauline. Later he learned that, in order to get back to the gay life of Paris that she so dearly loved, she had used as an excuse the death of her son. She had insisted that he should be buried beside his father at Montgobert, and Napoleon had not had the heart to refuse her. But Roger now found himself gazing at her with indifference.

When the crux of the ceremony was about to take place Napoleon suddenly took the crown from the hands of the startled Pope and crowned himself. Then among shouts of acclaim that made the lofty vault ring, he crowned Josephine.

At the reception afterwards, Roger had a few words with Pauline and expressed his sympathy at her loss of Dermid. 'It was too terrible,' she told him. 'Had I been there 'tis possible that I might have saved him. But I was suffering from the sickness that afflicts me and had had a relapse. When a courier arrived at Bagni de Lucca they thought me too ill to tell me, and by the time I had recovered it was all over.'

After a moment, she added with a smile, 'But I am over

378

the shock now and back in dear Paris. You must come to see me.'

He returned her smile and thanked her, but he had no intention of accepting her invitation. As he bowed himself away, he wondered if he would ever again want to make love to a woman. The long succession of them through the years had been only substitutes for Georgina, and it seemed that, somehow, her death had destroyed in him all desire to make love.

Soon after the Coronation there came a new development in the European situation that gave him great concern for Britain. While at Stillwaters he had learned that early in October Mr. Pitt's instructions had been carried out and the Admiralty had despatched four frigates to intercept the Spanish treasure ships. When they appeared, the Spanish squadron consisted of four slightly smaller frigates and, numbers being even, the gallant Spanish commander refused to surrender. During the ensuing fight one of the Spanish ships blew up and only then did the other three lower their colours.

Clearly the Admiralty had blundered badly in not having sent a larger force which the Spaniards would have decided they had no hope of resisting. But the damage had been done. Britain was indignantly accused of having committed both an act of war against a nation with whom she was at peace, and piracy. Godoy, as Mr. Pitt had anticipated, had done his utmost to avoid making this a cause for hostilities but the British Prime Minister had left Napoleon out of his calculations.

The Emperor had insisted that Spain must fight. Godoy had still resisted. Determined to make him, Napoleon had then charged Spain with being unfriendly to France, and had threatened to send an army to invade the Peninsula. The Spaniards had caved in and, on December 12th, declared war on Britain.

This brought about the very thing that Mr. Pitt had dreaded. The combined fleets of France and Spain outnumbered that of Britain. Now, at last, Napoleon had a real chance of achieving command of the seas, sweeping the Channel and, almost unopposed, launching his invasion.

It was two days after Spain had declared war that on entering the Tuileries to go on duty Roger was handed a letter. It was inscribed, '*M. le Colonel Breuc, Aide de Camp à Sa Majesté l'Empereur des Français, Palais de Tuileries, Paris.*' And the franks upon it showed that it had come via Cologne from Hamburg. Roger had a vague feeling that he knew the writing but could not imagine who would have written to him from the German port.

Tearing the packet open he saw that it contained several sheets of close writing in French. Then he recognized the hand of Colonel Thursby. Evidently the Colonel had had something urgent to communicate, sent the letter by the Captain of some neutral ship and had written in French so that, should it fall into the wrong hands, Roger would not be compromised as being in correspondence with an Englishman.

Quickly Roger carried the letter over to the embrasure of a window. As he skimmed the first line his heart missed a beat. It read:

'I felt I must endeavour to let you know that Jenny has returned to us. . . .'

Roger's mind reeled. He gave a gasp and clutched at the heavy curtain for support. If Jenny was alive Georgina might be too.

CHAPTER XXIV

JENNY'S STORY

R o g e r ' s hands were trembling so much that it was a few moments before he could steady them sufficiently to read the letter. Even then his eyes skipped from passage to passage, hoping for definite news of Georgina. Bit by bit he swiftly took in the main facts.

On the evening of March 20th when 'Enterprise' was a day's run to the north-east of the exit to the Windward Passage, she had been attacked by a buccaneer. The Captain and crew of 'Enterprise' had fought her gallantly but she had been outgunned and a fire started in her that could not be brought under control. Fearing that the fire would reach her magazine the order had been given to abandon ship. Several of the boats had already been rendered useless by the cannonade from the attacking ship, the Captain had been killed and there was an unseemly rush to get into the three that remained serviceable, during which Jenny had become parted from her mistress.

One of the three, in charge of the First Mate, had been overloaded and sank within a few minutes of being lowered. The other two, in an attempt to avoid capture, which would have meant their occupants being held to ransom, had headed for a small island about a mile away. The sun was setting and a calm had fallen; so the buccaneer, her sails hanging slack, was unable to go in pursuit but began to fire upon them. The boat containing Georgina, Lord Rockhurst and the Skiffingtons, was hit, several people in it were killed and it sank, leaving the others struggling in the water.

Jenny, in the remaining boat, had been near enough to see that Georgina and Lord Rockhurst were among the half dozen or so who were swimming towards the shore. The boat she was in was a jollyboat in charge of Mr. Small, the bos'n. She had pleaded with him to go to the rescue of her mistress and the others, but in vain. Shots were still falling round Mr. Small's boat and the six men in it were pulling desperately to get out of range; moreover, by turning away from the island they would stand a better chance of doing so and with that object he had just altered course. Had they turned back it seemed certain that they too would have been sunk before they could pick up the swimmers and get clear of the whistling cannon balls. So poor Jenny could only weep and pray as distance obscured the bobbing heads and soon afterwards the tropic night had descended, blacking out the scene.

During the night the jollyboat was carried a considerable distance by the current and when morning dawned there was no land in sight. Under the torrid tropical sun they had spent a gruelling day, but Mr. Small had cheered them by saying that to the northward, in which direction they were heading, there were hundreds of small islands; so their chances of coming upon one before their water ran out were good. And he had proved right.

At dawn on the second morning they had found themselves within a mile of a long, low, sandy spit, some way inland from which there was a good-sized grove of palm trees. Having rowed round to a small inlet that ran nearly up to the vegetation they drew the boat up well above the tide mark and, dividing into two parties, set about exploring the island. It proved to be about five miles long by two at its widest part, and more than half of it was sandy cay. But on the higher ground, as well as palms there were other trees and

382

shrubs and several springs of fresh water. It was uninhabited but a herd of wild pigs was rooting in the undergrowth and quite a number of the trees bore tropical fruit; so they considered themselves very lucky.

Apart from her distress about her mistress Jenny had, at first, been very worried on her own account—as a pretty woman marooned with seven seamen. But Mr. Small, a stalwart, handsome man with a head of ginger curls, had had his blue eyes on Jenny from the day she had gone aboard 'Enterprise', and on the first evening they spent in a rough camp they had made he had addressed his shipmates in the following sense:

That they should be grateful to their Maker for having preserved them from the perils of the sea, and guided them to a piece of land on which there was not only fresh water but meat and fruit as well as fish to be had; but it might be many weeks before a ship passed close enough for them to signal her, and during that time some of them might get thoughts of a kind he would not tolerate. In short, if any one of them so much as laid a finger on Miss Jenny he would belt the life out of him.

He had proved right in his prediction that they might remain marooned for a considerable time. Although they erected a flagstaff on the shore, from which to fly a shirt, lit a bonfire each night and kept a constant watch, it was not until July that the fifth ship they had sighted passed close enough to see their distress signals and send in a boat.

During their four months on the island they had fared none too badly on roast pig, shell fish and fruit but, as the boat approached, they were naturally overjoyed at the thought that they might now hope to be back in England within two months. In that they had been disappointed, as the ship had proved to be a Yankee trader on her homeward run, and it took the best part of that time before she landed them in Boston. There they had had to wait a fortnight before they could get a passage across the Atlantic; so Jenny had not reached home until mid-November.

She had brought the stalwart and devoted Mr. Small to

Stillwaters with her, and blushingly revealed to Colonel
Thursby that she had a mind to marry him; yet could not
abide the thought that, his profession being the sea, she
would be no more than a grass widow during the best years
of her life, and always fearing that tempest or some other
hazard would rob her of him for good.

On learning that the bos'n was willing to give up the sea
Colonel Thursby had gladly solved their problem by promising him employment on the estate and, as a wedding present
to Jenny, the free life-tenancy of a comfortable cottage as
their home.

Reading the letter through again Roger absorbed every
detail of it. He was delighted that dear Jenny had found a
good man as a husband and determined at the first opportunity to reward her faithful service by making over to her a
handsome sum as a wedding portion; but he swiftly dismissed
her from his thoughts to speculate excitedly upon what had
become of Georgina.

Jenny's statement confirmed in every particular the vision
he had had nearly ten months before, and when it had faded
Georgina, although still some distance from the shore, had
been swimming strongly towards the island. Now there was
real hope that she had reached it. If so it was probable that
Rockhurst, perhaps the Skiffingtons and a few members of
the crew had also done so. But what then?

If the island was similar to that upon which Mr. Small's
party had landed, Georgina and her companions should have
had no difficulty in surviving. Even if it had no pigs or fruit
trees on it, provided there was a freshwater spring, they could
have made do on shell fish. But, awful thought, if there had
been no spring they must all have died there.

Had they still been alive, surely from an island only a
day's sail from the exit to the Windward Passage they must
have been picked up within six months; and the odds against
their having been rescued by another American vessel that
had carried them to a port as far distant as Boston were
considerable. Even had they remained marooned for six
months and then been taken off by a local schooner they

should have got back to England before Jenny.

Weighing the pros and cons Roger was once more plunged into gloom. Then a few moments later a new idea struck him. In those lawless seas it was quite possible that they had not been picked up by an honest trader, or a warship, but by a Sea Rover. In fact it was highly likely that the buccaneer who had attacked 'Enterprise' had sent a party ashore and captured them within an hour of their landing.

Against that it was customary for pirates to take captives who were well off to a hideout on some desert islet where they careened their ships, and hold them there until they were ransomed. Yet if that was what had happened some crooked agent who acted for the pirates would have sent a demand for ransom that should have reached London months ago.

There remained still another possibility. Rockhurst and Skiffington, if they had reached the shore, might later have been killed in a fight with the pirates. At the sight of Georgina's beauty the pirate Captain might then have decided that rather than demand a ransom for her he would force her to become his mistress. It was therefore not to be ruled out that she was still alive but suffering a hideous captivity aboard the ship as a 'pirate's moll'. Still worse, having taken his pleasure with her, he might have decided that for such a lovely woman he could get nearly as big a sum by selling her into a brothel as by asking a ransom, and save both time in getting his money and the agent's heavy commission.

The more Roger thought of this last appalling possibility the more harrowed his mind became. Within the hour, he had decided that he must go out to the West Indies and, somehow, discover what had really happened to the love of his life.

That night he considered by what means he could most swiftly reach the Caribbean. From England he would have no difficulty, through Mr. Pitt's good offices, in getting a passage in the first frigate sailing for those waters. But now that it was next to impossible for smugglers to cross the eastern end of the Channel, he would have to go via Bordeaux and be landed somewhere in Devonshire or Cornwall. That would

385

mean a long ride through France, probably several days
before he could find a smuggler about to run a cargo, another
long journey by coach to London to see Mr. Pitt, still another
down to Portsmouth or Bristol and, even then, he might have
to wait for some time before the frigate sailed; so it could be
a month or more before he was actually on his way to the
Indies.

On the other hand wind and weather, particularly during
the winter months, together with the necessity for ships to be
detached in rotation to take in water, made the British
squadrons' blockade of the French ports far from constant.
In consequence French ships in considerable numbers had
fairly frequent opportunities of slipping out, and, once in the
vast open ocean, stood a very good chance of reaching the
Indies without meeting opposition. If, therefore, he could get
on a French ship the odds were that he would reach his
destination the sooner by several weeks.

Next morning he remained in bed and sent a note to Duroc
excusing himself from duty on the grounds that his weak lung
was again giving him trouble. Two days later he got up, went
to the Tuileries and asked for a private interview with his
master. An hour or so later Napoleon received him. As he
made his bow he gave vent to a fit of coughing, then said:

'Your Majesty, now that winter is upon us I must, with
great regret, ask for leave to quit Paris, otherwise I fear I
may be stricken with a pleurisy.'

Napoleon nodded, 'Your old trouble, eh? 'Tis wretched
for you that you should be so afflicted every winter.
However, I'll have no special use for you until early summer.
Now that the Spanish Fleet is as good as in my pocket,
together with our own and those of Northern Italy and
Holland, we'll drive the accursed English from the seas. But
not yet. The Spanish Fleet is in ill repair and several months
must elapse before it can be made battleworthy. 'Twould be
folly to strike before we can muster our maximum strength.
Meantime by all means go to that place of yours near St.
Maxime and enjoy the sunshine.'

'I thank you, Sire,' Roger replied. 'But it irks me to have

to spend long spells there idling my time away; and it has occurred to me that since my health prevents me from serving you in Paris I might do so elsewhere.'

'What have you in mind?'

'That you might send me in some capacity to the Indies. Not permanently, but perhaps to make a confidential report to you on the situation there. My mission could be covered by your appointing me as an Army liaison officer to your Admiral commanding on that station; and such a cruise would certainly benefit my health.'

'You have an idea there. My Army leaves nothing to be desired; but I am far from satisfied with our Navy. You are a shrewd observer, Breuc, and might well provide me with information which would enable me to weld it into better shape before I launch it in full force against the English. I'll think on it. Come to me tomorrow night at St. Cloud at ten o'clock.'

The following evening Roger rode out to the Palace and was duly shown into the Orangery. Napoleon was seated at his desk and for some minutes continued writing in his fast, sprawling hand. Then he stood up, took a big map from a drawer, threw it on the floor, lay down, spread out the map and signed to Roger to join him.

'This,' he said, 'is our situation. Our two main fleets are at Toulon and Brest. Villeneuve commands the first and Gantheaume the second. We have a third, consisting only of five ships of the line and five frigates, under Missiessy at Rochefort. My object during the Spring is to decoy the main English fleet under Nelson to the West Indies. I am sending Missiessy orders that in January, as soon as an opportunity offers to evade the blockade, he is to sail to the Caribbean and make as much trouble there as possible. To give him time to do so, Villeneuve will leave Toulon in March and make a feint towards Egypt. That should draw Nelson after him. Then, evading Nelson, he will turn back, pick up the Spanish Fleet at Cartagena and follow Missiessy across the Atlantic with it. By then the English should have learned that Missiessy has attacked, and I hope taken one or more of their islands. The Franco-Spanish fleet will be sighted as it passes Gibraltar. Nelson will learn of that a few days later and turn back in pursuit. But Villeneuve should have a good lead. He will join Missiessy at Martinique. The combined fleets will then at once recross the Atlantic while Nelson is hunting for them in the Caribbean. On Villeneuve's return he will pick up the second Spanish fleet from Cadiz. Gantheaume will break out of Brest and the Dutch fleet leave its ports. Having massed our entire seapower we shall overwhelm the English squadrons in the Channel and launch the invasion.'

'A magnificent conception,' Roger declared heartily. 'Magnificent. It cannot fail.'

'It will not. To achieve this combination has taken me four years. But now at last these devilish islanders who have thwarted my plans in every direction are about to face the day of reckoning.'

The Emperor paused for a moment, then he went on, 'With regard to Missiessy; it is my intention that he should take with him twelve thousand troops. His first objective will be the capture of Dominica. He may then use his judgment whether next to attack St. Kitts, Nevis or Monserrat. Such troops as he may still have after leaving garrisons in such islands as he succeeds in taking he will use to reinforce San Domingo. By then Villeneuve should have joined him and they will return together. You are to sail with Missiessy, but not as a liaison officer. Seeing that you are one of my personal staff, the Admirals would be certain to suspect that I had sent you to spy on them. You will go as Governor-designate of the island of Dominica.'

At this announcement Roger had all he could do to keep a straight face. In '94 Mr. Pitt had sent him out as Governor of the French island of Martinique which had recently been captured by the British; now Napoleon was sending him out to be Governor of the British island of Dominica which was to be captured by the French. It was a delightful piece of irony, but no time to laugh. Swiftly recovering himself, he expressed his gratitude at being given this lucrative appointment, upon which Napoleon said:

'You will not be there long, as you must return with the combined fleet to be with me for the invasion. But you have a good head on your shoulders, and six or eight weeks in the island should be sufficient for you to establish French rule firmly before handing over to a successor.' Getting to his feet Napoleon took a packet from his desk, handed it to Roger and added, 'Here is your Commission as Governor of Dominica, and a letter to Admiral le Comte de Missiessy informing him of your appointment. You may leave for Rochefort as soon as you wish. I hope that there you will find better weather and quickly recover your health.'

Having effusively thanked the Emperor again Roger left the Palace in high elation. Not only had he secured his passage to the West Indies but by a great stroke of luck he had learned the movements of the French fleets for several months to come. Nevertheless, as he rode back to Paris he had to face a most disconcerting problem. Clearly it was his duty to pass on to Mr. Pitt as soon as he possibly could the information he had come by, so that Nelson should not be lured to the West Indies; but Missiessy was to sail in January as soon as he had an opportunity to break out of Rochefort. If he crossed to England he might not be able to get back before Missiessy sailed.

By the time he reached *La Belle Etoile* he had taken his decision. Deeply as he loved Georgina and harrowed as he had been by thinking of the awful fate that might have overtaken her if she had fallen into the hands of pirates, he must put his country first and risk having to postpone going in search of her.

As it was now December 18th and the odds were that Missiessy would not find a chance to escape the blockade during the first few days of January, Roger reckoned that he would have at least a fortnight and, with luck, three weeks in which to get from Paris to London then back to Rochefort. But the only route open to him was via Bordeaux and Devon. For there to be any hope of his getting back early in the New Year, not a moment must be lost.

At the hostelry he ordered a fresh horse to be saddled for

him, crammed a suit of civilian clothes and a few other things into a valise, then from under a loose board in his bedroom took a money belt stuffed with gold pieces and two letters of credit that he always kept there against an emergency. Soon after midnight he was in the saddle and on his way out of Paris.

On the 22nd he reached Bordeaux but there met with a nasty setback. The smuggler who had put him over on his last two trips had not returned from a crossing he had made early the previous month, so was presumed to be either dead or captured by the English.

By frequenting seamen's taverns during the next two days he at length got in touch with another smuggler named Jubert. But in spite of an offer of lavish payment Jubert proved sullen and difficult. His craft was already loaded with a cargo of wine but he refused to put to sea on account of the weather, although Roger had several times made the crossing when it was worse.

At last, on the 28th, Jubert's avarice overcame his fears and for the highest sum Roger had ever paid he agreed to sail. The passage, although rough enough to make Roger ill, was not particularly bad but, only two hours after they had left Bordeaux, they ran into trouble. Out of the night there emerged a British sloop of war. They were hailed and ordered to heave to. Jubert ignored the order and put about in an attempt to get away, but the sloop sent a cannon ball crashing through his rudder. This lucky shot rendered the ship out of control, whereupon the sloop came alongside and grappled her.

The sound of the shot brought Roger on deck. At a glance he took in the situation and had swiftly to decide what to do. Suddenly it occurred to him that this apparent disaster might prove a blessing in disguise and enable him to send his information to London without landing in England.

Stepping up to Jubert—now haggard at the thought of not only losing his cargo but spending years in an English prison—Roger said quietly, 'Leave this to me. I have a big sum of money with me and may be able to buy them off.'

390

A young officer accompanied by six British tars with drawn cutlasses scrambled aboard. Jubert stood back, and Roger, addressing the officer in broken English, told him that he was responsible for the ship. He then asked to be taken to the Captain of the sloop. Ten minutes later he was in her after-cabin with her commander, a middle-aged Lieutenant.

As soon as they were alone Roger ceased all pretence of being a Frenchman and said, 'Lieutenant, I am a British agent in the personal service of the Prime Minister. Your having intercepted us is most fortunate. I have information regarding the future movements of the French fleet which should be conveyed to him with the utmost urgency. I pray you get it to him with all possible speed, and release this smuggler so that he can land me again in France and I can continue the important work I am doing there.'

In spite of his perfect English, the Lieutenant at first refused to believe him. But after twenty minutes, during which Roger answered innumerable questions for which he could hardly have provided the answers had he not been brought up in Hampshire and been acquainted with a number of prominent Englishmen, the Lieutenant was convinced of his *bona fides*. Pen and paper were provided and he sat down in the heaving sloop to write his despatch for Mr. Pitt. When he had done he gave it to the Lieutenant to read through. Realizing its vital nature, the officer said he would set a course for Plymouth and, although reluctant to do so, agreed to release the smuggler, provided he made no further attempt to land his illicit cargo.

Back aboard the smuggler Roger pulled a long face as he told Jubert that it had cost him twelve thousand five hundred francs to bribe the Englishman to let them go, but that for that sum he had also agreed to undertake certain business for him in England which now made it unnecessary for him to go there himself. He added that he had given his word that no further attempt should be made on this trip to land the cargo and that, even if he was prepared to break it, with the sloop still in the vicinity it would be suicidal to do so; but that there was nothing to prevent Jubert from attempting to put his cargo across in a few days' time.

Jubert, thanking his stars that he had had a passenger aboard rich enough to save himself and his ship from capture, at once agreed to put back to port, and in the early hours of the morning Roger was landed at the old harbour in Bordeaux.

It was now December 29th and Rochefort lay only a hundred miles to the north; so he had time in hand. On the afternoon of the 31st he arrived there and reported to Admiral Comte de Missiessy. The Admiral and his senior officers were about to celebrate the New Year of 1805. Roger was invited to join them and spent a hectic evening, now overjoyed to think that his vital information was on its way to Mr. Pitt by a safe hand, and that he was assured of a passage which, with any reasonable luck, would get him to the West Indies within six to eight weeks.

He would have been far from being so pleased with himself had he known that within twelve hours of his leaving the sloop of war she had encountered a French frigate. After a sharp engagement the sloop had got away but her after-structure had been set on fire, Roger's despatch had gone up in flames, and the sloop's Commander, who was the only man aboard who knew its contents, had been killed during the action. So, after all, Nelson's fleet was destined to be lured on a long, futile chase to the West Indies.

CHAPTER XXV

DISASTROUS VOYAGE

I T W A S not until January 11th that, bad weather during the preceding days having driven off the British ships blockading Rochefort, Missiessy's squadron was able to break out. Its ten ships, carrying nearly twelve thousand troops in addition to their crews, were crammed to suffocation. Between decks hammocks were slung in serried rows alternately head to foot as close as sardines in a tin, and each was shared by three men for stretches of eight hours in every twenty four. For the rest of the time those who were not sleeping either lay about playing cards beneath the hammocks or, by companies, were in turn taken up on deck to be exercised. The officers, too, had to share cabins, and Roger, being as Governor designate of Dominica a person of importance, considered himself lucky in having a small stateroom with a bunk to himself and only one other in it that was occupied by a Brigadier.

Even so, he was in for five weeks of unending misery. The French fleet had not yet fully recovered from the effects of the Revolution, when all but a very small percentage of its experienced officers had either become victims of the Terror or gone into exile. Since Napoleon's coming to power discipline had been restored; but for the best part of ten years the sailors had lazed about, refusing to do any but essential work, so almost nothing had been done to keep the ships in good repair and they were still in a deplorable state.

As soon as the squadron struck bad weather the condition of the ships, which had lain for so long in port, became terrifyingly evident. Half-rotten sails were split by the wind before they could be furled, frayed ropes snapped, capstan bars broke, spars snapped off and no fewer than ten masts crashed on to the crowded decks killing scores of men. Roger as usual, was terribly seasick; so too were over ninety per cent of those on board. For days on end he could keep nothing down and even when the storm had blown itself out the stench continued to be so appalling that periodically it still made him vomit.

He lost over a stone in weight and to add to his suffering could not rid his mind of the constant fear that they would encounter a British squadron. Even two or three line-of-battle ships manned by officers and men of the Royal Navy, trained to fight their ships with split-second efficiency and hardened by countless months at sea in all weathers, could have taken on Missiessy's whole squadron and wrought the most appalling carnage among the seething masses of men who packed his ships. But in that, at least, Roger was lucky; for throughout the voyage they did not sight a hostile sail and, despite the shortcomings of his ships and crews, Missiessy succeeded in getting his squadron to Martinique by February 20th.

When they dropped anchor in the splendid bay of Fort de France the scene Roger saw through his cabin porthole aroused very mixed memories. For seven months he had enormously enjoyed being Governor of the island and, by dealing harshly with malcontents but using sweet reason with its leading citizens, brought the French settlers to co-operate with him in administering British rule. Then, after being recalled to England by Mr. Pitt to undertake a special mission, he had returned four months later to find that his wife, Amanda, had just died in giving birth to little Susan. It had been a terrible shock for, although as with all the other

394

women he had known, had the need arisen he would have sacrificed Amanda for Georgina, she had been a good wife and a charming companion; so he had loved her dearly and had mourned her death for many months.

He remained in his cabin, rather than go up on deck, for a very good reason. In Fort de France there were hundreds of people who had known him as His Excellency Mr. Roger Brook; so to have gone ashore would have been fatal. As a reason for not doing so he had decided to sham illness as long as they were anchored off the town, and in preparation for this deception he had given out twenty four hours earlier that he had a slight fever which, he feared, heralded an attack of malaria. The ship's chief doctor had been to see him, given him some quinine pills, which it had recently been discovered were a good remedy for the disease and, without showing the reluctance Roger felt, he had allowed himself to be bled. His brother officers were too elated at the prospect of getting ashore to give much thought to him; and, having taken to his bunk with a number of books, he had reconciled himself to remaining there until the squadron sailed for Dominica. But at least he was able to relieve his self-inflicted captivity by enjoying meals of newly-killed poultry, fresh fish and tropical fruits.

Admiral Villaret-Joyeuse, who commanded in Martinique, proved most helpful in sending men to assist in making the repairs necessary in Missiessy's ships and revictualling them; so they were made fit to sail again in a little over a week.

But, Roger learned from the Brigadier who shared his cabin, Missiessy was by no means so helpful to Villaret-Joyeuse. The latter was much concerned about a small island called Diamond Rock, which lay a few miles to the southwest of Martinique. When, in accordance with the Treaty of Amiens, the British had returned Martinique to the French, a party of British subjects had retired to the Rock with their possessions and a number of small ships. During the peace the French had not interfered with them and they had succeeded in supporting themselves. When war was again declared they had promptly sent for help to Dominica, troops and cannon had been sent to garrison the island and, ever since, it had proved a thorn in the side of French shipping approaching Fort de France. Villaret-Joyeuse had attempted but failed to take this stronghold, and now he appealed to Missiessy to capture it for him. But Missiessy refused to delay his own mission, and set sail for Dominica.

The northern tip of Martinique lay only twenty five miles from the southern tip of Dominica, and Roseau, the capital of the latter, some forty five from Fort de France. The wind being fairly favourable the passage was made in a little under two days and, soon after dawn, the French squadron appeared off Roseau.

Roger, who meanwhile had declared himself recovered, knew that a great part of the island, dominated by a lofty extinct volcano, Morne Diablotin, was covered with dense jungle. In spite of that, had he been commanding the expedition he would have landed his troops on the eastern shore and, even had it taken a fortnight, had them cut their way through the jungle to assault the capital from the rear. As the garrison of such a place was unlikely to consist of more than a single battalion, and the French had twelve thousand men at their disposal, by adopting such a strategy they could not have failed to take it; and on the island there were no other towns of importance, so the surrender of Roseau would have completed the operation.

After landing his troops, Missiessy could, too, have sailed his squadron round to the west coast and, when they made their assault, have assisted them in a swift capture of the place by bombarding the fort and town. But the Admiral, confident that the broadsides of his ships would swiftly cause the British flag to be hauled down, elected to rely on a frontal assault.

That the garrison had been taken by surprise there could be no doubt as, but for the firing of a single alarm gun, nearly a quarter of an hour elapsed before the fort began to reply to its bombardment by the French. But once the British gunners got into action their fire soon began to tell. Not only were they better trained and reloaded their pieces more swiftly, but they had the advantage always enjoyed by shore batteries engaging ships. Their cannon were on a firm base. whereas those in the ships were in constant motion owing to the swell of the sea. In consequence, the shooting of the British was much more accurate. Soon the French squadron was taking heavy punishment. Cannon balls smashed great holes in the sides of the ships, ploughed through the soldiers massed on their decks and brought down spars and masts.

Roger could not escape the obligation to stand on the poop of the flag-ship near the Admiral and his staff. As the battle raged the palms of his hands became damp and he felt goose pimples on his skin from fear that at any moment a cannon ball might cut him in half. Then, to his great relief, soon after ten o'clock, it became so obvious to Missiessy that he was getting by far the worse of the engagement that he had a signal hoisted breaking off the action.

A quarter of an hour later the squadron was out of range of the fort and heading up the coast. In a quiet bay some miles north of Roseau the ships dropped anchor and lay there for two days while the dead were consigned to the sea and the damage that had been done to the ships was, as far as possible, repaired.

On the day following the assault Missiessy called his Captains aboard the flag-ship for a Council of War, at which Roger and other senior Army officers were present. The general opinion was that now the garrison at Roseau had been alerted and shown itself capable of putting up such a stout resistance there could be no hope of taking the island. It was then decided to sail north and see if they would meet with better fortune at Montserrat, Nevis and St. Kitts.

Had the French succeeded in taking Dominica Roger would then have been faced with the problem of getting from there to the exit of the Windward Passage where 'Enterprise' had been lost; which meant a voyage of twelve hundred miles across the Caribbean west of the arc of islands that enclosed that sea, and he had already planned how to set about it.

Now he had to think again, but he soon decided what to do. As he was only a passenger and not under Missiessy's

397

orders he went to the Admiral after the Council of War, and said, 'Since there is to be no further attempt to take Dominica, sir, it is pointless for me to remain in the West Indies and the Emperor will expect me to return to France as soon as possible. The speediest way for me to do so would be to get a ship from Guadeloupe, so I should be grateful if you would have me put ashore at Pointe-à-Pitre.'

Guadeloupe was the next island northwards in the chain from Dominica and the squadron had to pass it on its way to Montserrat, so Roger's request presented no difficulty. Two days later he said good-bye to his companions on the terrible Atlantic crossing and was landed at Pointe-à-Pitre.

There Roger had no fear of being recognized as Mr. Brook, as Guadeloupe was the only French-owned island in the Caribbean that had never been taken by the British. The Governor made him welcome as one of the Emperor's A.D.C.s and, eager to hear all about Napoleon's Imperial Court, said that he must be his guest at the Residency until he could get a ship. Roger thanked him and, now that Missiessy was out of the way, enquired, not for one to take him back to France, but one bound for San Domingo.

On account of his health he was not expected back in France until the early summer; so now he would say that he had employed his time by visiting several French islands in order to be able to report upon conditions in them.

If, haunted as he was by the nagging fear that Georgina had been sold into a brothel, it was unlikely that she would have been taken so far from the place where she had been captured as Guadeloupe. Nevertheless, during Roger's stay of six days on the island, on the excuse of amusing himself after a long voyage, he visited all the haunts of vice in Pointe-à-Pitre, and paid the 'Madams' handsomely to produce all their girls for his inspection, having said that he was searching for one girl in particular whom he had known on a previous visit to the West Indies.

The majority of the girls in the less expensive houses were Caribs or of mixed blood; but in the better ones more than half of them were French with here and there Spanish, Dutch and English trollops. Some of them had previously served in houses in other islands and these, having stood them wine, Roger closely questioned; but none of them could recall having known a woman at all resembling Roger's description of Georgina.

On March 10th he went aboard the ship that was to take him on the eleven hundred mile run north-west across the Caribbean. The winds proved fairly favourable and for day after day, now brown as a berry, he lay on deck shaded by a sail from the blazing sun, reading or idly watching the flying fish skim the blue water. It was April 2nd when they docked at Port-au-Prince, and there he paid only a formal call on the Governor, courteously refusing his offer of hospitality with the explanation that he meant to spend only long enough in the capital to hire a small sea-going craft in which he intended to sail up the coast.

This left him free to explore the vice haunts of the city; but after three days he had met with no success in his quest for news of Georgina. Meanwhile he had chartered a ketch owned by a grizzle-haired quadroon named Charbon, who knew those waters well. The crew were mulattos; one of them called Pepe Pepe being a half-caste Spaniard who could act as an interpreter in Cuba. On the 5th he sailed across the southern end of the Windward Passage for Santiago de Cuba, arriving there on the 10th.

As allies of the French, the Spaniards made no difficulties for him; and for the next three days, with Pepe Pepe as his companion, he continued his search, visiting a score of brothels, but with no more success than in Port-au-Prince. On the 13th he sailed again, this time up the Windward Passage and round the north-eastern end of Cuba to Baracoa. This was the nearest port to the place where 'Enterprise' had gone down and, again with Pepe Pepe's help, he spent forty eight hours visiting every vice spot in the town, until he had satisfied himself that Georgina had not been taken there.

On the 18th he left Cuba and recrossed the Windward Passage to Port de Paix on the northern tip of San Domingo. There he spent another two days, by now sick of the sight of

399

near-nude women and the stench of their cheap perfume. Still he failed to pick up any trail, but he remained convinced that Georgina was alive and was determined not to give up until he had found her; so he sailed along the north coast to the French stronghold of Cap Haïtien. Yet another two days' search proved unavailing.

He had by now explored the stews in all the most likely ports to which Georgina might have been taken. There remained only Port Royal outside Kingston in Jamaica. It was more distant from the scene of her disappearance than the others but there, down by the palisades, there was a whole town of houses of ill fame that was notorious throughout the Caribbean, and if she had become the victim of an English buccaneer it was in Port Royal that he would probably have sold her.

If Roger landed in Jamaica he could become Mr. Brook, but his crew, although half-castes, were French subjects; so for fear of capture it would be necessary to bribe them heavily before they would agree to put him ashore in some deserted bay. Moreover Kingston was four hundred miles distant from Cap Haïtien, whereas the place where the 'Enterprise' had gone down was only some hundred or so miles off and in the opposite direction. As there had always been the possibility that Georgina was still marooned on a desert island Roger intended, should he fail to trace her in any of the ports, to search the area for her. To go south to Kingston and return would take anything from a fortnight to three weeks; so he decided to save for the time being the money with which he would have had to bribe his crew, explore the islands first then, if need be, go down to Jamaica as a last resort.

Accordingly they sailed from Cap Haïtien on April 24th and set a north-west course, which would carry them about half way between the north-eastern tip of Cuba and the many shoals and sandbanks to the south-west of Great Inagua.

The only information Roger had to go on was Mr. Small's statement that 'Enterprise' had been attacked when a day's run outside the Windward Passage and, depending on wind

400

and weather, that might have taken the ship anything from twenty to a hundred miles or more beyond the point of Cuba; so the area to be searched was a considerable one.

On the 27th they sighted the first group of islands. During the next three days the ketch dropped anchor in the shallows off each in turn, and Roger had himself rowed ashore in the dinghy to explore them. Two of the largest were inhabited, but only by a few families of miserable-looking Carib Indians who contrived to eke out a bare existence on fish and coco-nuts and lived in palm leaf huts. Scared out of their wits at the sight of Roger they ran off and hid in the undergrowth; but he made no attempt to lure them out as, not knowing their language, he could not have questioned them.

During the past three weeks Roger had been favoured with good weather, only occasionally meeting with a wind strong enough to make the sea uncomfortably choppy; but soon after the ketch left the group the sky became overcast, the wind dropped and the atmosphere became ominously still. Realizing that a hurricane was blowing up, they hastily got out the oars and pulled with all their strength to get back to the nearest island. Fortunately they reached it near a creek up which they were able to pole the ketch a few hundred yards. By then the sky was black with great drops of rain spattering down. A few minutes later it was descending in torrents. Lightning flashed in great jagged streaks and thunder boomed like the discharge of whole broadsides of guns. The down-pour lasted for two hours, to be succeeded by a terrible wind that it seemed would tear the clothes from their bodies and bent a nearby group of palm trees so far over that their fronds at times brushed the sand. The sea had been churned into huge waves that rushed up the creek and caused the ketch to bounce wildly up and down, then beached her high and dry. By evening the worst of the hurricane was over, but they had to remain there for another three days before the weather was sufficiently settled for them to relaunch the ketch and set sail again.

In the nine days that followed they visited a score or more of other islands, among them several on which there were

401

wild pigs, and one of these, Roger felt sure, after finding the remains of a camp, must be that on which Jenny and Mr. Small's party had been marooned from March to June in the preceding year.

Then, on the morning of May 12th they sighted an island about two miles long with a shelving beach which ran up to higher ground on which there was dense vegetation. As they approached it recognition dawned in Roger's mind. Suddenly he was positive that it was the island to which in his vision he had seen Georgina swimming. The airs were light and with maddening slowness the ketch edged in towards the coast. Trembling with impatience, when they entered shallow water he cried:

'I'll not use the dinghy. Beach her! Run her ashore!'

Captain Charbon looked at him in astonishment but obeyed the order. Jumping from the bow Roger plunged waist deep into the water and waded the last twenty feet to dry sand. Looking swiftly about him he saw the entrance to a shallow valley some two hundred yards to his right. At a run he set off towards it. The valley had a small stream trickling through it and curved inland, the banks growing steeper until on one side he was hastening along beneath a fifteen-foot high cliff. After he had covered a quarter of a mile the little canyon widened into a clearing, in which there were two rough palm-leaf huts leaning crookedly against the cliff. As he stumbled towards the larger of the two he pulled up short and gave a horrified gasp. Sprawled in front of the rickety door lay a bundle of clothes. Inside them was a skeleton.

From the well-cut breeches, the rapier still clutched in the hand of bones and the fair hair that still covered the grinning skull, Roger realized instantly that it must be Lord Rockhurst. It was evident that he had been dead for a considerable time and that the ants had eaten every shred of flesh from his bones.

Sweating with fear Roger entered the rude hut. It contained two couches of leaves, a roughly made table and stools but was otherwise empty. Turning, he lurched towards the smaller hut, pulled back the doorway made of palm fronds and looked inside. The light there was dim but sufficient for him to see a couch of leaves on which lay another skeleton. It was much shorter than the other and clad only in a pair of sailcloth shorts, but from the skull there rose a mop of dead-black hair.

With a sob, Roger threw himself down beside it. He felt that his heart was breaking, for he had come to the end of his quest and, too late, found his beloved Georgina.

CHAPTER XXVI

THE FATE OF ENGLAND HANGS...

R O G E R W A S still crouching there in stricken silence when, half an hour later, Captain Charbon and two of his mulatto crew came upon him. On previous occasions he had often spent four or five hours on his own exploring islands while the seamen hunted for shell fish along the shore; but his excited behaviour that morning had given the ketch captain the idea that he might suddenly have become the victim of sunstroke. Knowing that Roger had been searching the islands for castaways, Charbon on seeing the two skeletons at once grasped the tragedy that had befallen his employer and endeavoured to comfort him.

But Roger was beyond all comfort and his mind so bemused by shock that he could only shake his head in dumb despair. After a while he allowed himself to be led away, back to the ketch. There Charbon made him swallow several mouthsful of liquid from a small grimy bottle. It contained a potent brew of herbs used by the Negroes in San Domingo to dull pain and, having been given such a large dose, ten minutes later Roger lapsed into unconsciousness.

When he roused the sun was setting. Memory of his terrible discovery that morning returned to him and he burst into tears. Again he refused to be comforted by Charbon and Pepe Pepe. Silently he made to climb out of the boat, but they gently restrained him and told him it was pointless to go ashore as they had buried the two skeletons that morning. Then they persuaded him to take another draught of the narcotic, which caused him to sleep dreamlessly through the night.

Next morning he had his grief sufficiently under control to speak of it and said he intended to go back to the clearing to see the graves. Charbon went with him and helped him to make two wooden crosses. As Roger had often been present at burials at sea he knew the burial service almost by heart and repeated over the graves all he could remember of it.

Only afterwards, as they knelt to pray, he suddenly remembered that Georgina had left him her hair. As he had seen it the day before it had been straight instead of curly and only about eight inches in length but, marooned there as she had been for many months, he had realized at once that she would have had no means of keeping it in curlers and must have cut off her long lovelocks because they would have bothered her in the intense heat. He had half a mind to disinter the skeleton and plait her hair into an armband that he would always wear; but he had no need of any such material thing to remember her by and, having said the burial service over the grave, felt that it would now be near-sacrilege to disturb it.

Before leaving the clearing they again looked round the two huts, finding in them a few things that had evidently been washed ashore from the wreck of 'Enterprise'. They also discovered in a little niche behind the head of one of the beds of leaves two tortoiseshell combs and a string of fine pearls that Roger knew of old to be Georgina's.

Being anxious to get his employer away from the scene of the tragedy as soon as possible, Charbon had given his men orders to get the ketch ready for sea and, as soon as he and Roger were aboard, they set sail. Without asking for instructions the Captain set a course back to his home port of Port-au-Prince and they arrived there six days later.

During those days Roger had remained in a lethargy of despair, but on landing he roused himself to thank his crew for all they had done for him, then he took Charbon to a bank, cashed one of his letters of credit, and paid him off with a handsome bonus. At the hostelry in which he had stayed for a few nights six weeks earlier he took a room and there endeavoured to concentrate on what he should do with himself.

It was now May 19th and in the midday hours the heat was grilling. There was no point in his staying longer in the West Indies so obviously the sooner he could get back to Europe the better. To meet Napoleon's wishes he should have sailed over a month before, but he could excuse the lateness of his return by saying that, after carrying out unofficial inspections in Martinique, Guadeloupe and San Domingo, he had decided to find out the state of the Allies' warships in the Cuban ports, but had been blown off course, wrecked and marooned for some weeks on a desert island.

On the other hand, did he really wish to continue in Napoleon's service? The knowledge that Georgina was definitely dead seemed to have killed all ambition in him; he wondered now if it would not be better for him to carry out his old plan of settling down in England. Colonel Thursby and Aunt Marsham, he knew, would be delighted for him to make his home at Stillwaters. There he could play the rôle of what Georgina had termed 'a proper man' to bring up her boy; and he would, too, derive much happiness from seeing his own little Susan grow up into a lovely girl. Whatever he might decide, situated as he was, the quickest way for him to get back to Europe was in a French warship.

With this in mind he called next day upon the Governor, who told him that a frigate would be sailing in a week or ten days' time and that he would secure him accommodation in her, then asked him to stay to dinner. Reluctantly, but out of politeness, Roger accepted. At the meal four other naval and military officers were present, and from their conversation he learned what had been happening in the Carribean during his ten-week search for Georgina.

Missiessy's squadron had alarmed the English by appearing off several of their ports and caused them considerable annoyance by capturing merchantmen whose value as prizes was estimated to be £60,000; but the cruise was accounted a failure because he had not succeeded in taking a single one of their islands.

Villeneuve had put to sea from Toulon in March, and orders had been sent to Missiessy to await him in the Indies, then return with him to European waters. But Nelson had headed Villeneuve off in the Mediterranean so he had had to put back to port. Missiessy had then received an order while at Martinique to return alone via the Canaries. Believing a British fleet to have reached the Caribbean he had been so eager to leave it that he had again refused Villaret-Joyeuse's request to reduce Diamond Rock, made all speed to San Domingo, landed his troops there and set sail for home

Meanwhile Villeneuve had again left Toulon, fooled Nelson by feinting towards Egypt and passed through the Straits of Gibraltar on April 9th. A fast frigate had been despatched to tell Missiessy to await him, after all, but Missiessy had been in such a hurry to obey the previous order that he was gone before the frigate arrived in the Indies. Villeneuve had made a good passage and arrived at Martinique soon after the frigate. Having captured Diamond Rock he had sailed again, it was believed with the intention of attacking Barbados; but for some days there had been no further news of him.

On May 28th Roger sailed in the frigate *Guillaume le Conquérant* which, with fair winds, should have landed him in Europe early in July; but during the first part of her voyage she suffered a severe check. When six days out she was struck by a hurricane, lost her foremast, sprang a leak and was driven from her north-eastern course hundreds of miles to the south.

Roger had a ghastly time, lying in his narrow cabin sick as a dog and praying that an end might be put to his misery by the ship going down. She survived the tempest, but only because good luck brought her on to the northern coast of Puerto Rico and she was able to put in to San Juan. Their Spanish allies there proved most helpful and hospitable; but time seemed to have no meaning for them, so it was June 14th before the repairs had been completed and they were able to put to sea again.

From then on they were favoured with good weather and on July 3rd, having spent a day scouting round the island of Madeira to make sure there were no British warships in the vicinity, they put into Funchal to water. They were still loading crates of live poultry, pigs and fresh fruit when Villeneuve's fleet came into view.

As soon as it had anchored in the bay, the Captain of *Guillaume le Conquérant* put off in his gig for the flagship to pay his respects to the Admiral, taking Roger with him. They were invited to stay to dine and after dinner, over some good bottles of old Madeira wine, Villeneuve gave them an account of his voyage to the Indies.

Having left Nelson hunting for him in the Mediterranean, after passing Gibraltar, he had picked up the Spanish squadron from Cadiz but it had proved in such ill condition as to be worse than useless and two of its ships had been lost during the ocean crossing. Frigates had later brought intelligence that after leaving the Mediterranean in pursuit Nelson had again been misled and, believing that Villeneuve was making for Ireland, had set a course for the Scillies. But, on learning the truth he had sailed with ten ships-of-the-line to 'save the West Indies', made a surprisingly swift passage and, having picked up two more ships-of-the-line at Barbados, set about scouring the Caribbean for the French.

Intent on obeying the Emperor's orders to clear the British out of the Antilles, Villeneuve had sailed from Martinique early in June with the intention of capturing Barbados. When approaching the island he had captured a convoy of merchantmen and from them learned that he had missed coming into collision with Nelson's fleet only by a few hours. Knowing that the Emperor's prime intention was that the combined fleets should, during the summer, sweep the

Channel in order to clear it for the invasion of England, he had cheerfully left Nelson hunting for him in the Caribbean and made all speed to recross the Atlantic.

After two days at Madeira while their reluctant allies, the Portuguese, slowly watered and revictualled the fleet, it sailed north to European waters. Adverse winds made their progress slow but on July 22nd they were off Finisterre in foggy weather. Out of the mist emerged Admiral Calder's squadron. He had only fifteen ships to oppose Villeneuve's twenty but, nevertheless, gave battle.

Stoically, Roger put the best face possible on having to stand on the poop of *Guillaume le Conquérant* and chance his luck whether he survived, while shot ripped through the sails, crashed through the bulwarks and made men utter agonizing screams.

To his relief the engagement proved a very minor battle compared to that of the Nile, which had raged with the most appalling carnage from sundown all through the night and, eventually, led to his having to go overboard from Admiral Brueys' flagship to save himself from being blown up in her. Here the lines of battle soon became confused and ship engaged ship then drifted away in the fog until each became visible to another enemy.

When night came Admiral Calder drew off so, on that account, it could be considered a French victory; but before the battle was over two of the ships under Villeneuve's colleague, the Spanish Admiral Gravina, struck their flags, whereas none of the British surrendered, and later it was learned that more than twice the number of French and Spanish seamen had been killed or wounded so, on points, the British had had the better of it.

On the 23rd Villeneuve put into Vigo to land his wounded and repair his ships. When they arrived in the port Roger took stock of his situation. Northern Spain was still a long way from England. If he remained with Villeneuve's fleet, as soon as it was fit to put to sea again it would head up Channel and he might easily become involved in another sea battle. Whereas if he had himself put ashore he could ride in safety to Bordeaux and, with less risk, cross from there.

It so happened that before he had even made up his mind his decision was taken for him. Villeneuve sent for him to come aboard the flagship and, after some general conversation, said:

'Colonel Breuc, I must, as soon as possible, send particulars to the Emperor of our action off Finisterre, and I know that you are anxious to rejoin him as swiftly as you can. I wish to inform him, too, that as soon as my fleet is shipshape I intend to move up to Ferrol. Are you willing to take a despatch to His Majesty?'

Roger at once agreed, returned to *Guillaume le Conquérant* to collect his baggage then picked up the despatch and went ashore. The following morning he set out on his long ride along the northern coast of Spain and round the Bay of Biscay to Bordeaux.

During those days of hacking along the dusty roads and sleeping in bug-ridden inns at Lugo, Oviedo, Santander, Bilbao, San Sebastian and several lesser places, he had ample time to think again about his future, and he decided that, at least for some time to come, he could not settle down at Stillwaters. The picture of Georgina's skeleton was still too clear in his mind; and he felt sure that in the lovely house where they had enjoyed such happiness together it would constantly haunt him.

As an alternative he could have occupied Thatched House Lodge. The two years he had spent there had been among the most enjoyable of his life. During them he had undertaken no dangerous missions and, Richmond being within easy distance of London, he and Amanda had thrown themselves with youthful enthusiasm into the social whirl. But Amanda, too, was dead, he had no inclination at all to dance or chatter among crowds of idle people and to live there alone with only old Dan to talk to must soon become terribly monotonous.

Since the battle off Finisterre other thoughts too had begun to stir his sluggish mind. It had brought home to him that a war was still raging upon which the fate of his country

410

depended. When, after his abortive peace mission, he had broken with Mr. Pitt, it had not seemed to him remotely possible that Napoleon would ever be in a position to invade England, and even a year ago his prospects of doing so had been extremely slender. But during the past six months the results of his shipbuilding programme had begun to show and this, together with the Spanish alliance, had made the picture very different.

When Roger had left Paris in December it was estimated that Britain had seventy five ships of the line against the Allies' sixty-four; but twelve of the British ships were known to be on far distant stations, so in Atlantic and home waters the Allies had actually achieved a superiority of one. Admittedly, ship for ship the British, being better equipped and their crews far better trained, were superior to the French and greatly superior to the Spanish. But should Napoleon's strategy prove successful and the main fleet under Nelson be kept out of the way for a few weeks, sheer weight of numbers would enable the Allies to drive the British squadrons from the Channel. The more Roger thought about this the more convinced he became that, not only did the best hope of escaping from his terrible depression lie in again actively occupying his mind, but that it was his definite duty to do his utmost to learn the latest French plans and, if possible, get information to England which would prevent the Allied fleets concentrating into another Armada. In consequence, instead of seeking out the smuggler Jubert at Bordeaux, he rode on through Poitiers, Tours and Orleans to Paris. His journey from Vigo had taken him sixteen days and he reached the French capital on August 8th.

Napoleon's blind spot was the hazards met with at sea. He expected fleets and frigates to move from place to place with the same precision as armies and despatch riders, taking no account of winds or weather, and that if a passage proved a bad one supplies sometimes ran so low that squadrons were compelled to delay further by going hundreds of miles off course to pick up food and water. So when Roger reported to him at St. Cloud he met with a rough reception and had to

411

remain silent for several minutes while the Emperor upbraided him for not having returned to France by May at the latest.

When the tirade subsided, Roger, without going into details, told his story: that he had been shipwrecked and for some while marooned on a desert island, then having given his master particulars of the battle off Finisterre, he went on to mollify him by saying that he had brought him a confidential report upon conditions in not only the fleet, but also in Martinique, Guadeloupe and the principal ports of San Domingo.

Taking the long document that Roger had written in the evenings in the hostelries at which he had stayed during his journey through France, the Emperor threw it on his desk and said:

'Well, well! That may prove useful and enable me to stir these lazy devils up a little, particularly my Admirals. Why I should be cursed with Naval Commanders who show such lack of initiative, I cannot think. That fool Gantheaume had the chance to break out of Brest weeks ago but never took it. And here is Villeneuve, instead of sailing up Channel while Nelson is out of the way, by now skulking like a sick dog in Ferrol. Do you know it? 'Tis the worst port in Spain, with a river entrance so narrow that a squadron rarely gets in or out of it without several of the ships becoming stuck on the mud banks and days being wasted getting them off. He should have gone to Cadiz, from where he could sally forth swiftly at any time. And I sent him orders that should he meet with serious opposition in the Channel that was what he was to do. I sent them, yes, on July 16th.'

'That is above three weeks ago, Sire,' Roger remarked soothingly. 'So he should have had them by now.'

'Yes, and I suppose he will now sit in Cadiz until I order him out. Had he had the stomach of a man he would by this time have driven the English off their beat outside Brest; then we would have had Gantheaume's fleet joined to his at sea and the Channel would be ours. But I have hopes yet that we will be able to launch the invasion this month. I would proceed to the coast now for a final inspection had I not so many things requiring my presence at the moment in Paris. Did you know that I was recently absent in Italy for three months?'

'I heard so on my way north, Sire; and am happy to congratulate Your Majesty upon now being King as well as Emperor, for I am told that you crowned yourself King of Italy in Milan Cathedral.'

'Yes. You should have been there, Breuc. It was a splendid spectacle. But while I was away a hundred matters got out of hand here; so I left young Beauharnais as my Viceroy and hurried back. We did the journey from Milan to Fontaine-bleau in eighty-five hours. Things here now are in better trim but I'll need another week or so before I can leave for the coast. You will, of course, come with me. In the meantime see Decrès at the Ministry of Marine. Give him an account of the battle off Finisterre, but of nothing else. I do not wish him to know that your voyage to the Indies had any other reason than to restore your health.'

The following morning Roger made his report to the Minister of Marine. When he had done Decrès said, 'I am inclined to agree with the Emperor that Villeneuve was wrong in not continuing up the Channel even if he had to engage Admiral Calder again. Although his superiority in ships was negligible, by detaching a fast frigate and sending it across the Bay of Biscay he could have brought the Rochefort squadron out to his assistance, which would have given him sufficient odds to win the battle. But His Majesty is far from being right in most of his naval appreciations. For example, it is his own fault that Gantheaume's fleet is not now at sea.'

'How so, Your Excellency?' Roger enquired.

The Minister made an unhappy grimace, 'His orders to Gantheaume were that he was not to break out of Brest should it entail a battle. When Admiral Nelson was known to be on his way to the West Indies, the blockading fleet at Brest became so reduced in numbers that Gantheaume could easily have defeated it. He asked permission to do so, but the

Emperor would not agree. Since then the English have been reinforced, so the opportunity was lost.'

'Before Nelson can return from the Indies there may come another,' Roger hazarded.

Decrès shrugged 'There may. If the Emperor orders Villeneuve up from Cadiz he could raise the blockade long enough for Gantheaume to break out; then, at last, we'd be masters of the Channel. But for how long? Unfortunately His Majesty refuses to face the fact that ship for ship we are not equal to the English, so basing operations simply on counting hulks leads to false assumptions. I have warned him of this many times but he refuses to listen. And my fear is that, even if we can concentrate a large enough fleet to cover the launching of the invasion, within a week or so Nelson will arrive on the scene and, even with one-third fewer ships than we have at our disposal, inflict a crushing defeat on us. Then our Army in England would be cut off.'

That, too, was Roger's belief, and he left the unhappy Decrès with the thought that of all posts the one he would least like to occupy was that of Napoleon's Minister of Marine.

Two days later he breakfasted with his old friend Talleyrand and found the Foreign Minister also in a far from optimistic frame of mind. After describing the Italian journey, on which he had accompanied the Emperor, he said:

'But I fear he may have to pay a price for his antics as cock-of-the-walk while in Italy. The Lombards were by no means averse to having their Republic converted into a Monarchy, but they would naturally have preferred to have as their ruler one of their own people rather than Josephine's boy Eugène, and they resent intensely the hordes of French officials that remain there battening upon them. The same applies to the territories of Piombino and Lucca which he has given to his sisters. Not content with that he has made the entire Ligurian Republic a part of France.

'Mr. Pitt, meanwhile, remains our deadly enemy. Soon after you sailed for the Indies, the Emperor sent another letter to King George III proposing a cessation of hostilities;

but the British Cabinet refused even to discuss the matter, and 'tis clear that they have strong hopes that Napoleon's ambitions may yet bring about his downfall.

'For many months past Mr. Pitt has been working tirelessly to bring about a third Coalition against us, and the Emperor has played into his hands. Our unpopularity in Italy has reached a point where the Italians would welcome the Austrians back if only they could get rid of us, and that has encouraged Vienna to contemplate another attempt to regain her old possessions in the peninsula. The Czar, too, displayed intense resentment at our incorporating the Ligurian Republic into France; so both Austria and Russia are, I am convinced, already secretly concerting measures with England. I'd willingly wager that we'll have another Continental war on our hands before the Autumn is out.,

'What view does the Emperor take of this new threat?' Roger enquired.

Talleyrand shrugged, 'Cher ami, he has become so confident of himself that he does not give a button. And should his invasion of England succeed he'll have no need to. Without the great subsidies that England always pays to keep her allies' armies in the field, they would not even start a war or, if they had, would promptly eat humble pie and sue for peace.'

'And what think you of his prospects of launching the invasion?'

'If he attempts it at all it should be this summer, otherwise that great Army of the Coast which has been training for so long will become stale. Therefore I think he will risk it provided he can achieve even temporary superiority in the Channel. To do that the fleets of Villeneuve and Gantheaume must unite. Were they defeated separately, or even one of them sufficiently crippled as to be useless for a year or more, I think it certain that the invasion project would have to be shelved for good.'

'After all these years of preparation and trumpet-blowing that would mean a great loss of face for Napoleon.'

'Not necessarily,' Talleyrand smiled. 'He is as slippery as

415

an eel when it comes to wriggling out of awkward situations. Measures would be taken to ensure it being known in every corner of France that he and the Army had been ready and eager to go; but that his first care was the lives of his men, and that his miserable Navy having refused to promise them a safe passage to the English beaches was his reason for cancelling the operation.'

Roger smiled back, 'And when does Your Excellency think we are likely to hear if it is to be or not to be?'

'Within a day or two of his carrying out his final inspection of the Army of the Coast. I and several other Ministers are to accompany him, and a Grand Council is to be held at which he will make known his decision.'

A week later the huge cavalcade set out for Boulogne. there on August 22nd the greatest military spectacle of that, and perhaps, any age, took place. The Emperor, followed by a glittering array of Marshals, Generals and Staff Officers reviewed the Grande Armée. With intervals of only a few yards between formations it stretched across the downs for nine miles.

By then it was known among Napoleon's intimate circle that Austria had accepted from England a subsidy of five and a half millions and that Russia and Sweden were actively preparing to renew the war against France; but the Emperor remained quite unperturbed. The only measure he took was to send Duroc to the ever-irresolute Frederick William, to offer Hanover to Prussia as the price of an alliance. Austria was not ready for war and many weeks must elapse before she could put an army in the field. The Army of the Rhine, with the aid of France's ally Bavaria, was capable of staving off any premature attacks. The Russian armies were so far away that they could not become a serious menace for several months. Meanwhile great events might alter the whole European scene.

The morning after the Grand Council the Emperor sent for Roger, gave him a despatch and said, 'You will take this to Villeneuve and hand it to him personally. I have chosen you rather than an ordinary courier because this is in a sense a

416

mission. You already know the Admiral and as one of my personal staff he will know you to be in my confidence. You are to inform him of the latest developments in Europe and discuss them, and the orders contained in this despatch, freely with him. My orders are that he is to put to sea, come up Channel, raise the blockade of Brest so as to free Gantheaume and make possible the invasion. Now, this is the delicate point. Should he again show reluctance to risk his ships you are to hint that I may deprive him of his command and give it to Admiral Rosily. You could say that you chanced to overhear a conversation between myself and Decrès. That should spur this mulish sailor into being of some use to me. Do you understand?'

'Perfectly, Sire,' Roger bowed. 'But Your Majesty will appreciate that to execute your order I'll have to ride near the whole length of France and Spain, so you can hardly expect Villeneuve to appear in the Channel much before mid-October.'

'Umph,' Napoleon gave a grunt. 'I know it. But that will be time enough. The weather is often excellent in the autumn. Unless the Admirals prove even more spineless than they have so far led me to suppose, we'll eat our Christmas dinners in what's left of London. Go now, and ride hard.'

Much perplexed as to what course to pursue, Roger set out on his long journey. More than ever now he regretted having quarrelled with Mr. Pitt before the Prime Minister's resignation for, had he not done so, the Foreign Office would have kept him informed during Addington's administration of the changes that occurred from time to time in the secret post offices maintained in France for conveying intelligence to England. Such pillar boxes rarely lasted more than a year or two before the static agents who ran them were detected by counter-espionage or decided that it was no longer safe to run them at the same address; so those that Roger had used in the old days of the Revolution and the Directory must have long since been closed down. In the previous year he had had to get his information across in person, and must do so again now.

417

How and when were the questions. If Jubert was still smuggling cargoes of wine across from Bordeaux, that was the answer to the first. The second was a much knottier problem. Normally, taking into consideration the bad posting service in Spain, horses going lame and other causes of delay, he could not be expected to accomplish his thirteen-hundred-mile journey in much under twenty six days. But if he rode all-out he could probably lessen that time by ten days. That should be sufficient for him to break his journey at Bordeaux, cross to England, recross to France and still reach Cadiz by about September 18th.

But should any mischance befall him during the crossing everything would go awry. Villeneuve would not receive his orders, so remain in port and the crux of the matter was to get him out of it, then ensure that he was intercepted and defeated.

Roger thought again of Talleyrand's remark that, if only one of France's two major fleets were crippled sufficiently to render it useless for a year or so, that would put an end to the invasion project. And he had no doubt that Talleyrand was right. It also entered his mind how fortunate it was that the shrewd Foreign Minister was evidently not aware that Napoleon had chosen for this mission *le Colonel Breuc* for, knowing him now to be still loyal to England, and therefore not to be trusted where operations against that country were concerned, Talleyrand would certainly have produced some plausible reason why one of the Emperor's other A.D.C.s should be charged with conveying his orders to Villeneuve.

After considerable cogitation Roger decided that he dared not risk a crossing from Bordeaux before delivering his despatch in Cadiz. Villeneuve would not put to sea immediately. Several days must elapse before he had watered and revictualled to capacity for a long cruise and got his ships into the best possible state to engage, as he would foresee he might have to, in a great naval battle. And Cadiz was only some sixty miles from Gibraltar.

Since Spain was at war with England the Rock was again besieged, so it might not be easy to reach, but Roger felt

418

fairly confident of his ability to do so one way or another within a few days of leaving Cadiz; and from Gibraltar, while Villeneuve was still in port fitting out his fleet for the great endeavour, a fast frigate could be despatched to England, to ensure that a fleet of sufficient strength would be waiting to give battle to him by the time he entered the Channel.

Alternatively, Roger decided, should it prove too difficult and dangerous to get through the Spanish lines to Gilbraltar, he could ride back at full speed to Bordeaux, cross with Jubert or some other smuggler to Devon and by the new semaphore telegraph send his information to London, still with enough margin of time for Villeneuve to be intercepted.

Having settled this question in his mind, Roger decided that there was nothing to be gained by exhausting himself in riding all-out to Cadiz. The longer Villeneuve's sailing was delayed the worse the weather would become; which meant that even if he succeeded in evading a battle with a British fleet and enabled Gantheaume's to emerge from Brest, the worse would be the prospects of the invasion being successful.

In consequence, Roger rode south through Rouen, Le Mans, Tours, Poitiers, Angoulême, Bordeaux, Bayonne, Vitoria, Burgos, Madrid, Cordoba and Seville by easy stages, averaging no more than fifty miles or so a day, and arriving at the little town of Jerez de la Frontera on September 19th.

Jerez was fewer than twenty miles from the coast but over thirty from Cadiz, because the road to the port ran first in a semi-circle round a wide bay then along a ten-mile spit of low-lying ground to the city, which lay at its northern extremity. It was this peninsula, running parallel to the coast and almost enclosing a great area of protected water, that made Cadiz the finest natural harbour in Europe.

Early on the morning of the 20th Roger rode out of Jerez; but when he came to the crossroads near the coast, instead of taking the road that curved round towards Cadiz, he continued on for another fifty miles until, in the afternoon, he reached Algeciras. Further thought had decided him that, if he could do so without difficulty, it would be better for him to inform the Governor of Gibraltar of his mission before

419

delivering the despatch to Villeneuve, as that should result in the Admiralty receiving news of French intentions several days earlier than if he had followed his original plan.

To the east, only a few miles across the bay from Algeciras, the great Rock of Gibraltar towered up clear in the evening light. The shipping lying under the guns of its forts and the houses on the terraced roads could be seen quite distinctly; but that evening Roger learned that to get there was a thing that could not be done without considerable risk and, anyway, not overnight.

The inn at which he had put up was much frequented by Spanish officers. On seeing his French uniform they saluted him with grave courtesy. He spoke a little Spanish and several of them spoke French so he had no difficulty in conversing with them and spent the evening drinking in their company. As an allied officer they freely discussed the progress of the siege with him and, although it had made no headway, it soon emerged that the fortress was so closely invested that it would be a most hazardous proceeding to attempt to get through the Spanish lines.

Next day he rode out round the perimeter encircling the approaches to the Rock, to La Linea and back, and his ride convinced him that he could not get through to it by land. He would have to use some of his gold to bribe a fisherman in some village along the coast to put him ashore on the Rock at night. But that meant a delay of two or three days, and as he had ridden down through France and Spain without hurrying he felt that he could no longer put off delivering his despatch. He reckoned it would be at least a week before Villeneuve was ready to put to sea; so he would have ample time to ensure a frigate's being despatched from Gibraltar before the French fleet sailed.

On the morning of the 23rd he left Algeciras and by afternoon was riding along the great natural breakwater that enclosed the harbour of Cadiz. Proceeding to the port on the inland curve of the promontory he stabled his horse at an inn on the waterfront called 'The Inca Queen'. He then hired a boat with a steersman and four oarsmen and had himself rowed towards the flagship. She lay about two miles south of the harbour and as the boat carried him towards her he had ample opportunity to take stock of the Allied fleet lying at anchor in the soft evening light.

His boat was about to pass within about sixty yards of a French frigate and his eye was caught by the bright dress of a young woman leaning out from the high stern gallery. Her hair was dressed high in the Spanish manner, rising to a big tortoiseshell comb from which a lace mantilla fell, partially covering her plump breasts. He was at once reminded of Georgina, for the woman's features, colouring and form were very similar to hers. But he had no doubt at all that she was some Spanish trollop that the Captain of the frigate had taken aboard to amuse himself with while the fleet was in harbour.

When his boat drew nearer, the woman suddenly began to wave and shout something at them. Taking it as an exhibition of *joie de vivre*, Roger waved back, then her cries gradually faded as his boatmen pulled on towards the flagship.

As he mounted the gangway, the officer of the watch observed his rank and had him ceremoniously piped aboard where he was received with every courtesy. But it transpired that Admiral Villeneuve was not on board. He had left that morning for Seville—in which city, associated with the ancient 'Board of the Indies', the Spanish Admiralty had its headquarters—to negotiate for further supplies for his fleet, and he was not expected back in Cadiz for several days.

Roger accepted a glass of Malaga wine from the senior officer on duty, then said that he must proceed to Seville to deliver personally a despatch to the Admiral. As his boat took him back towards the harbour it again passed fairly close to the frigate in which he had seen the woman who resembled Georgina. She was still leaning over the stern gallery, but twilight had now fallen so her features were less distinct. When they came nearer she gave a shout and waved a sheet of white paper to attract their attention. Roger was in no mood for a waterborne flirtation but he returned her hail. As he did so she quickly rolled the piece of paper into a spill,

421

pushed it into an empty bottle, rammed home the cork and threw the bottle as far as she could towards the passing boat.

Now considerably intrigued, Roger had his steersmen alter course until they were within fifty feet of the stern of the frigate; then he retrieved the floating bottle from the slightly choppy water. As he pulled the cork from the bottle neck and fished out the paper, he expected to find that the decidedly attractive Senorita had sent him a note to say that her lover was ashore and inviting him to come aboard to entertain her.

To his utter amazement he read, 'Roger, do you not recognize me? I dared not shout in English for fear of giving you away, but I am Georgina. I am held captive by the Captain of this frigate. For God's sake, rescue me.'

CHAPTER XXVII

NAPOLEON TRIUMPHANT

F O R A F E W moments Roger was so overcome by mingled surprise and joy that his wits refused to work. Then they snapped back with their usual resilience to an unexpected situation.

Three courses were open to him. He could have the boat rowed under the stern of the frigate and tell Georgina to jump for it. But the stern gallery over which she was leaning was a good twenty feet above the water, so that would mean a nasty drop and a chill wind was blowing. When they hauled her aboard she would be soaked to the skin and might catch her death of cold before he could get her to his inn.

Secondly, she could speak a little Spanish; so he could call up to her in that language that he would return after nightfall bringing with him a line to throw her and a rope ladder that she could then haul up, make fast and descend by to the boat. But while it was evident that the man who held her captive was not with her at the moment it was highly probable that he would be during the night. Not only would he prevent her escaping but, perhaps, grab up his pistols and fire down upon her defenceless would-be-rescuer.

The third course was to go boldly on board right away and claim her. And that Roger decided to do.

In his halting Spanish he called to Georgina, 'I am coming for you, Senorita. Get your things together quickly.' Then he said to the owner of the boat, 'That Senorita is an old friend of mine. She is being held on the ship against her will. Steer along to the gangway.'

As usual with ships in port for some time, instead of a rope ladder slung over the side, a flight of wooden steps had been rigged from her deck down to a platform a few feet above the level of the water. Much amused by this romantic encounter, the grinning sailors brought the boat alongside the platform and Roger jumped on to it.

Taking the wooden steps three at a time he mounted to the quarter deck. As the ship was in port only a skeleton watch was being maintained. Except for two seamen sitting on coils of rope smoking their long pipes at the entrance to the fo'c'sle no one was about, but at the sound of Roger's footsteps a young Lieutenant emerged from the after deck house. Saluting Roger politely he asked his business.

'I am here,' said Roger, 'to see the Señorita in the Captain's quarters.'

The Lieutenant looked startled and exclaimed, 'I. . . I fear that is not possible, *Monsieur le Colonel*. Nobody is allowed to see her without Captain Fournier's permission, and he is ashore.'

'I require nobody's permission,' returned Roger sharply. 'Come! Be good enough to take me to her.'

'But . . . but, *monsieur le Colonel*,' stammered the Lieutenant. 'I am under orders. The lady is English. She. . . she is a captive and held incommunicado.'

'Of that I am aware, as also are the authorities who sent me here.' Roger's blue eyes flashed as he added with a sneer, 'And since when did Frenchmen make war on women?'

The young man reddened. 'Please believe I am in no way responsible. But I have my orders. I cannot disobey them.'

'That I appreciate. However, by making your protest you

424

have done your duty. I will go find her for myself.' Turning on his heel Roger walked briskly towards the entrance under the poop that led to the ship's stern cabin.

Now sweating slightly with apprehension, the Lieutenant hurried after him and cried, '*Monsieur le Colonel*, will you not wait until Captain Fournier comes aboard? He is due back now, so should be here quite shortly. Wait and discuss this with him, I beg; otherwise I'll find myself in most grievous trouble.'

Ignoring the plea, Roger strode down the passage until he reached a door at the end which obviously gave on to the big stateroom. Seizing the handle of the door he rattled it, but it was locked. The noise he made brought a big, broad-shouldered man out of a nearby galley. A glance at the kit he was wearing led Roger to judge that he was the Captain's steward and he snapped:

'Where is the key to this door? Get it at once.'

The steward gave him a surly look then glanced at the Lieutenant, who quavered, '*Monsieur le Colonel*, we have our orders.'

'To hell with your orders! Refuse me the key and I'll kick the door in.' Roger drew back a pace as though about to raise his heavily-booted foot.

'These quarters is private,' said the steward aggressively. 'An' 'tis my job to see as no one enters 'em in Capn's absence.' Then he moved to step in front of Roger.

Drawing himself up, Roger said harshly, 'You know my rank. Observe also my sash. It is that of an A.D.C. to the Emperor. Lay a hand on me or endeavour to prevent me from entering this stateroom and by God you'll rue it. I'll have you sent to the galleys. Now, give me the key.'

The steward wilted and produced a long key from his jacket pocket. Taking it, Roger snarled at him, 'Get back to your galley.' Then he turned to the Lieutenant. 'I am about to relieve you of your prisoner. Should you make any attempt to stop me I shall report the matter personally to Monsieur Decrès, the Minister of Marine, and see to it that you are court martialled with your Captain for having aided him in an illegal act. You will now return to your quarter-deck.'

Still surly, but cowed, the steward shuffled back into his pantry. The Lieutenant, white to the gills, saluted then turned on his heel. Roger quickly inserted the key in the lock and opened the door. Georgina was standing near one end of a large table which occupied the centre of the big stateroom. She now had on a cloak and hood and was holding a big straw basket into which she had hurriedly crammed her belongings.

As Roger stepped through the doorway into the stateroom, Georgina, her great dark eyes shining with delight, started to run towards him. With a swift gesture he checked her, and put a finger to his lips enjoining silence. Then he bowed and asked:

'*Madame, parlez-vous français?*'

She nodded, and he went on in French, 'It has come to the knowledge of the authorities that you are being held here against your will. I have been sent to take you ashore. Permit me to relieve you of your basket.' He was playing this little comedy for the benefit of the steward, who he felt sure was listening behind the half-open galley door. And as he stepped up to Georgina to take the basket, he added in a whisper, 'Until we are alone it is better that we should pretend to be strangers.' Then he stood aside for her to precede him from the cabin.

On the quarter deck the Lieutenant was standing, still sweating at the thought of having to face his Captain's wrath; but he made no move to stop them and saluted as they stepped up on to the gangway.

The moment Roger could see over the ship's side he received a most unpleasant shock. His excitement at freeing Georgina had caused him momentarily to forget about the Lieutenant's having told him that Captain Fournier was expected back on board at any time. And there was the Captain just stepping out of his gig on to the platform below.

Quickly handing Georgina back her basket, he put her behind him and started down the steps. At the same moment the Captain glanced up. On seeing Georgina his mouth fell open in surprise. Then his face became black with anger and he bellowed at Roger:

'Who the devil are you? What's the meaning of this?'

Roger smiled at him and replied, 'I should have thought you could see for yourself. I am about to take this lady ashore.'

'You'll do nothing of the kind.'

'Indeed I shall. And you will attempt to stop me at your peril.'

Fournier was a tall, bronze-faced man of about forty, his good looks now marred by an ugly scowl. He had run up a dozen steps of the gangway and Roger had quietly walked down about the same number; so they were now within a few feet of one another.

'Who are you?' demanded the Captain. 'By what right are you in my ship?'

'My name is Galahad,' Roger grinned down at him. 'And I am about my normal business of rescuing damsels in distress.'

'Damn your insolence! I'll teach you manners before you are much older. Get back on deck this instant.'

'Manners? Oh come, Captain. Where are yours? Had you any you would not keep a lady waiting, but descend to the platform so that she could pass.'

Infuriated by this baiting, Fournier put his hand to his sword. Roger had been expecting that so was ready for it, but he had no intention of exchanging thrusts; for should either of them seriously wound the other he would have little hope of getting away with Georgina. If he got the worst of the encounter that would be that. If the Captain did it was certain that his men would prevent them from leaving the ship until some senior officer could be brought on the scene.

Instead he waited another moment until both Fournier's hands were engaged, the right gripping the hilt of the sword and the left grasping the scabbard. Then, grabbing with one hand the rope that ran alongside the gangway he went down

427

one step and, with the other, gave the Captain a terrific box on his right ear.

The blow sent Fournier reeling sideways. Roger followed it up with a swift kick that landed on the unfortunate man's right shoulder. His whole weight was thrown upon the rope, it gave outward, his feet slid from the step and he hurtled downward to land with a loud splash in the sea.

The Spaniards in Roger's boat had no love for their French masters and gave vent to loud *olés* of approval. The French sailors in the gig apparently had little affection for their Captain, as they had difficulty in hiding their grins at his discomfiture while putting off to rescue him before he was swept away by the tide. Georgina held her sides and roared with laughter.

Two minutes later Roger had her in his boat and the Spaniards were pulling lustily for the harbour. Eager as they were to question one another during the trip ashore, Georgina obeyed Roger's injunction to treat him as a stranger; so they could do no more than steal furtive eager glances at one another in the semi-darkness. It was not until they reached harbour and he had paid off the boatman that Roger could ask her:

'How in Heaven's name did you come to be here at Cadiz and in that ship?'

'I came in her from the Indies,' she replied quickly. 'She was one of Admiral Villeneuve's fleet.'

'Well, I'll be damned!' he exclaimed. 'And I was in another; at least from Madeira. To think we sailed in company and did not know it. You must then have been at the battle off Finisterre?'

'I was, and scared out of my wits.'

'But how came you to be in a French frigate?'

'The ship in which I left Jamaica eighteen months ago was attacked by buccaneers and. . .'

'I know it. I saw you in a vision and you were nearly drowning.'

She pressed his arm, 'Dearest Roger. It was you then who saved me. Had I not had the sense to free myself of my skirt

428

and petticoats before the boat I was in went down I would certainly have drowned. Even so I was nearly exhausted and the shore still distant. I recall thinking of you. Then new strength seemed to enter into me. I reached the beach of a desert island and was marooned there many months.'

'I know that, too. I went in search of you and found the place.'

'Oh, Roger, Roger. I might have known you would if you believed me to be still alive. But you came too late.'

'I did not get there till May 12th of this year; but I knew it for certain to be the island you had been on, for I found your pearls and have ever since worn them beneath my shirt.' Suddenly he halted and began to laugh.

Turning her face up to his she said gently, 'I see nothing humorous in that. It does but show that you treasured the memory of me.'

'Nay, not that,' he strove to control his laughter. 'On the island I came upon two skeletons. One, tall and with fair hair still on its skull, I had no doubt was that of my Lord Rockhurst, with whom you travelled out. The other was short and had black hair. I believed it to be you, and was so overcome with grief that my men took me from the place. When I returned I found they had buried both. Had they not done so I'd have taken that black hair, plaited it and would be wearing it now instead of your pearls.'

Georgina then burst out laughing too. 'My dear! My dear! Just to think of you going about Europe for years to come treasuring a hank of hair you believed to be mine when it was really that of a half-caste seaman.' After a moment she went on, 'His name was José. With Rockhurst and myself he was the only survivor from our boat. The poor Skiffingtons and the other men in it were all drowned.'

'But what happened later?' Roger asked quickly. 'How did Rockhurst and José come to die and you escape?'

'We had been on the island just on a year,' she replied, 'when the French frigate you found me in anchored off shore to water. A party of sailors from her came upon us. Little José had been taken with a fever and was lying in his own

429

hut, so was helpless and must have died shortly after. Seeing me skirtless and half-naked the sailors thought me fair game for a rape. Rockhurst endeavoured to defend me, but they were too many for him and he was struck down. Luckily for me a young officer appeared at that moment and called his men to order. He took me aboard the ship and I told my story to Captain Fournier. The gallant Captain was much taken with me.'

'And then?' Roger prompted her.

Georgina giggled, 'Surely you can guess the rest. Although something of a martinet he is a handsome fellow, and after a few days at sea I made a bargain with him. I agreed to become his mistress if he would take me back to Europe. The frigate lay for some while at Port-au-Prince, then sailed down to Martinique, joined Admiral Villeneuve's fleet and recrossed the ocean.

'After the battle off Finisterre we put in to Vigo. I asked Jules Fournier to put me ashore and give me sufficient money to journey down to Gibraltar, so that I could get back to England. But he had become quite besotted about me and behaved most ungenerously, declaring it to be his intention to keep me with him indefinitely. There have been occasions since when I could have escaped, but I dared not land penniless in a foreign port; and though I watched him like a hawk he was too clever to give me an opportunity to steal money from him.'

By this time they were approaching the 'Inca Queen', and even while listening to Georgina's story Roger had been giving half his mind to considering what it would be best to do in this most unexpected situation. Drawing Georgina into the shadow of an arch that led into the stable yard of the inn, he said quickly:

'Listen, my sweet. We are not yet out of the wood. Fournier will be coming ashore at any moment to hunt for us. If he finds us you may be certain he will force a duel upon me. I'm a good enough blade to back myself to get the better of him, but duels are tricky things and did he chance to wound me severely that would spell disaster for us both. For

430

me because I have information of the utmost importance that I must get to England; for you because you would be left stranded here without money or anyone to turn to. That we dare not risk, so we must get out of Cadiz as swiftly as we can.'

'Gibraltar is no great distance from here, is it?' Georgina said.

'Stap me!' Roger exclaimed as an idea suddenly came into his head. 'I have it. To Gibraltar you must go. Though I cannot.'

'But why?' she cried. 'Oh Roger, having found one another again must we part so soon?'

'Alas, beloved, I fear we must. I cannot go there because the place is besieged and the Spaniards would not let me through their lines. But they are chivalrous people and, unlike Napoleon, do not interfere with civilians from enemy countries caught in theirs by a war. You have only to tell some story to the Spanish officers at La Linea. Say that your husband is a merchant on the Rock and that when war was declared you were staying with friends in Madrid; that you have recently heard that he has met with a serious accident and wish to rejoin him. I am confident they will let you through.'

'But, Roger,' Georgina was in tears now. 'Since... since you cannot go to Gibraltar, I've no wish to go. We'll go to some other place. Anywhere as long as I can remain with you.'

'Hush, dear heart, hush,' he pleaded. 'Stop crying, I beg, and listen. In this we must think not of ourselves but of our country. It is of the utmost importance that I get a message to the Governor of Gibraltar as swiftly as possible. And you can take it for me.'

He then told her of Napoleon's orders to Villeneuve to leave port and join Gantheaume's fleet from Brest which, unless Villeneuve could be intercepted, would make the French masters of the Channel.

Georgina realized at once how vital it was to get the information through and that by taking it to Gibraltar she could get it there perhaps as much as a week earlier than Roger could himself. So she dried her tears and made no further protest about being separated from him again so soon.

While they had been talking in the shadow of the arch several people had passed them, and back in the big yard of the inn a team of horses was being harnessed to a coach while it was loaded up. Glancing in that direction, Roger said:

'Wait here one moment, dearest, while I enquire of an ostler where that coach is bound for. It is most probably going to Seville, as that is the main road into central Spain; but he will be able to tell me the hour at which the one for Algeciras leaves in the morning, then we'll find some small inn at which Fournier is unlikely to enquire for us, and there pass the night.'

Two minutes later he returned to her and said huskily, 'My sweet Georgina, I've bad news for us; but good in that we'll not have to take the risk of Fournier running us to earth during the night and forcing a duel on me that might ruin everything. That vehicle about to start is the overnight diligence for Algeciras. And you must take it.'

'Oh, Roger! If I must, come with me.'

'Dearest, I dare not. I have to deliver my despatch to Villeneuve and it is already overdue. Besides, if you were seen in Algeciras with a French officer, since the French are the bitterest enemies of the English the Spaniards might suspect that I was an Englishman in a French uniform. It is, too, essential that you should play the part of a woman alone and in great distress on account of her injured husband.'

While he was speaking he had undone his tunic so that he could get at his money belt. From it he took a handful of Spanish gold pieces and gave them to Georgina. As she was stowing them away she said:

'Should the Spanish officers not after all prove as gallant as you expect and refuse to let me through, what am I to do?'

'I should have thought of that.' He paused a moment to consider, then went on. 'As soon as you have gone I shall set out for Jerez and pass what remains of tonight there. You

432

should be across the frontier tomorrow, but we'll allow an extra day, and it is no more than a day's journey up from Algeciras to Jerez. Tomorrow is the 24th. Although it means still further delay in delivering my despatch I'll bide at the best inn in Jerez until the morning of the 27th. Should you not have joined me by then I'll take it as certain that you have got through to Gibraltar. And now, most beloved of all beloveds, you must leave me to get a place in the diligence.'

For a good three minutes they embraced while he kissed her eyes, her neck, her mouth and felt her tears wet on his cheeks; then she tore herself away and walked resolutely towards the coach. He remained under the arch until ten minutes later the diligence clattered past him.

Immediately it was out of sight he had his horse saddled, paid the livery and bait fee, and set off for Jerez. Just outside the city he passed the diligence at a canter but he did not give it a glance. He dared not, for fear that his resolution would break down and he would, after all, accompany her to Algeciras.

He reached Jerez soon after one o'clock in the morning, knocked up the inn and went to bed. For a long time he lay awake, his mind filled by the miracle that Georgina was alive and that sometime, somewhere, he would again hold her lovely naked body in his arms. Then he slept soundly until well on in the morning.

When he awoke the events of the previous evening flooded back to him, but he thought they could have been only a vivid dream. Then the strange room brought home to him that they could not have been. He really was in Jerez and Georgina alive and well and on her way to Gibraltar.

For a while he lay there in ecstatic happiness. The years seemed to have fallen from him. When he got up he felt a buoyancy that he had not known since the terrible day when she had betrayed him to the tipstaffs. She had made no mention of that, or that she had forgiven him for having killed John Beefy. But the time they had spent together had been so short—apart from their silent trip from ship to shore in the boat—not much more than twenty minutes. And every

433

moment had been occupied by her telling him how she had got back to Europe, the urgency of their leaving Cadiz before Fournier found them and his giving her the information that she must take to Gibraltar.

Although he had ridden down from Boulogne by easy stages, he had been for thirty-one days almost continuously in the saddle; so the prospect of a few days' rest was an added joy and, after a hearty breakfast, he strolled round the little town.

It was a pleasant place and the centre of the sherry industry. As he was aware, several of the principal shippers were Englishmen; but the chivalrous Spaniards had left them at liberty to continue conducting their businesses, except for the restriction that they were no longer allowed to send cargoes to England. As a French officer Roger naturally avoided contact with them, but he met several of the Spanish growers. Members of both the Gonzalez and Domecq families took him round the great *bodegas* where the wine was stored and entertained him most hospitably.

Nevertheless, during the three days he spent in Jerez for most of the time his mind was on the miracle of Georgina being alive and wondering if she had succeeded in getting to Gibraltar. By the morning of the 27th he felt confident that all was well so, still in the highest spirits, he took horse for Seville.

Late in the afternoon he entered the ancient city and dismounted at the great building that housed the Board of the Indies. To his relief he learned that Villeneuve was still in Seville and, half an hour later, he was received by him at the *Casa* that the Spaniards had placed at the disposal of the Admiral and his staff.

The evenings were still warm enough to sit out in the sheltered patio of the *Casa* and there, seated beside a tinkling fountain, they held a long conference, during which Roger learned that Austria had declared war on France some three weeks before and that the Russians and Swedes had soon afterwards proclaimed their intention to join the Third Coalition against France. Villeneuve then said that he had not brought his fleet down to Cadiz for fear of further encounters with the English but because the last direct order he had received from the Emperor had enjoined him, should he meet serious opposition when sailing north, to retire into that port. He then spoke of the difficulties he would have to overcome before again putting to sea.

The Spaniards were politeness personified but unbelievably dilatory about carrying out their promises. Supply problems, which in France could be dealt with in a week, in Spain took a month. Admiral Gravina, who commanded the Spanish squadron in Cadiz, was a charming man but his ships were in a wretched condition and several, by French standards, unseaworthy. This made them so cumbersome to handle that they became a drag upon the remainder of the fleet and hampered its manoeuvres.

Another matter that gave Villeneuve grave concern was that both navies had been cooped up in port for so long that many of the Captains had had no opportunity to practise any but the most elementary evolutions. In fact the only one they could be relied on to carry out, without throwing the fleet into disorder, was to form line-of-battle; and that was a terrible disability when going into action against the English, who had been trained at a given signal to change formation with perfect precision.

He then lamented the fact that they were so far from Paris that time did not permit of his going there and attempting to dissuade the Emperor from staking everything on the autumn campaign; and Roger got the impression that, in spite of Napoleon's order, he might still not leave the port, later making the excuse that the Spanish fleet was unfit to sail and that without it he would find himself heavily outnumbered.

In spite of what Talleyrand had said about the Army becoming stale, it was Roger's view, too, that Napoleon would stand a greater chance of success if he waited until the Spring, because the worst-found ships in the Allied fleet would meet with less trouble in better weather. On the other hand, if they sailed in October rough weather would favour the British and, if caught in a bad storm, Villeneuve's fleet might well suffer the same fate as had the Spanish Armada.

It being Roger's object to do everything he could to bring about the destruction of the Allied Fleet, and the Admiral's reactions being much as Napoleon had anticipated, he did not scruple to use the spur he had been given. As tactfully as he could, he spoke to Villeneuve about the conversation he was supposed to have overheard and told him that if his fleet lingered in port until the weather became too bad for it to put to sea it was probable that he would be replaced by Admiral Rosily.

Having thanked him for the warning, the Admiral asked him to remain at the *Casa* as his guest until his negotiations with the Spaniards were completed; so Roger spent the following two days seeing the sights of Seville. He found the huge Cathedral very impressive, but was much more interested in the fascinating collection in one wing of the House of the Indies consisting of maps, gear and weapons used by Columbus and the great Conquistadores.

On the 30th Villeneuve told him that he now hoped to be able to sail from Cadiz in about a fortnight, then gave him a despatch for the Emperor containing detailed information upon the state of the fleet. At midday Roger again reluctantly mounted his horse and started on his long journey north. Anxious now to get back to Paris he covered longer daily stages than he had while coming south and reached Bayonne on October 9th.

Having stabled his horse at a good inn and sent his valise up to a room in it, he walked round to the Cavalry Barracks to get the latest military news. The officers there made him welcome in their Mess and, to his astonishment, told him that the whole of the Grande Armée had left the coast towards the end of August; but nobody there yet knew if the Emperor had sent it to the Rhine with the intention of invading Austria or down into Italy where it was believed that the Austrians had taken the offensive.

Puzzling over the matter later, it seemed to Roger at first sight a crazy business for Napoleon to have sent him with orders for the Allied Fleet to clear the Channel in preparation

436

for an invasion then, within a few days of having despatched him with them, withdrawn the troops who were to make the invasion should Villeneuve prove successful. But he knew the subtle mind of the Corsican far too well to believe that he had acted on impulse. Napoleon always had an alternative plan for every situation but if he did use it, invariably kept it to himself until the last moment.

That, given a reasonable chance of success, he would have invaded England Roger had no doubt at all. But evidently he had come to the conclusion that he could place no reliance on his Navy and, therefore, was using it only as a factor in a vast deception plan. By setting his Army in motion more than a week before the ill-prepared Austrians had even declared war, he had already stolen a march on them, and it would probably still be several weeks before his enemies learned that the Grande Armée had left the coast. If, before that, Villeneuve put to sea and the fact was reported by watching British frigates it would be assumed that he was about to launch the invasion. Reports of French troop movements towards the Rhine or Italy would be discounted as no more than the despatch of reinforcements. Then, one fine morning, the Austrians in one theatre or another would wake up to find the mightiest army in the world arrayed against them.

That night, before he went to sleep, Roger felt happier about the European situation than he had done for a long time. It was certain now that Mr. Pitt had succeeded in his great undertaking of welding together a Third Coalition against France. In whichever direction the Grande Armée was marching it could not be in two theatres of war at once. So even if the Austrians were defeated between the Rhine and the Danube they might hope to be victorious in Italy; or vice versa. And behind Austria was ranged Sweden and the might of Russia. Last, but not least, much against his will Villeneuve was being forced to come out of Cadiz. If he could be intercepted and his fleet destroyed that would put an end for years to come of any fear of England being invaded.

Next day Roger pressed on, covering over a hundred miles,

and reached Bordeaux. There nothing more was known than he had learned in Bayonne. Early the following morning he set out for Angoulême. But when he was a little more than half way there, disaster overtook him.

Shortly after he had passed through the little town of Chalais the road ran through a wood and stretches of the highway were covered with long drifts of fallen autumn leaves. Beneath a drift there lay a deep pothole. The off fore hoof of his horse plunged into it and he was flung from the saddle to crash heavily on the same shoulder he had injured in his fall on the night he had had his vision of Georgina drowning.

Half dazed, he stumbled to his feet, to find that his mount had broken a leg. There was nothing to be done but take one of his pistols from a holster and shoot the animal; then, in great pain, walk back to Chalais.

The inn there might have been worse. The local sawbones was called in to set his broken collar bone and the landlady proved to be a kindly body who did her best to make him comfortable. But he was delayed there six days before, having bought another horse, he felt fit enough to continue his journey; and, even then, his injury compelled him to go by easy stages.

It was not until the 18th that he reached Poitiers, where rumour had it that the Grande Armée had crossed the Rhine and that the Emperor was commanding it in person. At Tours reports were conflicting, but at Orléans on the 21st it was said that he had gained a great victory somewhere in Bavaria.

As Roger's shoulder was still paining him it took him two days to cover the last eighty miles to Paris. After a happy reunion with his old friends the Blanchards and an excellent dinner with them in their parlour, he went to bed greatly relieved to think that his seemingly endless ride was over.

First thing next morning he hurried round to the Tuileries to get authentic news of what had been happening. There, to his surprise, he found Duroc; as it was unusual for Napoleon to set off on a campaign without this faithful friend. But

Duroc explained that he had only recently returned from his mission to Berlin, which had been only partially successful. The avaricious but cowardly Frederick William had agreed to accept Hanover from France, not as a fee for becoming an ally, but as the price only of maintaining a benevolent neutrality. Duroc then gave Roger such intelligence as was known about the enemy and an account of the great battle that had taken place between the 12th and 17th of the month.

From captured despatches and the reports of spies it had emerged that the Emperor Francis had decided to despatch into Italy his largest army, some ninety thousand strong, under his ablest General, the Archduke Charles; while a smaller one of about thirty thousand, under the Archduke Ferdinand, with the veteran General Mack as his adviser, stood on the defensive to cover Austria; on the assumption that, before it could be attacked, it would be reinforced by a Russian army, also thirty thousand strong, that was advancing under Kutusoff.

Meanwhile the Coalition had in preparation two other offensives. In the north, from Swedish Pomerania, a combined Swedish and Russian army was to strike at Holland with the object of freeing that country from French domination, and a joint expedition of Russians from Corfu and English from Malta was to land in the south of Italy.

Napoleon had ignored these threats to the extremities of his dominions, left Masséna to do the best he could in northern Italy and decided to concentrate the maximum possible strength against Austria. Only skeleton forces had been left in Holland and on the Channel coast. The rest, by swift night marches, undetected by the enemy, had passed the Rhine and penetrated the Black Forest.

Although the movement had begun towards the end of August, in order to mask his intentions the Emperor himself had remained in Paris right up to September 23rd and, to publicize his presence there, had issued a decree that had set all Europe talking—no less than the abolition of the Revolutionary calendar and a reversion to the old Gregorian one.

It appeared that the Austrians, presumably on Mack's

advice, had decided to march through Bavaria and take their stand on the line of the river Iller thereby having the great fortress of Ulm, where the Iller flowed into the Danube, as a buttress to their northern flank and some fifty miles south another considerable fortress, Memmingen, to buttress their southern flank.

Totally unaware that a great French army was approaching, Mack had advanced from the line of the Iller into the Black Forest, possibly with the idea, if he met no resistance, of invading Alsace. The Emperor, playing for time, had opposed him only with light troops and led him on. Meanwhile, the Corps of Bernadotte, Ney, Soult and Lannes were coming down from the north-west towards the Danube and, on the 6th, the troops of the two last, with the help of Murat's cavalry, captured Donauwörth, fifty miles down the river from Ulm.

By the 13th, while the advance guard of the Russian army was only just crossing the river Inn and still a hundred and fifty miles away, the French were already far to the south behind the Austrian lines and Soult had cut off the big garrison in the fortress town of Memmingen. On the same day Ney, by a brilliant dash across the Danube from Elchingen, inflicted a severe defeat on the Austrians outside Ulm. Having encircled both wings of Mack's army, the Emperor had then ordered his whole force to go in for the kill. Ney, the hero of the campaign, had stormed the Michaelsberg, the key position in the Ulm defences, and the Austrians had asked for an armistice.

Having been in Naples when Mack, lent by the Austrians to the Neapolitans, had made a hopeless mess of their campaign and lost their country for them to a mere two divisions of French troops, Roger thought the Emperor Francis must be crazy to have entrusted another army to such an aged and incompetent General. But the damage was now done. While displaying for the benefit of Duroc enthusiastic delight at Napoleon's triumph, he could only secretly bemoan the fact that the new war on the Continent had opened so badly for the Coalition.

440

His next visit was to Decrès; for, although he would have taken Villeneuve's despatch direct to the Emperor had he been in Paris, it was obviously a matter for the Minister of Marine. After glancing through the document, Decrès said:

'Poor Villeneuve; fortune has been most unkind to him. He is a good and courageous sailor. Through no fault of his, the tools he has been given to work with are only third-rate; but, try as I will, I cannot make the Emperor understand that. And now, unless he left port by the middle of this month, he is finished. Before leaving for the Rhine the Emperor decided to replace him and Admiral Rosily is now on the way south to take over his command.'

Roger nodded, 'Even should he have left port before Rosily reaches Cadiz, I do not envy him. He will be terribly hampered by those almost useless Spanish ships, and you may be sure that the English will fight him tooth and nail as he makes his way up Channel.'

'*Mon cher Colonel*, you are out of date,' Decrès smiled. 'The Emperor deceived the enemy brilliantly by his forced march to the Rhine, but before he left Paris he realized that if Villeneuve reached the Channel at all it would be too late for his fleet to play any useful part in the deception. Fresh orders were sent some time after your departure, that when he left Cadiz he was to re-enter the Mediterranean and use his ships to protect our lines of communication between Marseilles and Genoa, so that we can continue to supply our army in Italy.'

That was another and far worse blow for Roger; but he concealed his dismay and, soon after, took his leave of the Minister.

On the following day, October 25th, a special bulletin was published in *Le Moniteur*. A full account of the battle of Ulm was given, then the great news that the Austrians had surrendered. On the 20th, at the foot of the great Michaelsberg that Ney, 'the bravest of the brave', had stormed, the Emperor sat his white charger. Behind him were his Marshals and his brilliant staff, and behind them the serried ranks of the Imperial Guard. To either side were four columns of troops each thousands strong, the standard bearers holding aloft their Eagles. From Ulm there filed out a long, sad procession headed by old General Mack. When he had handed over his sword, twenty thousand infantry and three thousand cavalry laid down their arms before their conquerors.

No more was said, but Roger could foresee the sequel. Kutusoff and his thirty thousand Russians could have saved the day if only Mack had had the simple sense to withdraw while there was still time and fall back upon them; but on their own, they could not possibly check the advance of the Grande Armée; so they could only retreat while Napoleon, the way now open to him, entered Vienna in triumph.

Sadly, Roger contemplated the situation. In England the new Coalition, brought about by Mr. Pitt with such tireless labour and a great outpouring of British gold, must have raised high hopes. They had been shattered at the very first encounter. In Vienna Napoleon would impose a peace on Austria that would bring the war in Italy to a close, and he had troops enough to defeat both any Russian advance in Central Europe and from Swedish Pomerania.

Still more in Roger's mind was the fact that he had sent by Georgina misleading information to England. A British fleet might now lie in wait for Villeneuve in the Channel, but he would not appear. If he, or Rosily, left port at all it would be for the Mediterranean; so both his fleet and that of Gantheaume in Brest would remain intact. That meant that when Napoleon had dealt with his enemies on the Continent, he might, after all, next Spring succeed in combining the two fleets, clear the Channel and invade England.

There was nothing more that Roger could do, and his depression was lightened only by the belief that Georgina was alive. Yet, at times, he had worrying misgivings even about that. They had been together for so short a time and all that had occurred that evening in Cadiz now seemed so improbable. He had since often wished that he had returned there, found his boat's crew and through them verified his belief that he really had brought her off from the frigate. Even at the risk of an encounter with the infuriated Fournier, he felt

442

now that he should have done so; for that in itself would have been proof that the whole episode was not a vivid dream.

During his long journey north he had told himself again and again that had he not seen her in the flesh he would never have relied on her taking his information to Gibraltar but have gone there himself. Yet why had no mention of her betrayal of him and of John Beefy's death passed between them; and why had he not given her back her pearls?

Now that he had completed his mission and had nothing else to think about, these unsubstantial but worrying doubts began to obsess him and, after another day in Paris, he decided that he would have no peace of mind until he settled them. Suddenly, too, it dawned upon him that if, as he really felt sure, his encounter with Georgina had not been a dream, only a crossing of the Channel lay between them and a glorious reunion.

His mind made up, he hastened to the Tuileries, saw Duroc again and said to him, 'Old friend, in another week it will be November. As you know, the weakness of my wretched lungs compels me each year to winter in the south of France. In your next despatch to the Emperor please be good enough to inform him that I have taken leave to go thither.'

Duroc readily agreed and later that morning Roger set out for Bordeaux. Now imbued with fresh energy he reached the city on the 28th. To his relief he found the smuggler Jubert still operating. He was not due to sail with another cargo of Bordeaux wine until November 1st but Roger, seized with impatience to be off, paid him handsomely to speed up his loading and, in spite of the weather not seeming very propitious, to set sail at midday the next day. But using his gold to overcome Jubert's better judgment was to cost him dear.

When they put to sea it was already choppy and a few hours later when darkness fell, owing to heavy cloud that hid the moon and stars, it became black as pitch. During the night the weather worsened, the little ship rolled and pitched and Roger, lying in one of the only two bunks aft, was very ill. In the cabin it was atrociously stuffy and when morning came he staggered out on deck to get some fresh air. A bitter wind was blowing that sent showers of spray hissing over the side. White horses crested every wave and no other ship was in sight.

For a while he clung to a handrail as the lugger bucked and lurched, striving it seemed, to drag him from his hold. Rain came, at first in drifts that stung his face and forced him to close his eyes. Then the wind eased a little and it began to rain in earnest. It sheeted down so that visibility was reduced to a few feet. Within ten minutes, in spite of the oilskin cape that Jubert had lent him, he was soaked to the skin. The downpour had run off his bare head and down his neck both behind and in front so that his underclothes had become saturated and as he moved the water squelched in his boots. Yet he was loath to take cover in the frowsty cabin, so he continued to hang on there.

The deck was awash with flying spume and the torrents of rain. It had become bitterly cold but the water, pouring from side to side with each roll of the ship, had sloshed so high against the galley that it had penetrated it and put out the stove; so there was no possibility of getting a hot drink, or even luke-warm soup. Roger had a big flask of cognac and, from time to time, swallowed a mouthful. The raw spirit made him gasp but eased the pain in his heaving stomach.

About midday, after what had seemed to Roger endless hours of torment, Jubert, skilfully judging from long practice the lurch of the vessel, crossed the deck to him and bellowed in his ear:

'You are unlucky for us, *Monsieur*. The last time I took you across we were caught by an English sloop and turned back. And now this. I said we'd meet bad weather, but you refused to heed my warning. For all your gold I'll not take you as a passenger again.'

White, shaking, breathless and with his eyes half-closed, Roger could only mutter, 'You could have refused. Grumbling won't help matters now. Go look to your ship and leave me be.'

444

The smuggler gave a crooked grin, 'It'll be worse yet, and since you've no stomach for it, you'd best get back to the cabin.'

As Roger's arms were aching from holding on he knew that the advice was sound, yet he hated to lose face by admitting that he could not stand up to the storm; so he ignored Jubert's advice and remained where he was.

The Captain proved right. During the afternoon the waves became mountain-high so that the lugger seemed to race through the sea as though she were a car on an endless switchback. For minutes on end she soared up one green slope to hit the wave crest then career like a toboggan down into another valley. Lest she be pooped, Jubert was holding the lugger head-on to the storm but, having been up all night, by late in the afternoon he was very tired. As they rushed up a great wave he made a slight miscalculation, so that instead of the bow of the ship cutting through the foaming crest she struck it at a slight angle.

At that moment Roger was holding on with only one hand. In the other he held his flask tilted high, his head thrown back, as he sucked from it the last drops of brandy. The lugger gave a frightful lurch. The tug on his arm tore his fingers from their hold. A second later he was flat on his back.

A wave swept the deck, lifting him high. With both arms outflung he made a desperate effort to seize on something by which he could save himself. The fingers of his left hand fastened on a grating. The breath driven from his body, he clung to it while the water cascaded away beneath him. The suction was terrific. Suddenly the fastenings of the grating gave and it came away. Still clutching it, he was carried across the deck to the low gunwhale of the lugger. It hit him in the back but was not high enough fully to check his headlong descent caused by the heavy list as the ship plunged down the far slope of the wave. His legs were flung up and with a gasp of horror he realized that he had been swept overboard.

445

CHAPTER XXVIII

BUT BRITAIN RULES THE WAVES

A S R O G E R went under, his mouth filled with water. The salt in it rasped his throat and nostrils. A great darkness engulfed him. Clinging desperately to the grating with both hands, he kicked out wildly. After a few moments that seemed an eternity he surfaced. Shaking the water from his eyes, he looked about him. The lugger was thirty feet away and now rocketing up another steep slope of dark green foam-flecked water. In her stern he glimpsed Jubert and another man at the wheel. Both had lashed themselves to nearby structures, but neither of them was looking in his direction.

Seized with panic, he gave a loud shout. It was drowned by the roaring of the wind. A wave slapped into his face, blinding him and again filling his mouth with water. He realized then that it was impossible for him to attract their attention. His seasickness forgotten, now that his life was in peril, he made an effort to fight down his panic and assess his chances.

Although he was a strong swimmer, he knew that without the wooden grating to support him, in such a sea he could not have kept himself afloat for a quarter of an hour, if that.

Only one thing was in his favour; it had been much colder in the cutting wind on deck than it was in the water, for the sea still retained a degree of the warmth it had absorbed during the long summer and autumn. But how long would it be before, tossed hither and thither by the waves and at intervals submerged as their crests broke over him, he became too exhausted any longer to keep his hold on the grating?

He had only a very vague idea of his whereabouts. On leaving Bordeaux a strong wind had favoured them and, although Jubert had put the lugger about to face the storm, it must have driven them still further to the north-westward. When Roger had gone overboard they had been close on thirty hours at sea, so he guessed himself to be somewhere in the northern end of the Bay of Biscay. There was, therefore, just a chance that he might be driven ashore on the southern coast of Brittany. But no land had been in sight all day, so that hope was a poor one. There was the possibility that before he became exhausted he might be sighted from a ship and picked up. But in such weather no fishing smacks would be at sea and the main shipping route from Spain across the Bay was, almost certainly, a considerable way further out. Grimly he faced the fact that his chances of survival were very slender.

From time to time, as the lugger mounted a big wave, or he was heaved high on one, he continued to catch glimpses of her, but after a quarter of an hour she was lost to sight. Twilight was already falling and soon darkness hid everything from him except the white foam crests in his immediate vicinity.

Every now and then he changed his grip on the grating, sometimes holding it in front of him, at others clutching it with only one hand while gently swimming beside it so as to keep his circulation going. It measured about four feet by three and to have used it as a raft was out of the question as it would have tipped over; but after he had been in the water for an hour or so he tried putting both his arms right over it so that the greater part of it was below his chest. The disadvantage to that position was that even when holding his head

447

back wavelets slapped into his face; but, at intervals, it enabled him to relieve his arms of the strain of hanging on to it.

The wind lessened and gradually the storm went down, but the night seemed endless and towards morning he began to fear that he could not last much longer. The thought of death brought into his mind Georgina and how she had so nearly drowned in the West Indies. Again he saw the vision he had had of her, then it seemed to change and, instead of him looking down on her, she was looking down on him. A moment later her voice came clearly to him in an urgent, anxious cry:

'Tie yourself to the grating, Roger. Tie yourself to it. Use your cravat.'

Rousing from the lethargy that was overcoming him, he attempted to undo his cravat. As the long strip of white linen was soaking wet it proved a veritable struggle to get it off. At length he succeeded. Terrified, now that he had to use both his hands, that he would be washed away from the grating, he half lay on it while, in fits and starts, he made slip knots in both ends of the cravat. Next he was faced with the hardest task of all—to get both the slip knots under the grating and up through holes in it that were well apart. Again and again he failed and had to lie panting for a few minutes until he had recovered sufficiently to try again. By sheer dogged persistence he eventually had about fifteen inches of the stock stretched under the grating near the far edge, and the two ends protruding above it. With a final effort he wriggled both his hands through the slip knots and the next roll of the grating pulled them tight over his wrists. Now, with his arms stretched out, he lay face down with his head between them while the lower half of his body and legs dangled in the water. Then he lost consciousness.

When he came to he saw Georgina again and she was bending over him. He smiled feebly, thinking it to be another vision. Then it dawned upon him that he was in a ship's cabin, lying in a bunk wrapped in blankets with hot bottles packed all round him. Still he could not believe that he was

not the victim of a fantasy, or dead, and that it was his spirit
that was looking up into her lovely face.

Tears of happiness were running down her cheeks as she
kissed him and said, 'Roger, my heart, just as you saved me,
the dear Lord has enabled me to save you. Early this morning I woke and had a vision. I saw you there alone and
drowning and knew you to be about to abandon hope. I
called to you to tie yourself to the grating you were holding.
Then the vision faded. But something told me you were not
far off. I pulled on my robe and rushed out to find the
Captain of this frigate. He would not believe me, but on my
insistence humoured me by agreeing that a special look-out
should be kept. When he had called the watch on deck I
offered a thousand guineas reward for the man who first
sighted you. While I waited, scanning the vast, empty waters
for a speck, I thought I'd die of suspense. At last a man in
the mizzen top saw you, for the others had failed to catch a
sight of you as we passed nearly a mile off. A boat was
lowered and they picked you up. To my utter horror, when
they brought you aboard I thought it was too late and that
you were already a corpse. I pray that never again may I go
through such a half hour as that while they were forcing the
water from your lungs. Twice they would have given up had
I not begged and insisted that they continued. At last you
breathed again but were still unconscious and it is two hours
since they carried you to my cabin with the sweet assurance
that you would live.'

Although Roger's mind took in all that she had said, he
was still half bemused and his thoughts went back to their
last meeting. In a croaking voice he said, 'There have been
times when I could not really credit that we had been
together in Cadiz.'

'I've felt that, too,' she agreed, 'but knew it must be so;
for else how could I have come to be in Gibraltar?'

He smiled, 'I had no such means of proving to myself that
our meeting was not a dream. 'Twas to set my awful doubts
at rest that I was on my way to England. Since then I have

cursed myself a thousand times for failing to take the opportunity to ask you two questions.'

'What were they?'

'From the joy you showed at seeing me again and your reluctance that we should part I have good hopes but . . .' He hesitated a moment, 'well. . . I beg you to give me reassurance that you have at last forgiven me for . . . for robbing you of John Beefy.'

'Dear Roger,' the tears again welled up into her splendid eyes. 'About that it is I who should crave forgiveness. On that terrible night you were as drunk as a lord, mad with jealousy of George Gunston and bitterly angry with me for declaring that I would not let you come again to Stillwaters. Poor John was the cause of that and you clearly held him in contempt. All this combined to make me believe that the ruthlessness without which, at times, you could not carry out your missions when abroad, had come uppermost in your drink-addled brain, and you had deliberately swept him from your path. In that I did you a great injustice. But I did not know it until shortly before I sailed for the Indies. I chanced to meet Gunston again, and John's death then being long past we talked of it. He made no pretence of being any friend of yours, but had the honesty to tell me that when two men fight as you and he did, both must watch each other's eyes. That even to look away for a second could mean receiving a deadly thrust. So as your eyes were fixed on his, your lunge could not have been aimed at John.'

'Thank God you realize the truth, my sweet; for, as I've always sworn, it was an accident. Though seeing the state I was in and all that led up to it, I cannot greatly blame you for disbelieving me. But tell me now—why on that day when I escaped from prison and hid in the stable loft at Stillwaters, instead of bringing me money as you had promised, did you betray me to the tipstaff?'

'Betray you!' Georgina's eyes grew round and her mouth fell open. 'I. . . No! Oh, Roger, how could you ever have believed that I would do such a thing? It was that dastardly new groom of mine whom I sent in to Guildford for the money. When he reached the town he heard the town crier ringing his bell and crying a reward for your capture. 'Twas he who brought the tipstaffs to the stable. When I heard what had occurred I was shaking mad with rage. I took my whip to him and lashed him until he fell writhing on the ground. I'd not have stopped there had not others who witnessed the scene restrained me.'

'Oh, Georgina,' Roger hung his head and his voice was very low. 'For having such thoughts of you can you ever forgive me?'

Leaning forward, she kissed him on the forehead, 'My dearest love, without cause each of us has harboured harsh thoughts of the other; so we are both to blame. Yet the bond between us has never really broken. I saved your life by committing perjury for you when you were on trial for murder, and saved it yet again this morning; while you saved me in the Indies then went those many thousands of miles to search for me although you thought then that I had betrayed you. Let us now think only of the future, and of the joys we will again know when in a week or so we are once more together at Stillwaters.'

Roger put his arms round her and held her to him. After a long embrace and many kisses, between which they murmured of their abiding love for one another, as she at last drew away from him he noticed that she was wearing a black silk scarf round her neck, and said:

'Why are you wearing that scarf? You have always told me that you hated black, and I've never seen you in it except for mourning.'

Her expression became grave as she replied, 'It is mourning, dear heart. But, of course, you could not know. Our wonderful Admiral, the great Nelson, is dead.'

'Nelson dead!' cried Roger, starting up. 'No, you cannot mean it. 'Tis a mortal blow. All England will be stricken with grief as never before.'

She nodded, 'This frigate is carrying the awful news. I should have come home in the ship that carried your message to Mr. Pitt that Villeneuve was preparing to leave harbour, but in Gibraltar I was laid low by a fever for more than three weeks. Then I had to wait until this ship came out from the Mediterranean on her way home. Not far from Gibraltar we passed the scene of the battle two days after it took place.'

'Battle! D'you mean that Nelson engaged Villeneuve's fleet?'

'Yes. The French were sailing south from Cadiz and on the 21st Nelson caught them off Cape Trafalgar. They had thirty-three ships-of-the-line against his twenty-six; but only fifteen of the Franco-Spanish fleet got away and those were severely damaged. Eighteen were destroyed or captured and not a single British ship struck her colours. Poor Nelson was shot down on his quarter deck in the hour of his triumph; but he lived long enough to know that he had achieved a decisive victory.'

'Georgina! Georgina!' Roger held out his hands to her and he was almost weeping. 'Do you realize what this means, and that we two have helped to bring it about? With Villeneuve's fleet destroyed our dear country is made safe at last. England need no longer fear the horrors of an invasion.' Hoarsely, half sobbing, he burst into song:

'Rule Britannia: Britannia rules the waves!
Britons never, never, never shall be slaves.'

This book, designed by
William B. Taylor
is a production of
Edito-Service S.A., Geneva

Printed in France
Bound in Switzerland